YO-KAI WATCH™

14

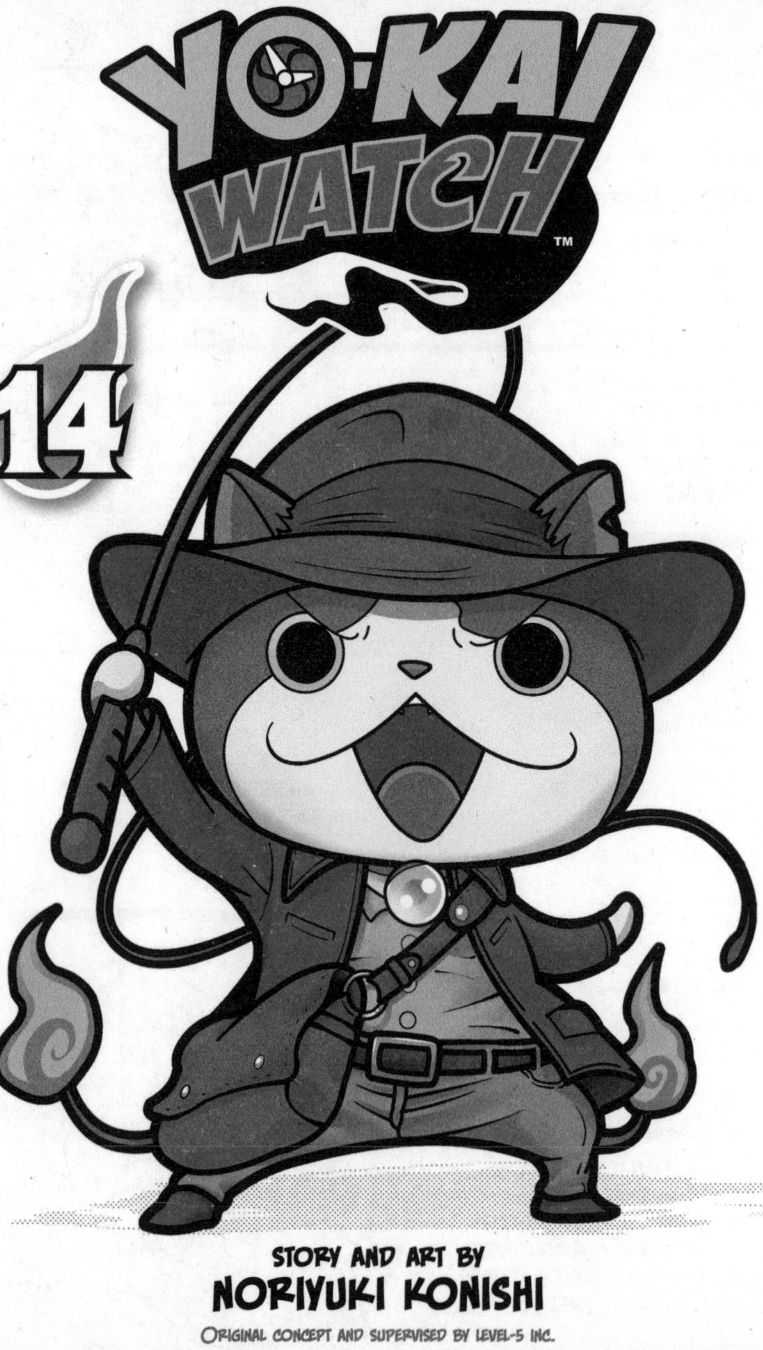

STORY AND ART BY

NORIYUKI KONISHI

ORIGINAL CONCEPT AND SUPERVISED BY LEVEL-5 INC.

CHARACTER INTRODUCTION

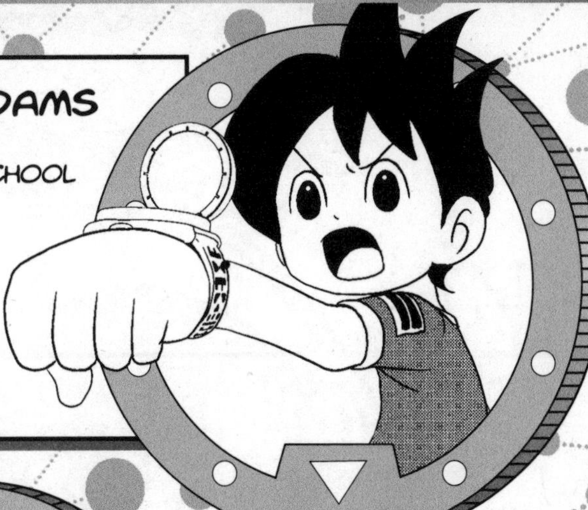

NATHAN ADAMS

AN ORDINARY ELEMENTARY SCHOOL STUDENT. WHISPER GAVE HIM THE YO-KAI WATCH, AND THEY HAVE SINCE BECOME FRIENDS.

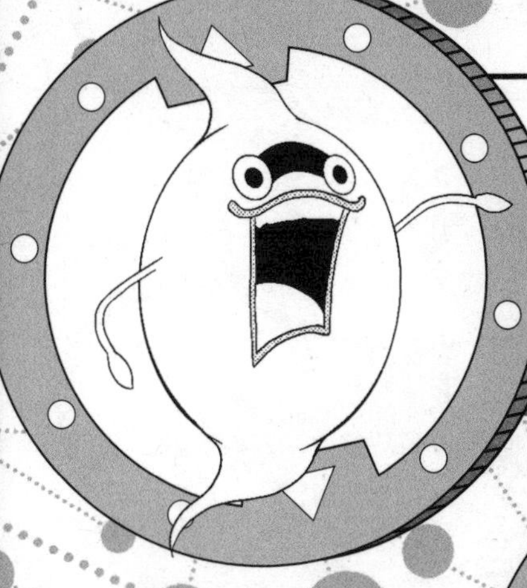

WHISPER

A YO-KAI BUTLER FREED BY NATE, WHISPER HELPS HIM WITH HIS EXTENSIVE KNOWLEDGE OF OTHER YO-KAI.

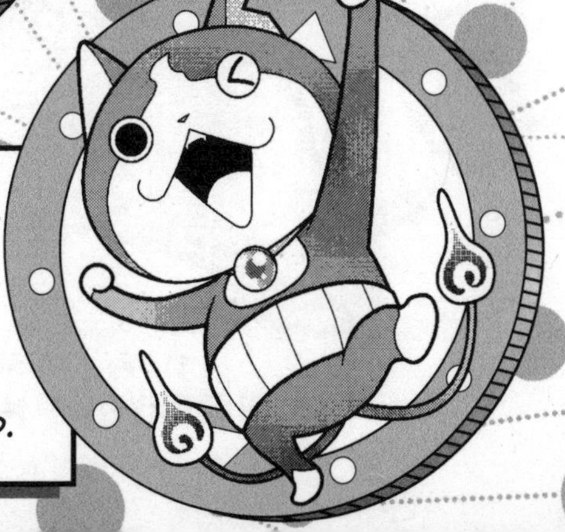

JIBANYAN

A CAT WHO BECAME A YO-KAI WHEN HE PASSED AWAY. HE IS FRIENDLY, CAREFREE, AND THE FIRST YO-KAI THAT NATE BEFRIENDED.

BARNABY BERNSTEIN

NATE'S CLASSMATE.
NICKNAME: BEAR.
CAN BE MISCHIEVOUS.

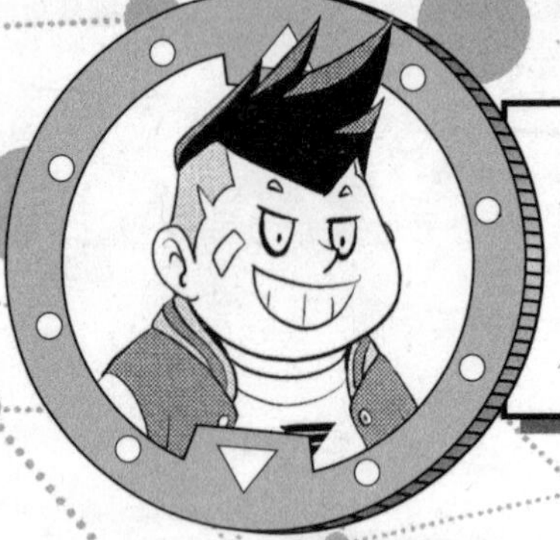

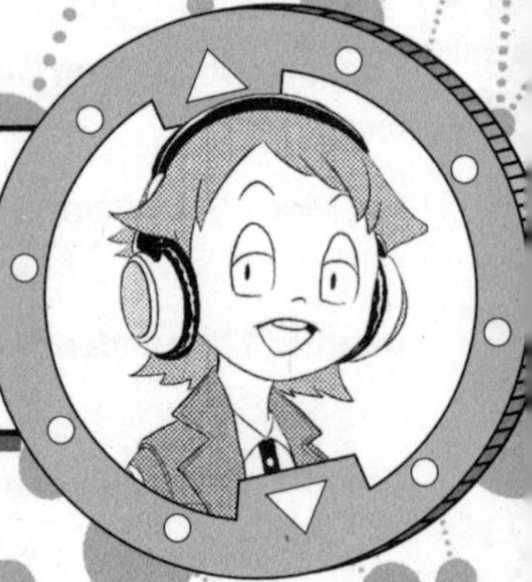

EDWARD ARCHER

NATE'S CLASSMATE.
NICKNAME: EDDIE.
HE ALWAYS WEARS HEAPHONES.

HAILEY ANNE THOMAS

A FIFTH GRADER WHO IS A SELF-PROCLAIMED SUPER-FAN OF ALIENS AND SAILOR CUTIES.

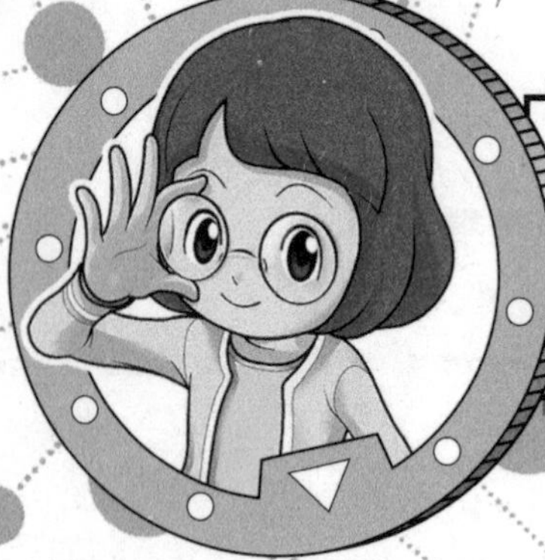

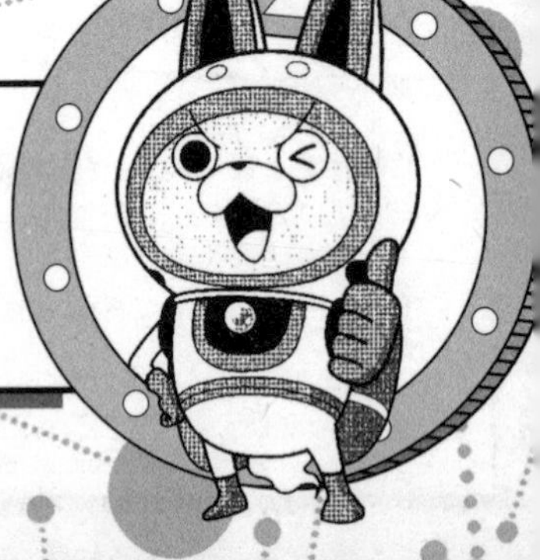

USAPYON

A RABBIT-LIKE YO-KAI WEARING A SPACESUIT. HE'S SEARCHING FOR SOMEONE.

TABLE OF CONTENTS

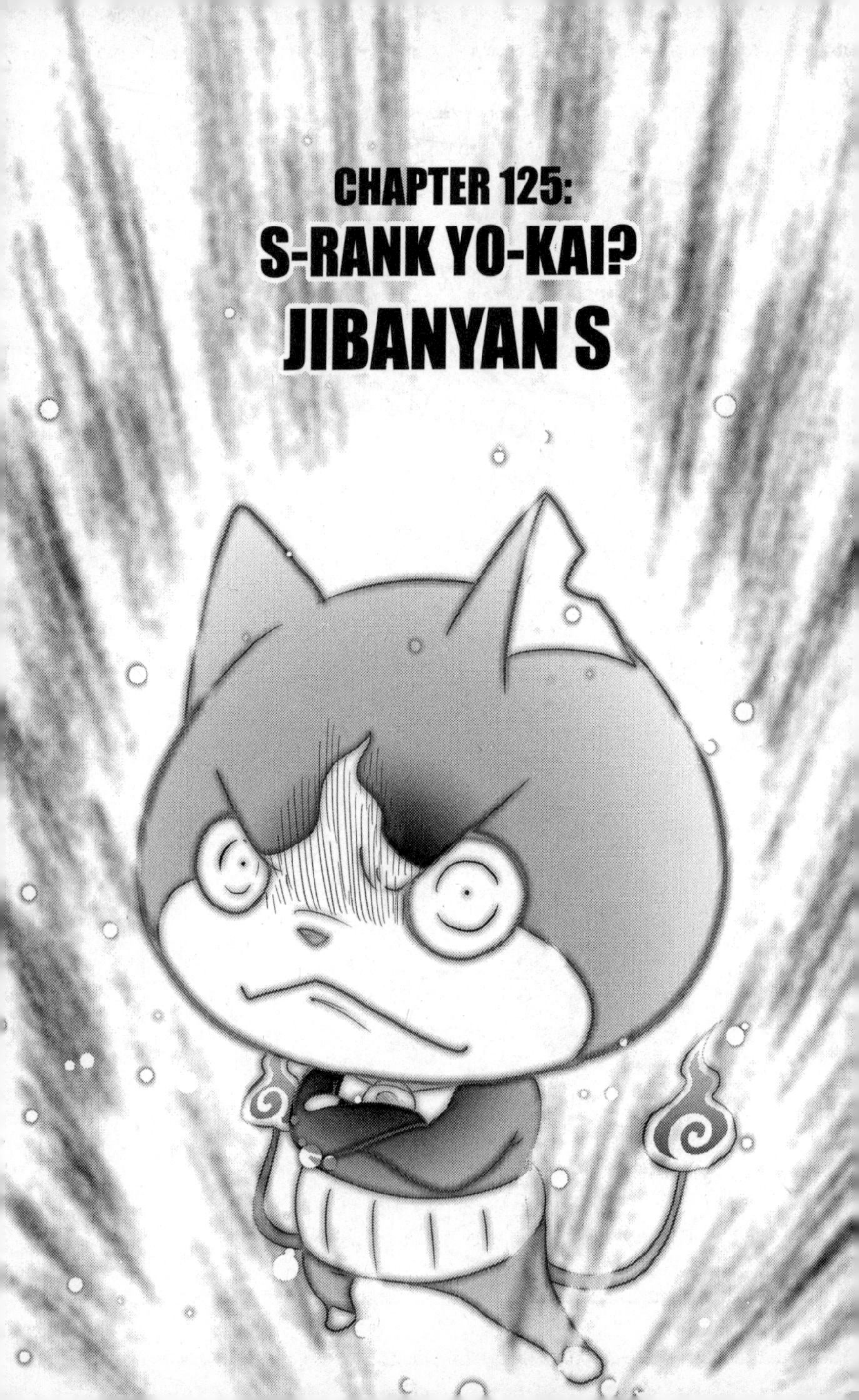
CHAPTER 125:
S-RANK YO-KAI?
JIBANYAN S

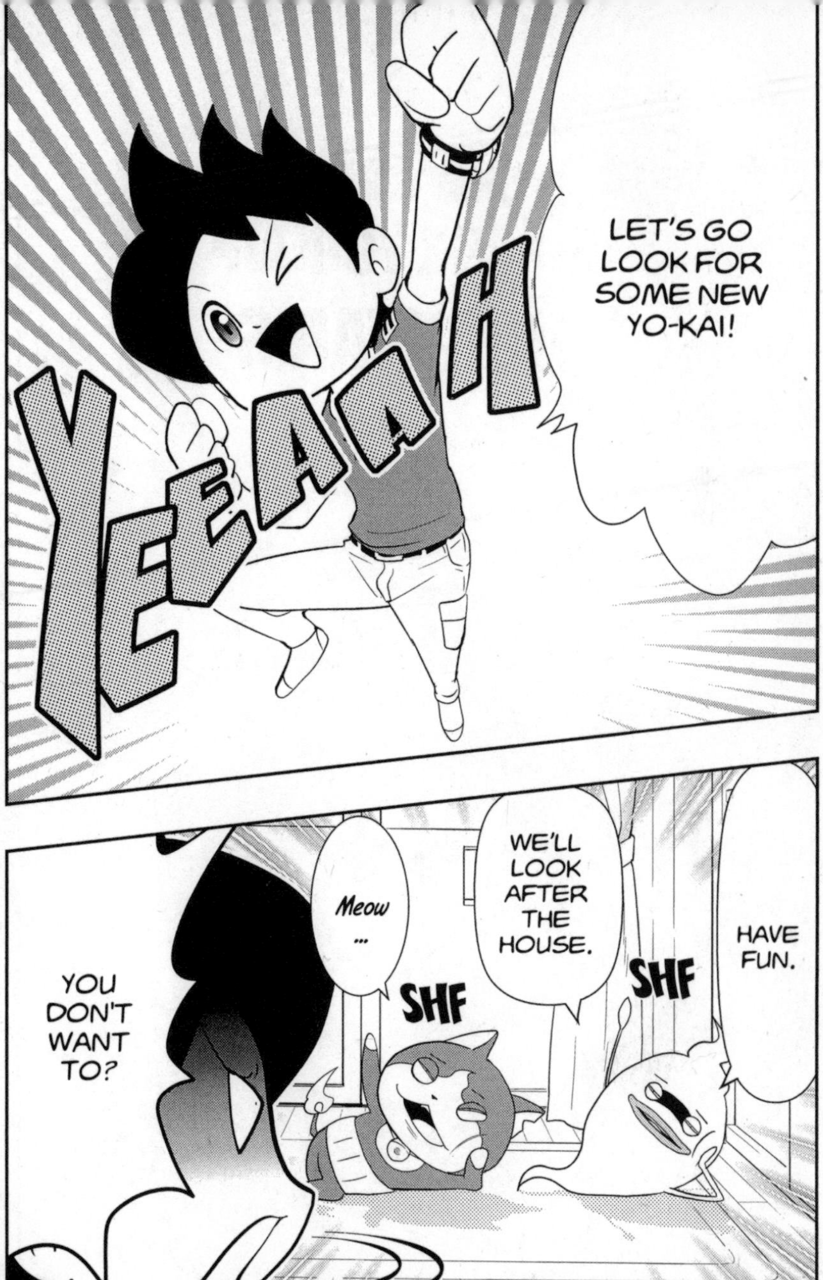
LET'S GO LOOK FOR SOME NEW YO-KAI!
YEEAAH
HAVE FUN.
SHF
WE'LL LOOK AFTER THE HOUSE.
SHF
Meow ...
YOU DON'T WANT TO?

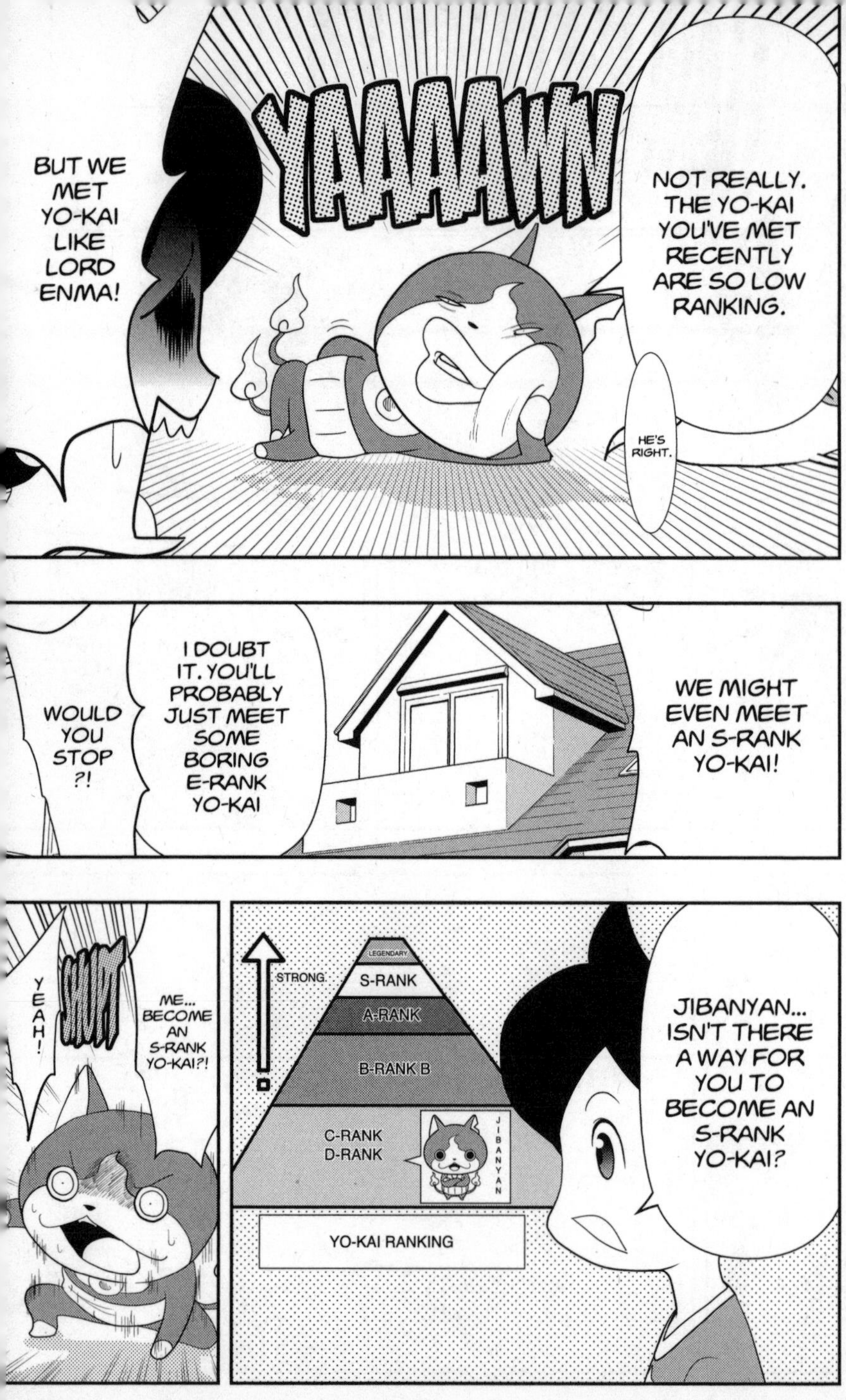
NOT REALLY. THE YO-KAI YOU'VE MET RECENTLY ARE SO LOW RANKING.
YAAAAWN
HE'S RIGHT.
BUT WE MET YO-KAI LIKE LORD ENMA!
WE MIGHT EVEN MEET AN S-RANK YO-KAI!
I DOUBT IT. YOU'LL PROBABLY JUST MEET SOME BORING E-RANK YO-KAI
WOULD YOU STOP ?!
JIBANYAN... ISN'T THERE A WAY FOR YOU TO BECOME AN S-RANK YO-KAI?
STRONG
LEGENDARY
S-RANK
A-RANK
B-RANK B
C-RANK
D-RANK
JIBANYAN
YO-KAI RANKING
ME... BECOME AN S-RANK YO-KAI?!
YEAH!

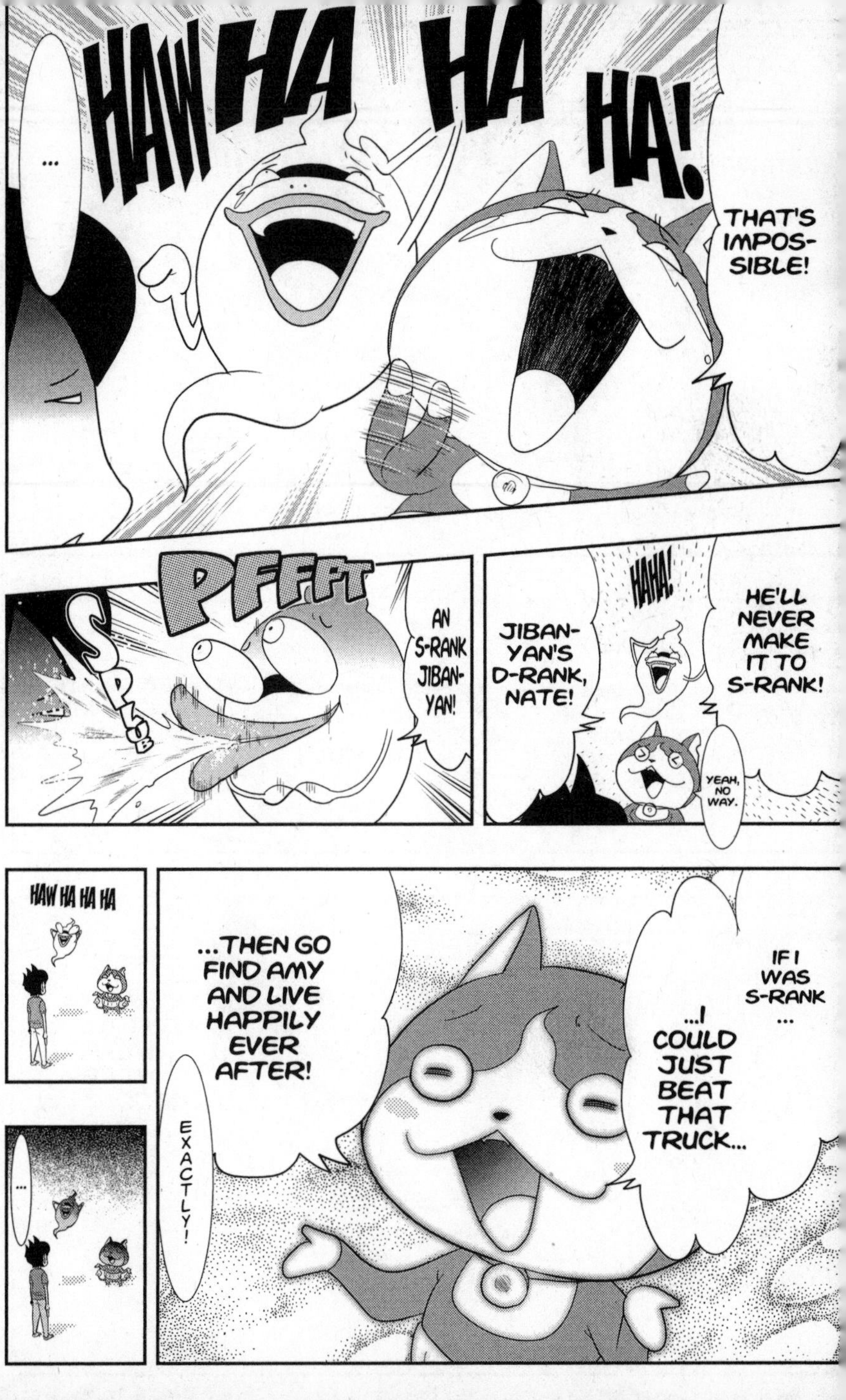
THAT'S IMPOSSIBLE!
HAW HA HA HA!
...
HE'LL NEVER MAKE IT TO S-RANK!
HAHA!
JIBANYAN'S D-RANK, NATE!
YEAH, NO WAY.
AN S-RANK JIBANYAN!
PFFFT
SPLUB
IF I WAS S-RANK...
...I COULD JUST BEAT THAT TRUCK...
...THEN GO FIND AMY AND LIVE HAPPILY EVER AFTER!
EXACTLY!
HAW HA HA HA
...

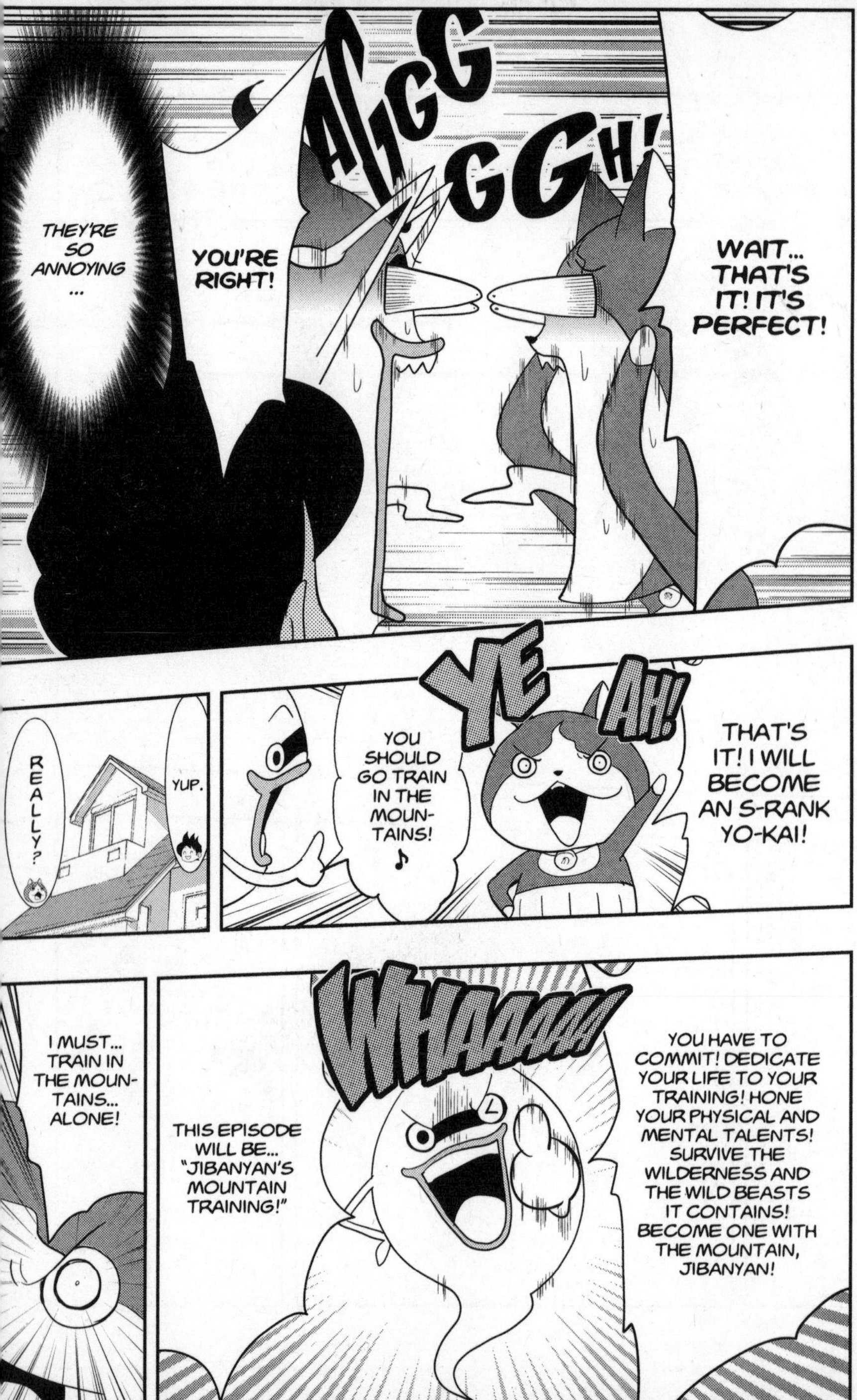
AIGGGGH!
WAIT... THAT'S IT! IT'S PERFECT!
YOU'RE RIGHT!
THEY'RE SO ANNOYING ...
YEAH!
THAT'S IT! I WILL BECOME AN S-RANK YO-KAI!
YOU SHOULD GO TRAIN IN THE MOUN-TAINS! ♪
YUP.
REALLY?
WHAAAA!!
YOU HAVE TO COMMIT! DEDICATE YOUR LIFE TO YOUR TRAINING! HONE YOUR PHYSICAL AND MENTAL TALENTS! SURVIVE THE WILDERNESS AND THE WILD BEASTS IT CONTAINS! BECOME ONE WITH THE MOUNTAIN, JIBANYAN!
THIS EPISODE WILL BE... "JIBANYAN'S MOUNTAIN TRAINING!"
I MUST... TRAIN IN THE MOUN-TAINS... ALONE!

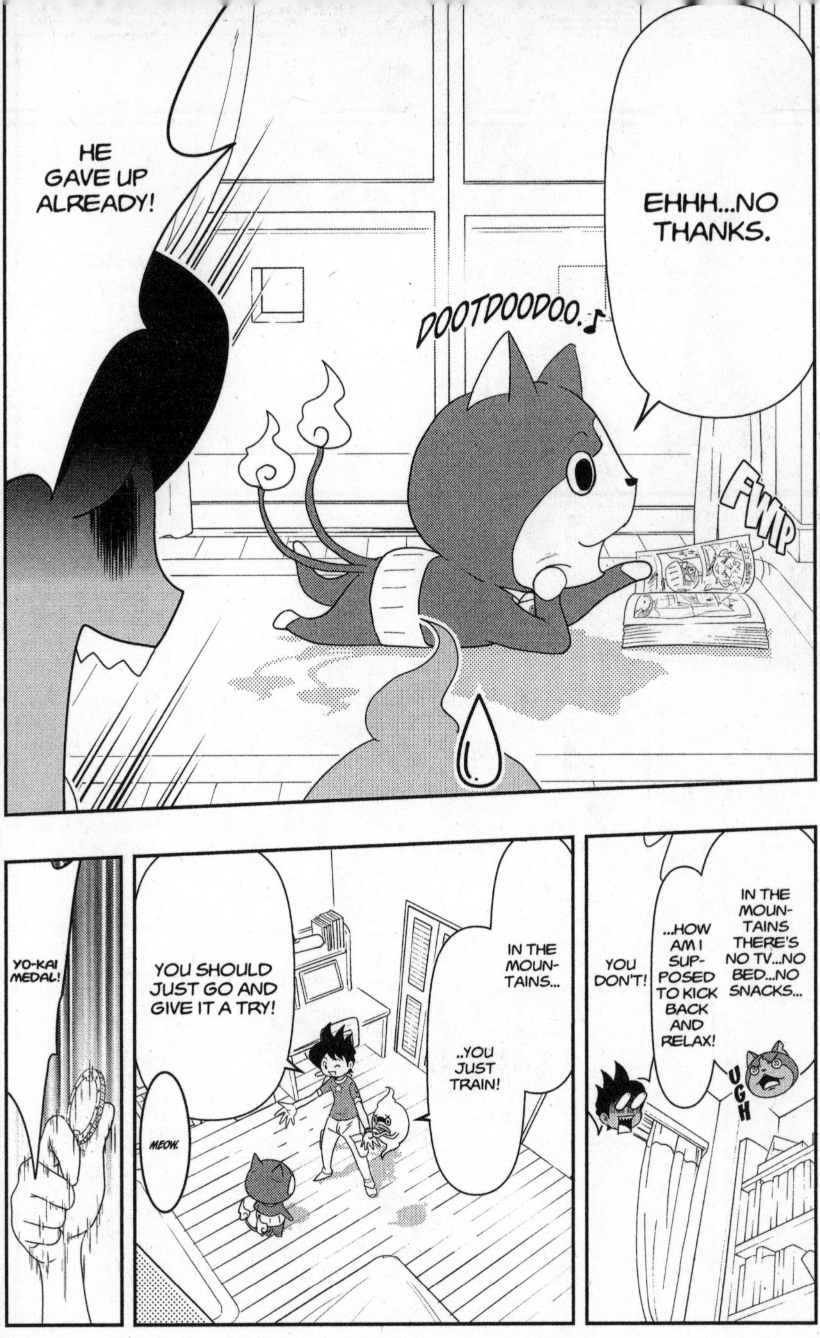
EHHH...NO THANKS.
DOOTDOODOO.♪
FWP
HE GAVE UP ALREADY!
IN THE MOUNTAINS THERE'S NO TV...NO BED...NO SNACKS...
...HOW AM I SUPPOSED TO KICK BACK AND RELAX!
UGH
YOU DON'T!
IN THE MOUNTAINS...
..YOU JUST TRAIN!
YOU SHOULD JUST GO AND GIVE IT A TRY!
MEOW.
YO-KAI MEDAL!

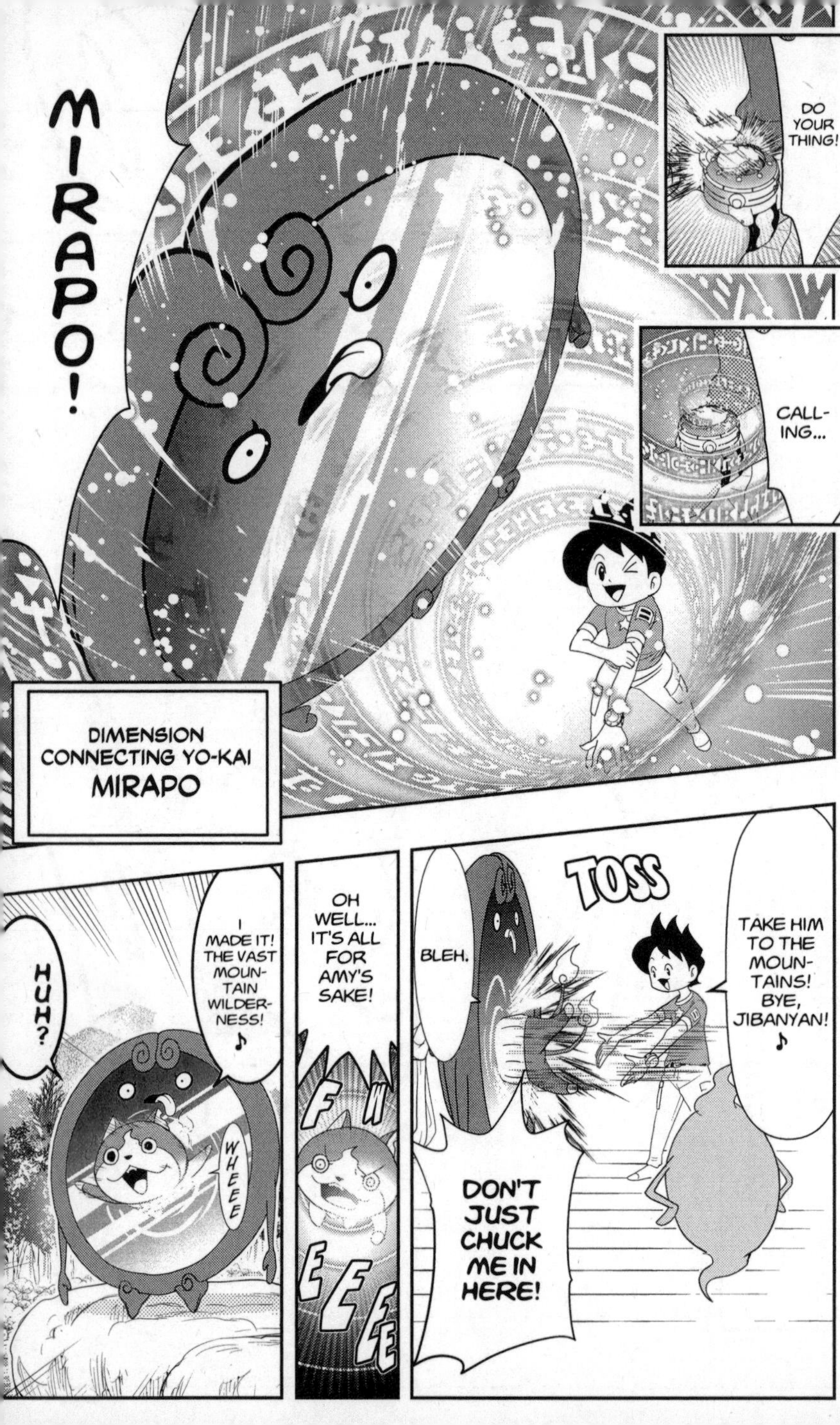

DO YOUR THING!
CALLING...
MIRAPO!
DIMENSION CONNECTING YO-KAI MIRAPO
TAKE HIM TO THE MOUNTAINS! BYE, JIBANYAN! ♪
TOSS
BLEH.
DON'T JUST CHUCK ME IN HERE!
OH WELL... IT'S ALL FOR AMY'S SAKE!
FWEEEE
I MADE IT! THE VAST MOUNTAIN WILDERNESS! ♪
HUH?
WHEEE

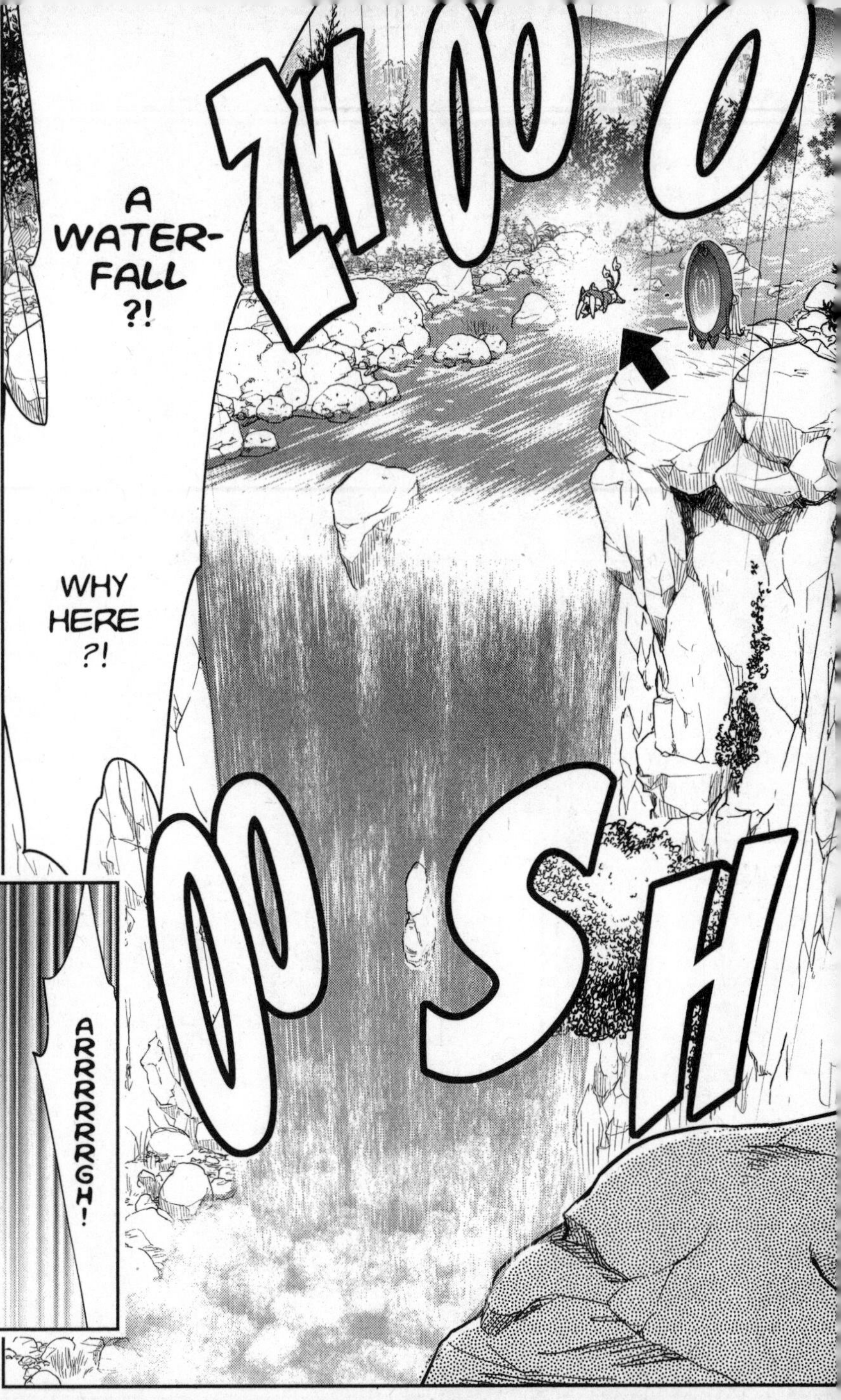
ZWOOOOOOSH
A WATER-FALL ?!
WHY HERE ?!
ARRRRRRGH!

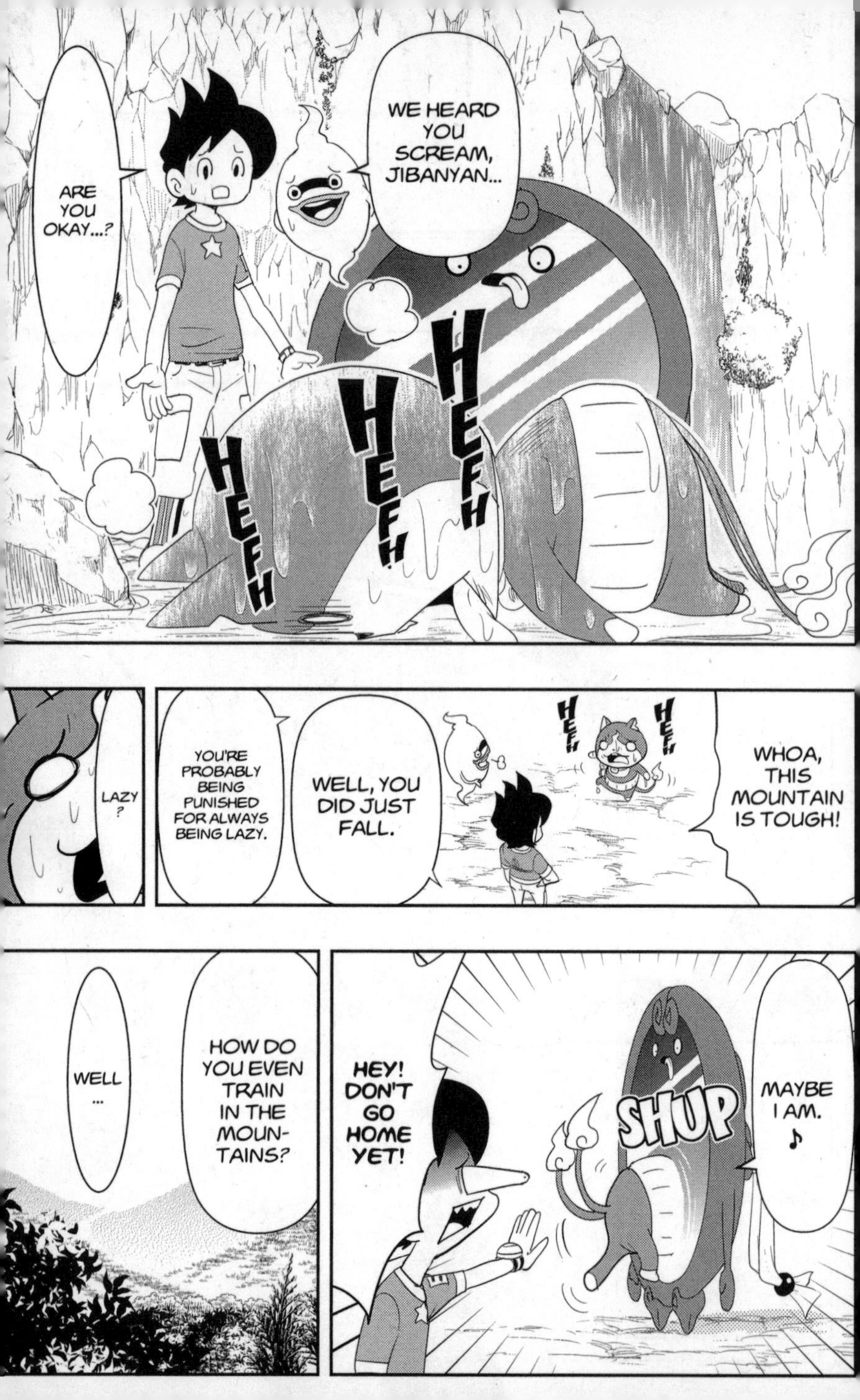
WE HEARD YOU SCREAM, JIBANYAN...
ARE YOU OKAY...?
HEFH
HEFH
HEFH
WHOA, THIS MOUNTAIN IS TOUGH!
HEFH
HEFH
WELL, YOU DID JUST FALL.
YOU'RE PROBABLY BEING PUNISHED FOR ALWAYS BEING LAZY.
LAZY?
MAYBE I AM. ♪
SHUP
HEY! DON'T GO HOME YET!
HOW DO YOU EVEN TRAIN IN THE MOUN-TAINS?
WELL...

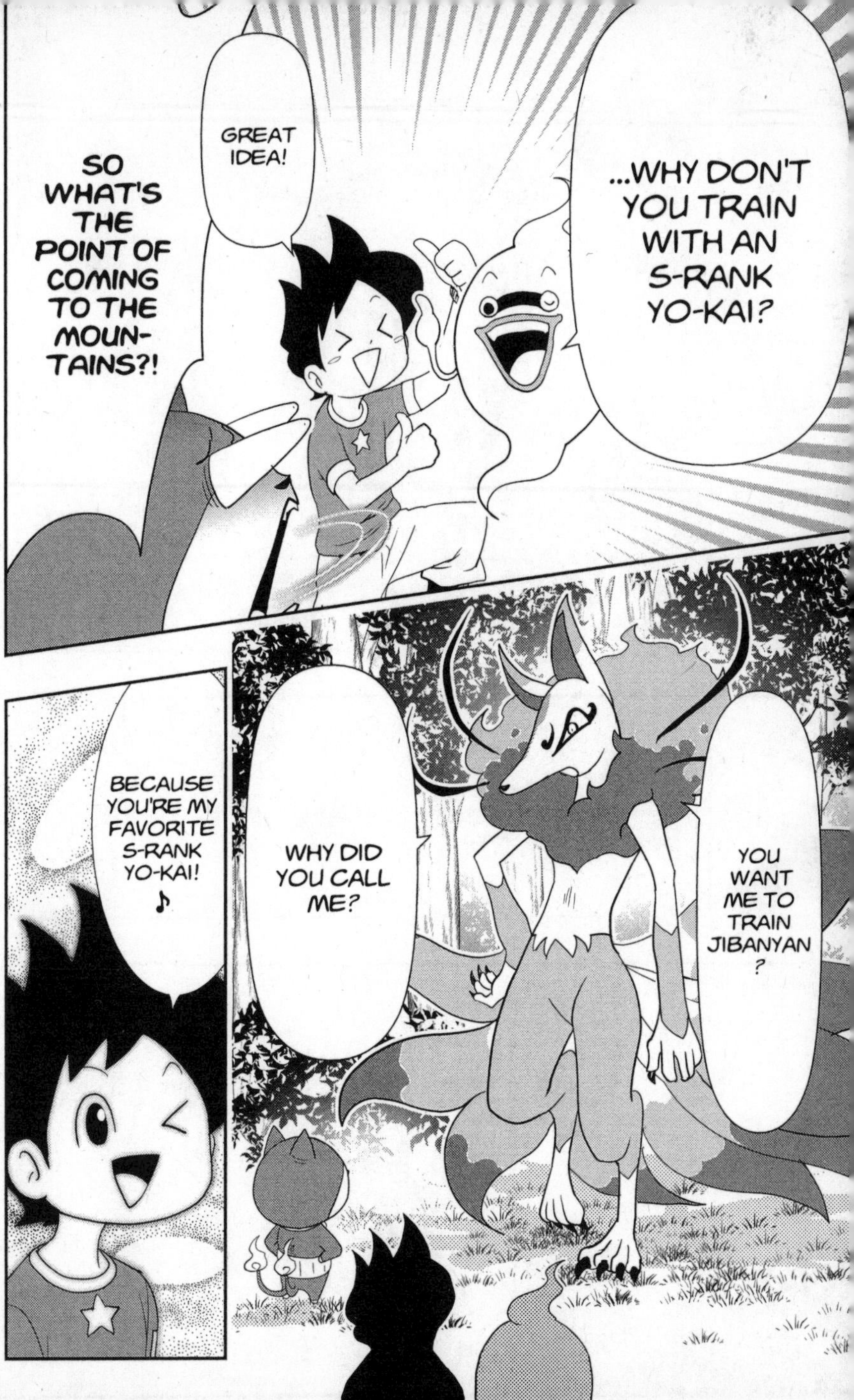
...WHY DON'T YOU TRAIN WITH AN S-RANK YO-KAI?
GREAT IDEA!
SO WHAT'S THE POINT OF COMING TO THE MOUN-TAINS?!
YOU WANT ME TO TRAIN JIBANYAN?
WHY DID YOU CALL ME?
BECAUSE YOU'RE MY FAVORITE S-RANK YO-KAI! ♪

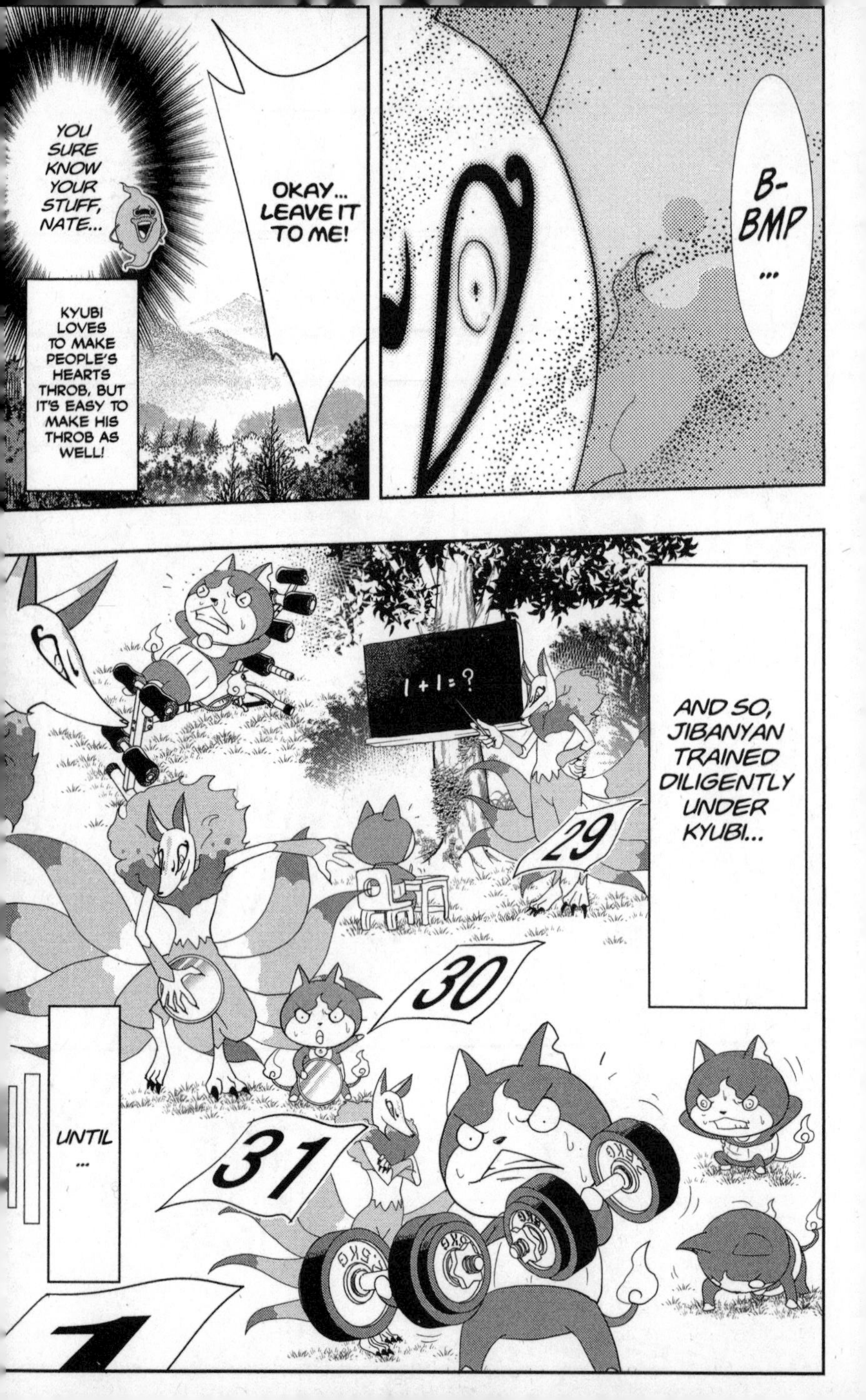
B-BMP...
OKAY... LEAVE IT TO ME!
YOU SURE KNOW YOUR STUFF, NATE...
KYUBI LOVES TO MAKE PEOPLE'S HEARTS THROB, BUT IT'S EASY TO MAKE HIS THROB AS WELL!
AND SO, JIBANYAN TRAINED DILIGENTLY UNDER KYUBI...
1+1=?
29
30
31
UNTIL ...

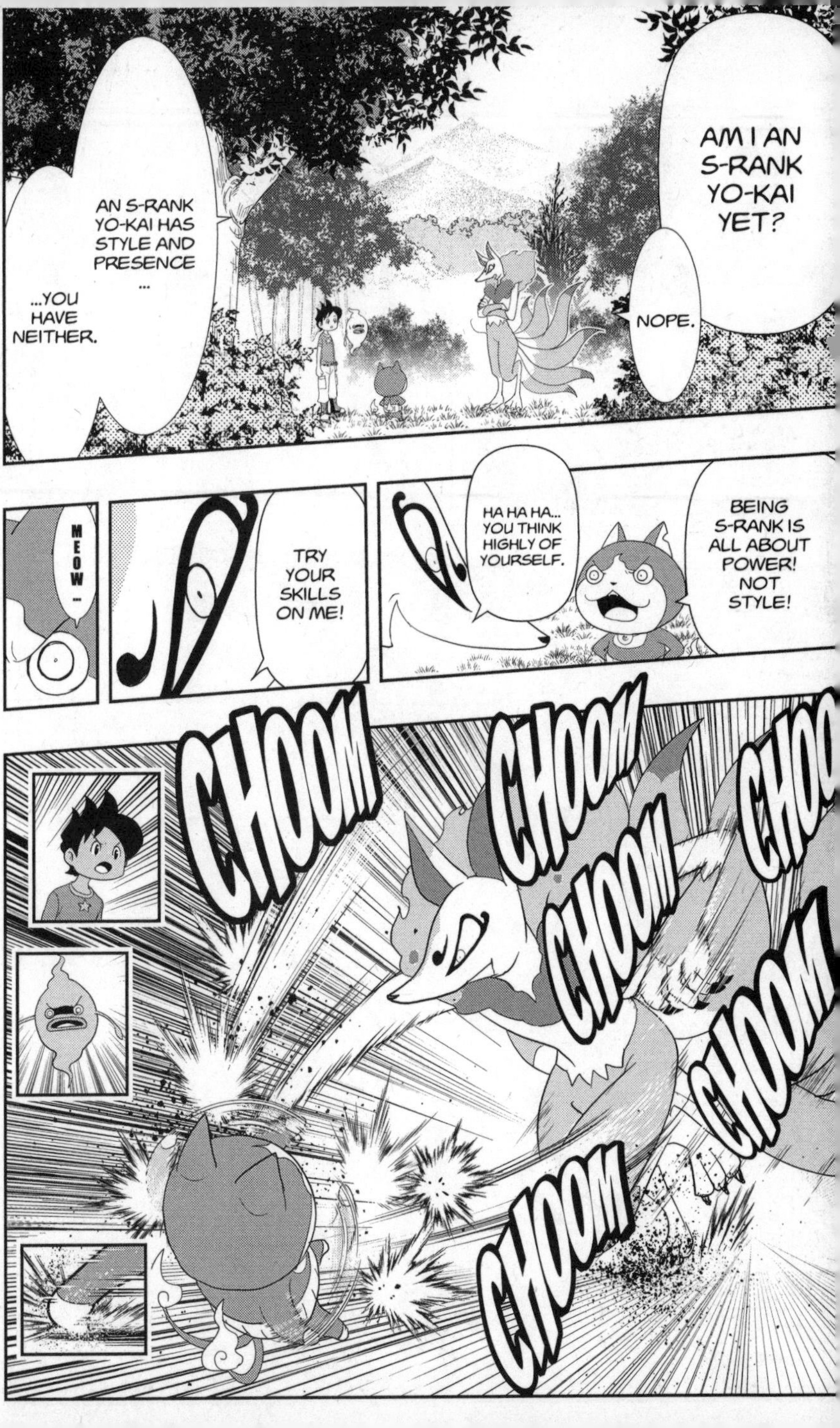
AM I AN S-RANK YO-KAI YET?
NOPE.
AN S-RANK YO-KAI HAS STYLE AND PRESENCE ...
...YOU HAVE NEITHER.
BEING S-RANK IS ALL ABOUT POWER! NOT STYLE!
HA HA HA... YOU THINK HIGHLY OF YOURSELF.
TRY YOUR SKILLS ON ME!
MEOW...
CHOOM
CHOOM
CHOOM
CHOOM
CHOOM
CHOOM

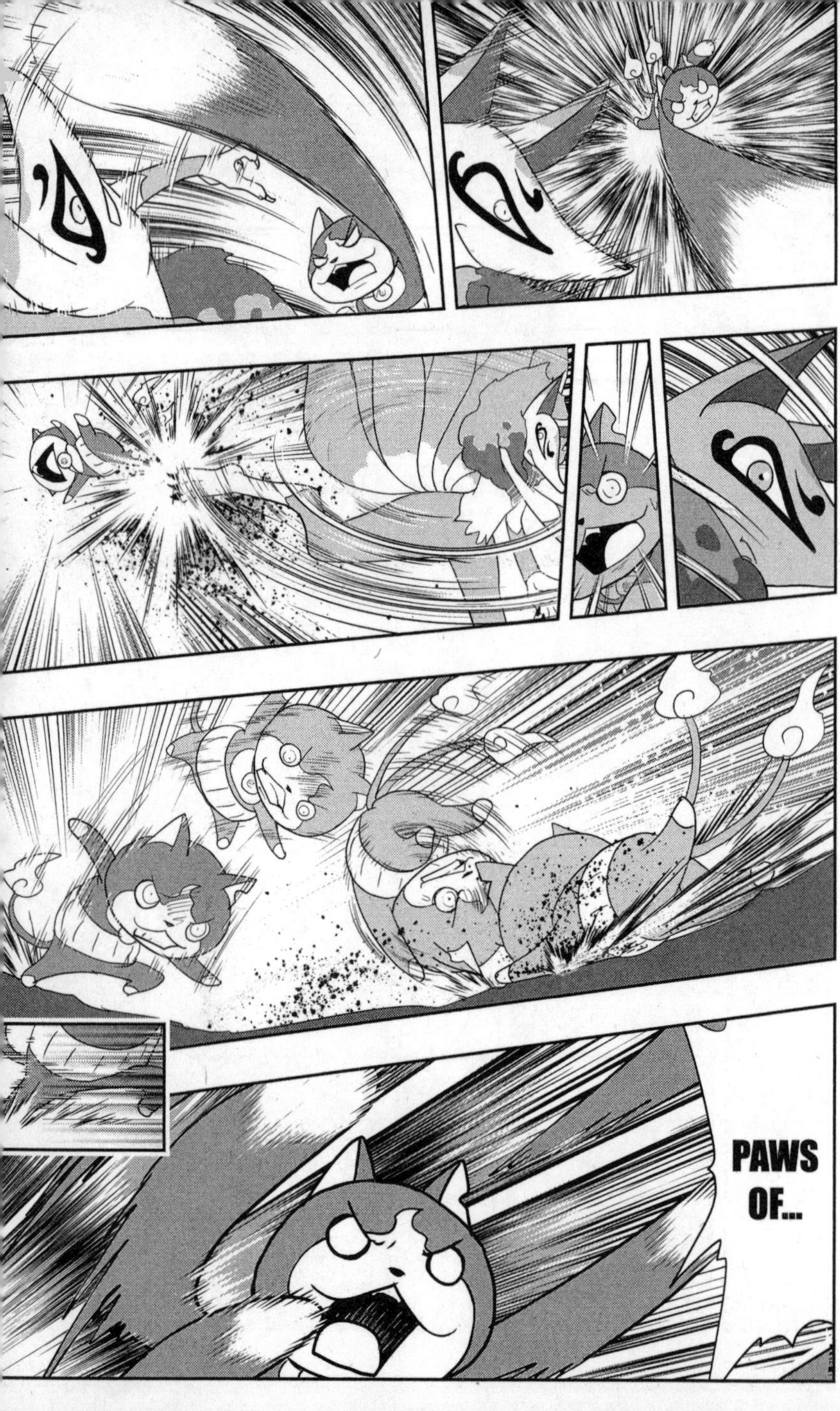
PAWS OF...

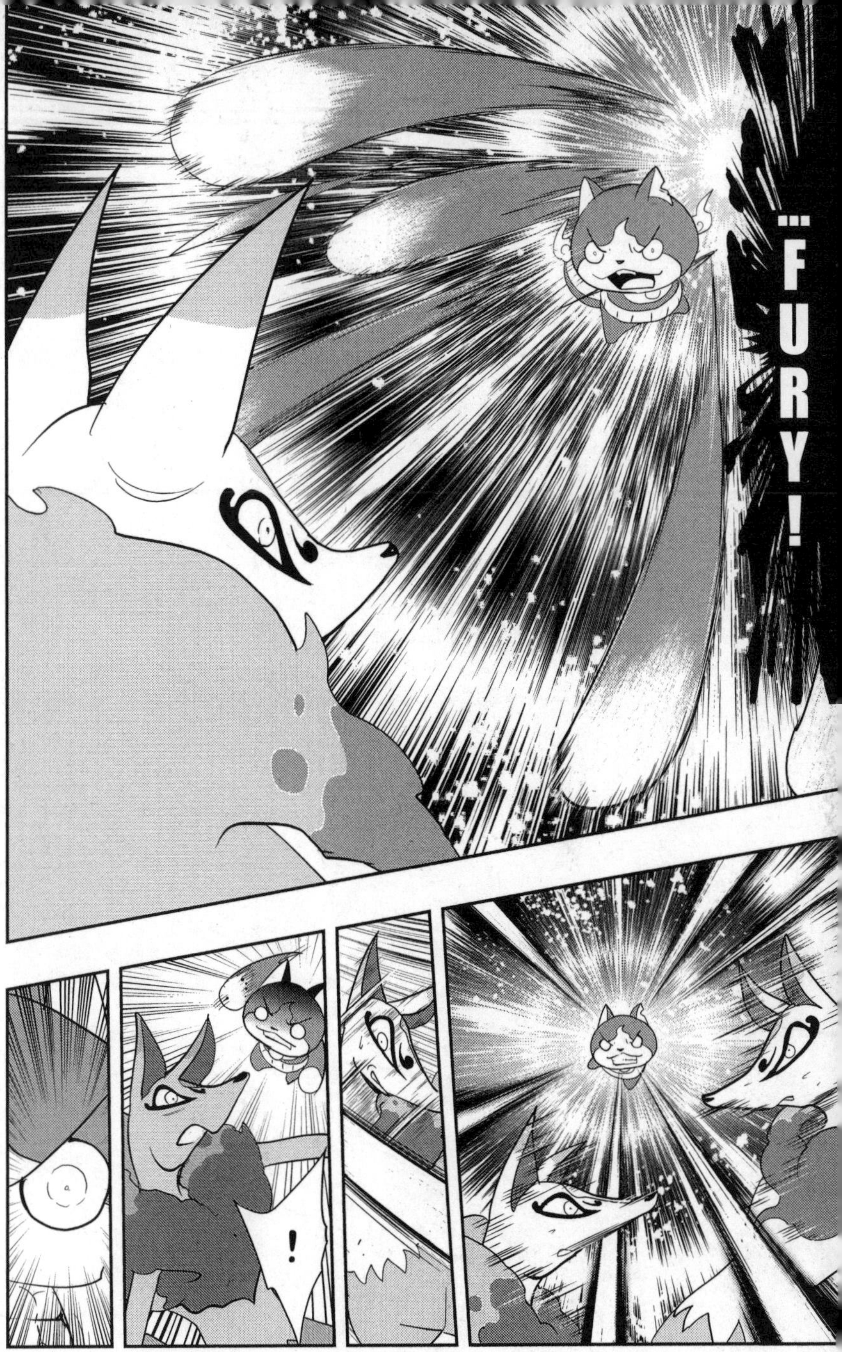
...FURY!
!

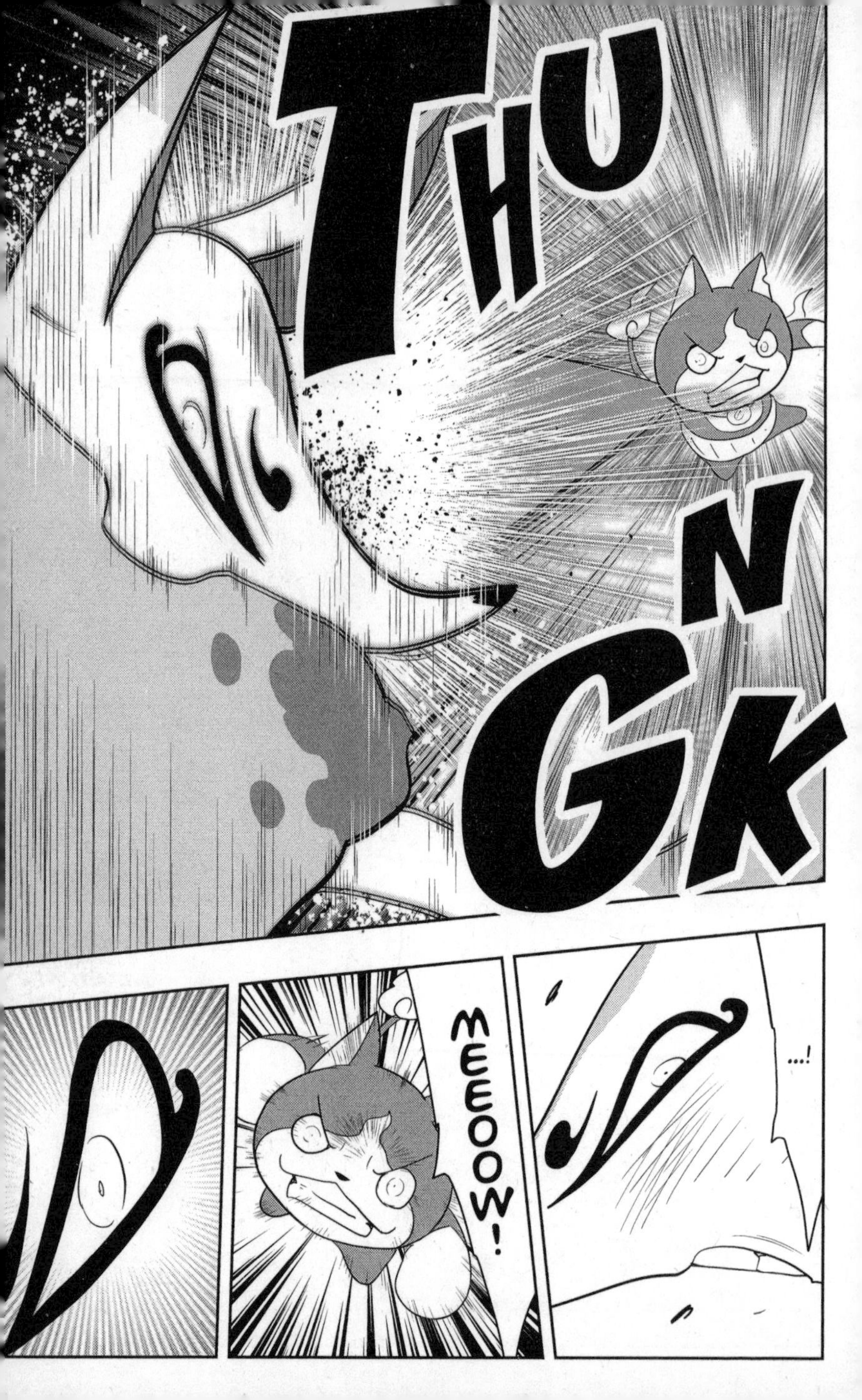
THUNGK
...!
MEEOOW!

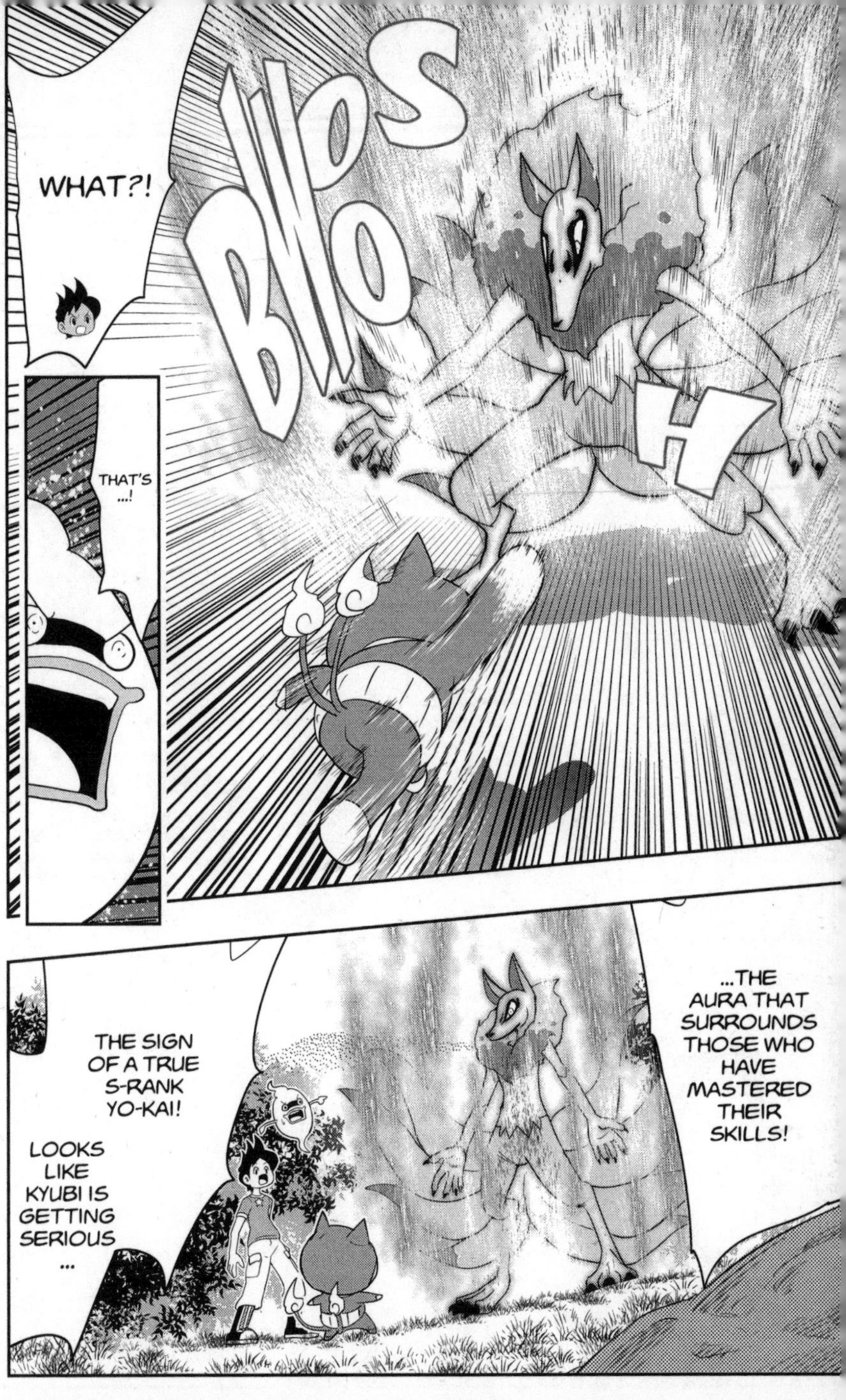
BWOOSH
WHAT?!
THAT'S ...!
...THE AURA THAT SURROUNDS THOSE WHO HAVE MASTERED THEIR SKILLS!
THE SIGN OF A TRUE S-RANK YO-KAI!
LOOKS LIKE KYUBI IS GETTING SERIOUS ...

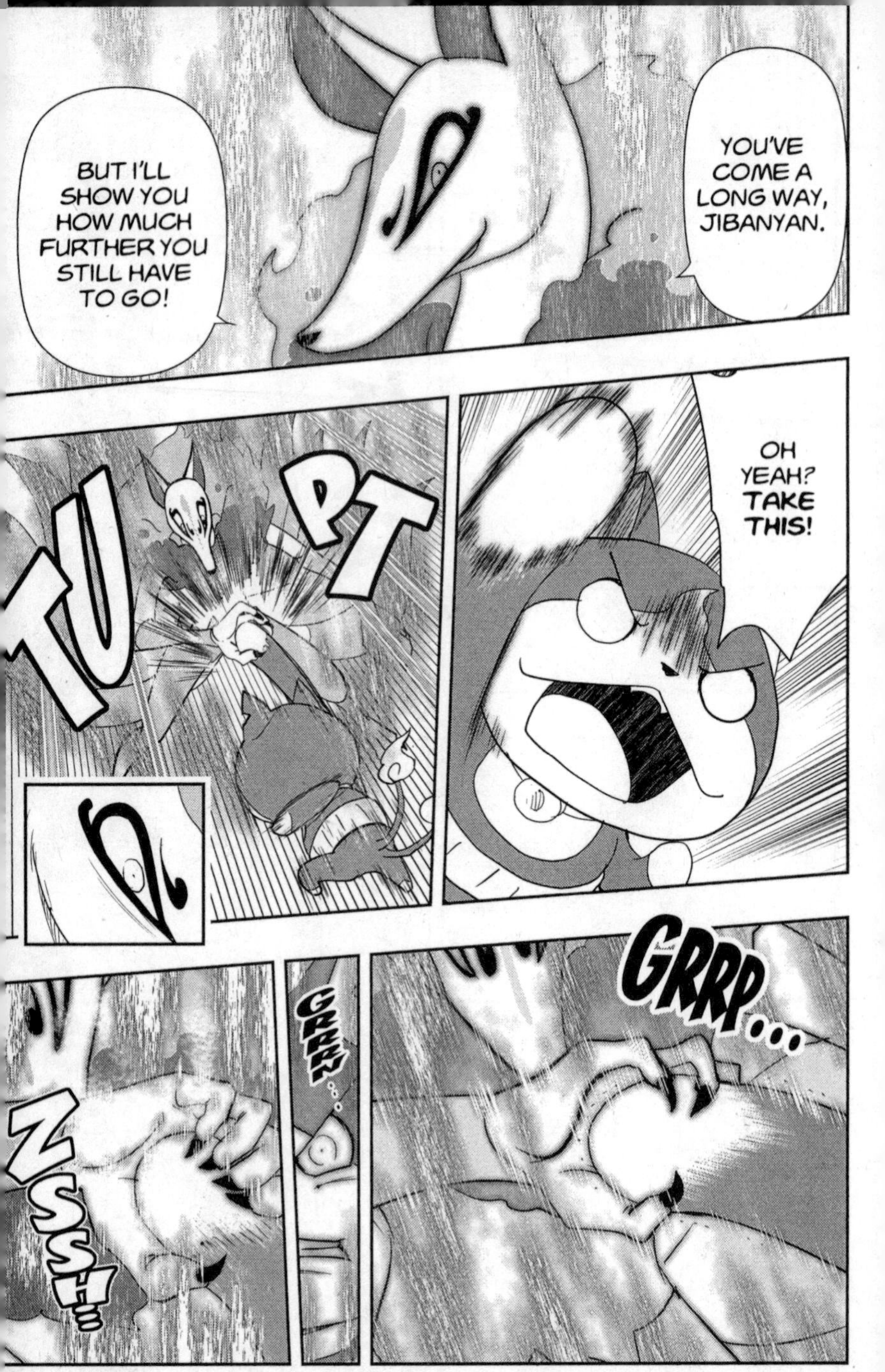
YOU'VE COME A LONG WAY, JIBANYAN.
BUT I'LL SHOW YOU HOW MUCH FURTHER YOU STILL HAVE TO GO!
OH YEAH? TAKE THIS!
TU
PT
GRRP...
GRRRN...
NSSH!!

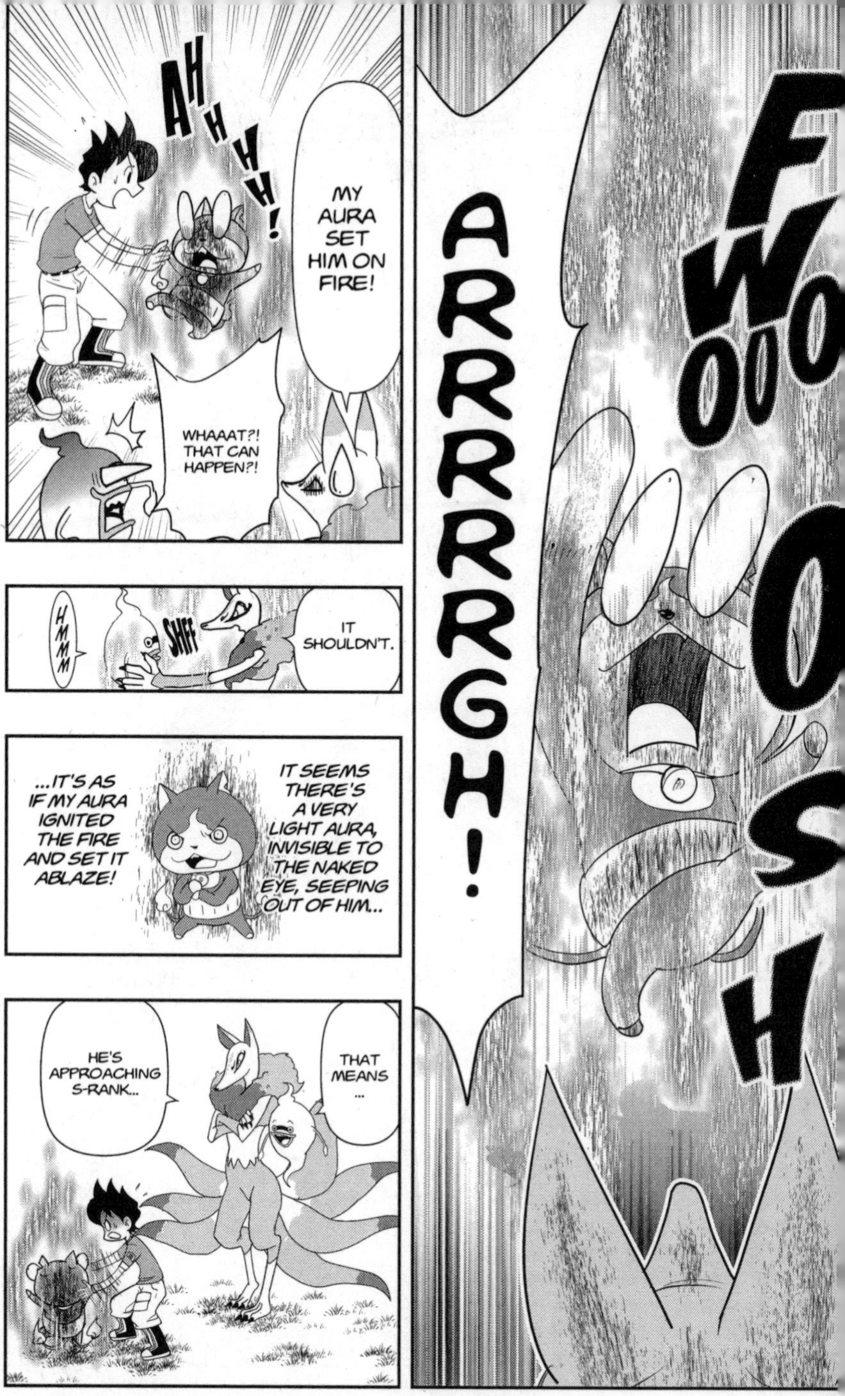
ARRRRGH!
FWOOOOOSH
MY AURA SET HIM ON FIRE!
AHHHH!
WHAAAT?! THAT CAN HAPPEN?!
IT SHOULDN'T.
SHFF
HMMM
IT SEEMS THERE'S A VERY LIGHT AURA, INVISIBLE TO THE NAKED EYE, SEEPING OUT OF HIM...
...IT'S AS IF MY AURA IGNITED THE FIRE AND SET IT ABLAZE!
THAT MEANS ...
HE'S APPROACHING S-RANK...

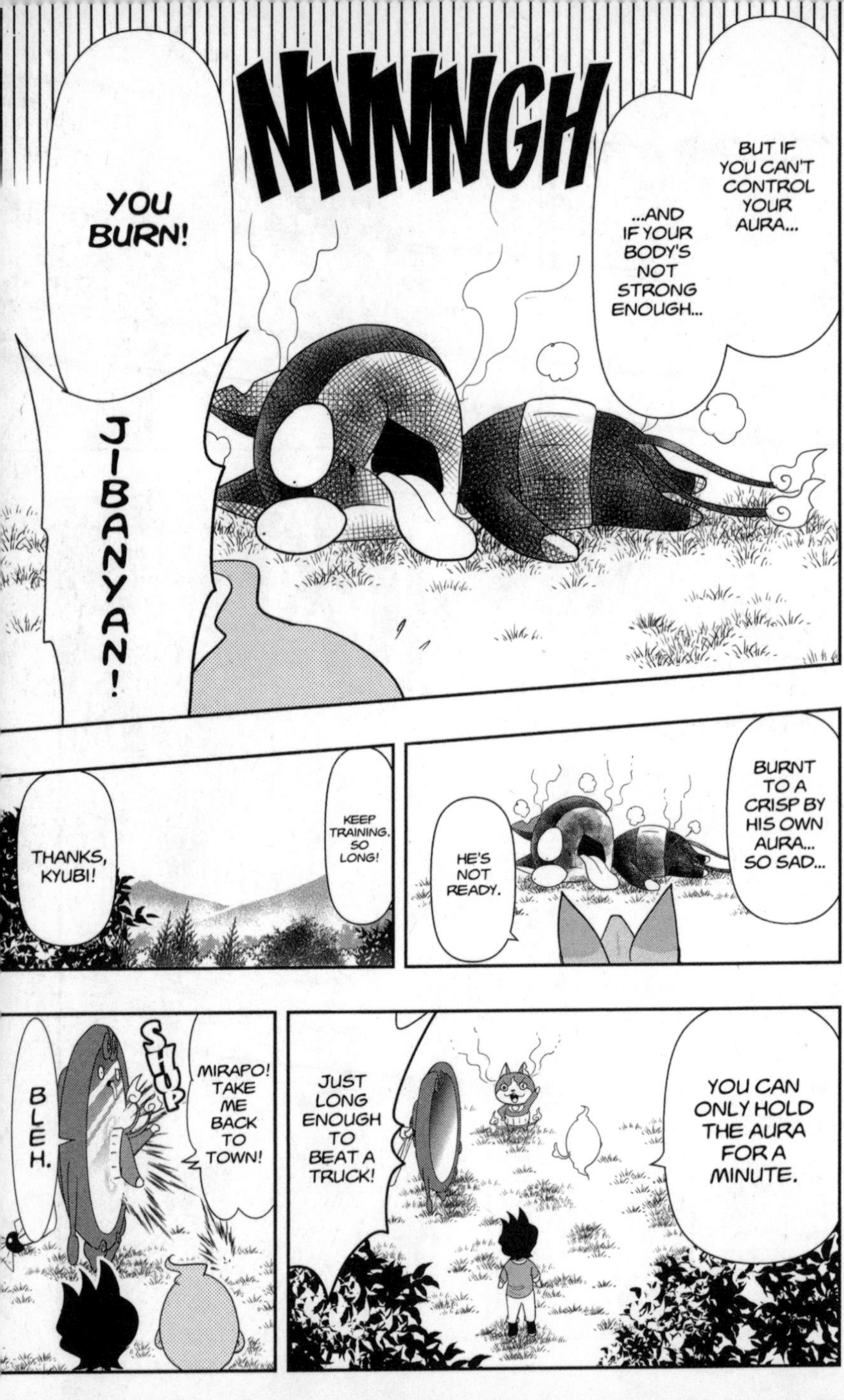
BUT IF YOU CAN'T CONTROL YOUR AURA...
...AND IF YOUR BODY'S NOT STRONG ENOUGH...
NNNNNGH
YOU BURN!
JIBANYAN!
BURNT TO A CRISP BY HIS OWN AURA... SO SAD...
HE'S NOT READY.
KEEP TRAINING, SO LONG!
THANKS, KYUBI!
YOU CAN ONLY HOLD THE AURA FOR A MINUTE.
JUST LONG ENOUGH TO BEAT A TRUCK!
MIRAPO! TAKE ME BACK TO TOWN!
SHUP
BLEH.

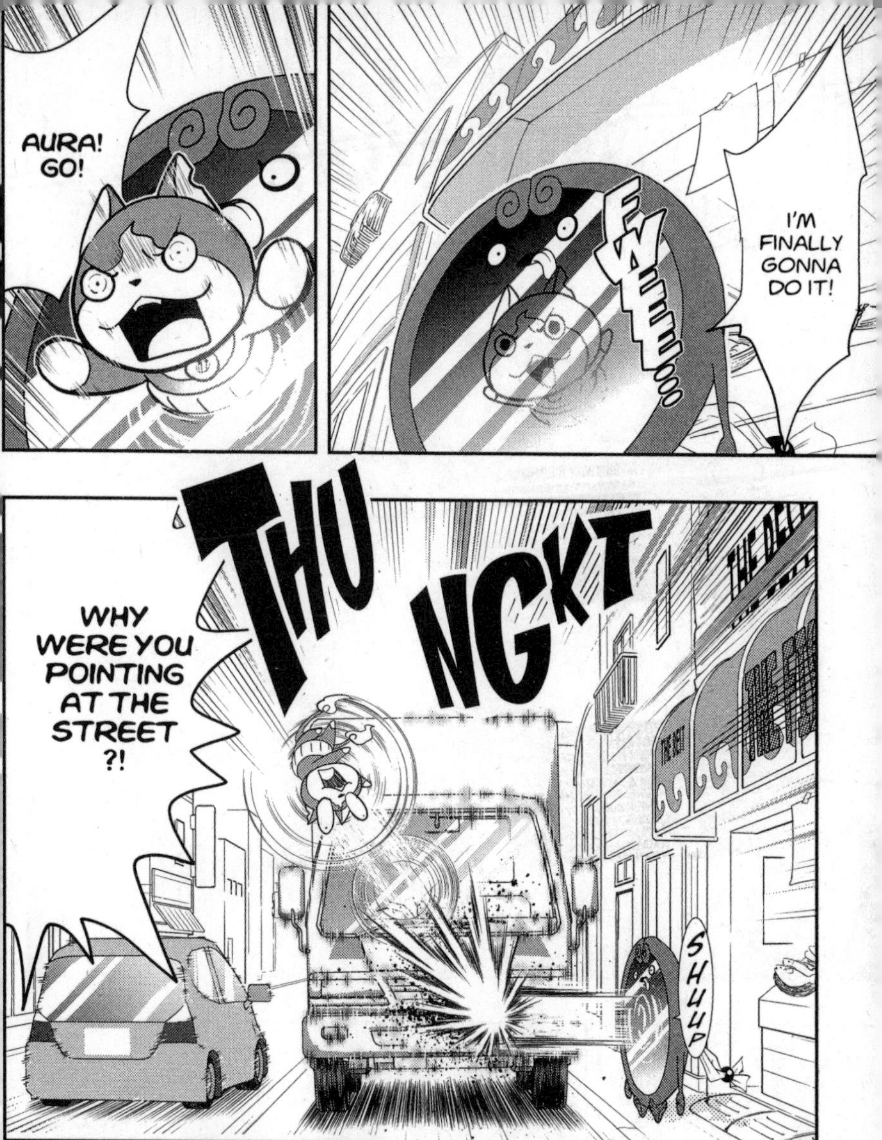
I'M FINALLY GONNA DO IT!
AURA! GO!
THUNGKT
WHY WERE YOU POINTING AT THE STREET?!
SHUUP
...
JIBANYAN CAN NOW BECOME S-RANK FOR A LIMITED AMOUNT OF TIME!

CHAPTER 126: BOILING BATH LOVER YO-KAI SPROINK

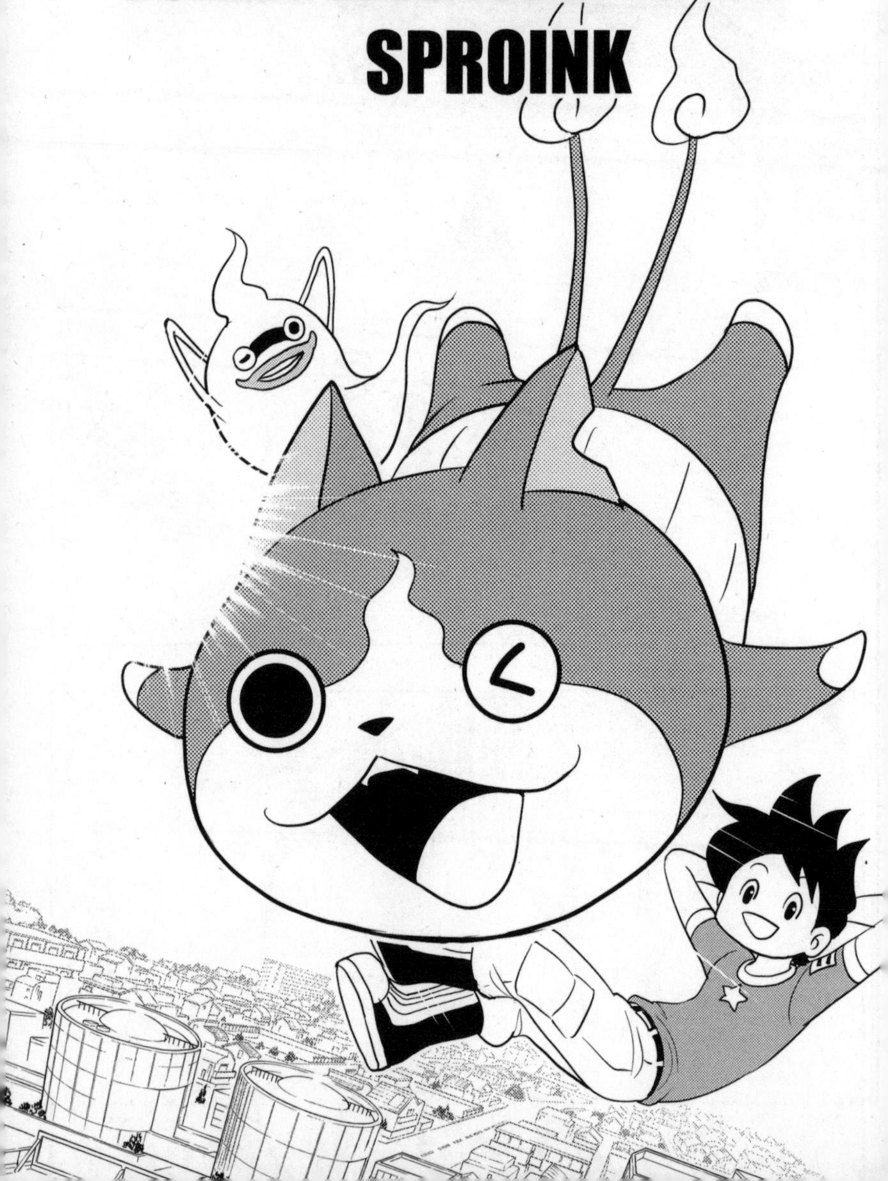

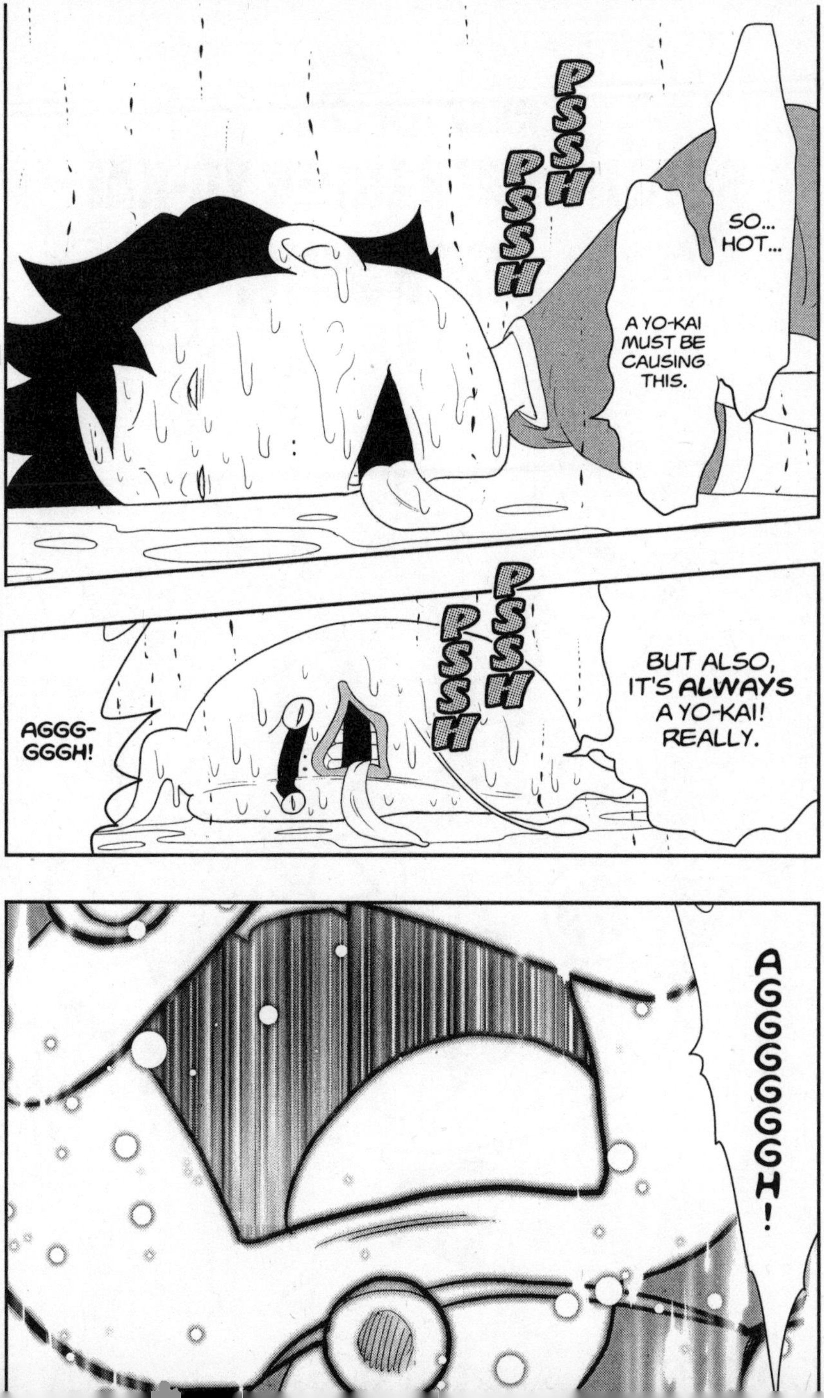
PSSH PSSH
SO... HOT...
A YO-KAI MUST BE CAUSING THIS.
PSSH PSSH
BUT ALSO, IT'S ALWAYS A YO-KAI! REALLY.
AGGG-GGGH!
AGGGGGGGH!

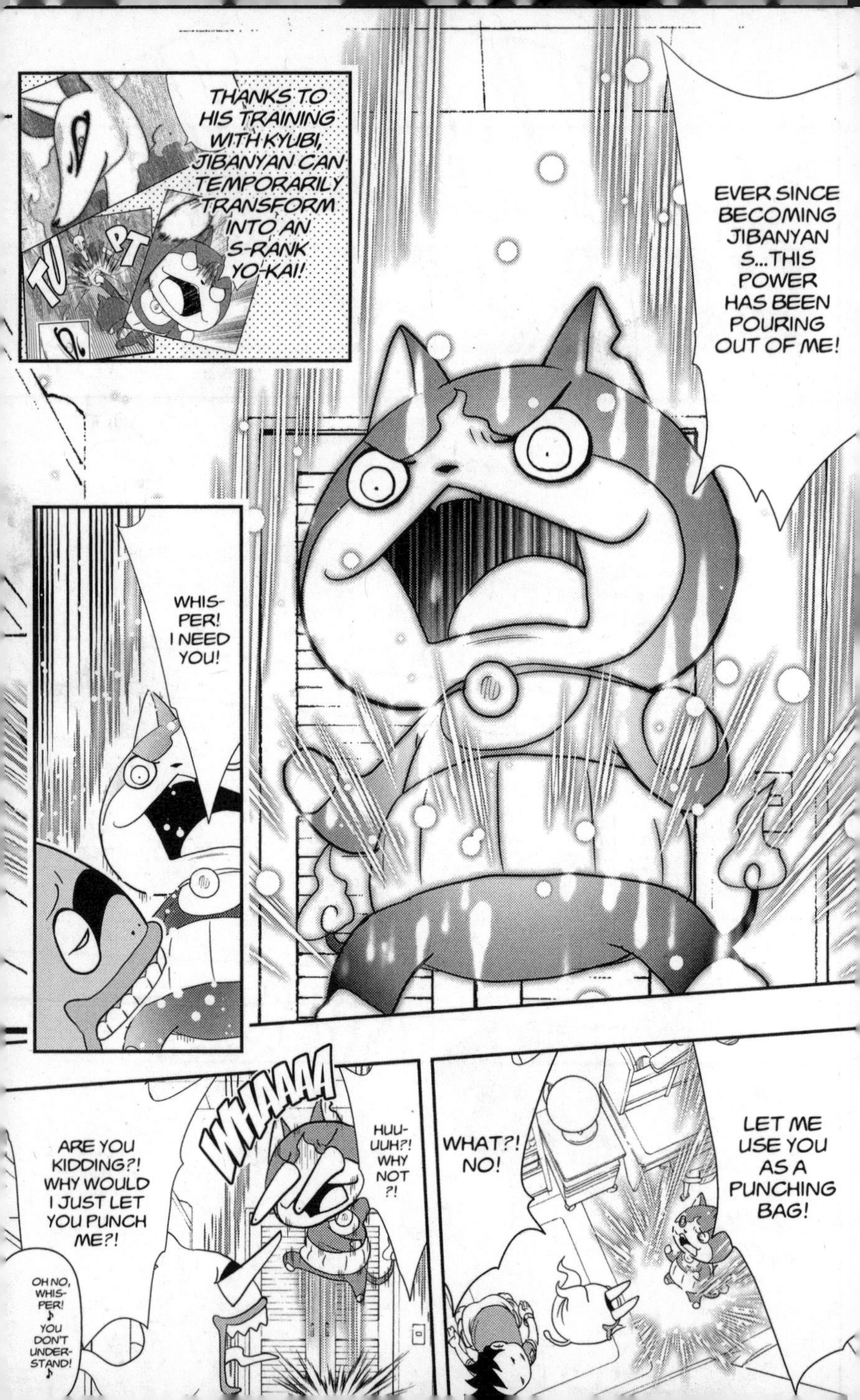
EVER SINCE BECOMING JIBANYAN S...THIS POWER HAS BEEN POURING OUT OF ME!
THANKS TO HIS TRAINING WITH KYUBI, JIBANYAN CAN TEMPORARILY TRANSFORM INTO AN S-RANK YO-KAI!
PT
TU
WHIS-PER! I NEED YOU!
LET ME USE YOU AS A PUNCHING BAG!
WHAT?! NO!
HUU-UUH?! WHY NOT ?!
WHAAAA
ARE YOU KIDDING?! WHY WOULD I JUST LET YOU PUNCH ME?!
OH NO, WHIS-PER! ♪ YOU DON'T UNDER-STAND! ♪

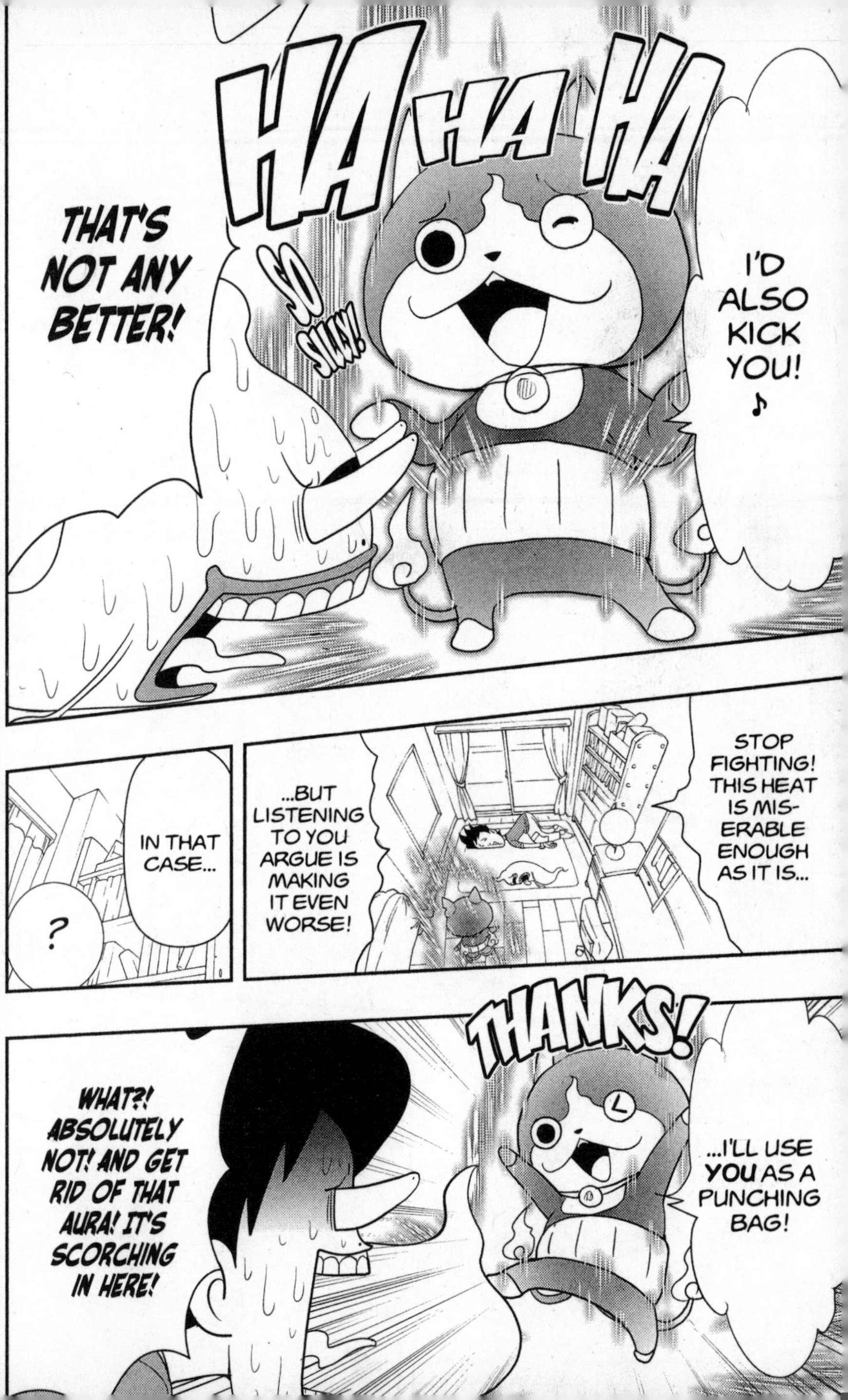
HA HA HA
I'D ALSO KICK YOU! ♪
SO SLASH!
THAT'S NOT ANY BETTER!
STOP FIGHTING! THIS HEAT IS MIS-ERABLE ENOUGH AS IT IS...
...BUT LISTENING TO YOU ARGUE IS MAKING IT EVEN WORSE!
IN THAT CASE...
?
THANKS!
...I'LL USE YOU AS A PUNCHING BAG!
WHAT?! ABSOLUTELY NOT! AND GET RID OF THAT AURA! IT'S SCORCHING IN HERE!

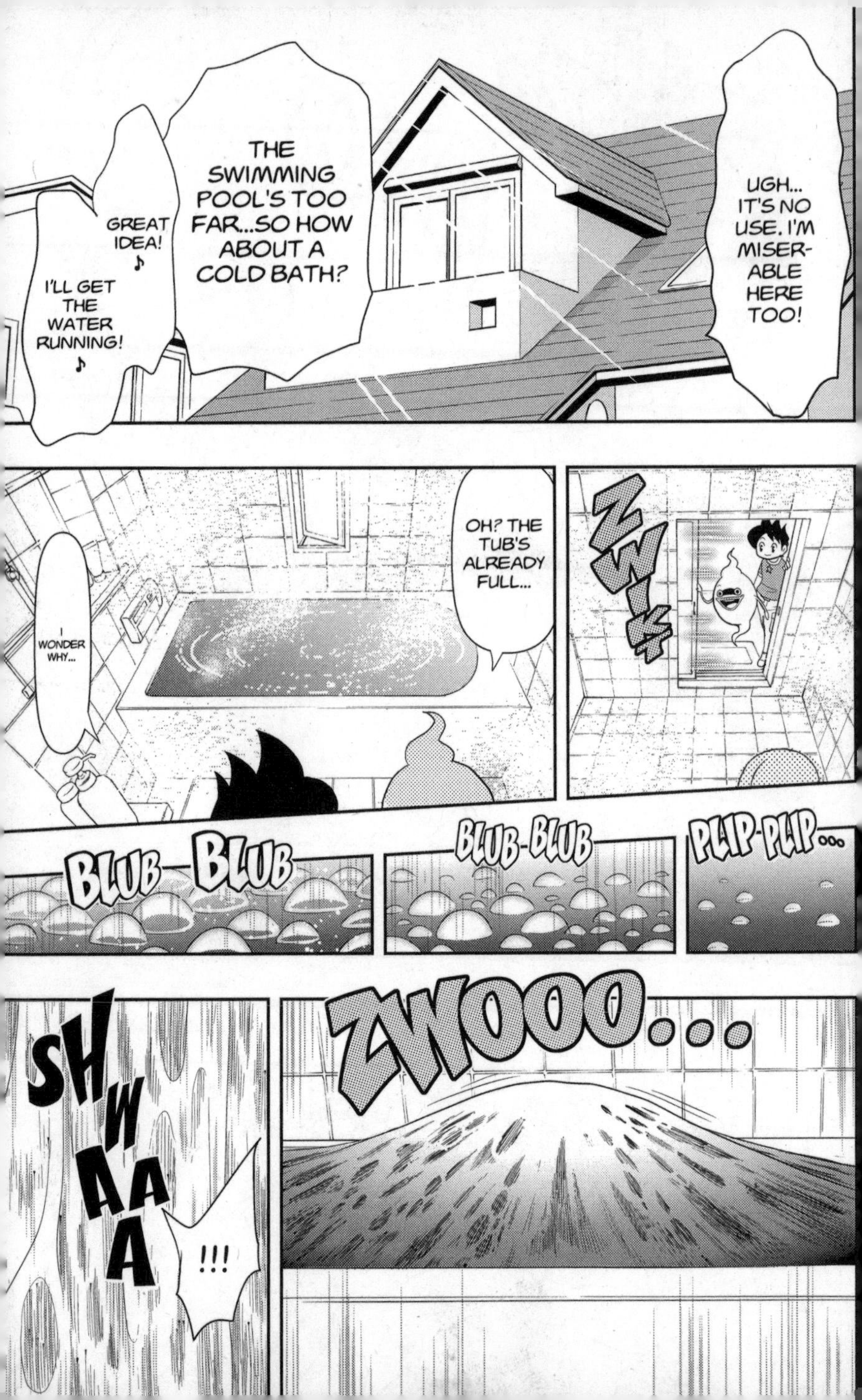
UGH... IT'S NO USE. I'M MISER-ABLE HERE TOO!
THE SWIMMING POOL'S TOO FAR...SO HOW ABOUT A COLD BATH?
GREAT IDEA! ♪
I'LL GET THE WATER RUNNING! ♪
ZWIK
OH? THE TUB'S ALREADY FULL...
I WONDER WHY...
PLIP-PLIP...
BLUB-BLUB
BLUB-BLUB
ZWOOO...
SHWAAA
!!!

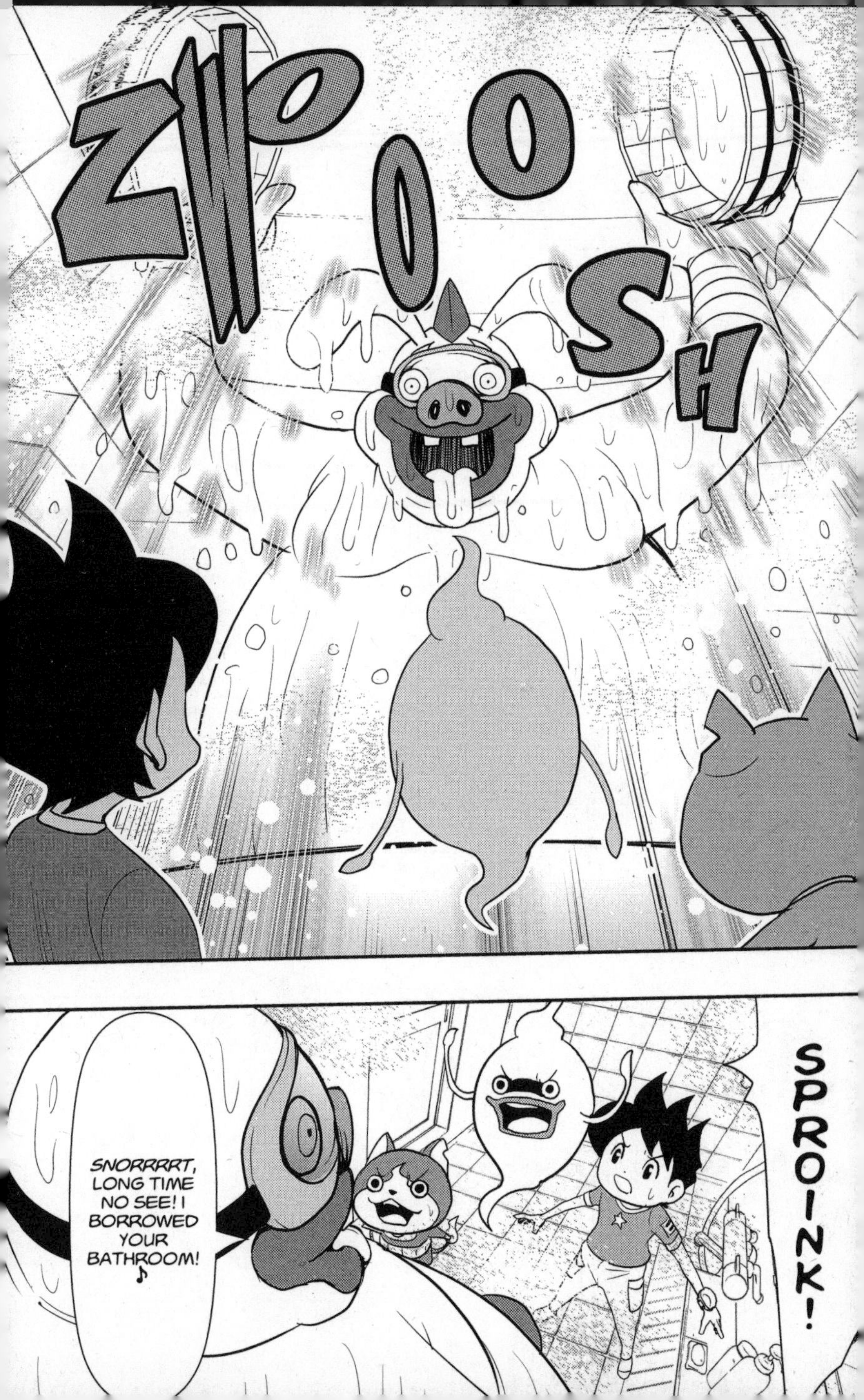
ZWOOOSH
SPROINK!
SNORRRRT, LONG TIME NO SEE! I BORROWED YOUR BATHROOM! ♪

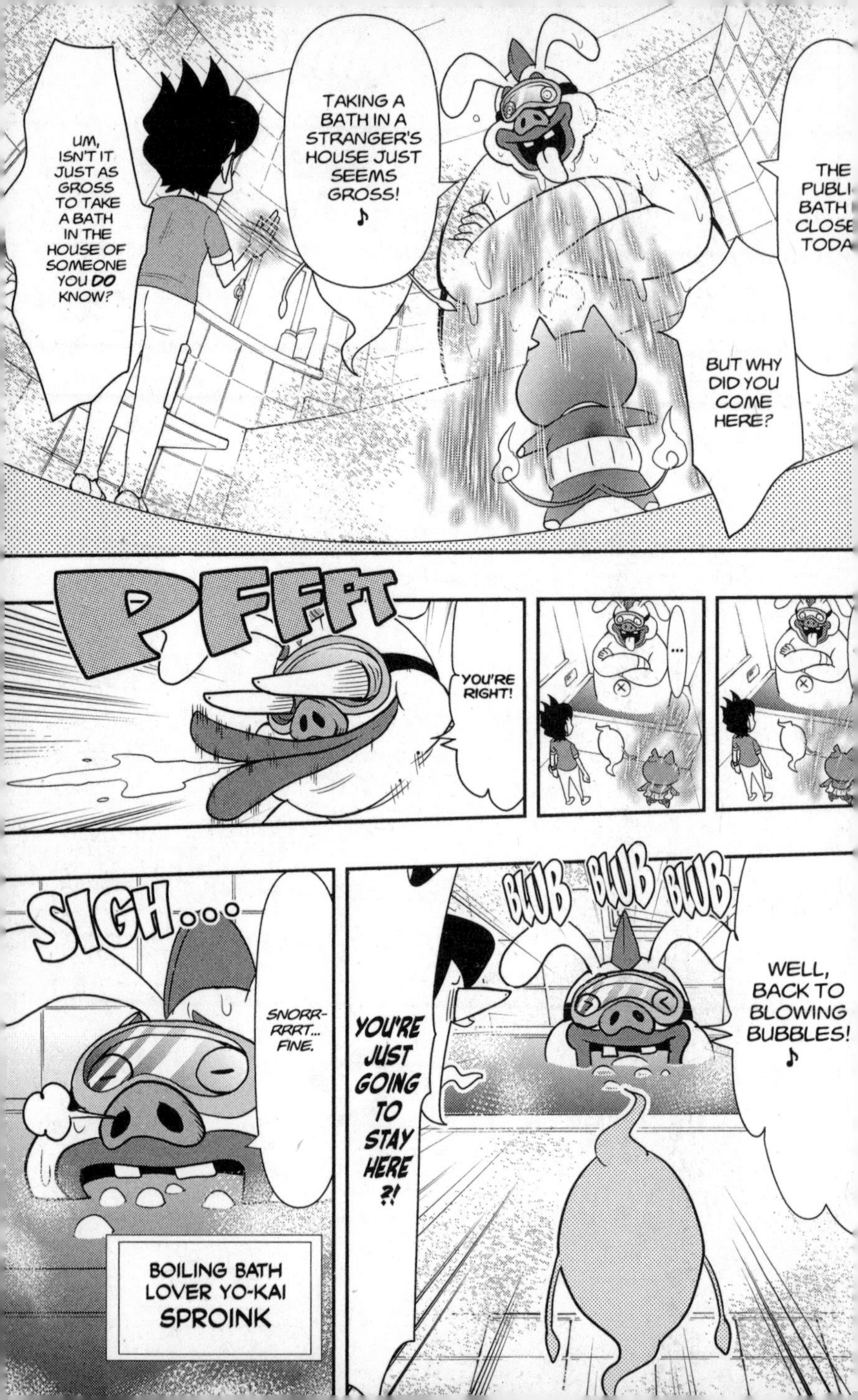
THE PUBLI BATH I CLOSE TODA
BUT WHY DID YOU COME HERE?
TAKING A BATH IN A STRANGER'S HOUSE JUST SEEMS GROSS! ♪
UM, ISN'T IT JUST AS GROSS TO TAKE A BATH IN THE HOUSE OF SOMEONE YOU **DO** KNOW?
...
YOU'RE RIGHT!
PFFFT
WELL, BACK TO BLOWING BUBBLES! ♪
BLUB BLUB BLUB
YOU'RE JUST GOING TO STAY HERE?!
SIGH...
SNORR-RRRT... FINE.
BOILING BATH LOVER YO-KAI SPROINK

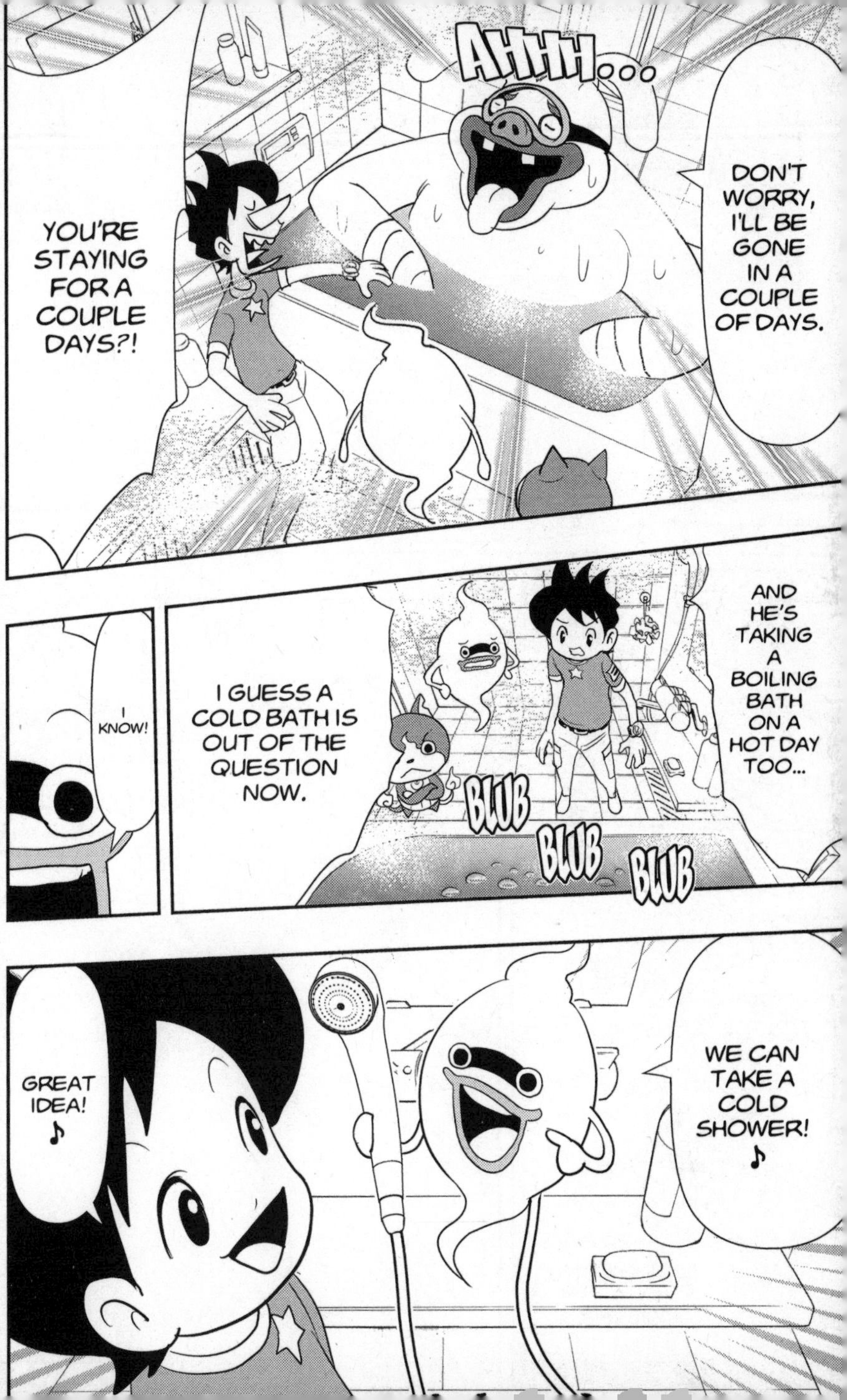
AHHHH ooo
DON'T WORRY, I'LL BE GONE IN A COUPLE OF DAYS.
YOU'RE STAYING FOR A COUPLE DAYS?!
AND HE'S TAKING A BOILING BATH ON A HOT DAY TOO...
I GUESS A COLD BATH IS OUT OF THE QUESTION NOW.
BLUB
BLUB
BLUB
I KNOW!
WE CAN TAKE A COLD SHOWER! ♪
GREAT IDEA! ♪

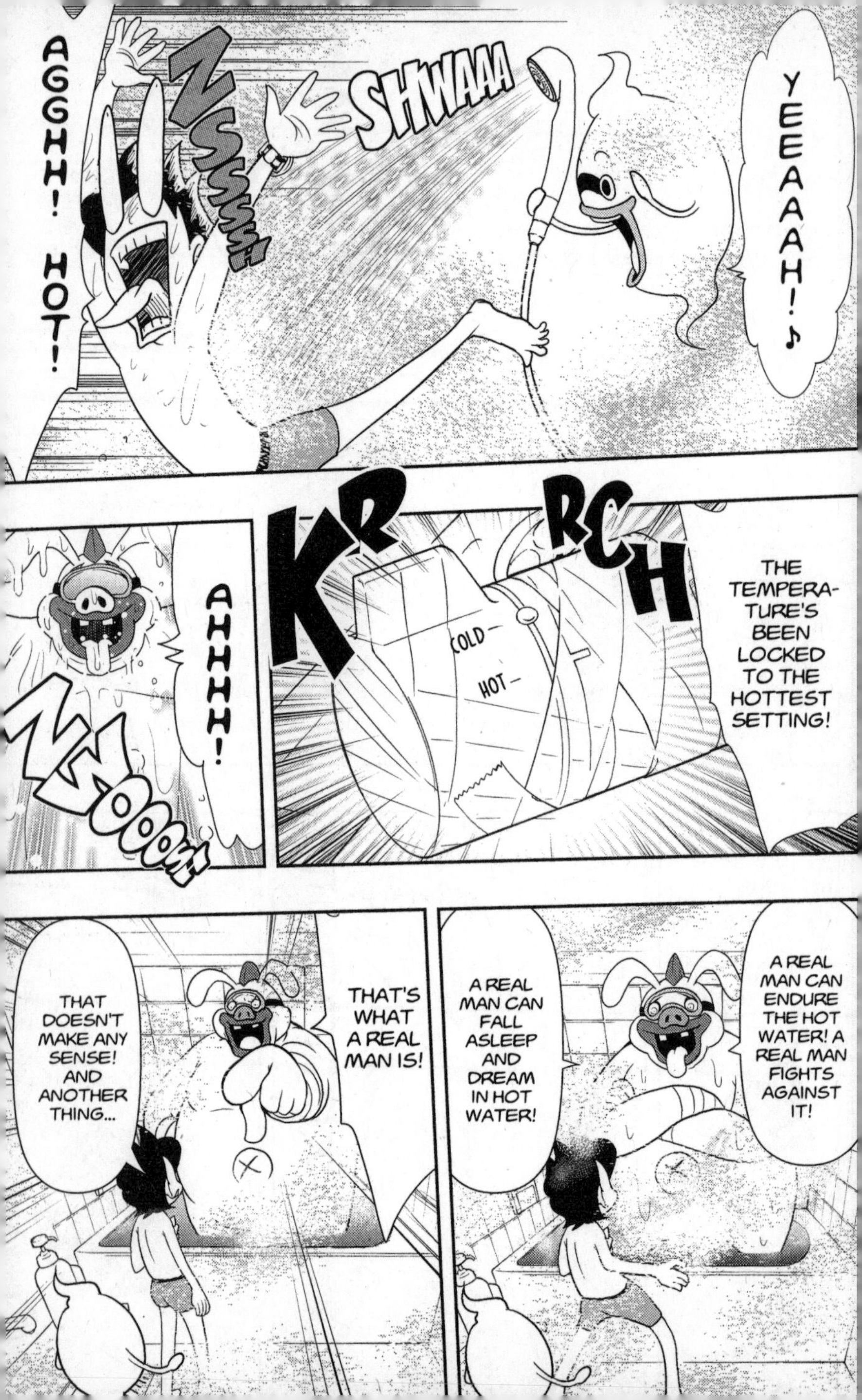
YEEAAAH!♪
SHWAAA
AGGHH! HOT!
THE TEMPERA-TURE'S BEEN LOCKED TO THE HOTTEST SETTING!
KRRCH
COLD
HOT
AHHHH!
A REAL MAN CAN ENDURE THE HOT WATER! A REAL MAN FIGHTS AGAINST IT!
A REAL MAN CAN FALL ASLEEP AND DREAM IN HOT WATER!
THAT'S WHAT A REAL MAN IS!
THAT DOESN'T MAKE ANY SENSE! AND ANOTHER THING...

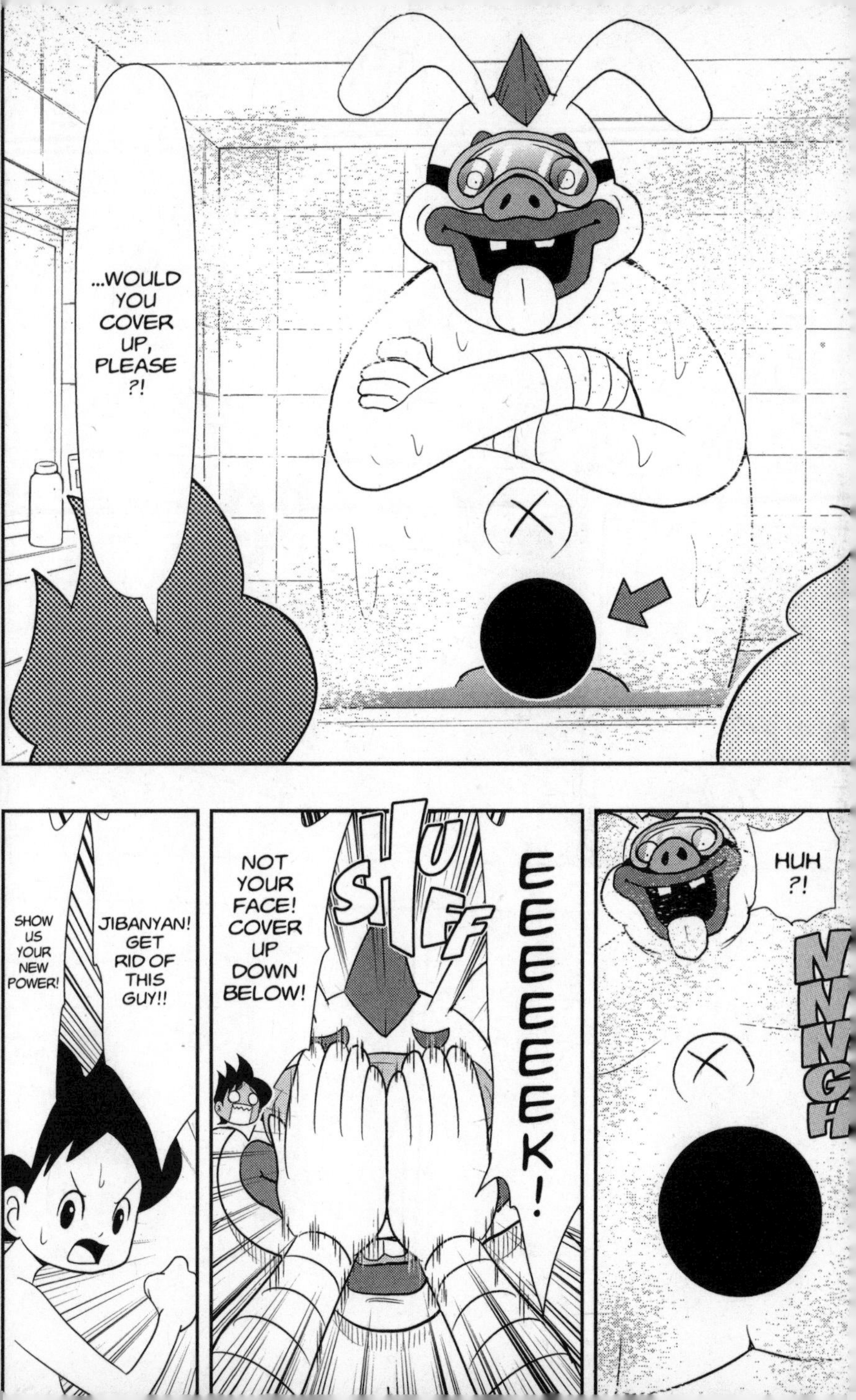
...WOULD YOU COVER UP, PLEASE?!
HUH?!
NNNGH
EEEEEEEK!
SHUFF
NOT YOUR FACE! COVER UP DOWN BELOW!
JIBANYAN! GET RID OF THIS GUY!!
SHOW US YOUR NEW POWER!

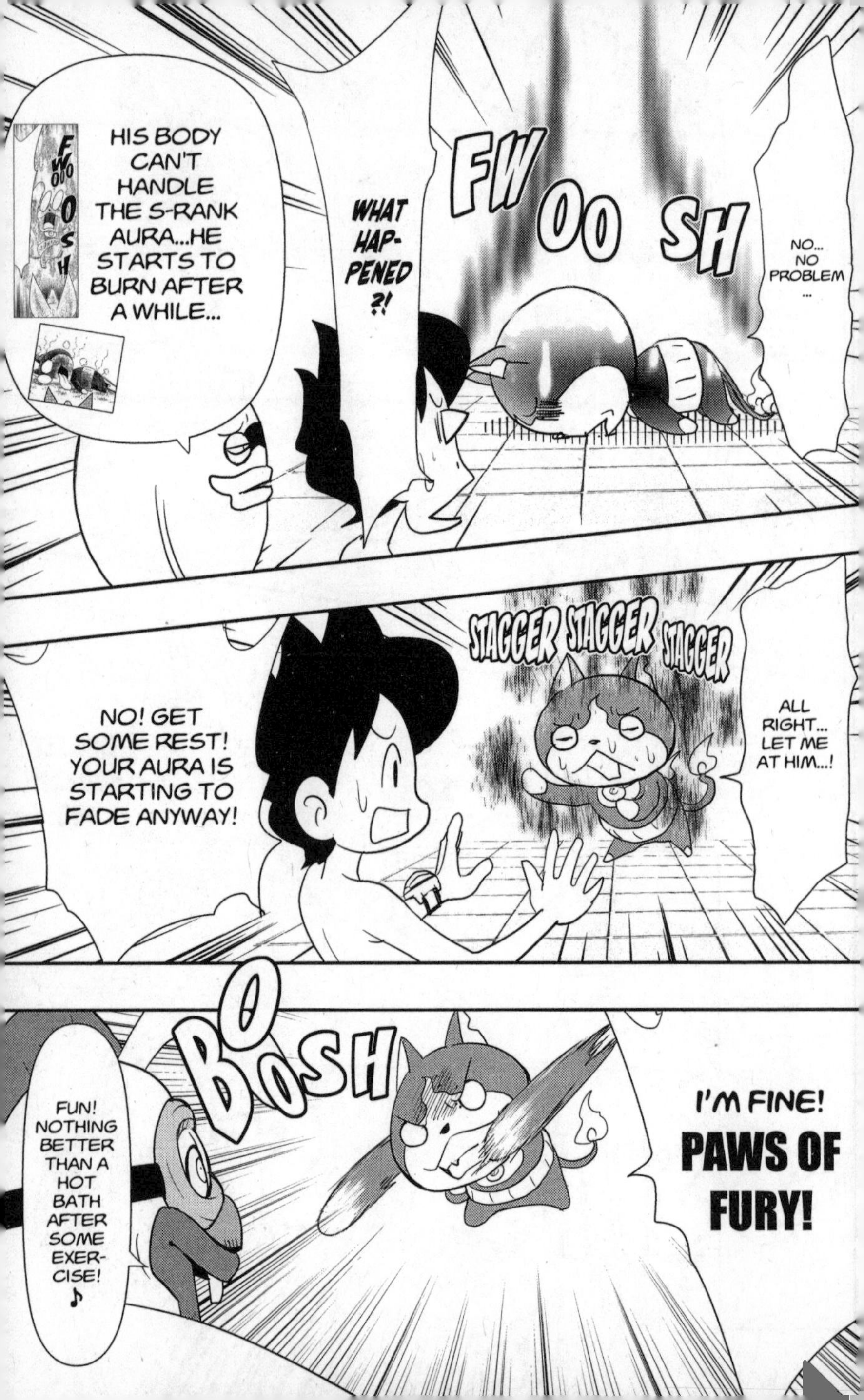
FWOOSH
NO... NO PROBLEM ...
WHAT HAP-PENED?!
HIS BODY CAN'T HANDLE THE S-RANK AURA...HE STARTS TO BURN AFTER A WHILE...
FWOOOSH
ALL RIGHT... LET ME AT HIM...!
STAGGER STAGGER STAGGER
NO! GET SOME REST! YOUR AURA IS STARTING TO FADE ANYWAY!
I'M FINE! PAWS OF FURY!
BOOSH
FUN! NOTHING BETTER THAN A HOT BATH AFTER SOME EXER-CISE! ♪

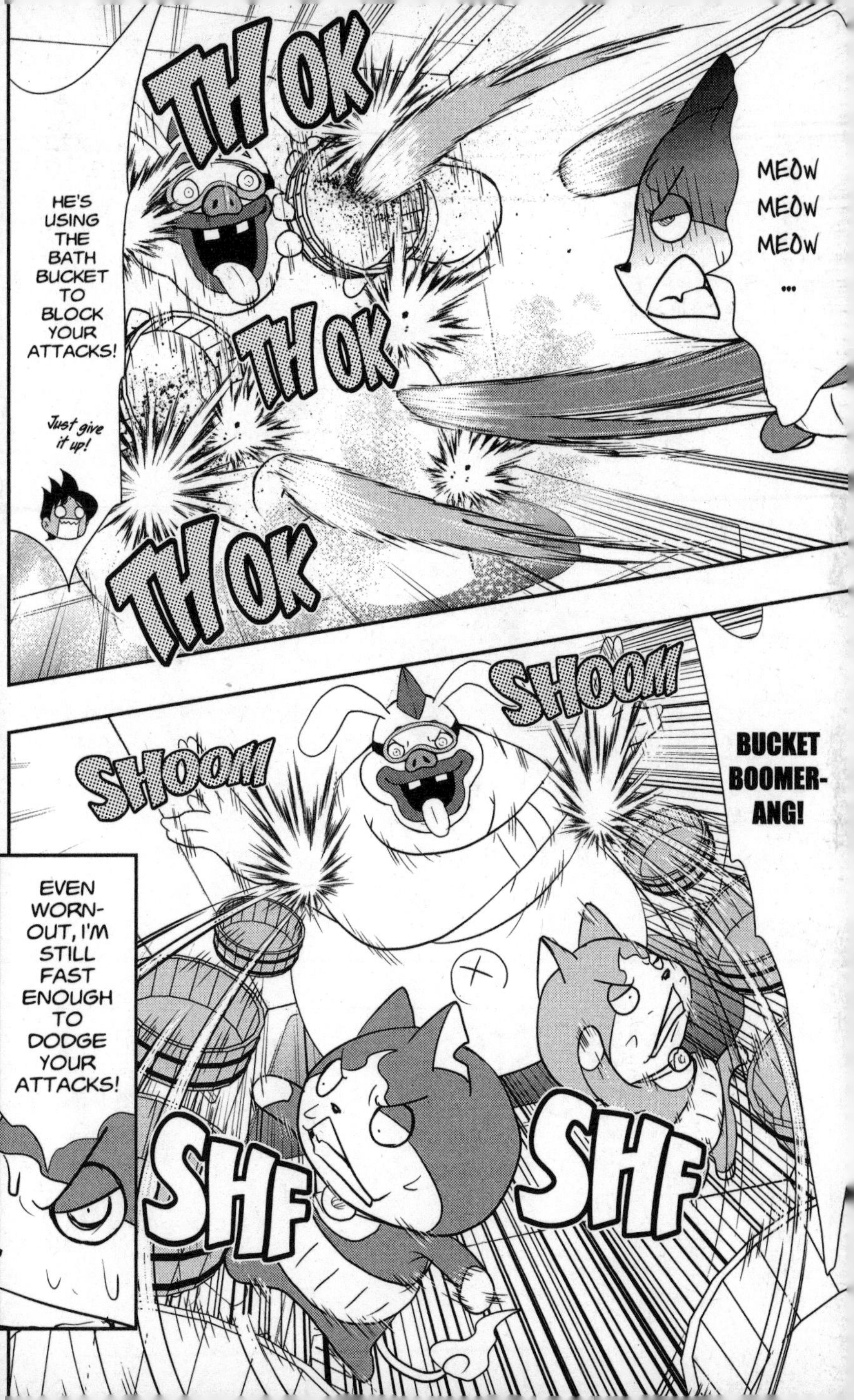
MEOW MEOW MEOW ...
THOK
HE'S USING THE BATH BUCKET TO BLOCK YOUR ATTACKS!
THOK
Just give it up!
THOK
BUCKET BOOMER-ANG!
SHOOM
SHOOM
EVEN WORN-OUT, I'M STILL FAST ENOUGH TO DODGE YOUR ATTACKS!
SHF
SHF

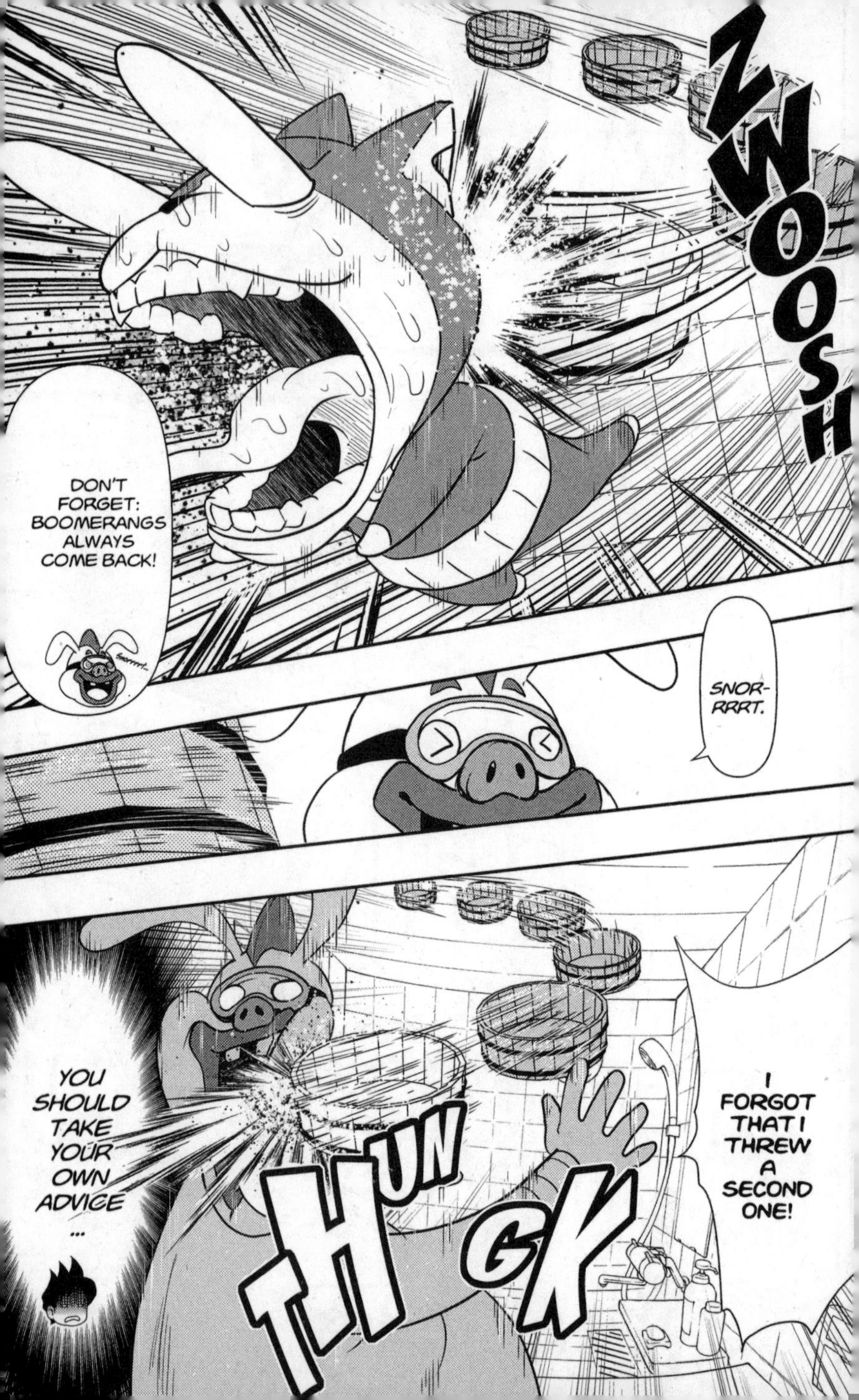
WHOOSH
DON'T FORGET: BOOMERANGS ALWAYS COME BACK!
SNORRRRT.
I FORGOT THAT I THREW A SECOND ONE!
THUNCK
YOU SHOULD TAKE YOUR OWN ADVICE...

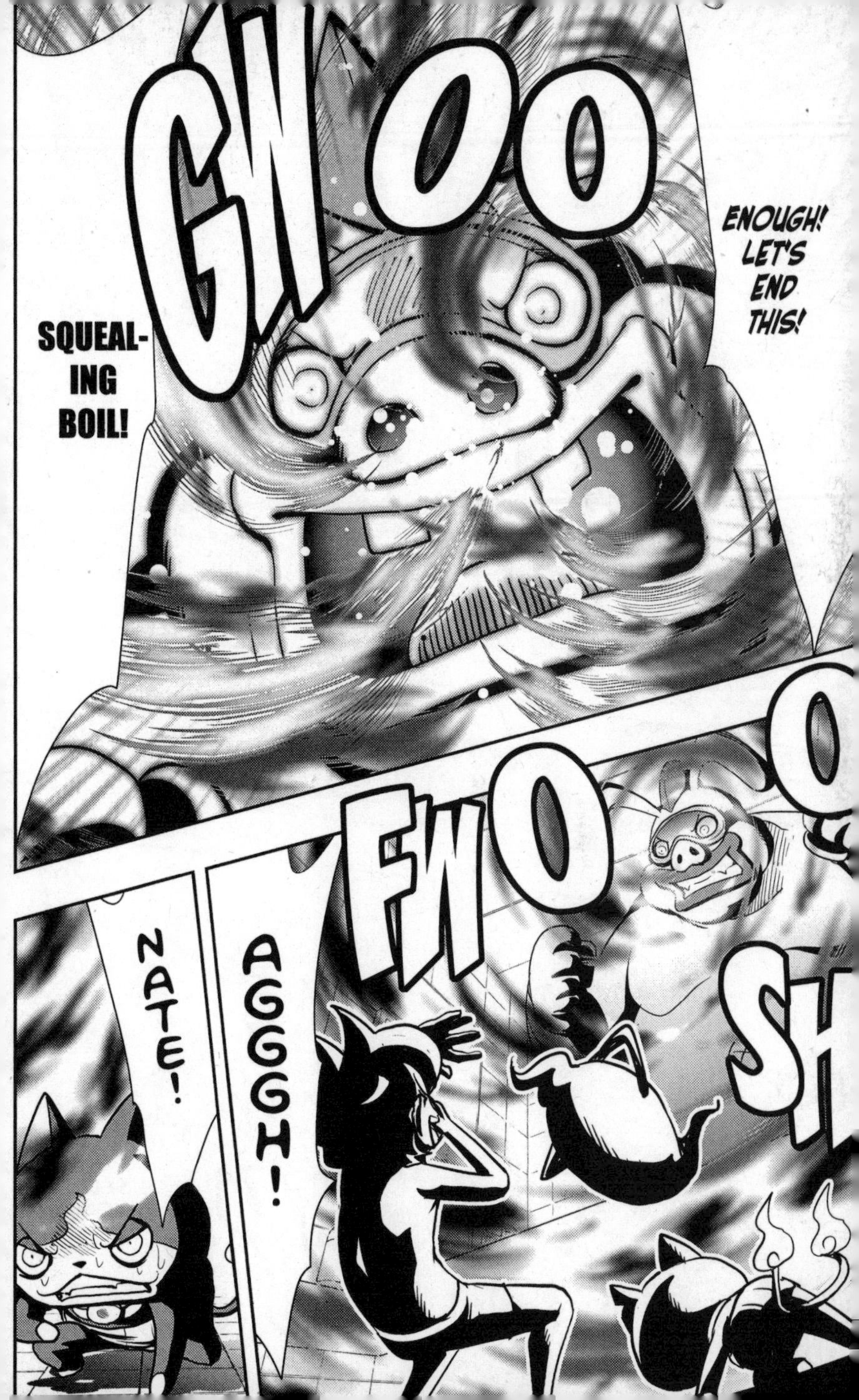
ENOUGH! LET'S END THIS!
GNOO
SQUEAL-ING BOIL!
FWOO
SH
AGGGH!
NATE!

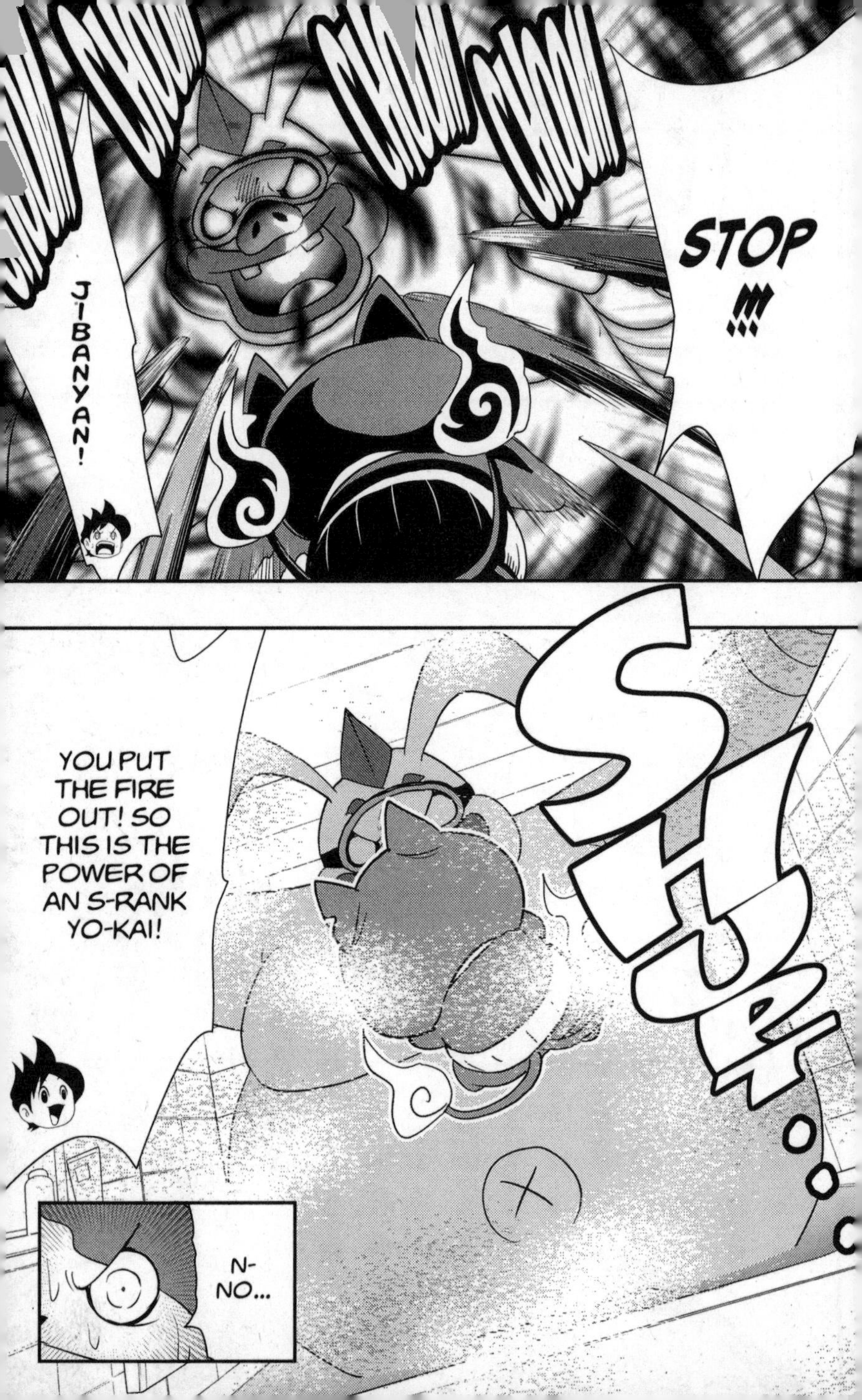
STOP!!!
JIBANYAN!
YOU PUT THE FIRE OUT! SO THIS IS THE POWER OF AN S-RANK YO-KAI!
N-NO...

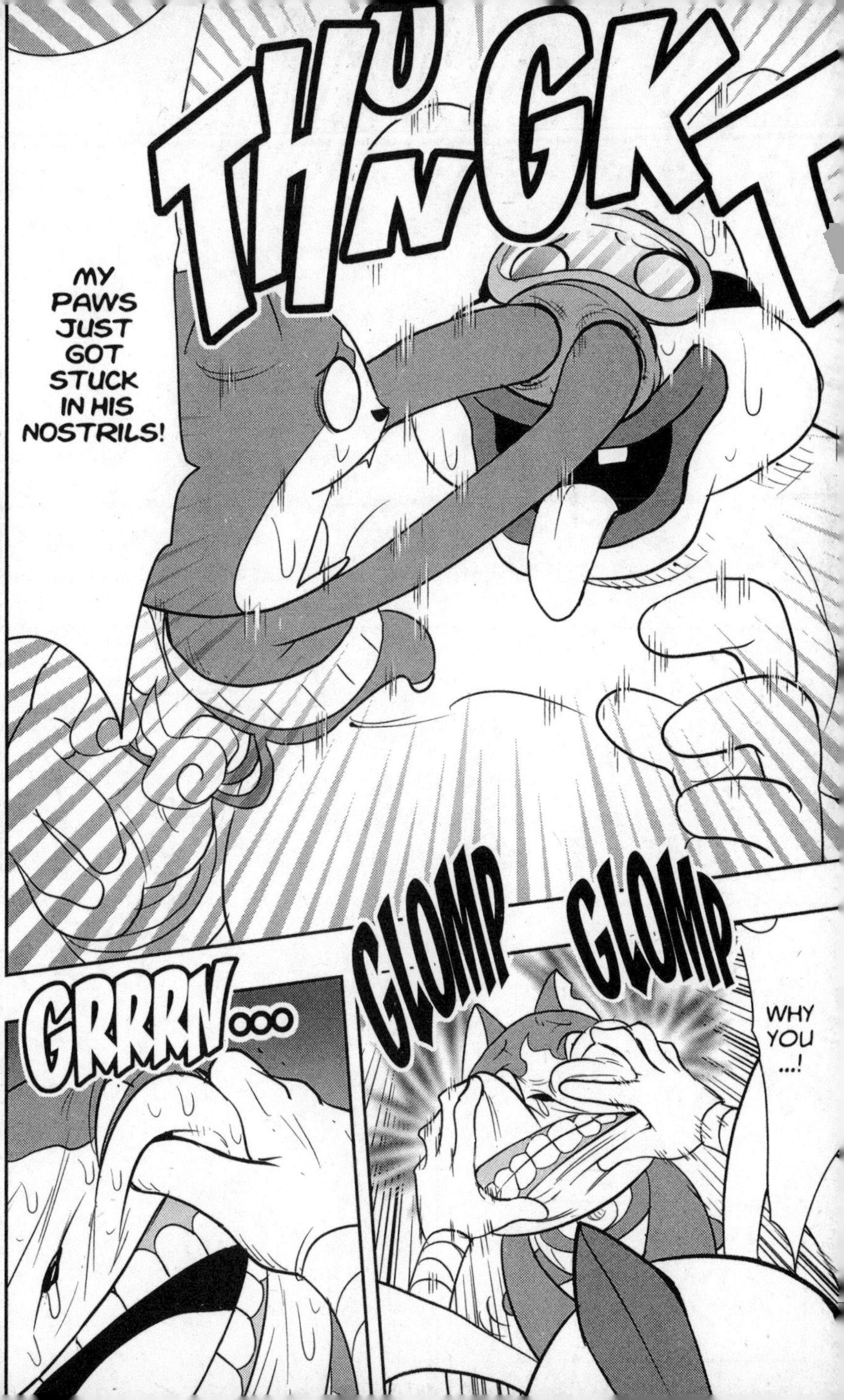
THUNGK
MY PAWS JUST GOT STUCK IN HIS NOSTRILS!
GLOMP GLOMP
WHY YOU ...!
GRRRN...

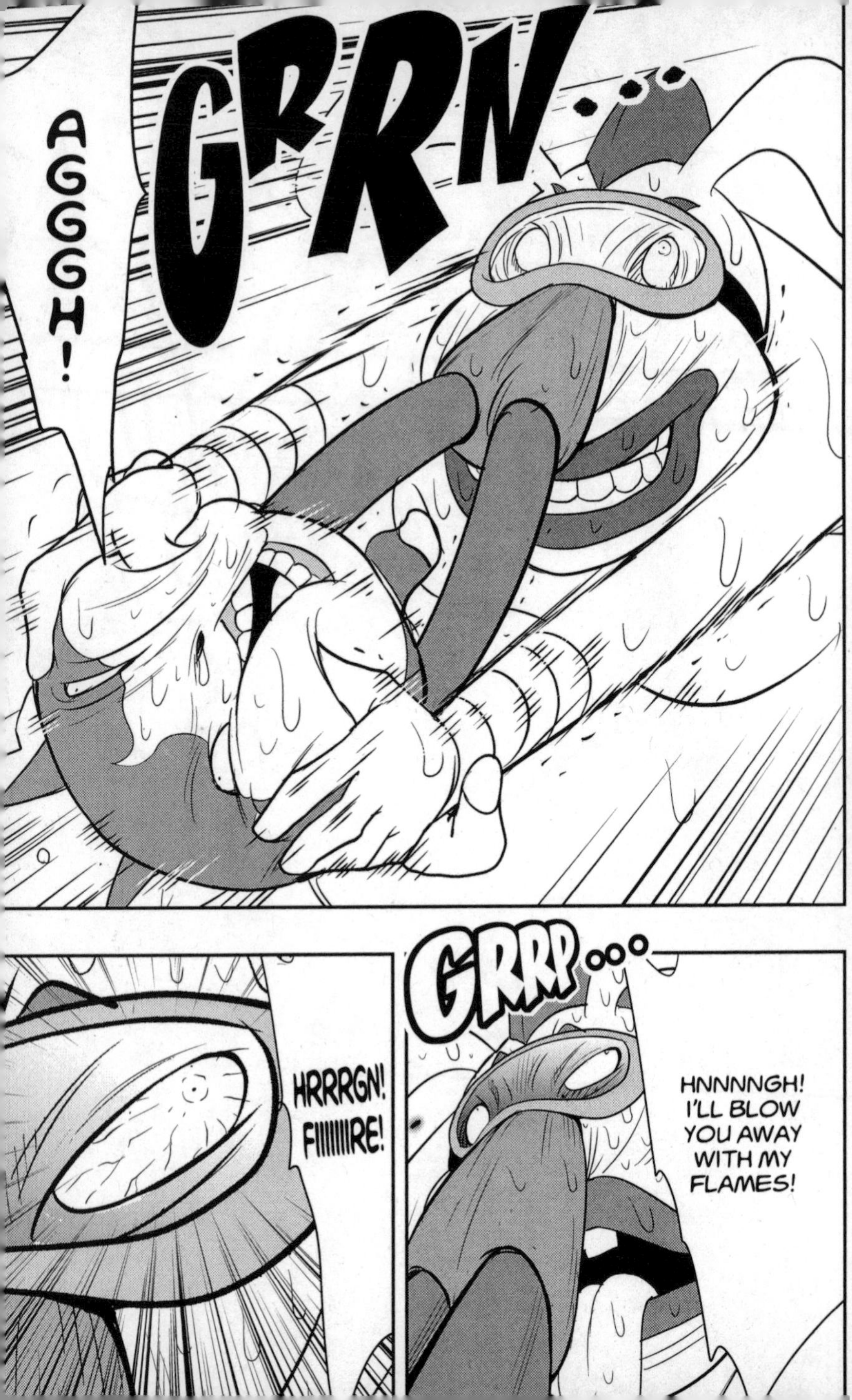
GRRN...
AGGGH!
GRRP...
HNNNNGH! I'LL BLOW YOU AWAY WITH MY FLAMES!
HRRRGN! FIIIIIIRE!

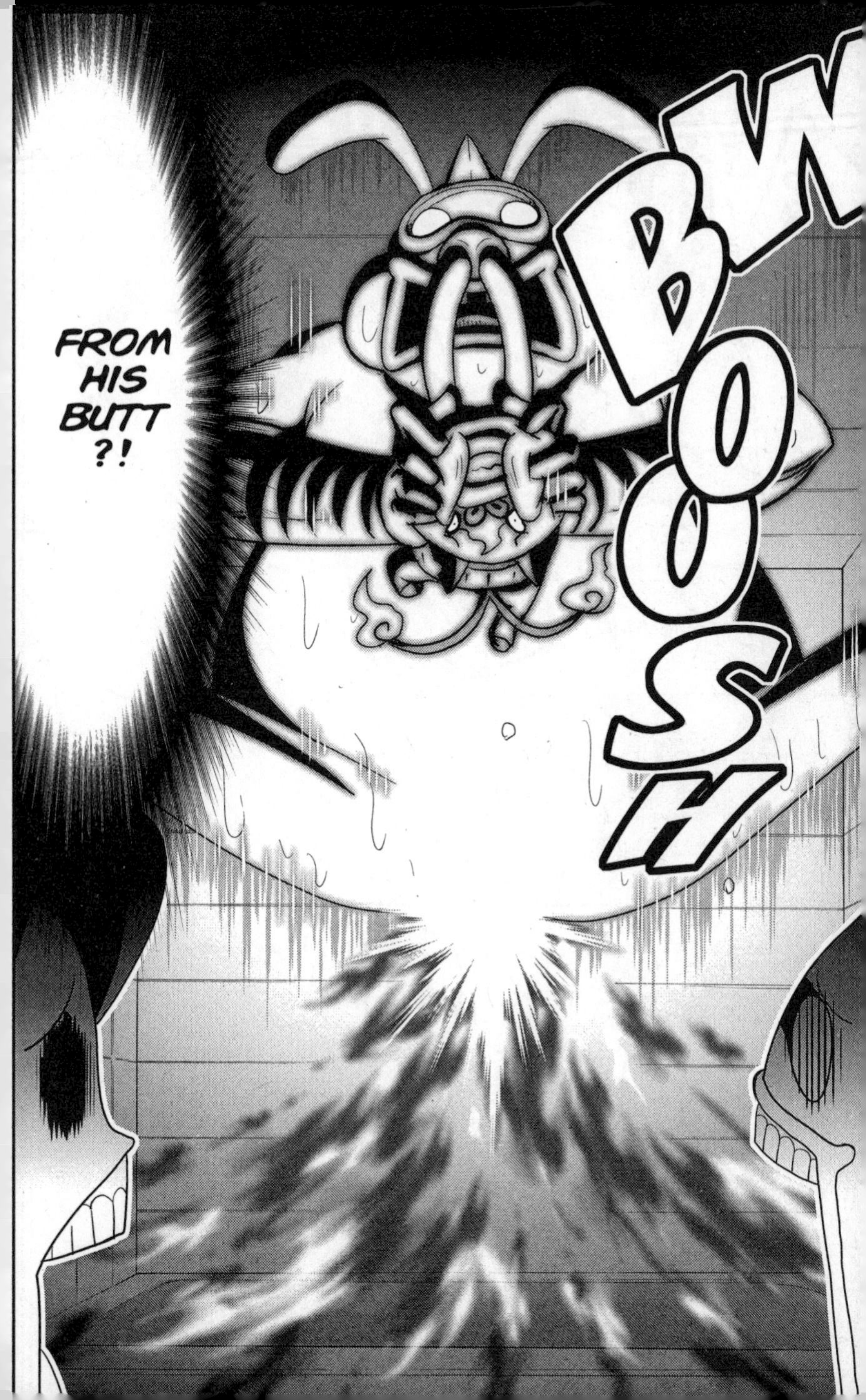
BWOOOSH
FROM HIS BUTT?!

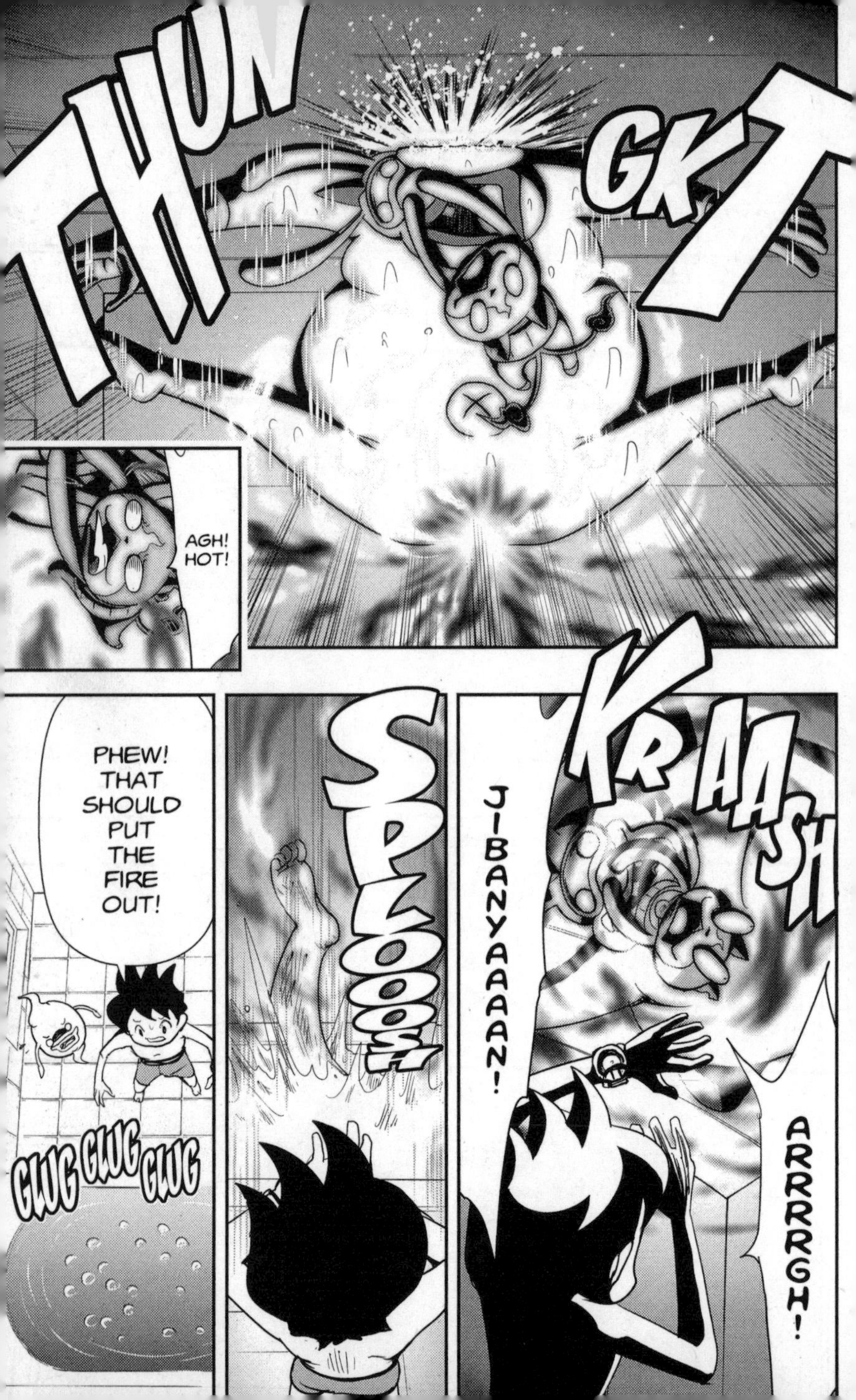
THUN
GKT
AGH! HOT!
KRAASH
JIBANYAAAAAN!
ARRRRGH!
SPLOOOSH!
PHEW! THAT SHOULD PUT THE FIRE OUT!
GLUG GLUG GLUG

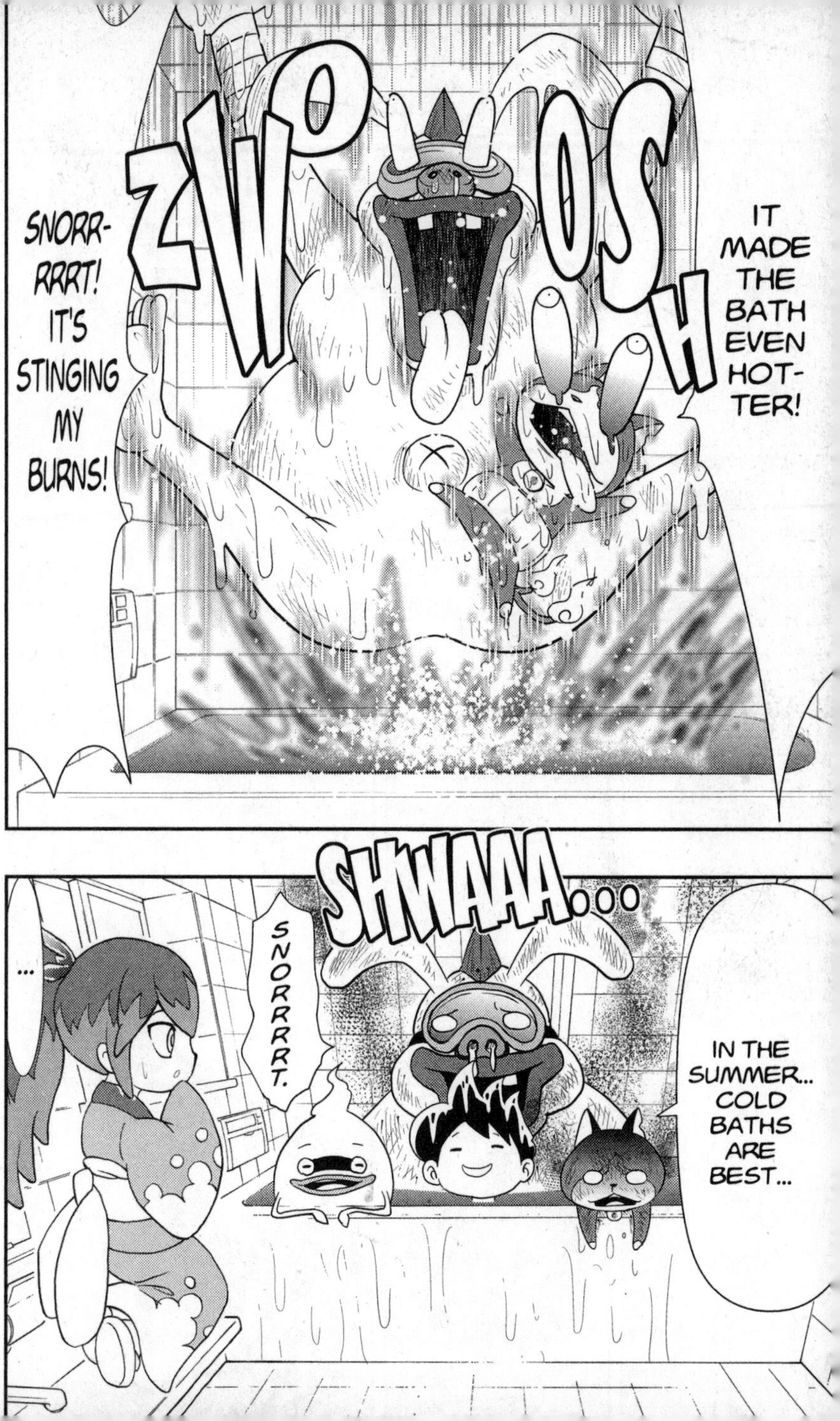
IT MADE THE BATH EVEN HOT-TER!
ZWOOSH
SNORR-RRRT! IT'S STINGING MY BURNS!
SHWAAA...
IN THE SUMMER... COLD BATHS ARE BEST...
SNORRRRRT.
...

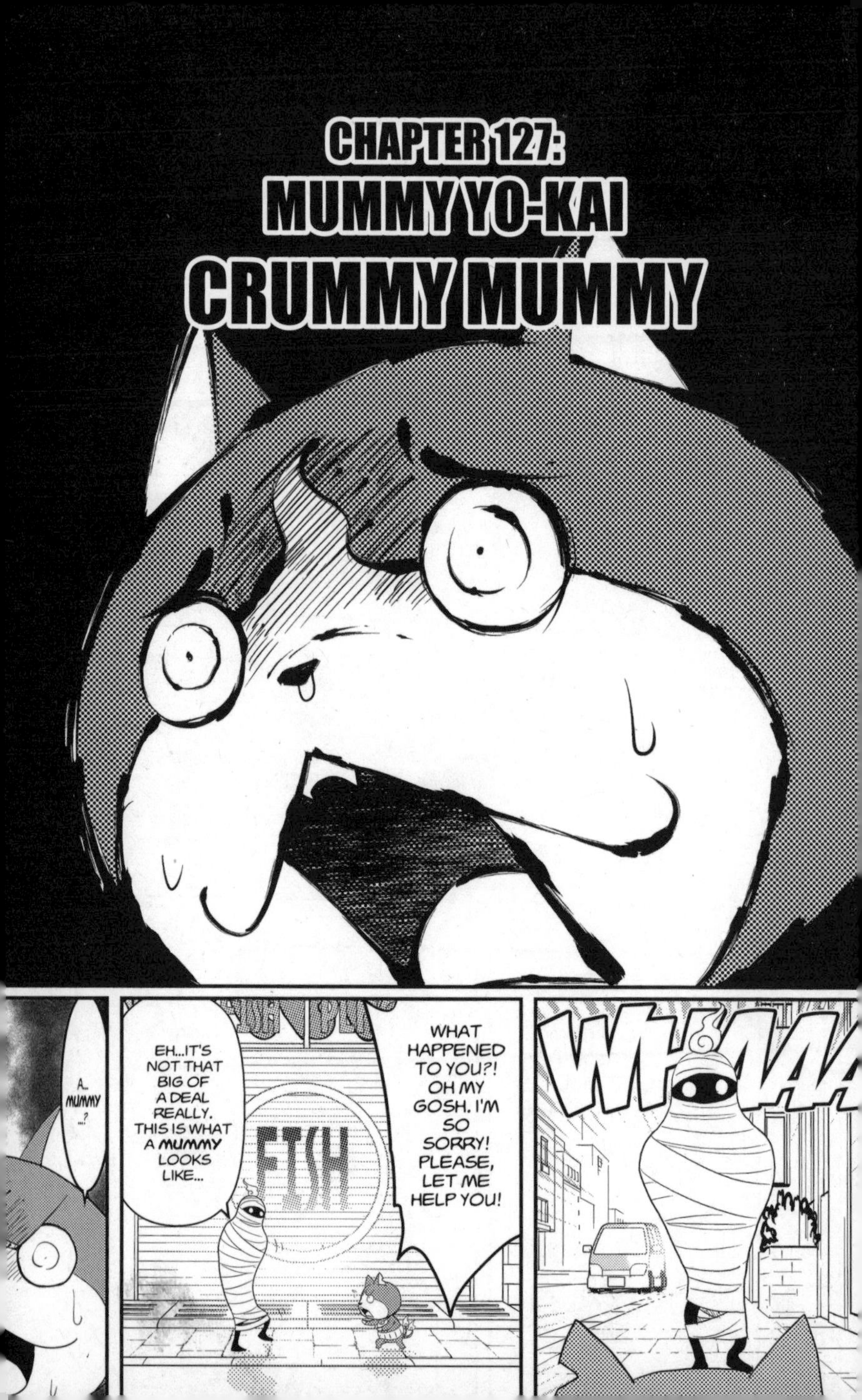
CHAPTER 127:
MUMMY YO-KAI
CRUMMY MUMMY
WHAAA
WHAT HAPPENED TO YOU?! OH MY GOSH. I'M SO SORRY! PLEASE, LET ME HELP YOU!
EH...IT'S NOT THAT BIG OF A DEAL REALLY. THIS IS WHAT A MUMMY LOOKS LIKE...
FISH
A... MUMMY ...?

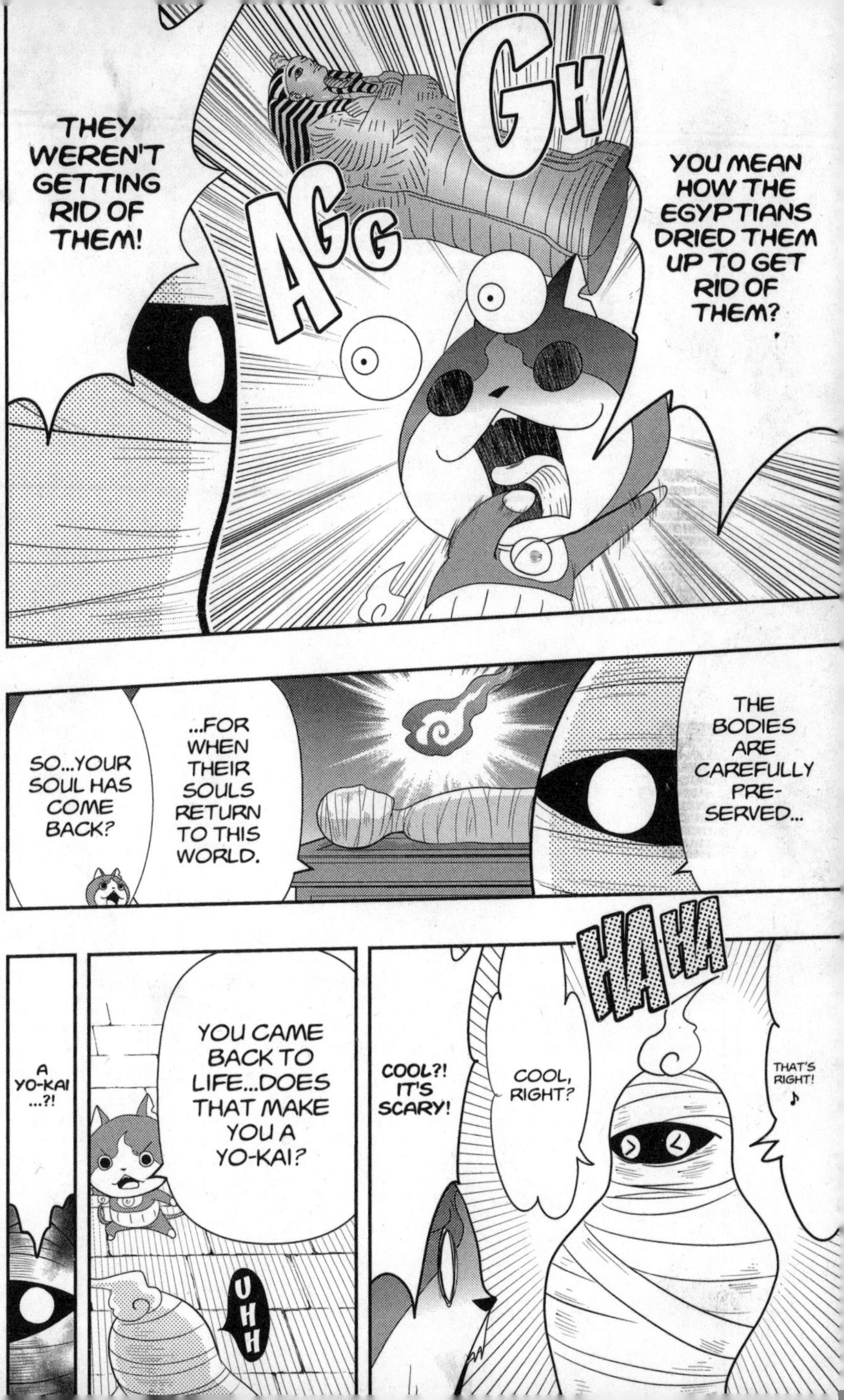

YOU MEAN HOW THE EGYPTIANS DRIED THEM UP TO GET RID OF THEM?
AGGGH
THEY WEREN'T GETTING RID OF THEM!
THE BODIES ARE CAREFULLY PRE-SERVED...
...FOR WHEN THEIR SOULS RETURN TO THIS WORLD.
SO...YOUR SOUL HAS COME BACK?
HAHA
THAT'S RIGHT! ♪
COOL, RIGHT?
COOL?! IT'S SCARY!
YOU CAME BACK TO LIFE...DOES THAT MAKE YOU A YO-KAI?
UHH
A YO-KAI ...?!

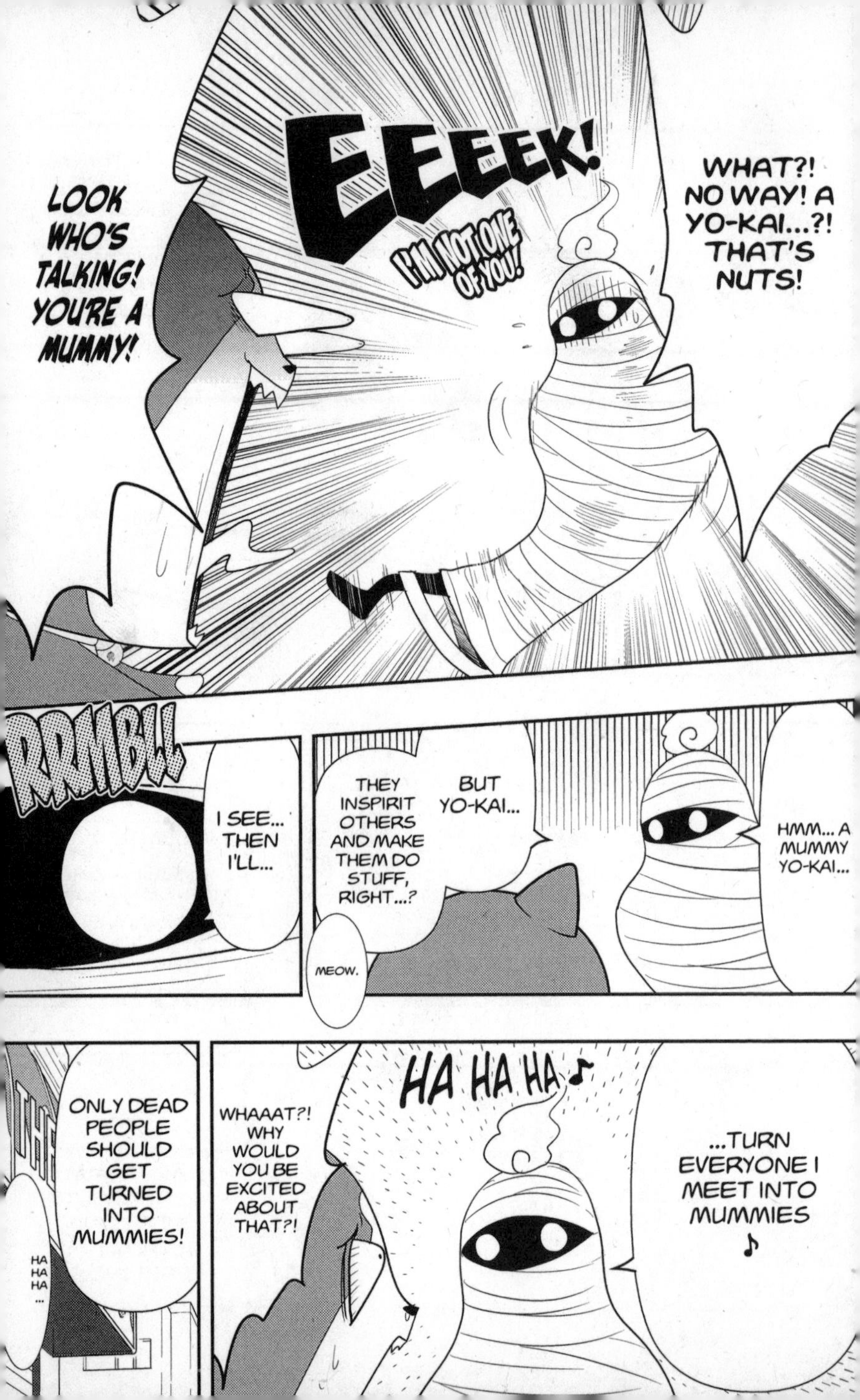
WHAT?! NO WAY! A YO-KAI...?! THAT'S NUTS!
EEEEK!
I'M NOT ONE OF YOU!
LOOK WHO'S TALKING! YOU'RE A MUMMY!
HMM... A MUMMY YO-KAI...
BUT YO-KAI...
THEY INSPIRIT OTHERS AND MAKE THEM DO STUFF, RIGHT...?
MEOW.
RRMBL
I SEE... THEN I'LL...
...TURN EVERYONE I MEET INTO MUMMIES ♪
HA HA HA ♪
WHAAAT?! WHY WOULD YOU BE EXCITED ABOUT THAT?!
ONLY DEAD PEOPLE SHOULD GET TURNED INTO MUMMIES!
HA HA HA ...

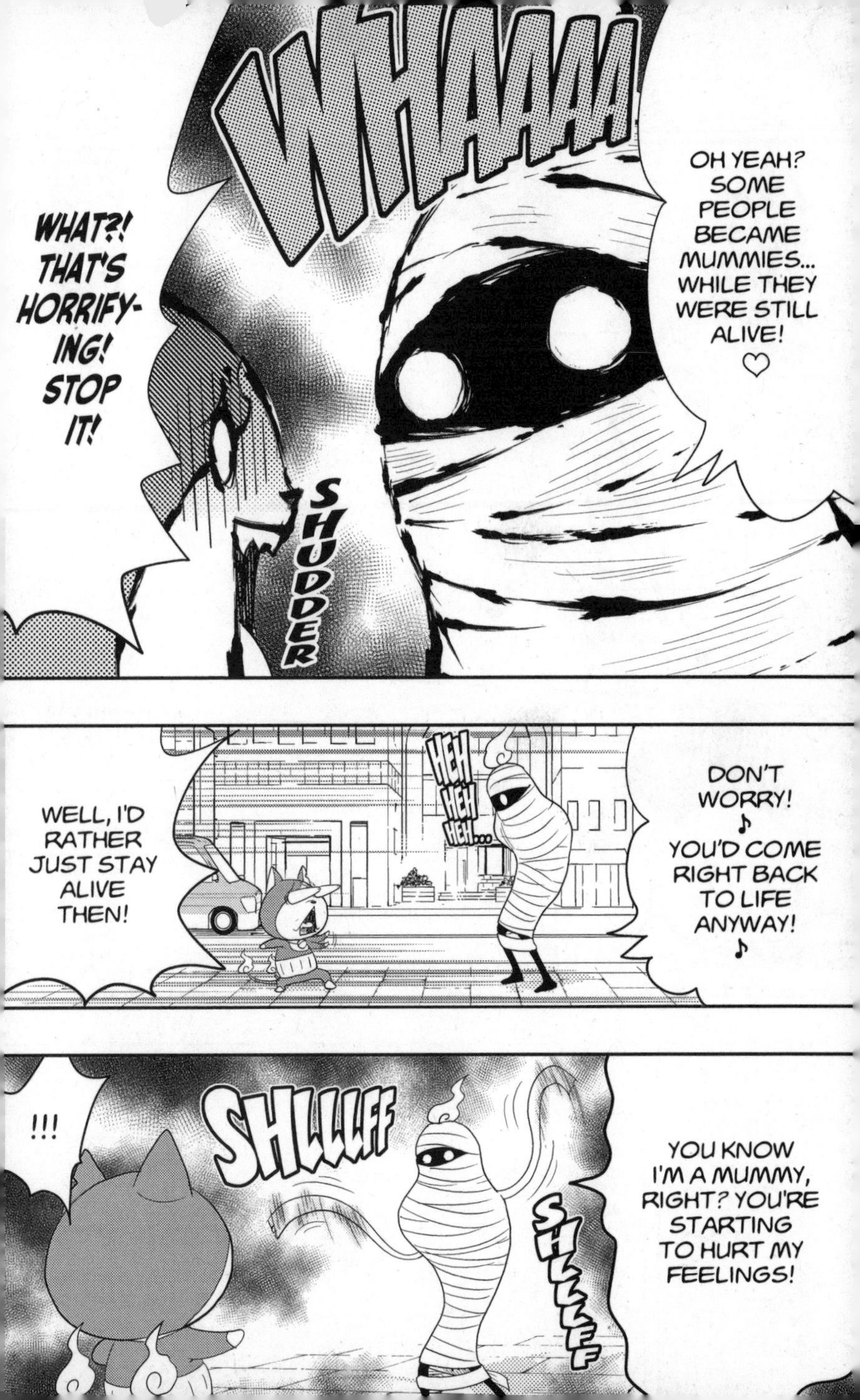
WHAAAA
OH YEAH? SOME PEOPLE BECAME MUMMIES... WHILE THEY WERE STILL ALIVE! ♡
WHAT?! THAT'S HORRIFY-ING! STOP IT!
SHUDDER
DON'T WORRY! ♪ YOU'D COME RIGHT BACK TO LIFE ANYWAY! ♪
HEH HEH HEH...
WELL, I'D RATHER JUST STAY ALIVE THEN!
YOU KNOW I'M A MUMMY, RIGHT? YOU'RE STARTING TO HURT MY FEELINGS!
SHLLLFF
SHLLLFF
!!!

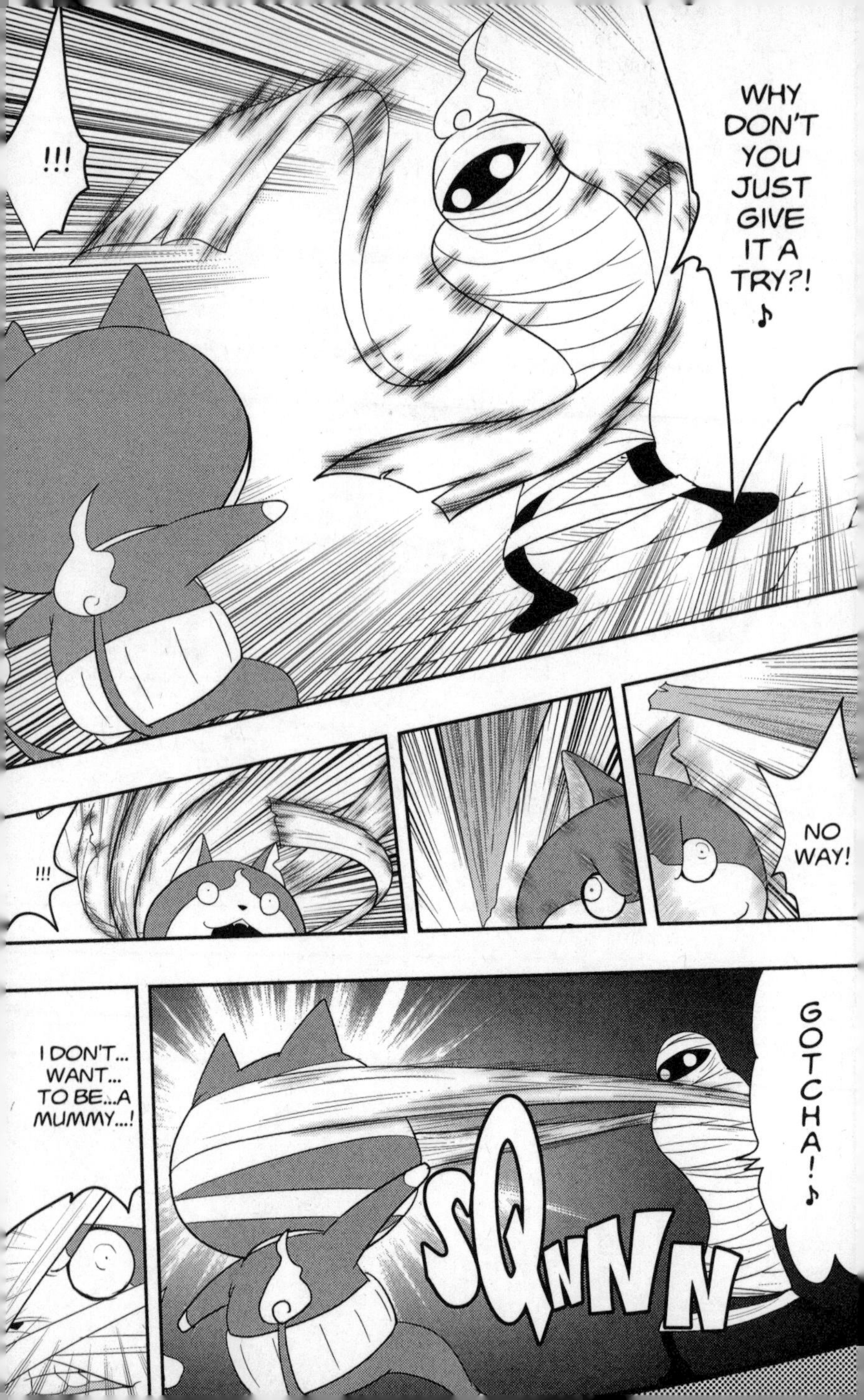

WHY DON'T YOU JUST GIVE IT A TRY?! ♪
!!!
NO WAY!
!!!
GOTCHA!♪
SQNNNN
I DON'T... WANT... TO BE...A MUMMY...!

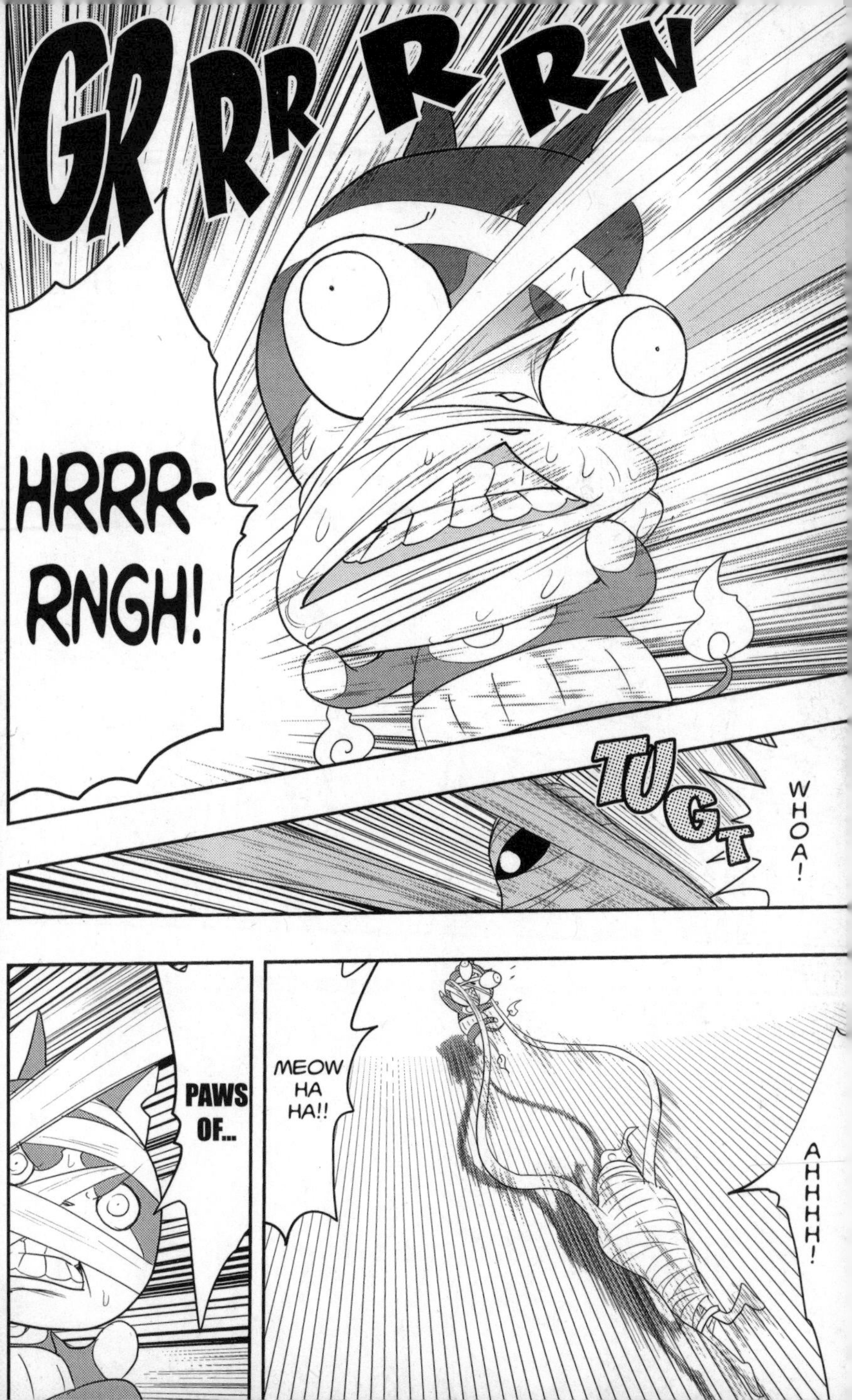
GRRRRRN
HRRR-RNGH!
TUGT
WHOA!
AHHHH!
MEOW HA HA!!
PAWS OF...

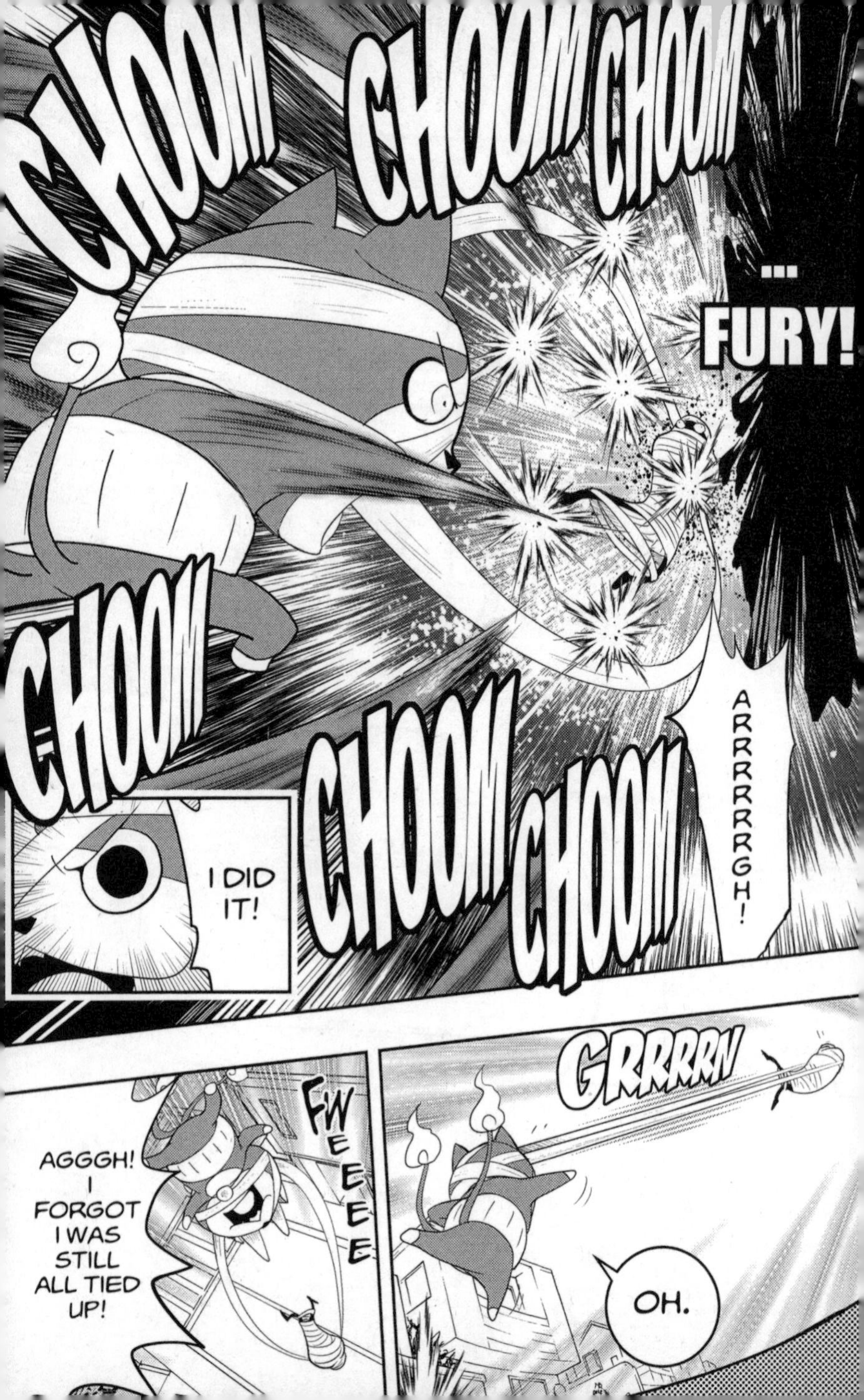
...FURY!
CHOOM CHOOM
CHOOM
ARRRRRRGH!
CHOOM
CHOOM
CHOOM
I DID IT!
GRRRRN
OH.
FWEEEEE
AGGGH! I FORGOT I WAS STILL ALL TIED UP!

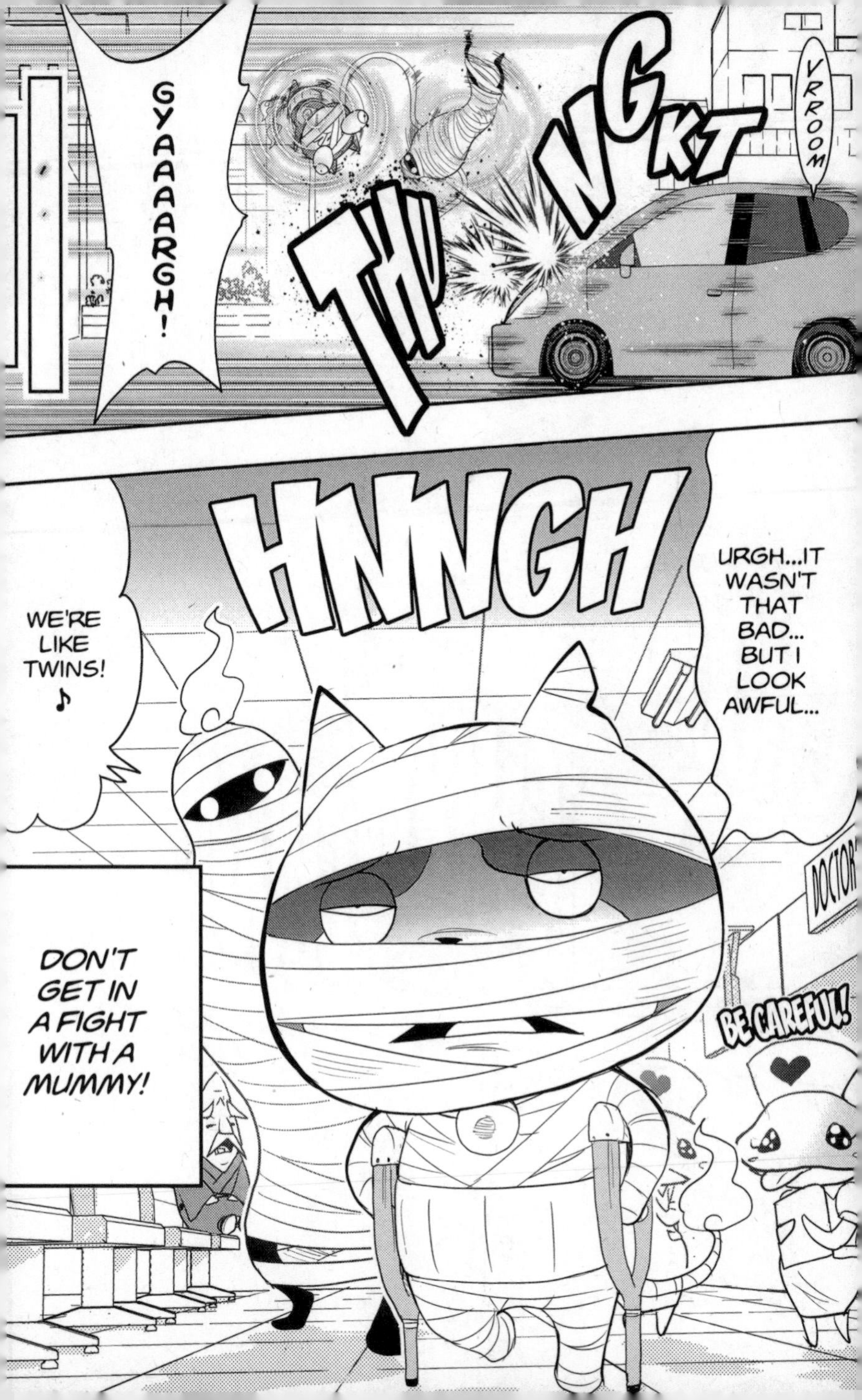
VRROOM
THUNGKT
GYAAAARGH!
URGH...IT WASN'T THAT BAD... BUT I LOOK AWFUL...
HNNGH
WE'RE LIKE TWINS! ♪
DOCTOR
BE CAREFUL!
DON'T GET IN A FIGHT WITH A MUMMY!

CHAPTER 128:
HIDDEN TALENT DRAW-OUT YO-KAI UNSHELLTERED

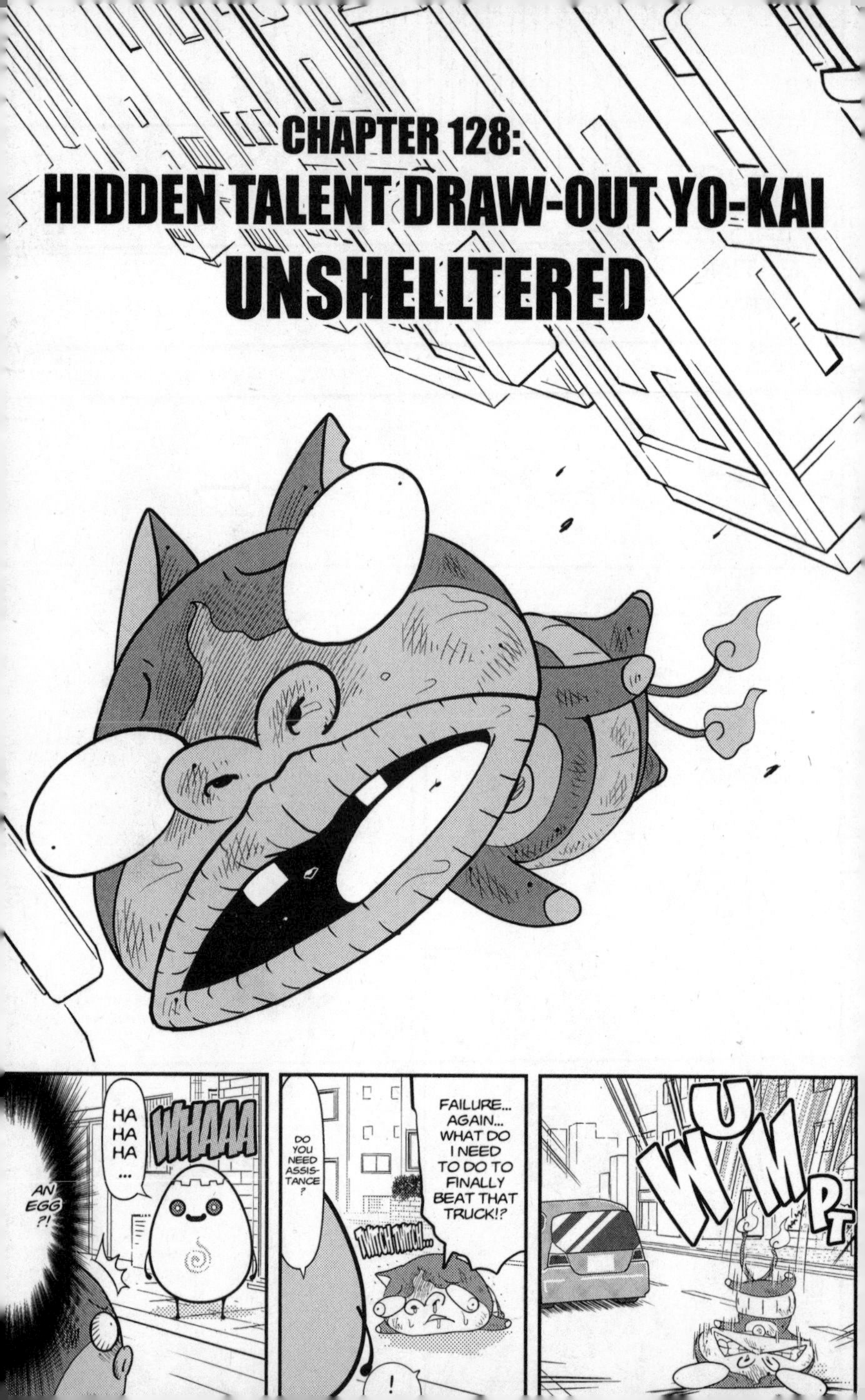

WUMPT
FAILURE... AGAIN... WHAT DO I NEED TO DO TO FINALLY BEAT THAT TRUCK!?
TWITCH TWITCH...
DO YOU NEED ASSIS-TANCE?
!
WHAAA
HA HA HA...
AN EGG?!

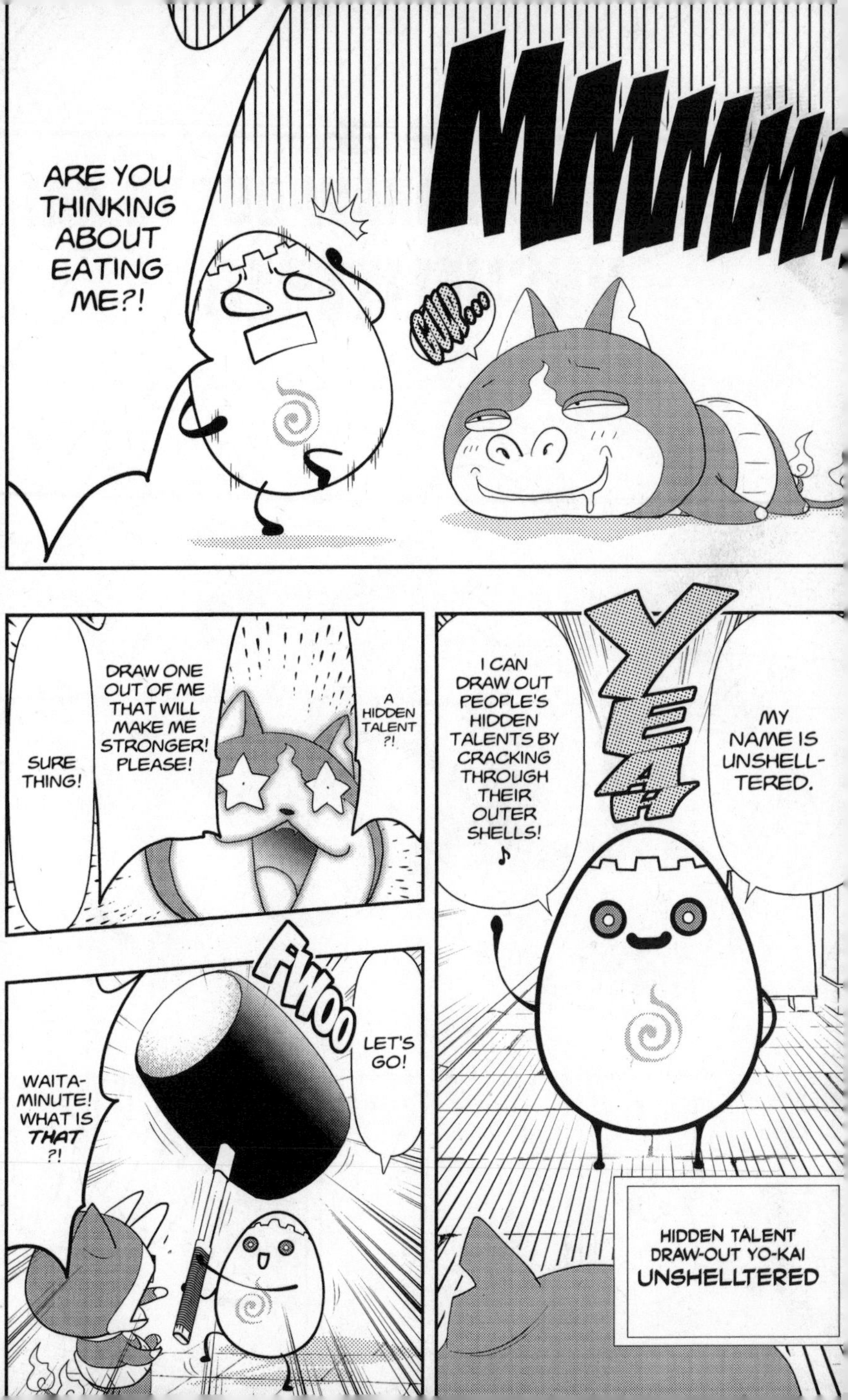
MMMMM
ARE YOU THINKING ABOUT EATING ME?!
YEA
MY NAME IS UNSHELL-TERED.
I CAN DRAW OUT PEOPLE'S HIDDEN TALENTS BY CRACKING THROUGH THEIR OUTER SHELLS! ♪
HIDDEN TALENT DRAW-OUT YO-KAI UNSHELLTERED
A HIDDEN TALENT?!
DRAW ONE OUT OF ME THAT WILL MAKE ME STRONGER! PLEASE!
SURE THING!
LET'S GO!
FWOO
WAITA-MINUTE! WHAT IS THAT?!

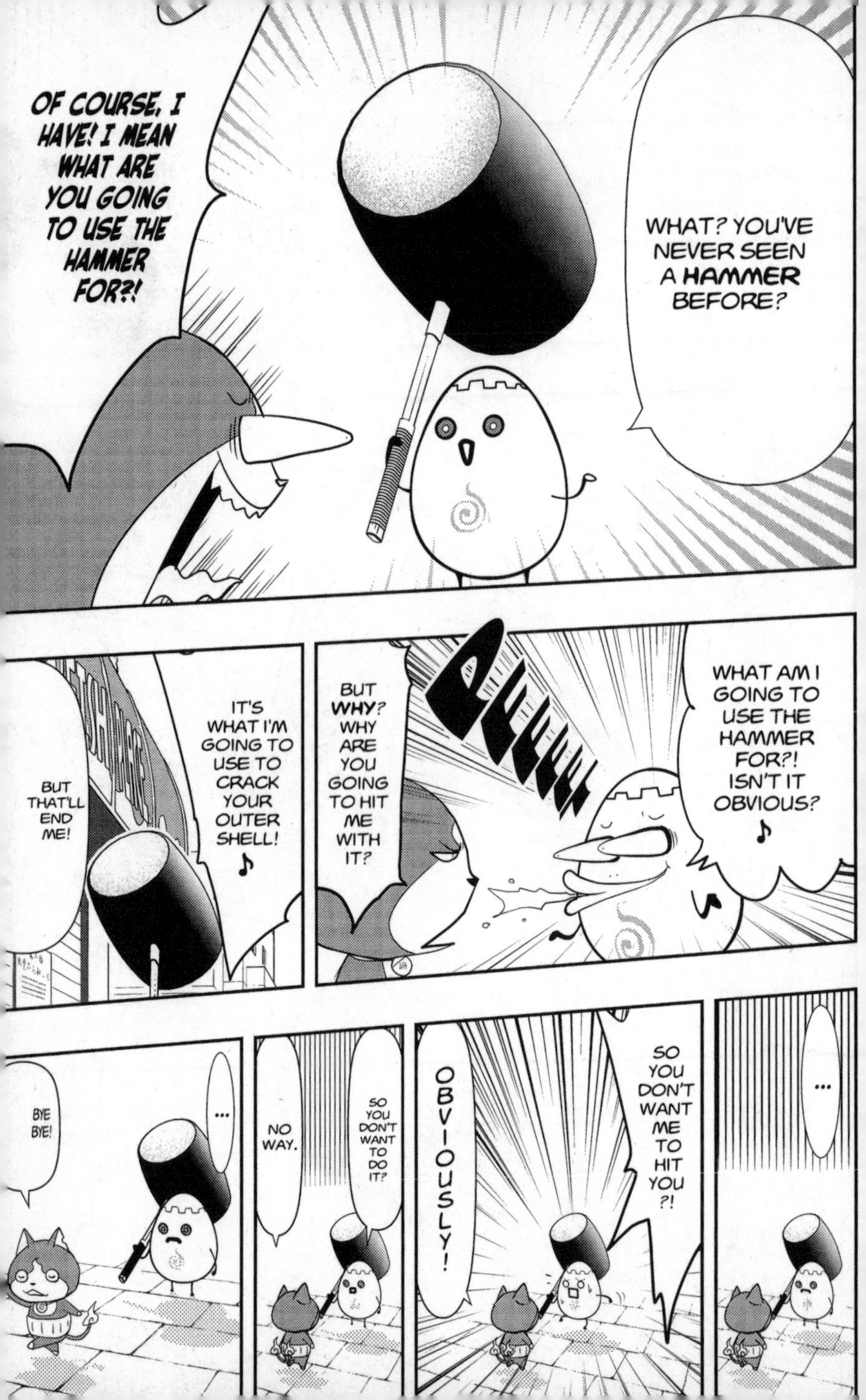
WHAT? YOU'VE NEVER SEEN A **HAMMER** BEFORE?
OF COURSE, I HAVE! I MEAN WHAT ARE YOU GOING TO USE THE HAMMER FOR?!
WHAT AM I GOING TO USE THE HAMMER FOR?! ISN'T IT OBVIOUS? ♪
BUT **WHY**? WHY ARE YOU GOING TO HIT ME WITH IT?
IT'S WHAT I'M GOING TO USE TO CRACK YOUR OUTER SHELL! ♪
BUT THAT'LL END ME!
...
SO YOU DON'T WANT ME TO HIT YOU?!
OBVIOUSLY!
SO YOU DON'T WANT TO DO IT?
NO WAY.
...
BYE BYE!

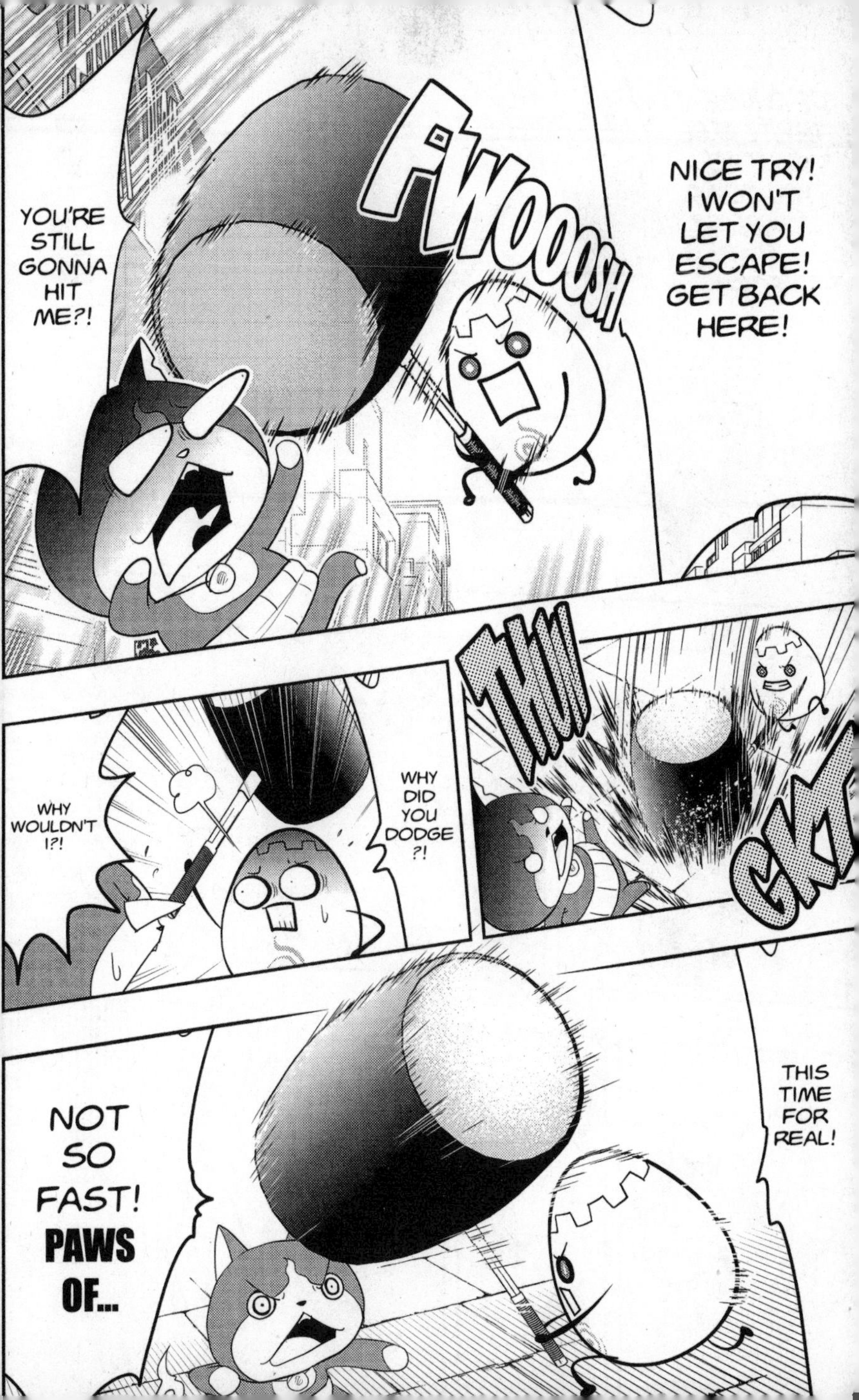
NICE TRY! I WON'T LET YOU ESCAPE! GET BACK HERE!
FWOOOSH
YOU'RE STILL GONNA HIT ME?!
WHY DID YOU DODGE?!
WHY WOULDN'T I?!
THIS TIME FOR REAL!
NOT SO FAST! **PAWS OF...**

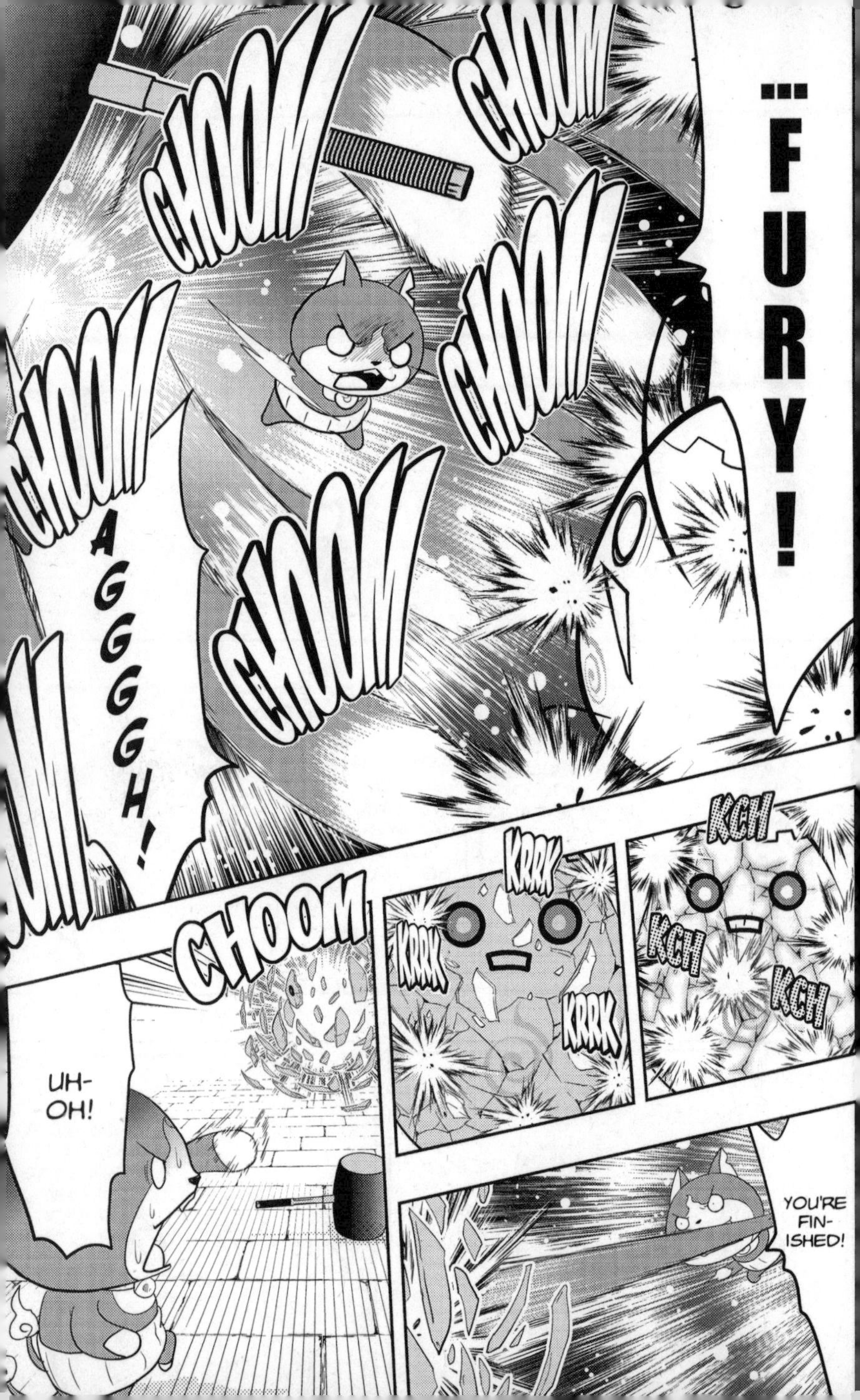

...FURY!
CHOOM
CHOOM
CHOOM
CHOOM
CHOOM
CHOOM
AGGGGH!
KCH
KCH
KCH
KRRK
KRRK
KRRK
CHOOM
YOU'RE FIN-ISHED!
UH-OH!

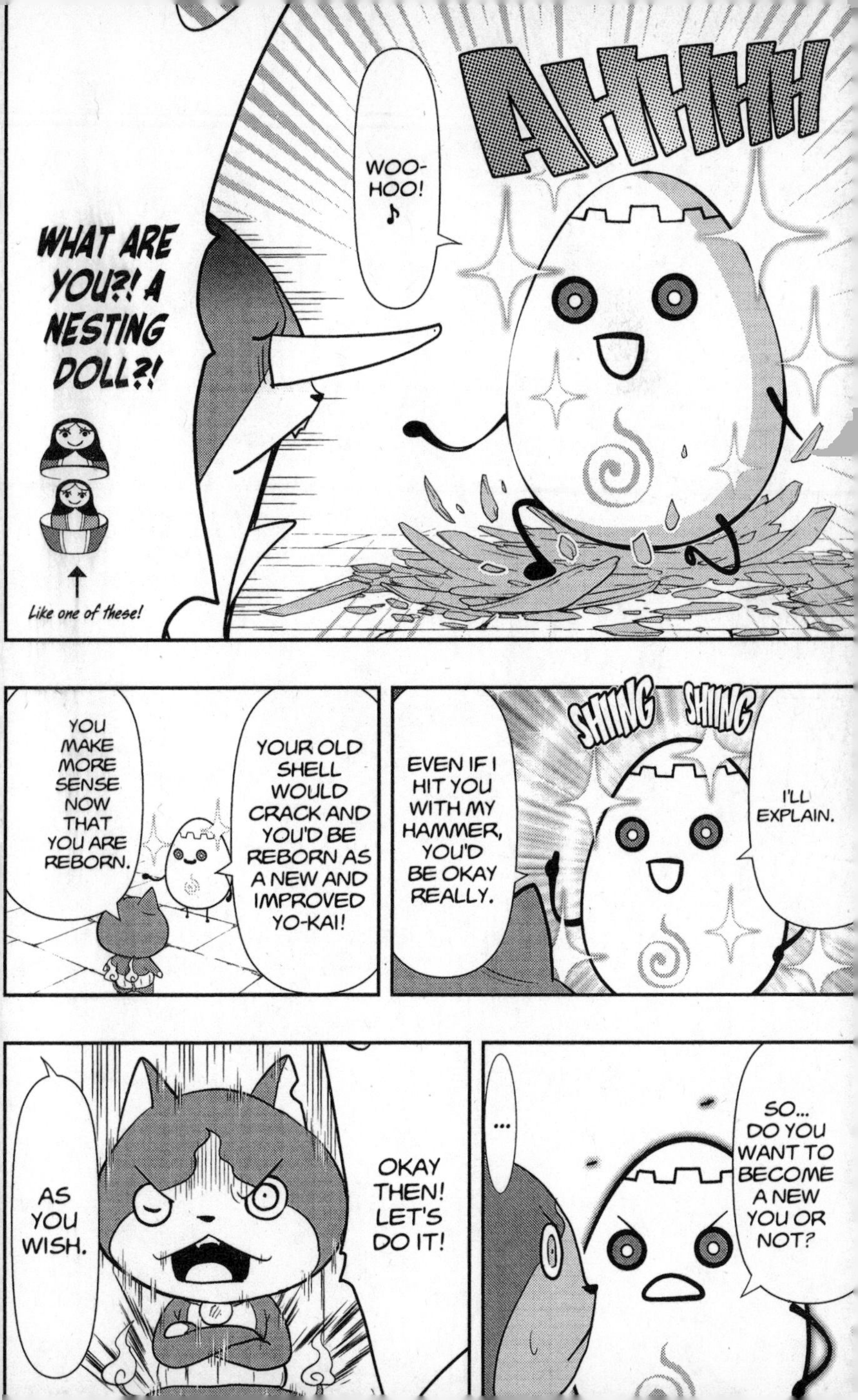
AHHHHH
WOO-HOO! ♪
WHAT ARE YOU?! A NESTING DOLL?!
Like one of these!
SHIING SHIING
I'LL EXPLAIN.
EVEN IF I HIT YOU WITH MY HAMMER, YOU'D BE OKAY REALLY.
YOUR OLD SHELL WOULD CRACK AND YOU'D BE REBORN AS A NEW AND IMPROVED YO-KAI!
YOU MAKE MORE SENSE NOW THAT YOU ARE REBORN.
SO... DO YOU WANT TO BECOME A NEW YOU OR NOT?
...
OKAY THEN! LET'S DO IT!
AS YOU WISH.

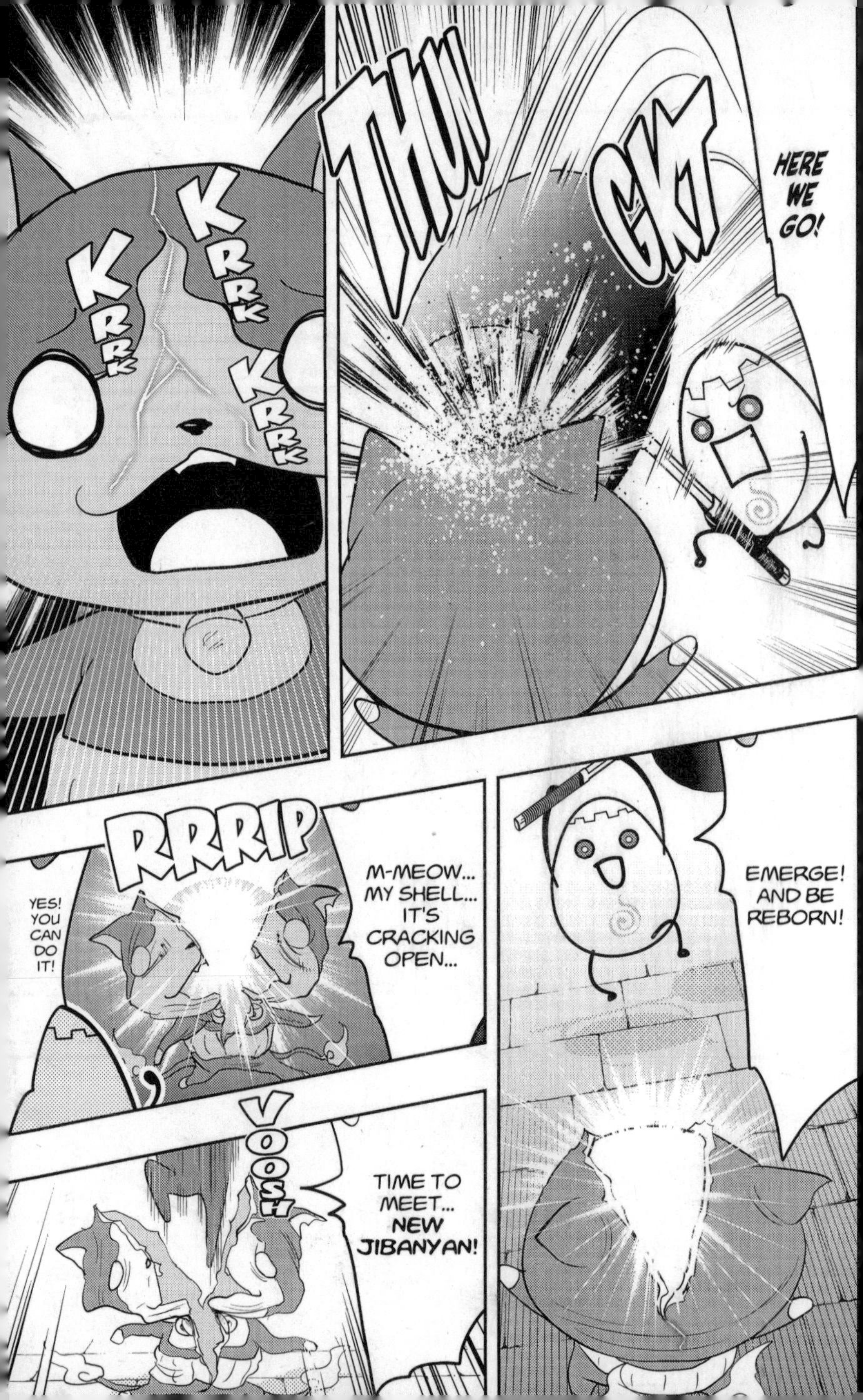
THUN
GKT
HERE WE GO!
KRRRK
KRRRK
KRRRK
EMERGE! AND BE REBORN!
RRRIP
M-MEOW... MY SHELL... IT'S CRACKING OPEN...
YES! YOU CAN DO IT!
VOOOSH
TIME TO MEET... **NEW JIBANYAN!**

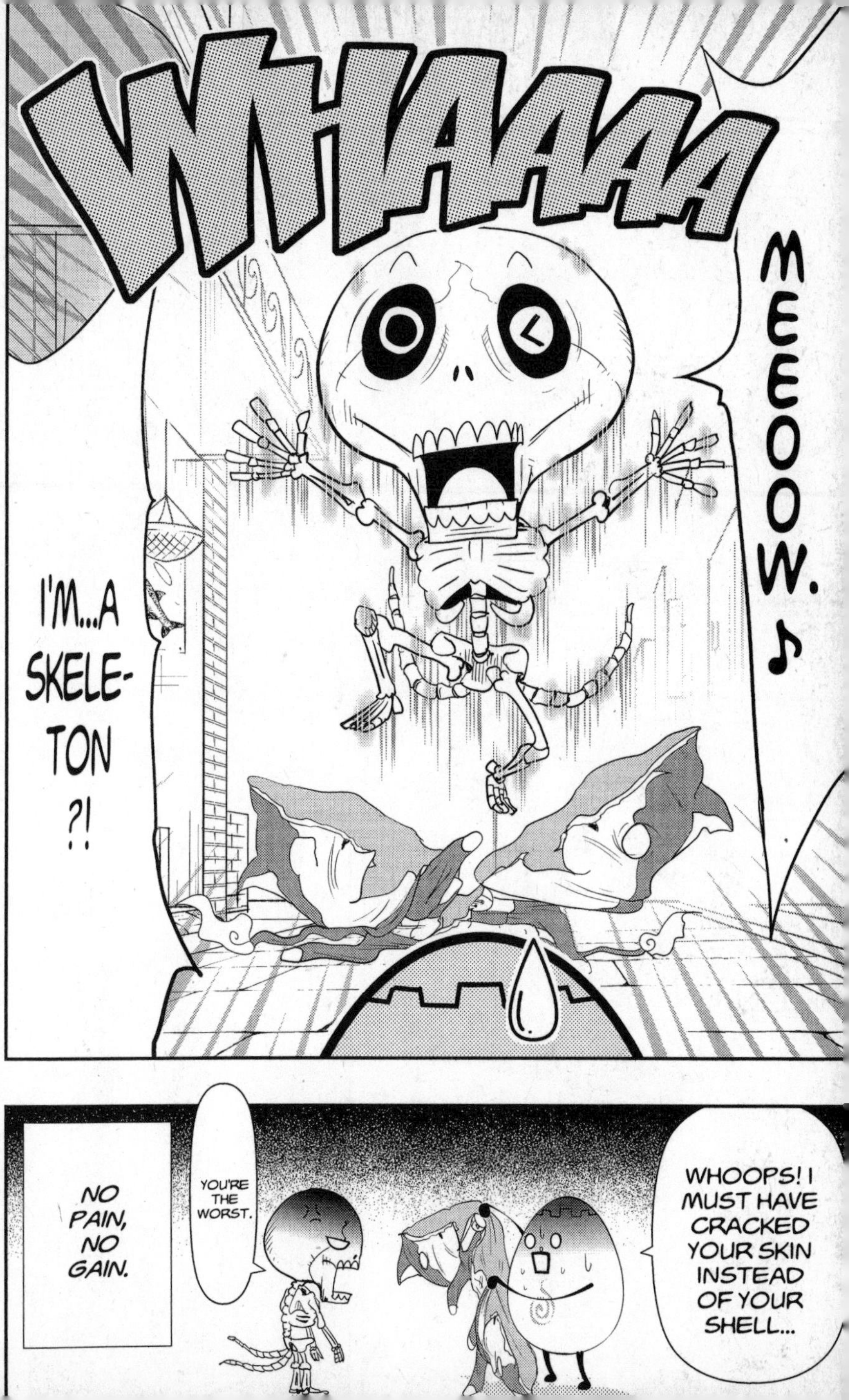
WHAAAA
MEEOOW.♪
I'M...A SKELE-TON ?!
WHOOPS! I MUST HAVE CRACKED YOUR SKIN INSTEAD OF YOUR SHELL...
YOU'RE THE WORST.
NO PAIN, NO GAIN.

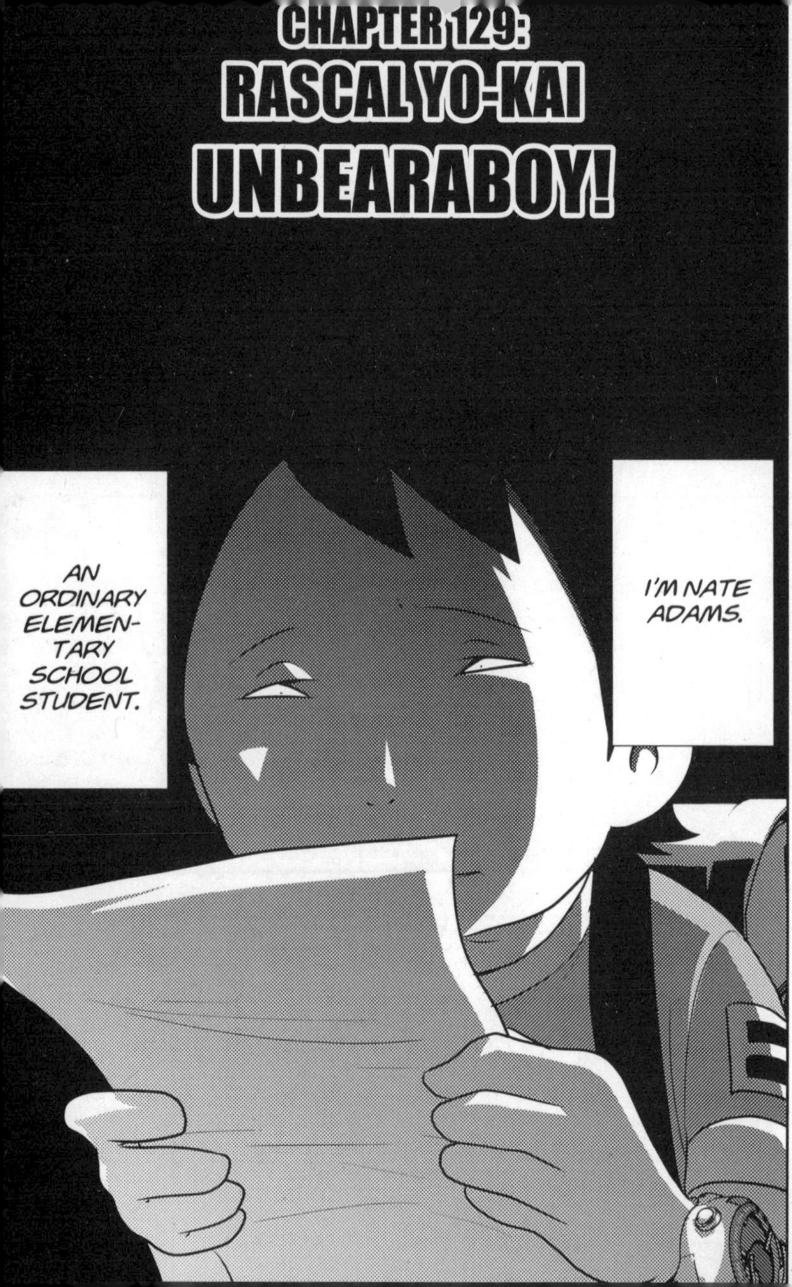
CHAPTER 129:
RASCAL YO-KAI
UNBEARABOY!
I'M NATE ADAMS.
AN ORDINARY ELEMENTARY SCHOOL STUDENT.

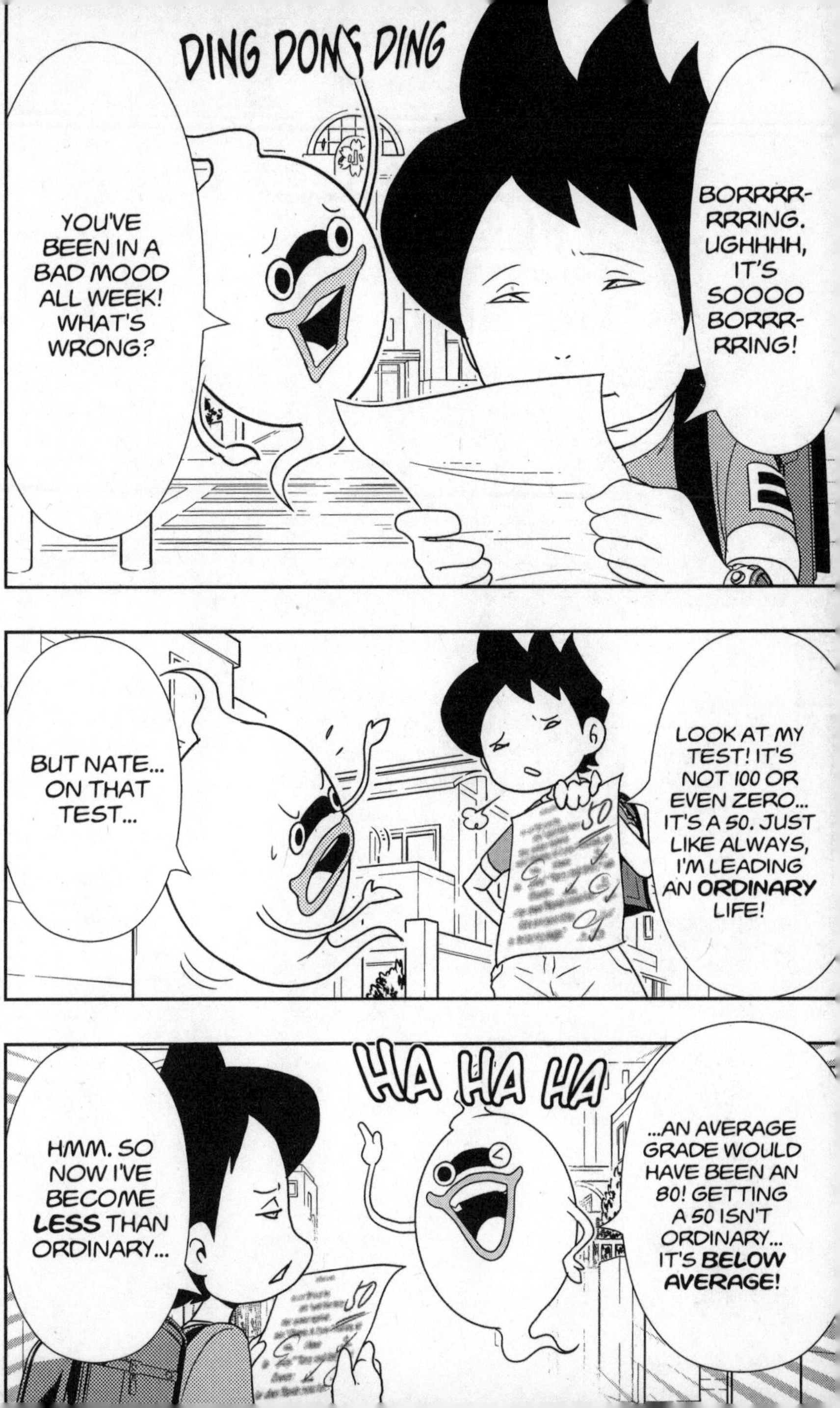
DING DONG DING
BORRRRR-RRRING. UGHHHH, IT'S SOOOO BORRRR-RRING!
YOU'VE BEEN IN A BAD MOOD ALL WEEK! WHAT'S WRONG?
LOOK AT MY TEST! IT'S NOT 100 OR EVEN ZERO... IT'S A 50. JUST LIKE ALWAYS, I'M LEADING AN **ORDINARY** LIFE!
BUT NATE... ON THAT TEST...
...AN AVERAGE GRADE WOULD HAVE BEEN AN 80! GETTING A 50 ISN'T ORDINARY... IT'S **BELOW AVERAGE!**
HA HA HA
HMM. SO NOW I'VE BECOME **LESS** THAN ORDINARY...

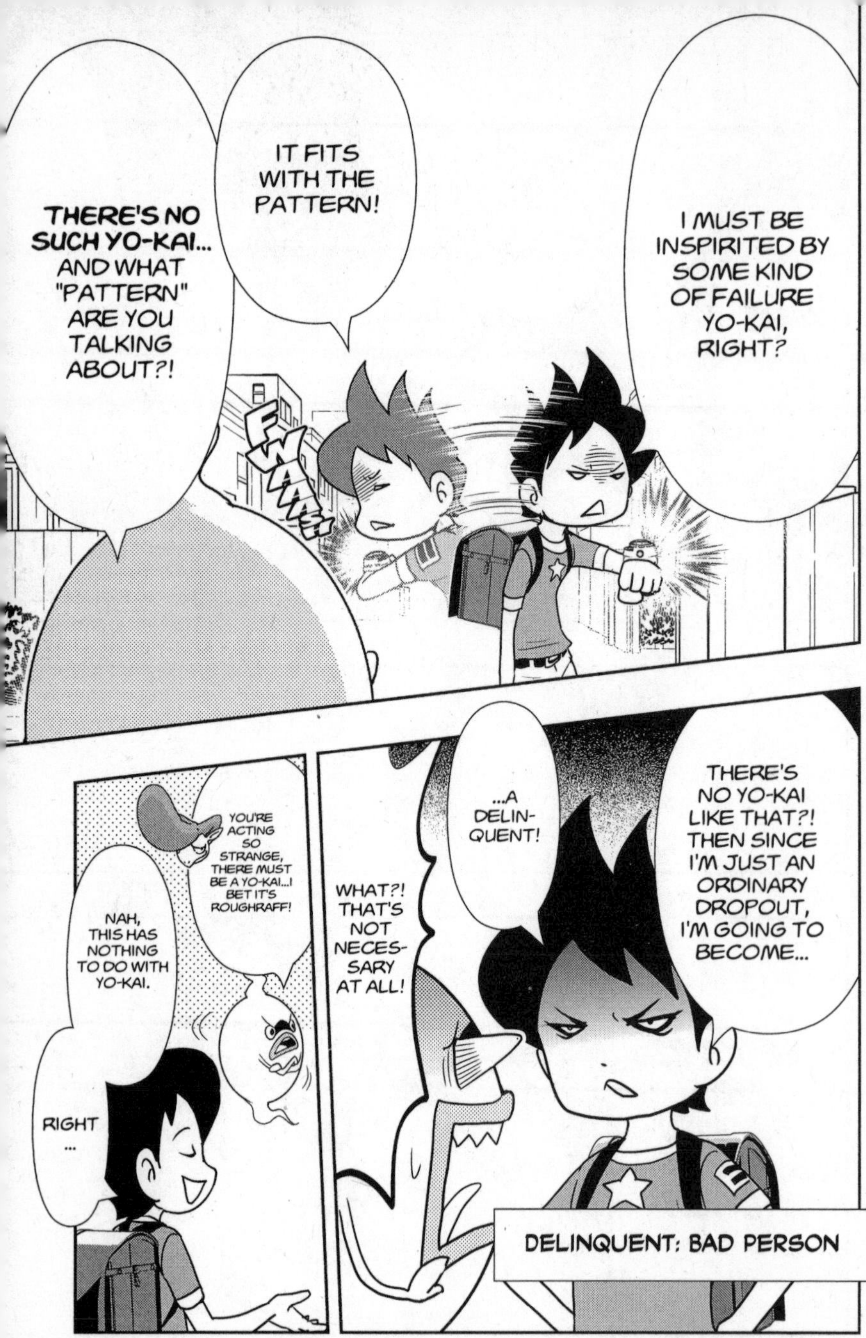
I MUST BE INSPIRITED BY SOME KIND OF FAILURE YO-KAI, RIGHT?
IT FITS WITH THE PATTERN!
THERE'S NO SUCH YO-KAI... AND WHAT "PATTERN" ARE YOU TALKING ABOUT?!
FWAAS!
THERE'S NO YO-KAI LIKE THAT?! THEN SINCE I'M JUST AN ORDINARY DROPOUT, I'M GOING TO BECOME...
...A DELIN-QUENT!
WHAT?! THAT'S NOT NECES-SARY AT ALL!
DELINQUENT: BAD PERSON
YOU'RE ACTING SO STRANGE, THERE MUST BE A YO-KAI...I BET IT'S ROUGHRAFF!
NAH, THIS HAS NOTHING TO DO WITH YO-KAI.
RIGHT ...

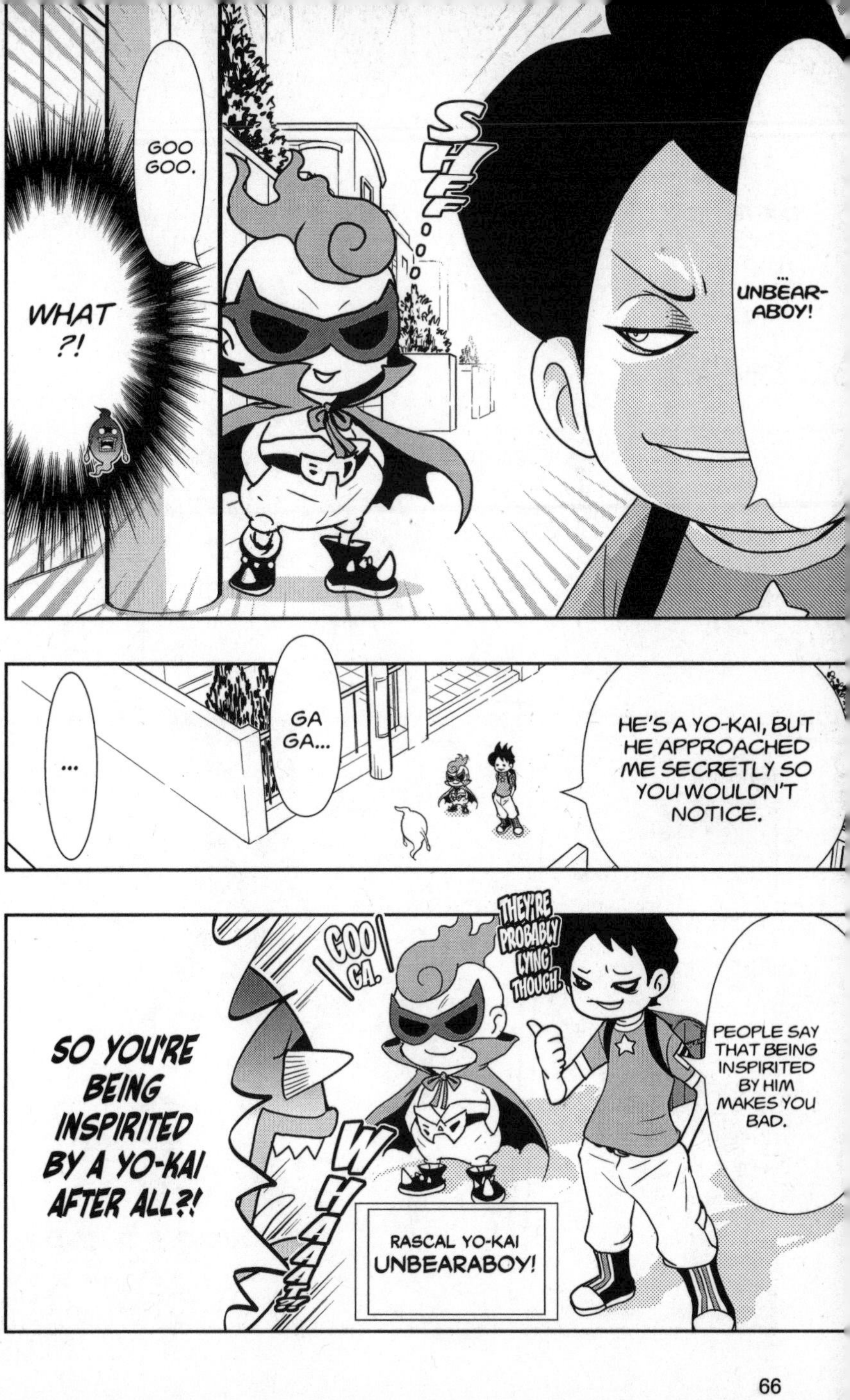
...UNBEARABOY!
SHFF
GOO GOO.
WHAT?!
HE'S A YO-KAI, BUT HE APPROACHED ME SECRETLY SO YOU WOULDN'T NOTICE.
GA GA...
...
PEOPLE SAY THAT BEING INSPIRITED BY HIM MAKES YOU BAD.
THEY'RE PROBABLY LYING THOUGH.
GOO GA.
RASCAL YO-KAI UNBEARABOY!
WHAAAT
SO YOU'RE BEING INSPIRITED BY A YO-KAI AFTER ALL?!

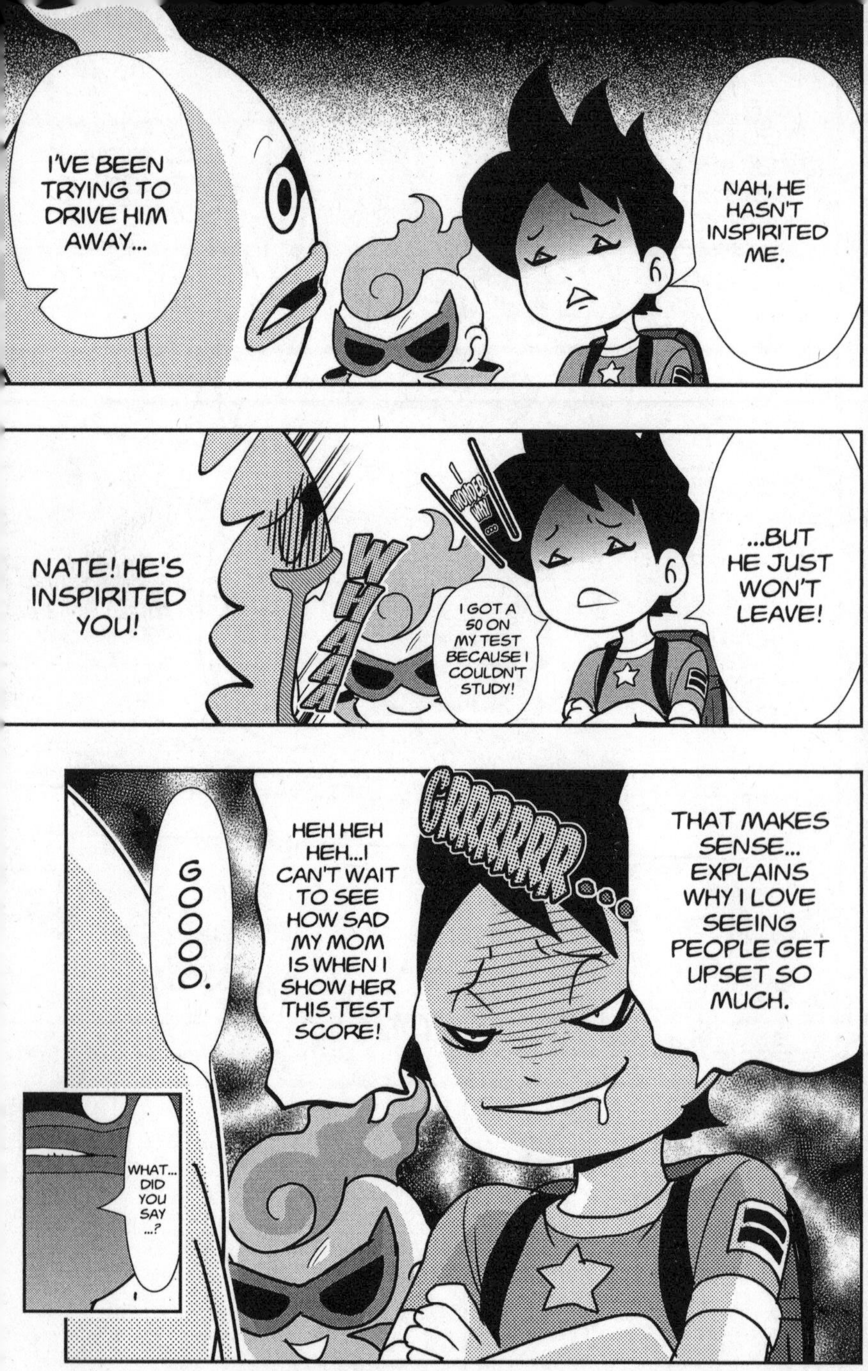
NAH, HE HASN'T INSPIRITED ME.
I'VE BEEN TRYING TO DRIVE HIM AWAY...
...BUT HE JUST WON'T LEAVE!
I WONDER WHY...
I GOT A 50 ON MY TEST BECAUSE I COULDN'T STUDY!
NATE! HE'S INSPIRITED YOU!
THAT MAKES SENSE... EXPLAINS WHY I LOVE SEEING PEOPLE GET UPSET SO MUCH.
GRRRRRR...
HEH HEH HEH...I CAN'T WAIT TO SEE HOW SAD MY MOM IS WHEN I SHOW HER THIS TEST SCORE!
GOOOO.
WHAT... DID YOU SAY ...?

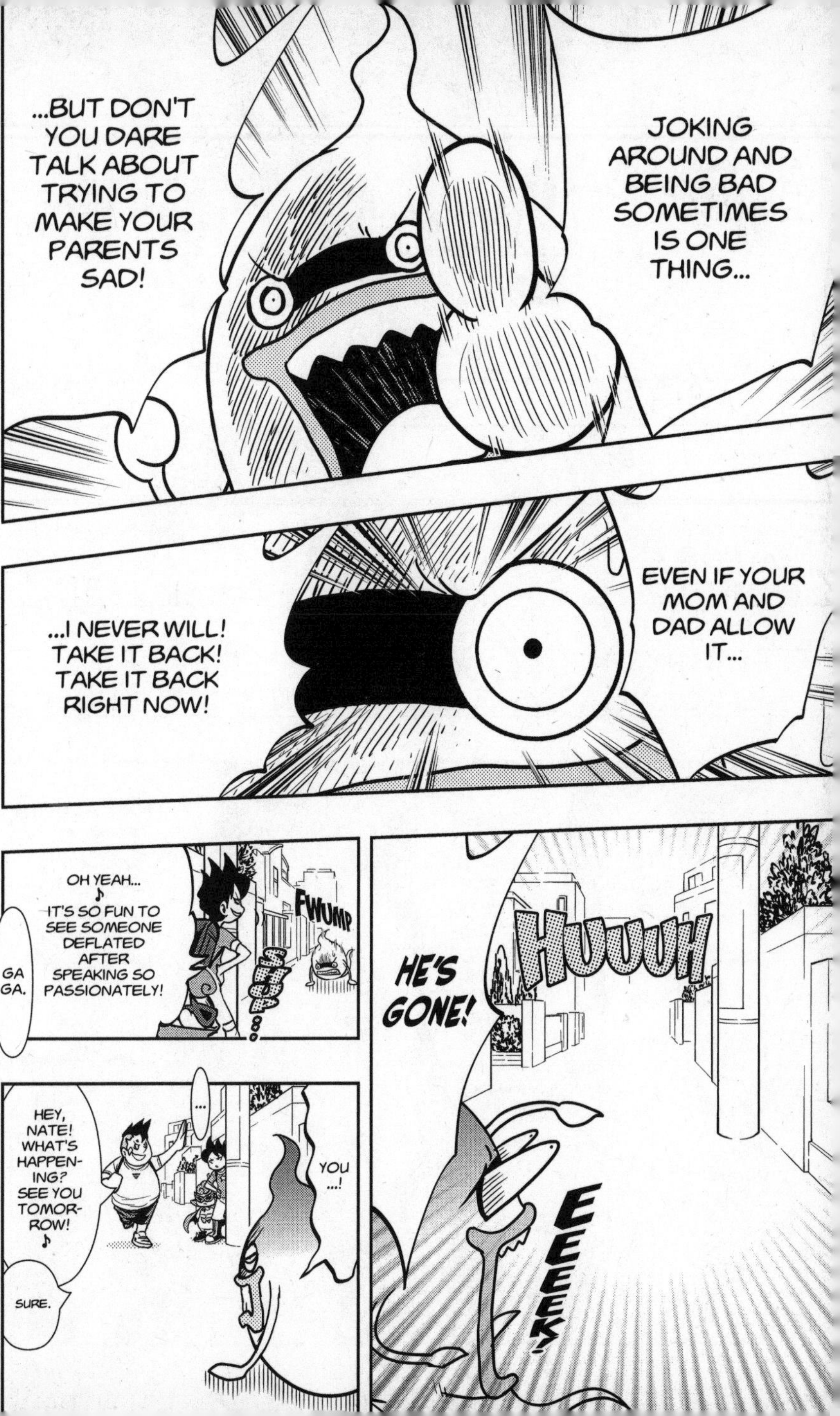
JOKING AROUND AND BEING BAD SOMETIMES IS ONE THING...
...BUT DON'T YOU DARE TALK ABOUT TRYING TO MAKE YOUR PARENTS SAD!
EVEN IF YOUR MOM AND DAD ALLOW IT...
...I NEVER WILL! TAKE IT BACK! TAKE IT BACK RIGHT NOW!
HUUUH
HE'S GONE!
EEEEEK!
OH YEAH... ♪ IT'S SO FUN TO SEE SOMEONE DEFLATED AFTER SPEAKING SO PASSIONATELY!
FWUMP
SHUP...
GA GA.
...
YOU ...!
HEY, NATE! WHAT'S HAPPEN-ING? SEE YOU TOMOR-ROW! ♪
SURE.

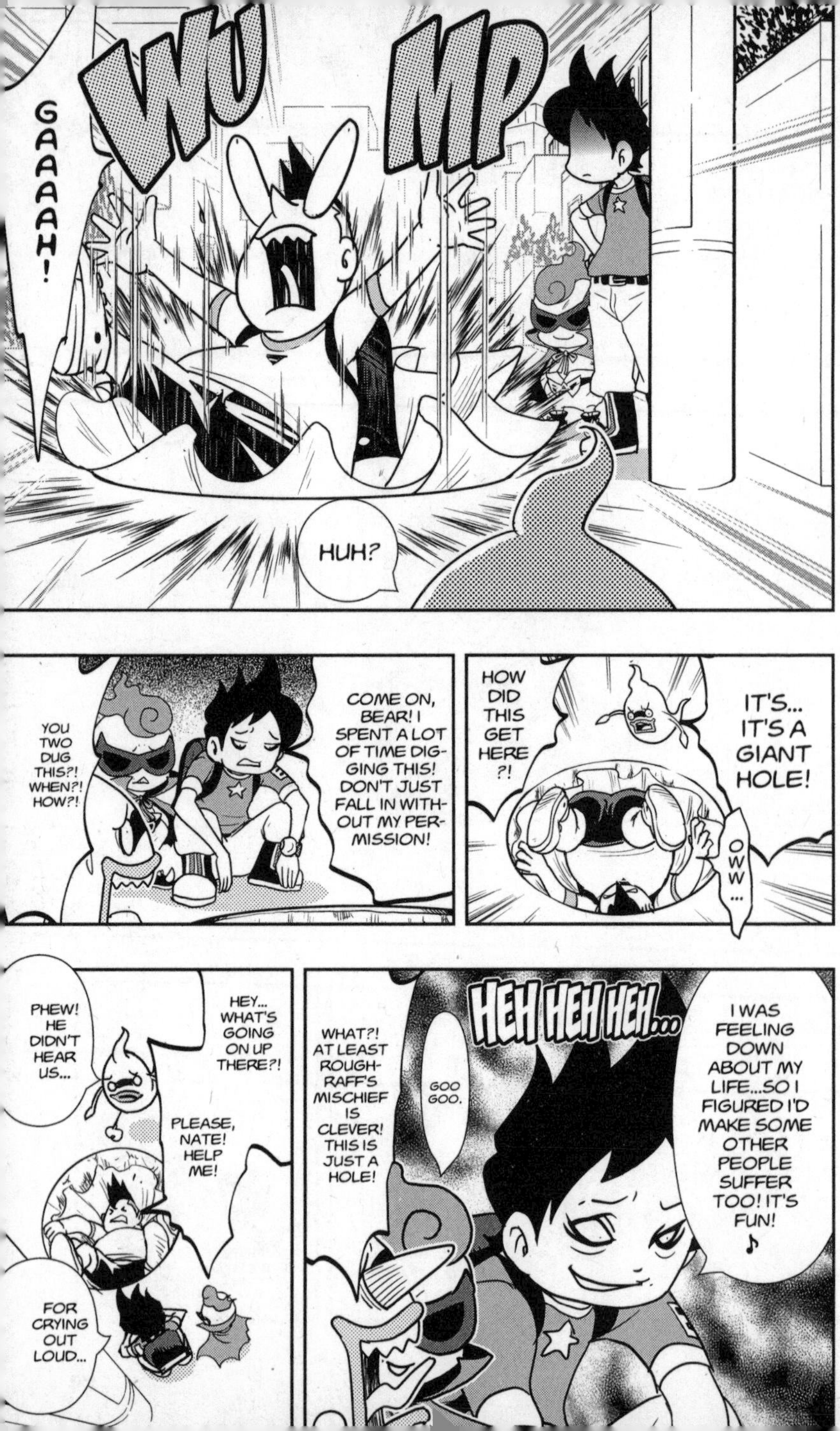
WUMP
GAAAAAH!
HUH?
IT'S... IT'S A GIANT HOLE!
HOW DID THIS GET HERE?!
OWW...
COME ON, BEAR! I SPENT A LOT OF TIME DIGGING THIS! DON'T JUST FALL IN WITHOUT MY PERMISSION!
YOU TWO DUG THIS?! WHEN?! HOW?!
I WAS FEELING DOWN ABOUT MY LIFE...SO I FIGURED I'D MAKE SOME OTHER PEOPLE SUFFER TOO! IT'S FUN! ♪
HEH HEH HEH...
GOO GOO.
WHAT?! AT LEAST ROUGHRAFF'S MISCHIEF IS CLEVER! THIS IS JUST A HOLE!
HEY... WHAT'S GOING ON UP THERE?!
PHEW! HE DIDN'T HEAR US...
PLEASE, NATE! HELP ME!
FOR CRYING OUT LOUD...

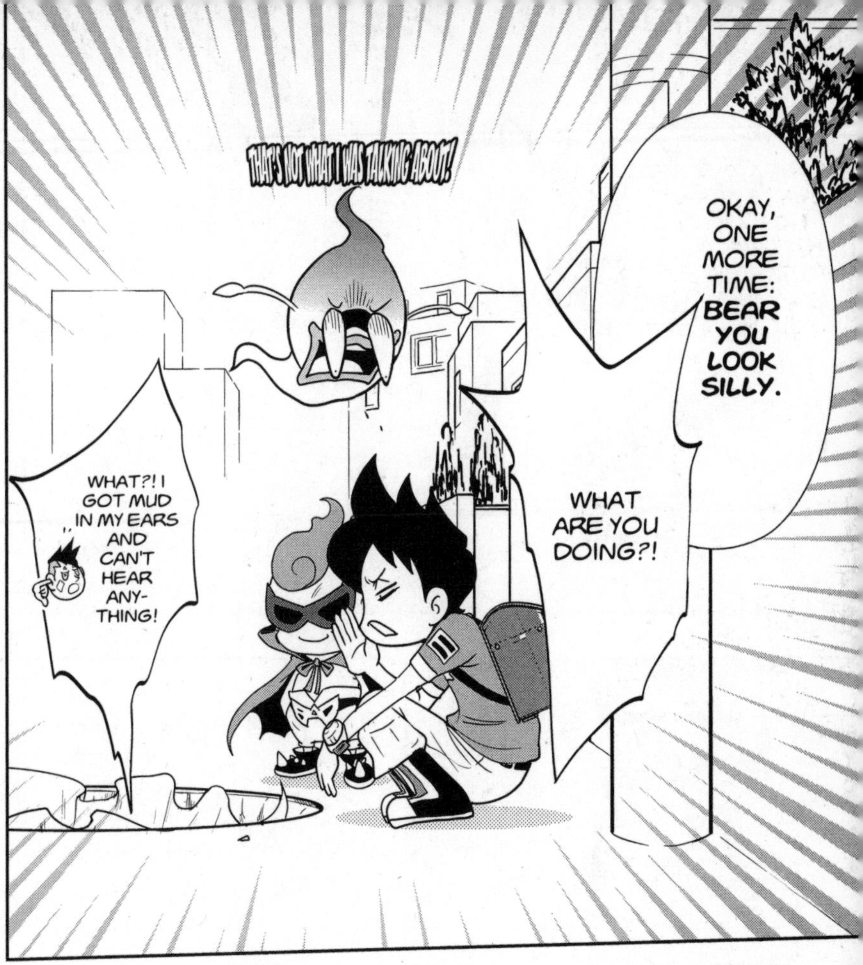
OKAY, ONE MORE TIME: BEAR YOU LOOK SILLY.
THAT'S NOT WHAT I WAS TALKING ABOUT!
WHAT ARE YOU DOING?!
WHAT?! I GOT MUD IN MY EARS AND CAN'T HEAR ANY-THING!

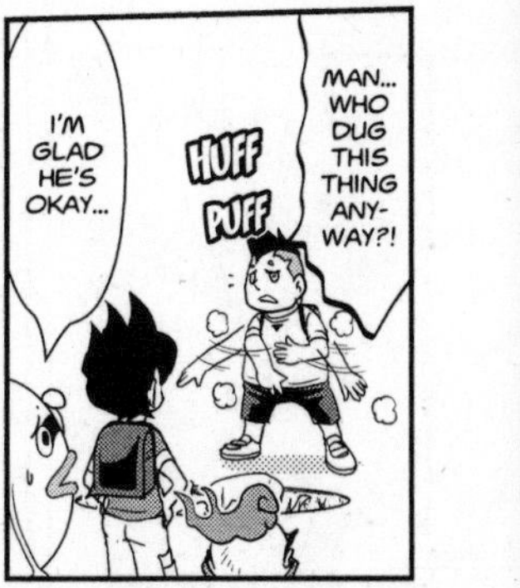
MAN... WHO DUG THIS THING ANY-WAY?!
HUFF PUFF
I'M GLAD HE'S OKAY...

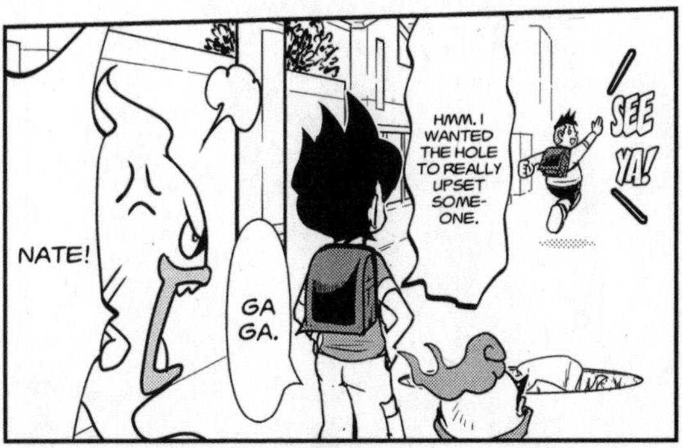
SEE YA!
HMM. I WANTED THE HOLE TO REALLY UPSET SOME-ONE.
GA GA.
NATE!

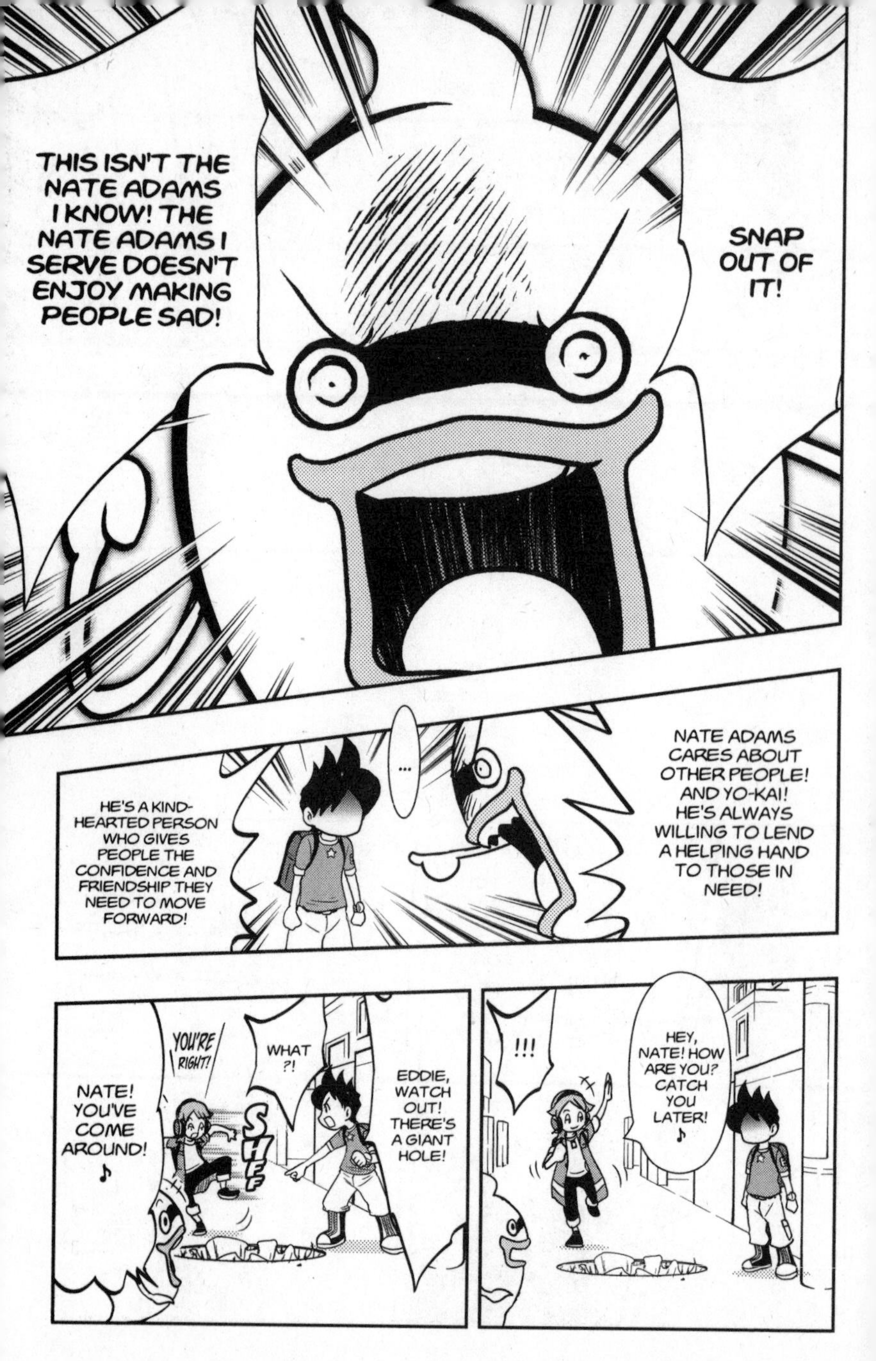
THIS ISN'T THE NATE ADAMS I KNOW! THE NATE ADAMS I SERVE DOESN'T ENJOY MAKING PEOPLE SAD!
SNAP OUT OF IT!
NATE ADAMS CARES ABOUT OTHER PEOPLE! AND YO-KAI! HE'S ALWAYS WILLING TO LEND A HELPING HAND TO THOSE IN NEED!
...
HE'S A KIND-HEARTED PERSON WHO GIVES PEOPLE THE CONFIDENCE AND FRIENDSHIP THEY NEED TO MOVE FORWARD!
HEY, NATE! HOW ARE YOU? CATCH YOU LATER! ♪
!!!
EDDIE, WATCH OUT! THERE'S A GIANT HOLE!
WHAT?!
YOU'RE RIGHT!
SHFF
NATE! YOU'VE COME AROUND! ♪

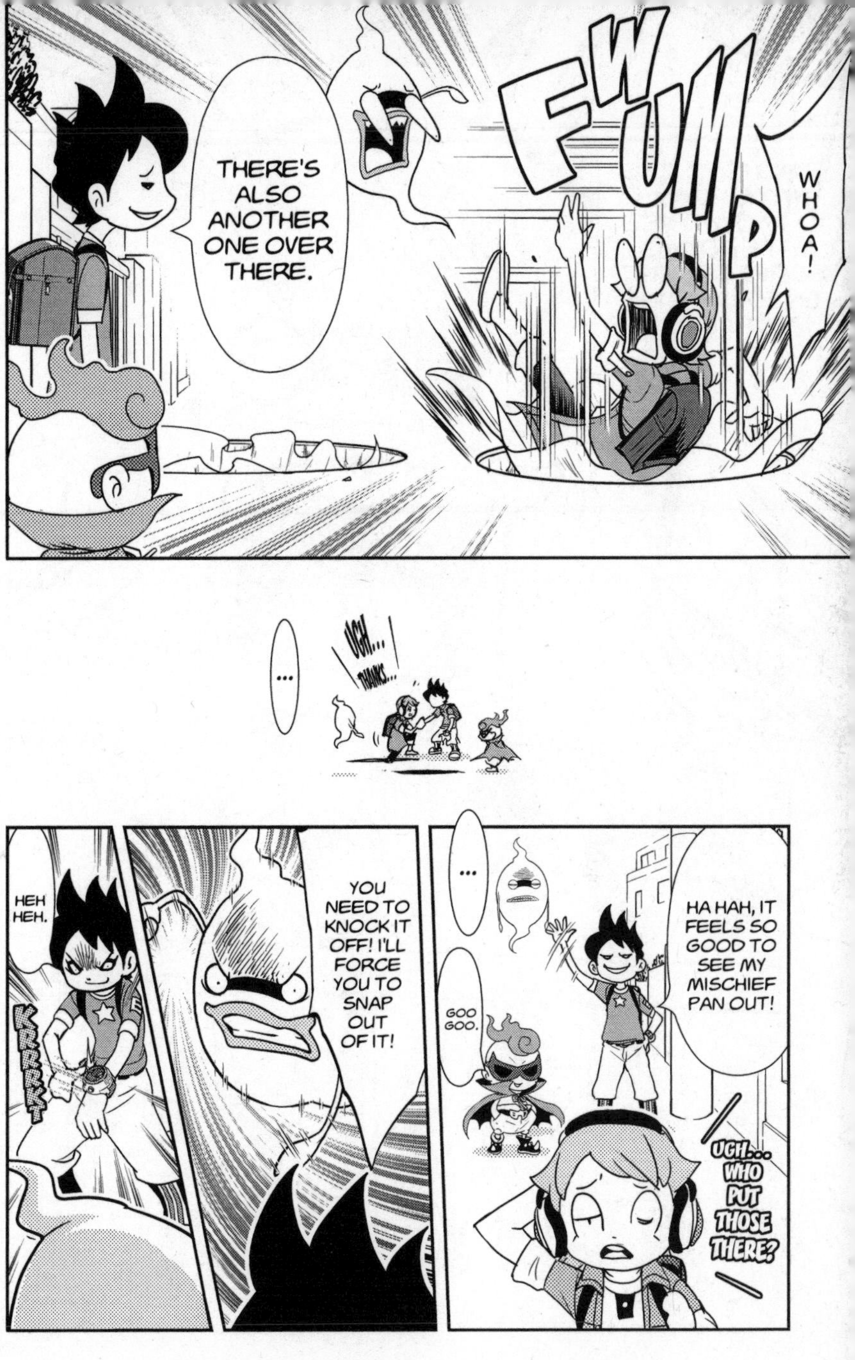
FWUMP
WHOA!
THERE'S ALSO ANOTHER ONE OVER THERE.
UGH... THANKS...
...
HA HAH, IT FEELS SO GOOD TO SEE MY MISCHIEF PAN OUT!
...
GOO GOO.
UGH... WHO PUT THOSE THERE?
YOU NEED TO KNOCK IT OFF! I'LL FORCE YOU TO SNAP OUT OF IT!
HEH HEH.
KRRRKT

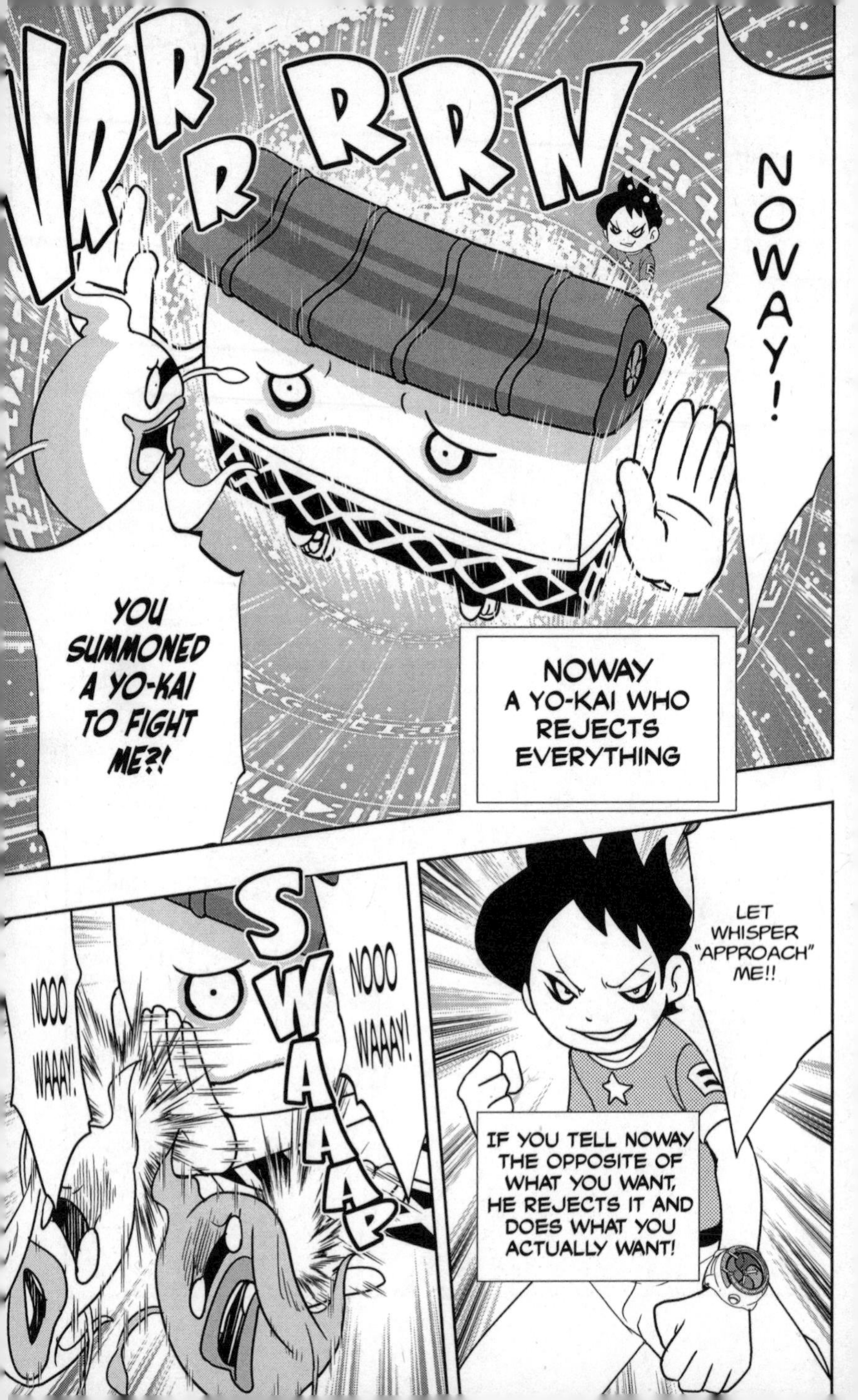
VRRRRRN
NOWAY!
YOU SUMMONED A YO-KAI TO FIGHT ME?!
NOWAY A YO-KAI WHO REJECTS EVERYTHING
LET WHISPER "APPROACH" ME!!
IF YOU TELL NOWAY THE OPPOSITE OF WHAT YOU WANT, HE REJECTS IT AND DOES WHAT YOU ACTUALLY WANT!
SWAAAP
NOOO WAAAY!
NOOO WAAAY!

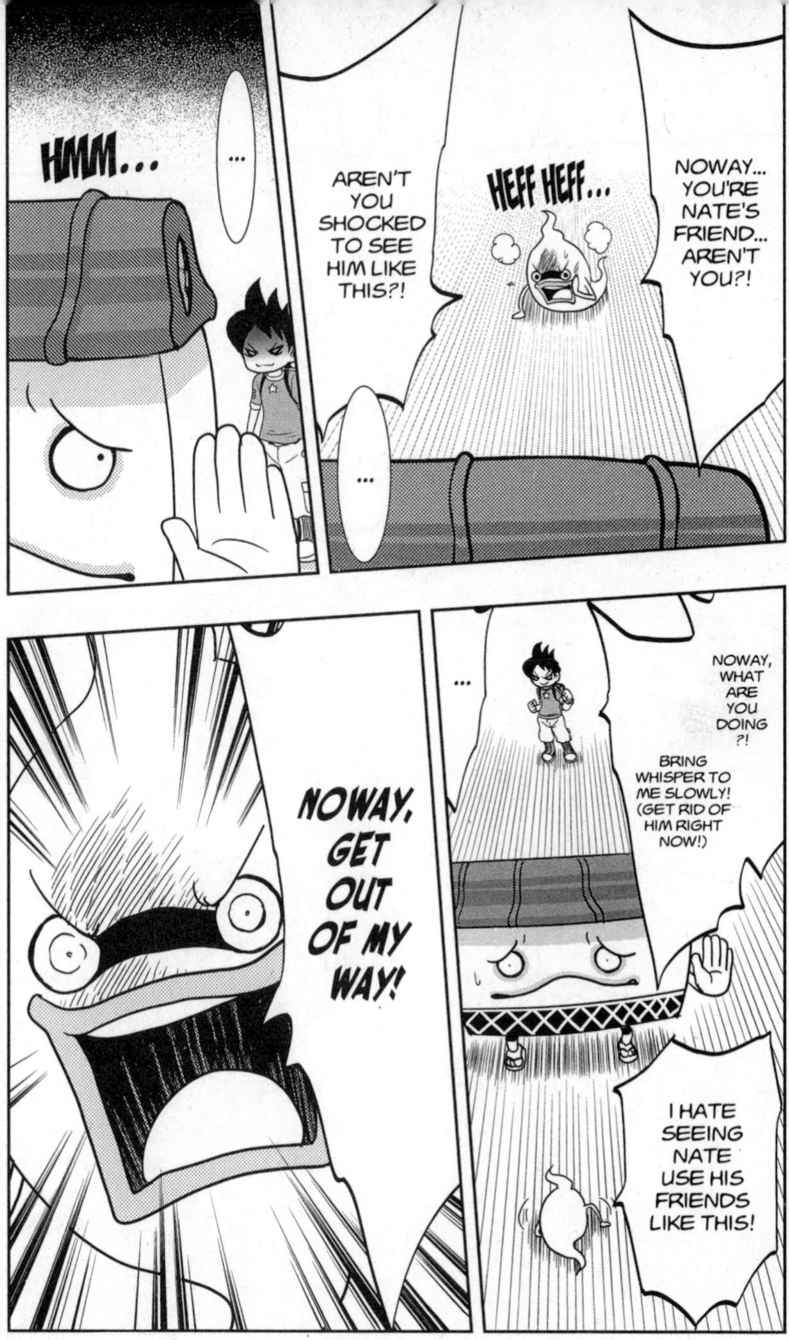
NOWAY... YOU'RE NATE'S FRIEND... AREN'T YOU?!
HEFF HEFF...
AREN'T YOU SHOCKED TO SEE HIM LIKE THIS?!
...
...
HMM...
NOWAY, WHAT ARE YOU DOING?!
BRING WHISPER TO ME SLOWLY! (GET RID OF HIM RIGHT NOW!)
...
I HATE SEEING NATE USE HIS FRIENDS LIKE THIS!
NOWAY, GET OUT OF MY WAY!

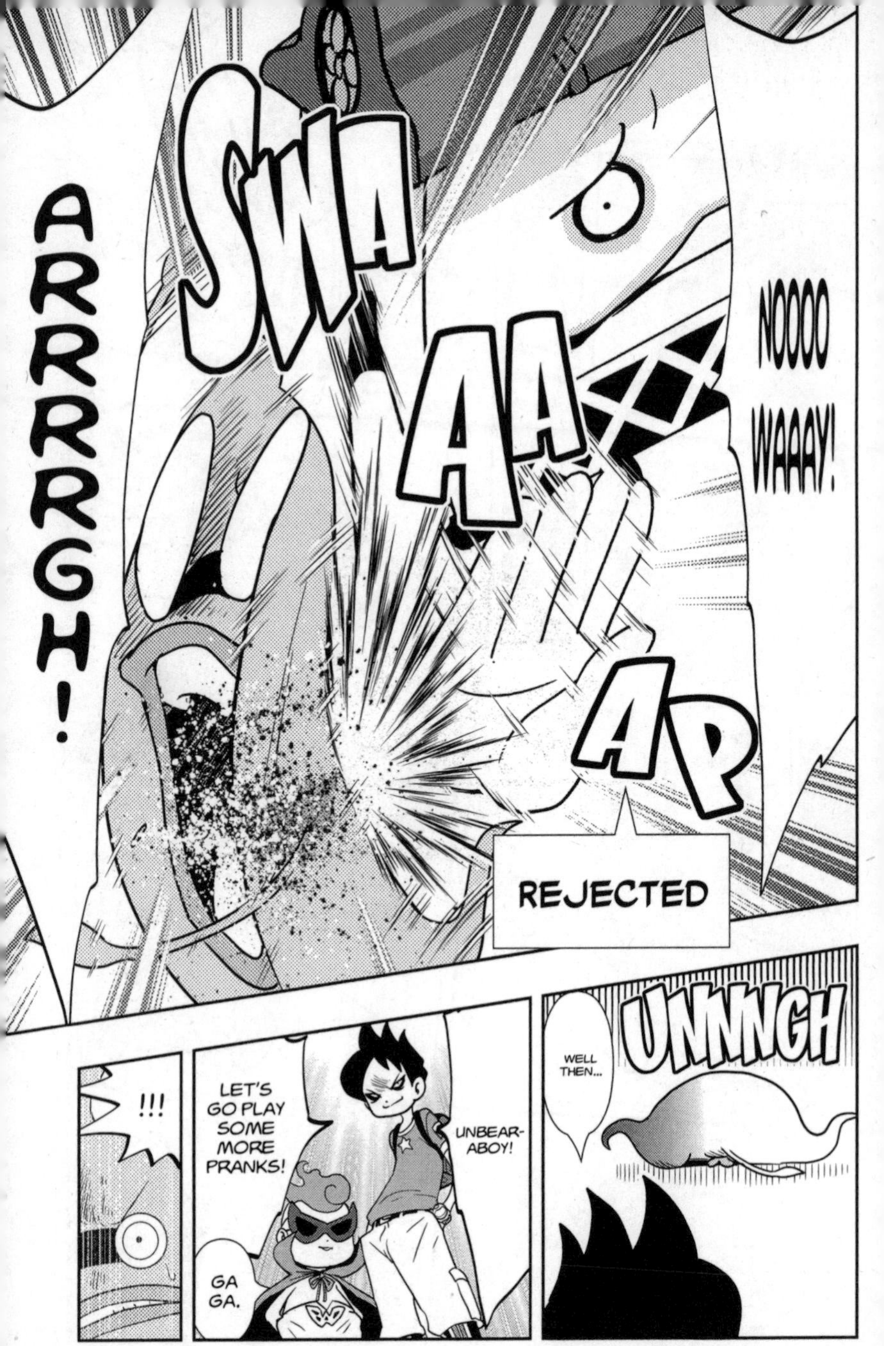
NOOOO WAAAY!
SWAAAAP
REJECTED
ARRRRGH!
UNNNGH
WELL THEN...
UNBEAR-ABOY!
LET'S GO PLAY SOME MORE PRANKS!
GA GA.
!!!

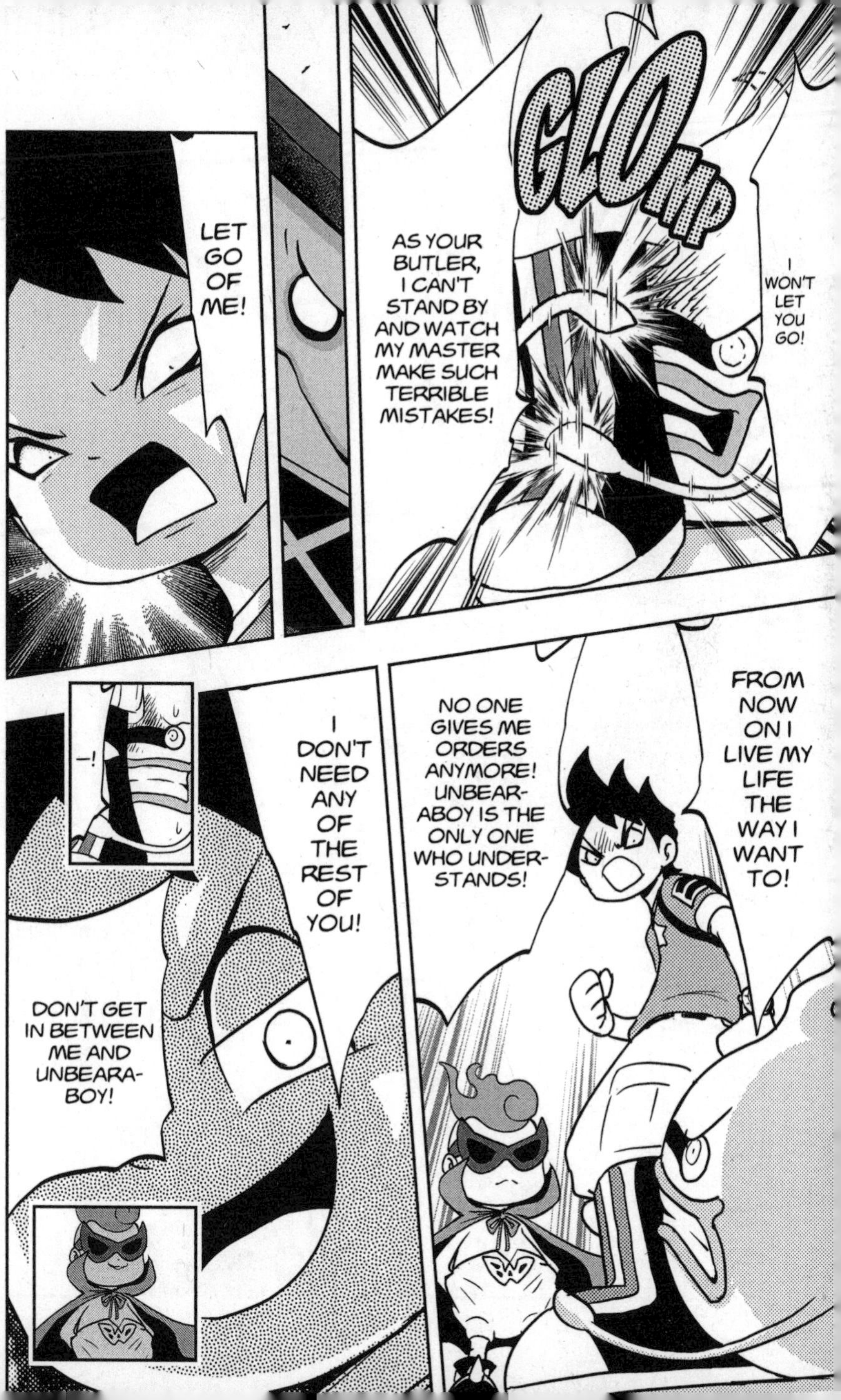
GLOMP
I WON'T LET YOU GO!
AS YOUR BUTLER, I CAN'T STAND BY AND WATCH MY MASTER MAKE SUCH TERRIBLE MISTAKES!
LET GO OF ME!
FROM NOW ON I LIVE MY LIFE THE WAY I WANT TO!
NO ONE GIVES ME ORDERS ANYMORE! UNBEARABOY IS THE ONLY ONE WHO UNDERSTANDS!
I DON'T NEED ANY OF THE REST OF YOU!
—!
DON'T GET IN BETWEEN ME AND UNBEARABOY!

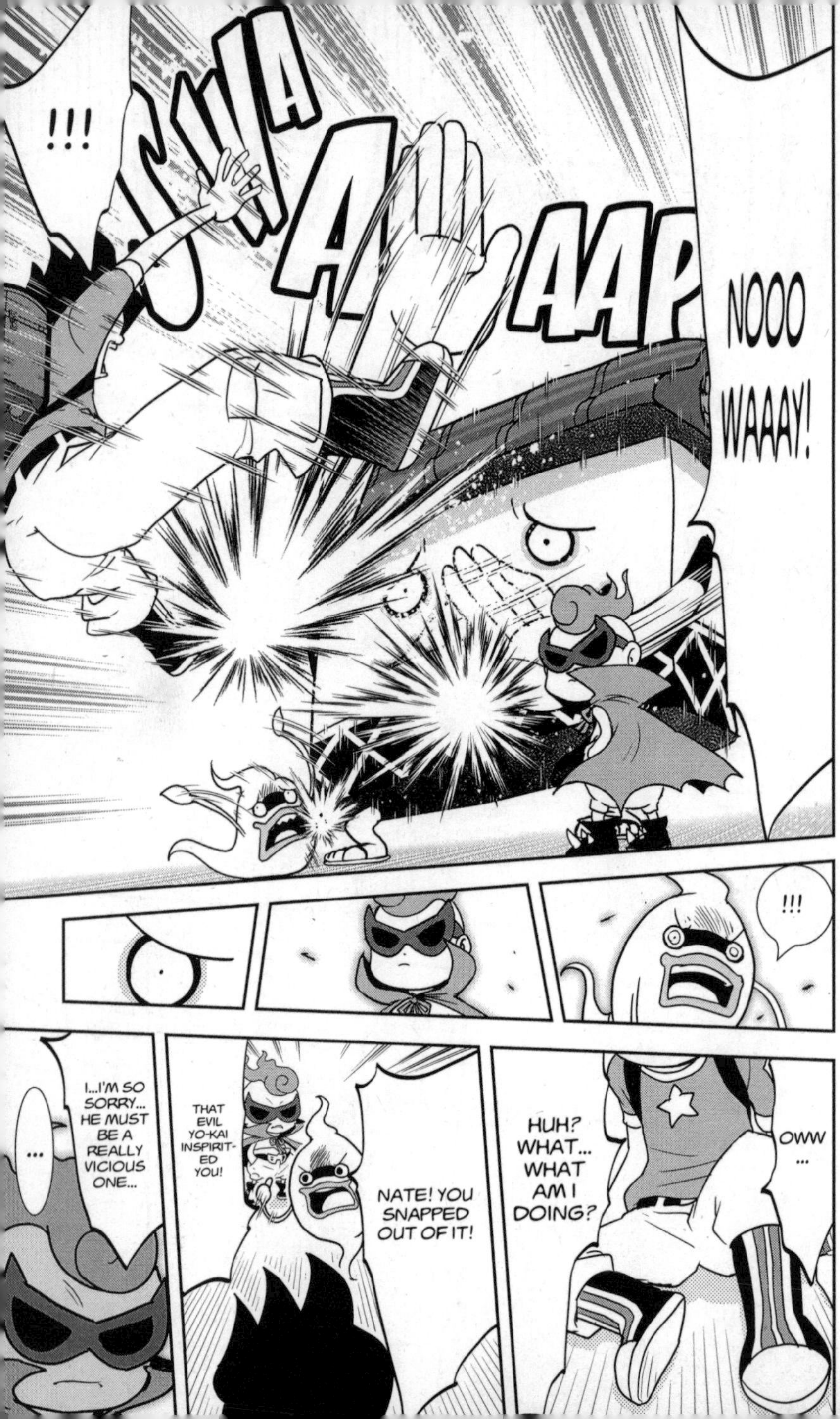
NOOO WAAAY!
SWAAAAP
!!!
!!!
OWW ...
HUH? WHAT... WHAT AM I DOING?
NATE! YOU SNAPPED OUT OF IT!
THAT EVIL YO-KAI INSPIRIT-ED YOU!
I...I'M SO SORRY... HE MUST BE A REALLY VICIOUS ONE...
...

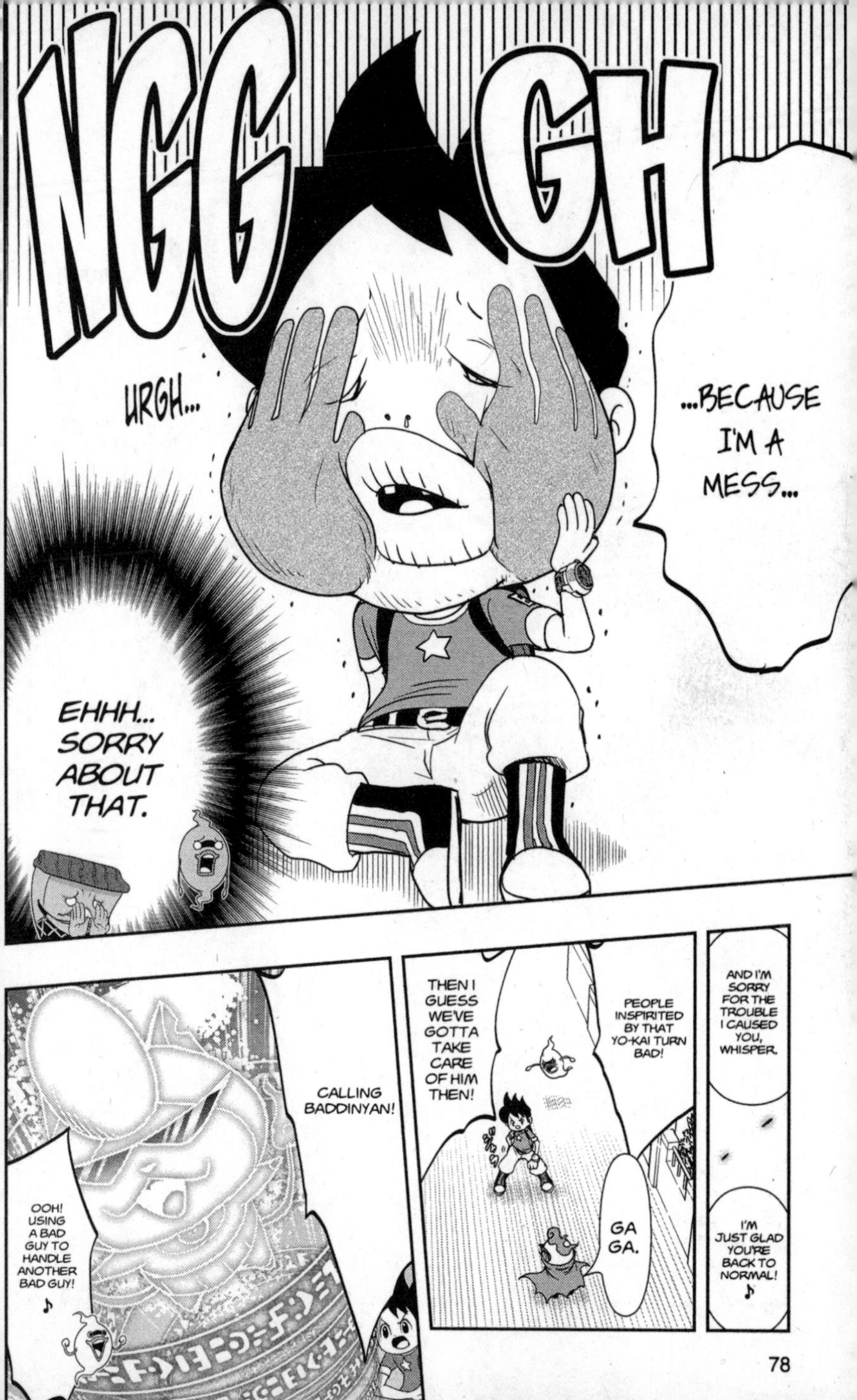
NGG GH
...BECAUSE I'M A MESS...
URGH...
EHHH... SORRY ABOUT THAT.
AND I'M SORRY FOR THE TROUBLE I CAUSED YOU, WHISPER.
I'M JUST GLAD YOU'RE BACK TO NORMAL! ♪
PEOPLE INSPIRITED BY THAT YO-KAI TURN BAD!
THEN I GUESS WE'VE GOTTA TAKE CARE OF HIM THEN!
GA GA.
CALLING BADDINYAN!
OOH! USING A BAD GUY TO HANDLE ANOTHER BAD GUY! ♪

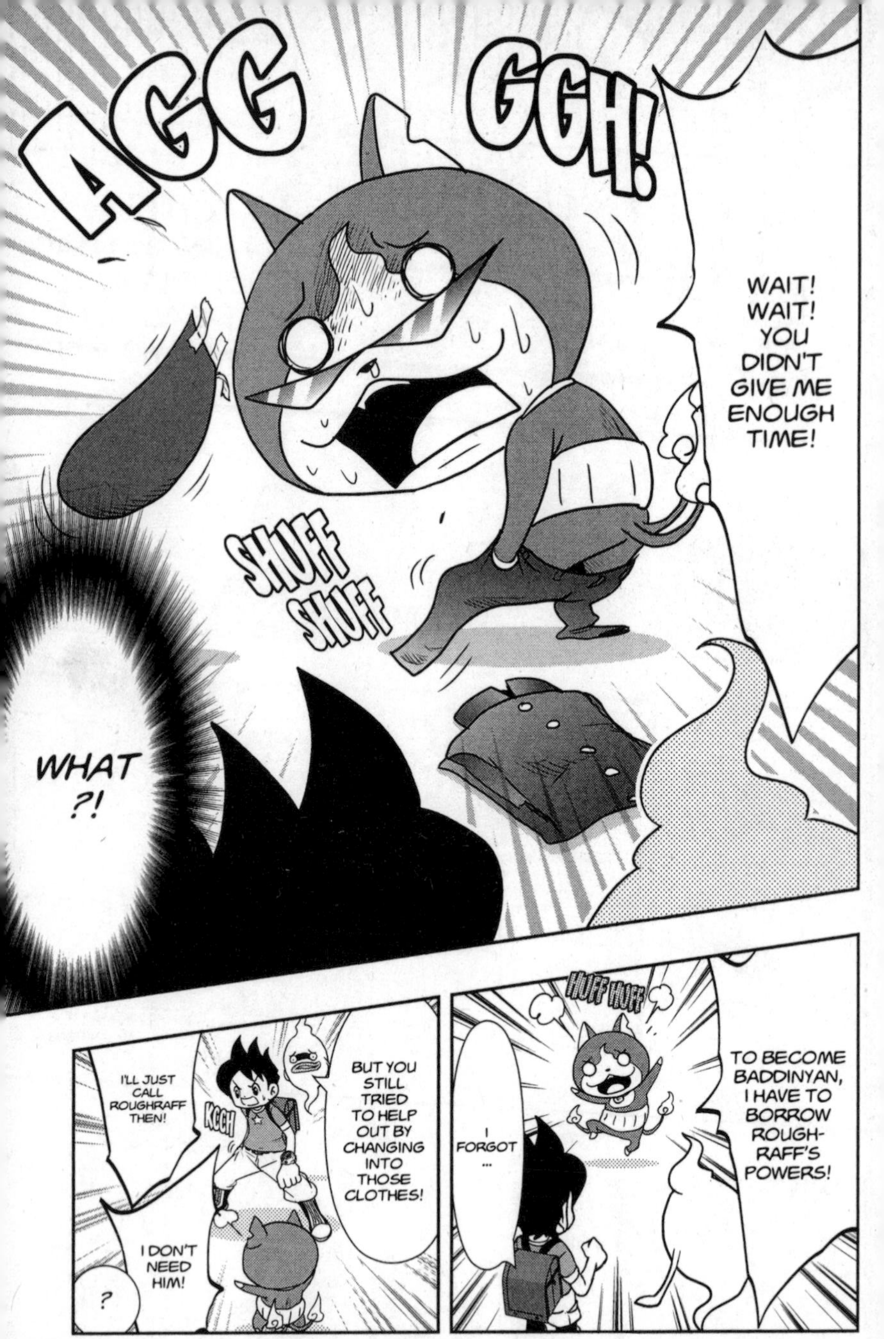
AGGGGH!
WAIT! WAIT! YOU DIDN'T GIVE ME ENOUGH TIME!
SHUFF SHUFF
WHAT?!
HUFF HUFF
TO BECOME BADDINYAN, I HAVE TO BORROW ROUGH-RAFF'S POWERS!
I FORGOT...
BUT YOU STILL TRIED TO HELP OUT BY CHANGING INTO THOSE CLOTHES!
I'LL JUST CALL ROUGHRAFF THEN!
KCCH
I DON'T NEED HIM!
?

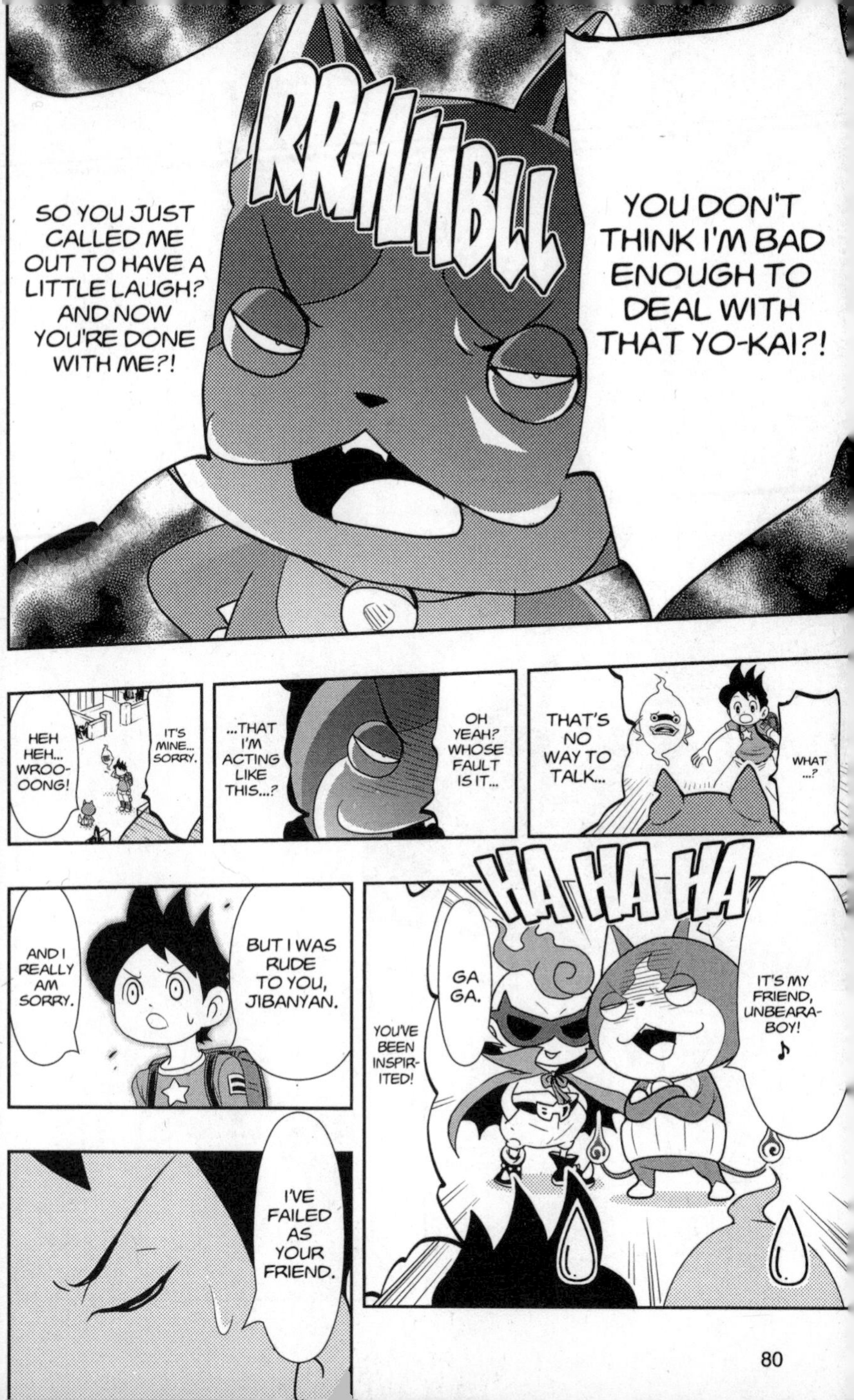
YOU DON'T THINK I'M BAD ENOUGH TO DEAL WITH THAT YO-KAI?!
RRMMBLL
SO YOU JUST CALLED ME OUT TO HAVE A LITTLE LAUGH? AND NOW YOU'RE DONE WITH ME?!
WHAT...?
THAT'S NO WAY TO TALK...
OH YEAH? WHOSE FAULT IS IT...
...THAT I'M ACTING LIKE THIS...?
IT'S MINE... SORRY.
HEH HEH... WROOO-OONG!
HA HA HA
IT'S MY FRIEND, UNBEARA-BOY! ♪
GA GA.
YOU'VE BEEN INSPIR-ITED!
BUT I WAS RUDE TO YOU, JIBANYAN.
AND I REALLY AM SORRY.
I'VE FAILED AS YOUR FRIEND.

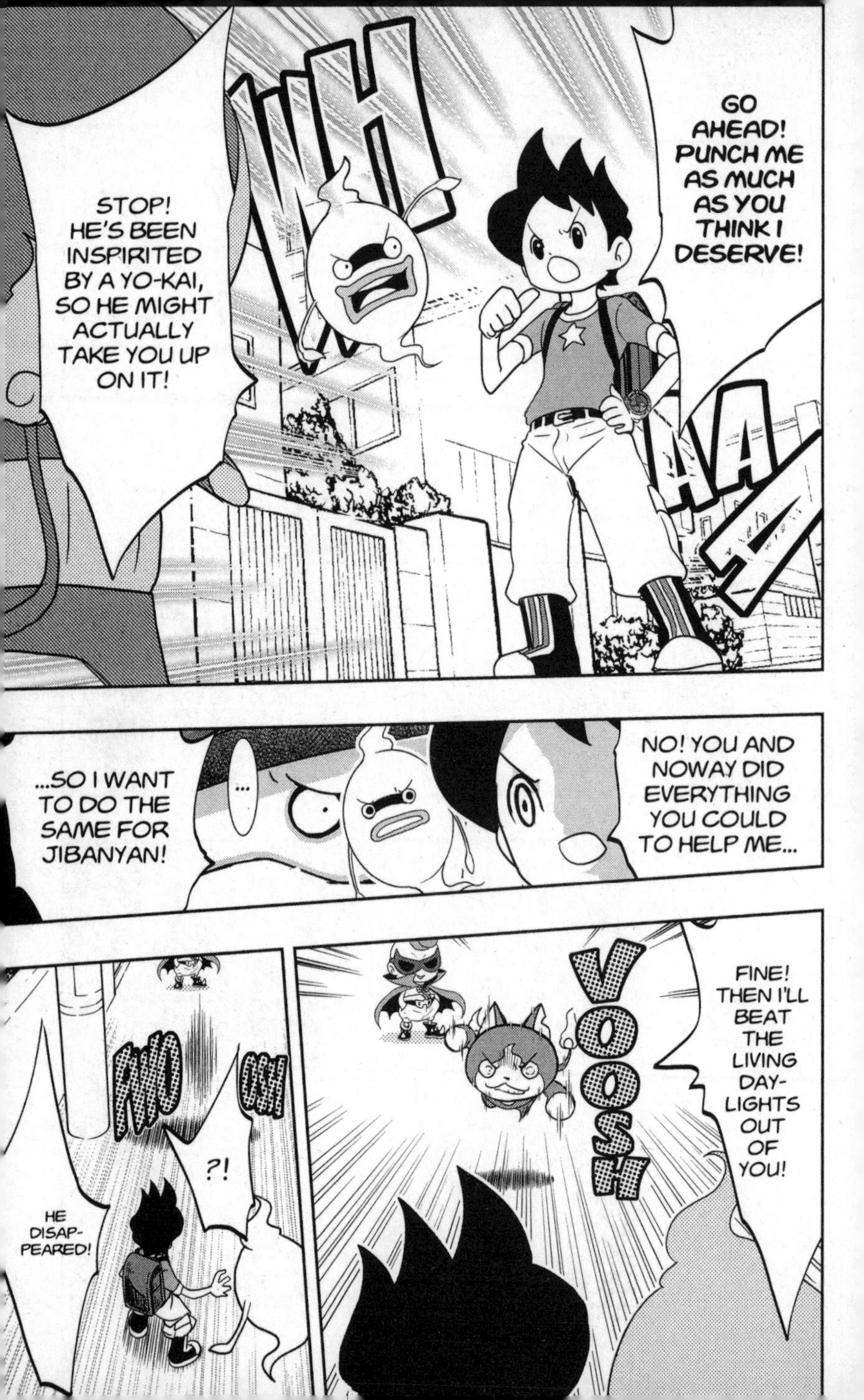
GO AHEAD! PUNCH ME AS MUCH AS YOU THINK I DESERVE!
WH
AA
STOP! HE'S BEEN INSPIRITED BY A YO-KAI, SO HE MIGHT ACTUALLY TAKE YOU UP ON IT!
NO! YOU AND NOWAY DID EVERYTHING YOU COULD TO HELP ME...
...
...SO I WANT TO DO THE SAME FOR JIBANYAN!
FINE! THEN I'LL BEAT THE LIVING DAY-LIGHTS OUT OF YOU!
VOOSH
PWO OSH
?!
HE DISAP-PEARED!

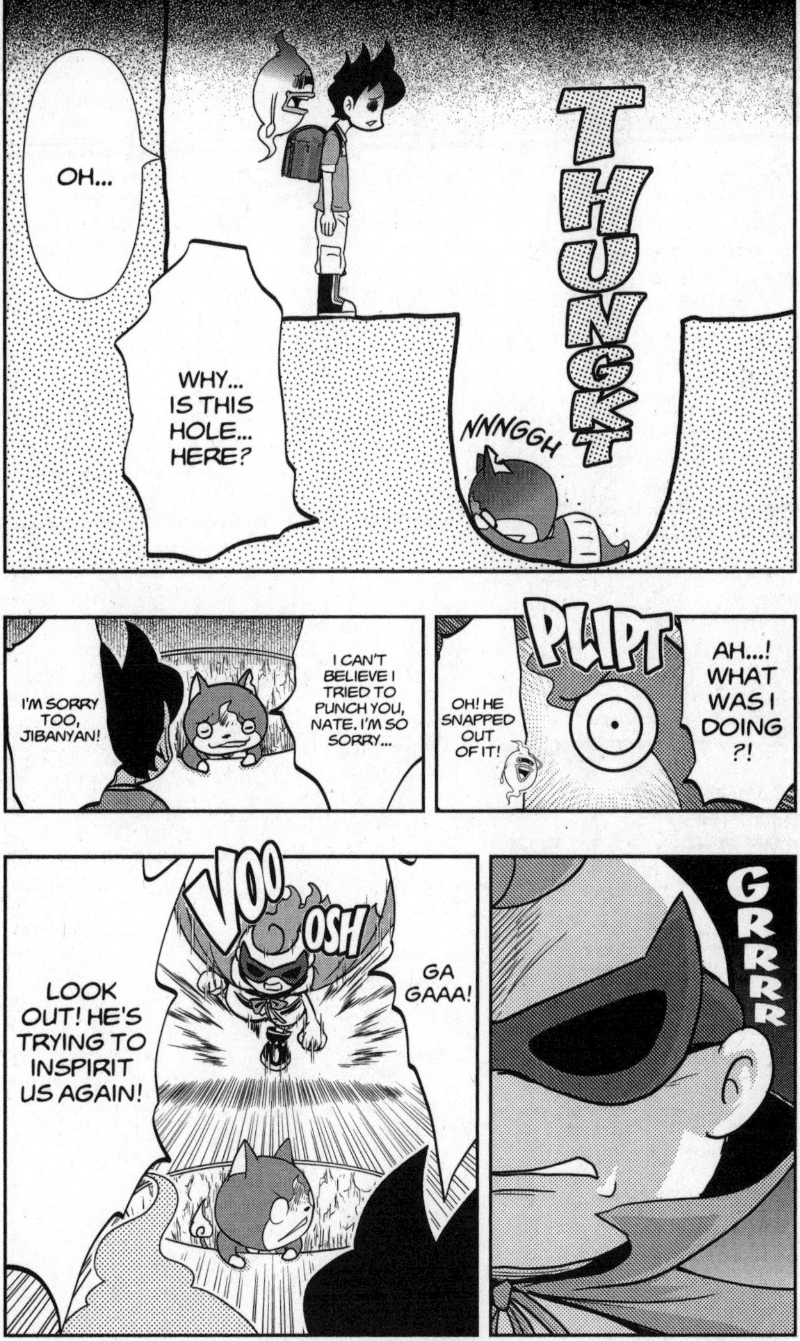
THUNGK
OH...
WHY... IS THIS HOLE... HERE?
NNNGGH
PLIPT
AH...! WHAT WAS I DOING ?!
OH! HE SNAPPED OUT OF IT!
I CAN'T BELIEVE I TRIED TO PUNCH YOU, NATE. I'M SO SORRY...
I'M SORRY TOO, JIBANYAN!
GRRR
VOOOSH
GA GAAA!
LOOK OUT! HE'S TRYING TO INSPIRIT US AGAIN!

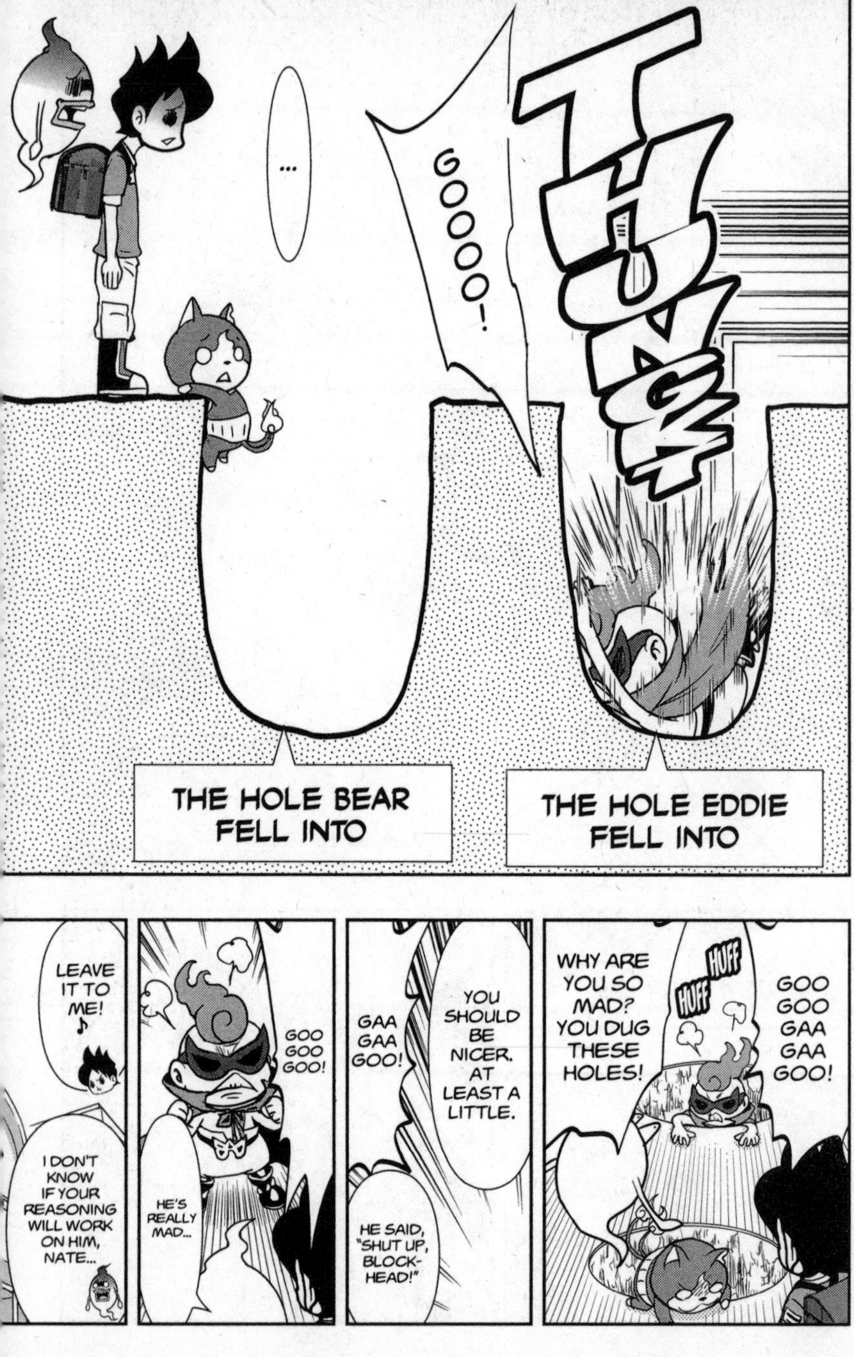
THUNK
THE HOLE EDDIE FELL INTO
GOOOOO!
...
THE HOLE BEAR FELL INTO
GOO GOO GAA GAA GOO!
HUFF HUFF
WHY ARE YOU SO MAD? YOU DUG THESE HOLES!
YOU SHOULD BE NICER. AT LEAST A LITTLE.
GAA GAA GOO!
HE SAID, "SHUT UP, BLOCK-HEAD!"
GOO GOO GOO!
HE'S REALLY MAD...
LEAVE IT TO ME! ♪
I DON'T KNOW IF YOUR REASONING WILL WORK ON HIM, NATE...

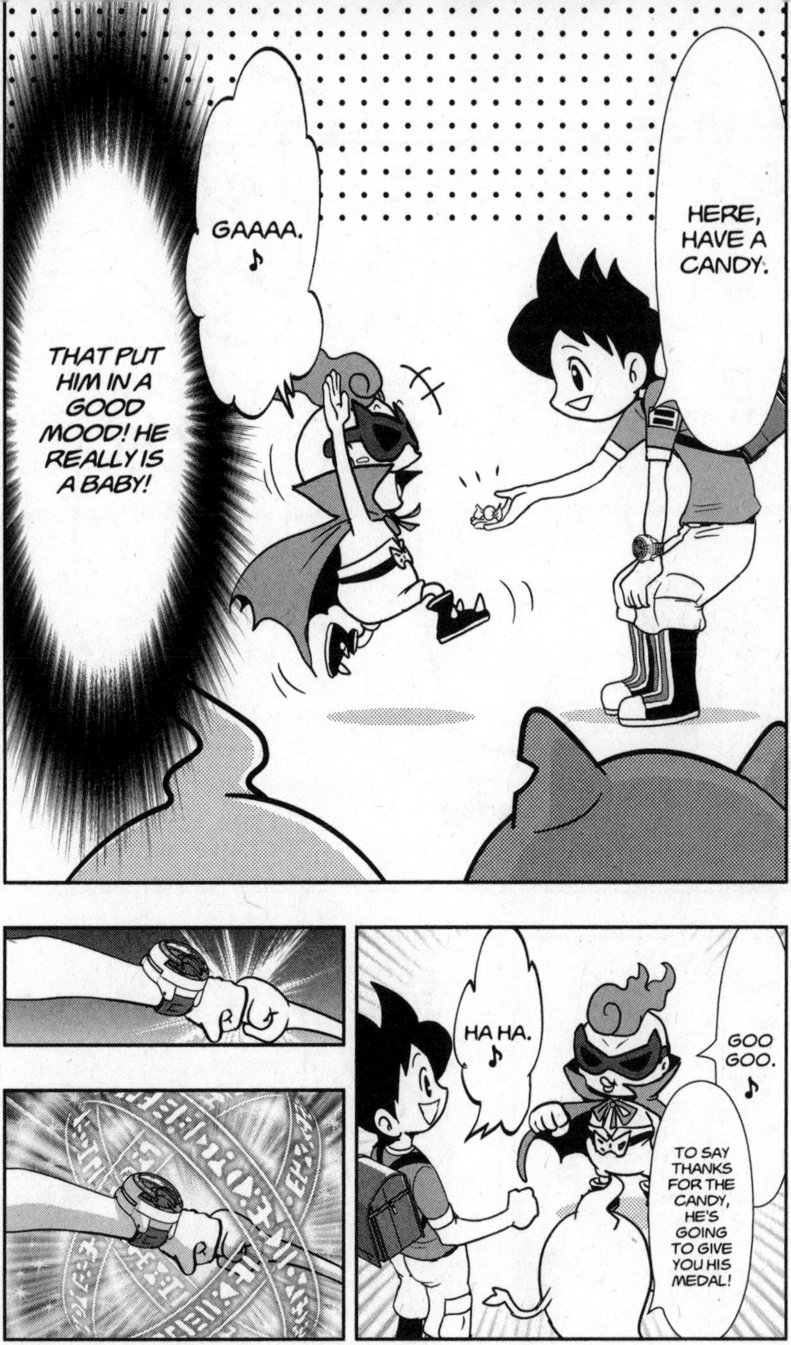
HERE, HAVE A CANDY.
GAAAA. ♪
THAT PUT HIM IN A GOOD MOOD! HE REALLY IS A BABY!
GOO GOO. ♪
HA HA. ♪
TO SAY THANKS FOR THE CANDY, HE'S GOING TO GIVE YOU HIS MEDAL!

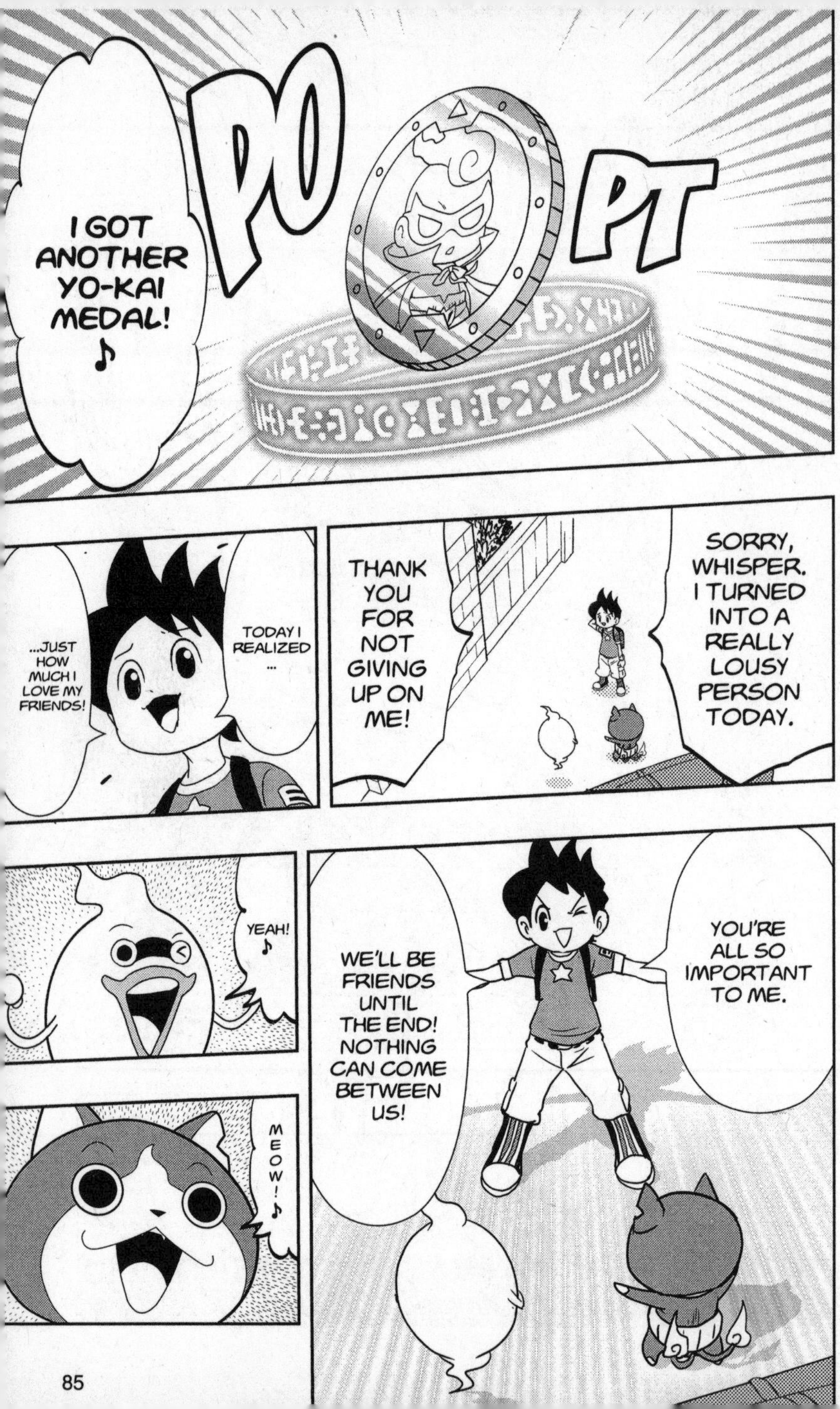
PO PT
I GOT ANOTHER YO-KAI MEDAL! ♪
SORRY, WHISPER. I TURNED INTO A REALLY LOUSY PERSON TODAY.
THANK YOU FOR NOT GIVING UP ON ME!
TODAY I REALIZED ...
...JUST HOW MUCH I LOVE MY FRIENDS!
YOU'RE ALL SO IMPORTANT TO ME.
WE'LL BE FRIENDS UNTIL THE END! NOTHING CAN COME BETWEEN US!
YEAH! ♪
MEOW! ♪

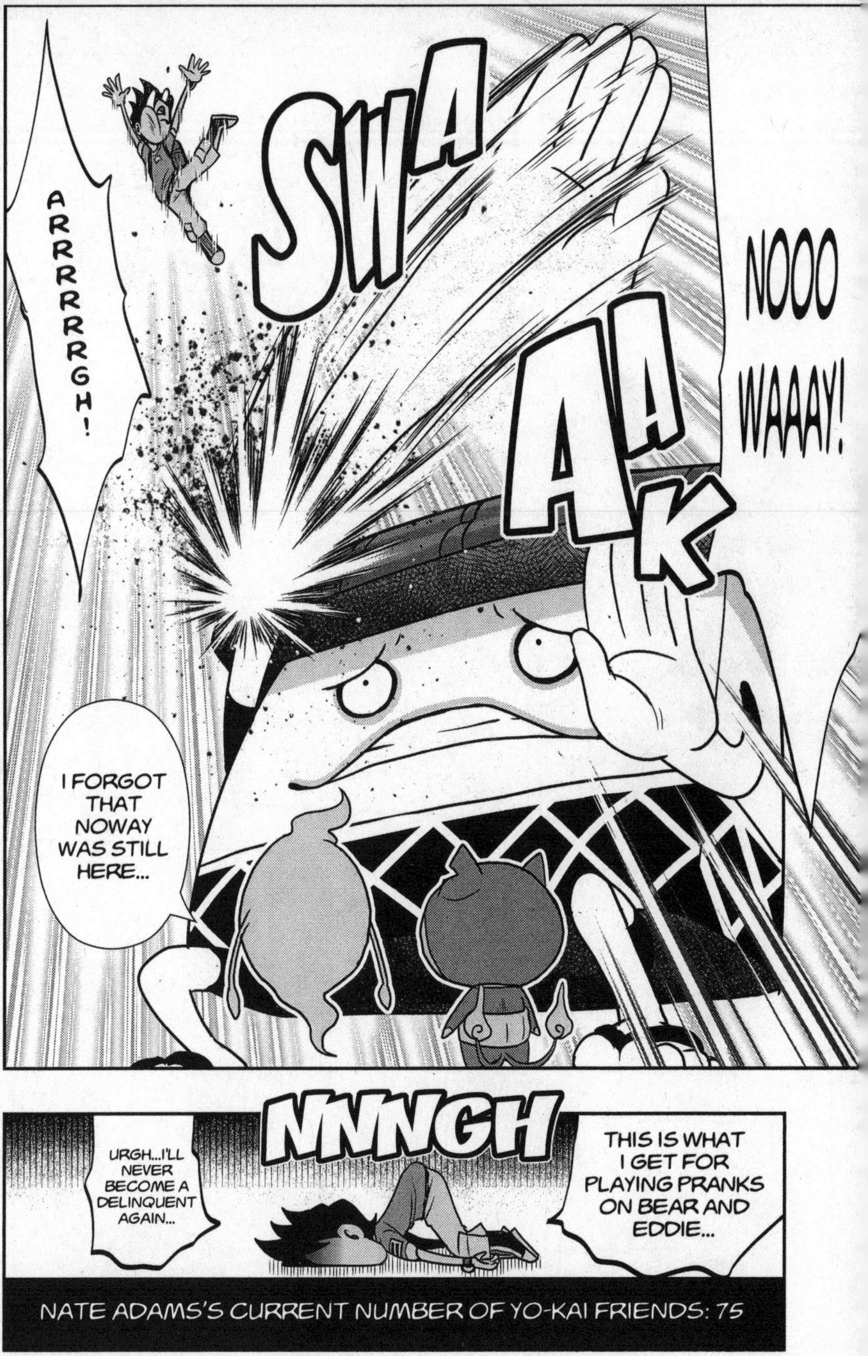
NOOO WAAAY!
SWAAAK
ARRRRRRGH!
I FORGOT THAT NOWAY WAS STILL HERE...
THIS IS WHAT I GET FOR PLAYING PRANKS ON BEAR AND EDDIE...
NNNGH
URGH...I'LL NEVER BECOME A DELINQUENT AGAIN...
NATE ADAMS'S CURRENT NUMBER OF YO-KAI FRIENDS: 75

CHAPTER 130:
PILOT YO-KAI AERONAUT 13

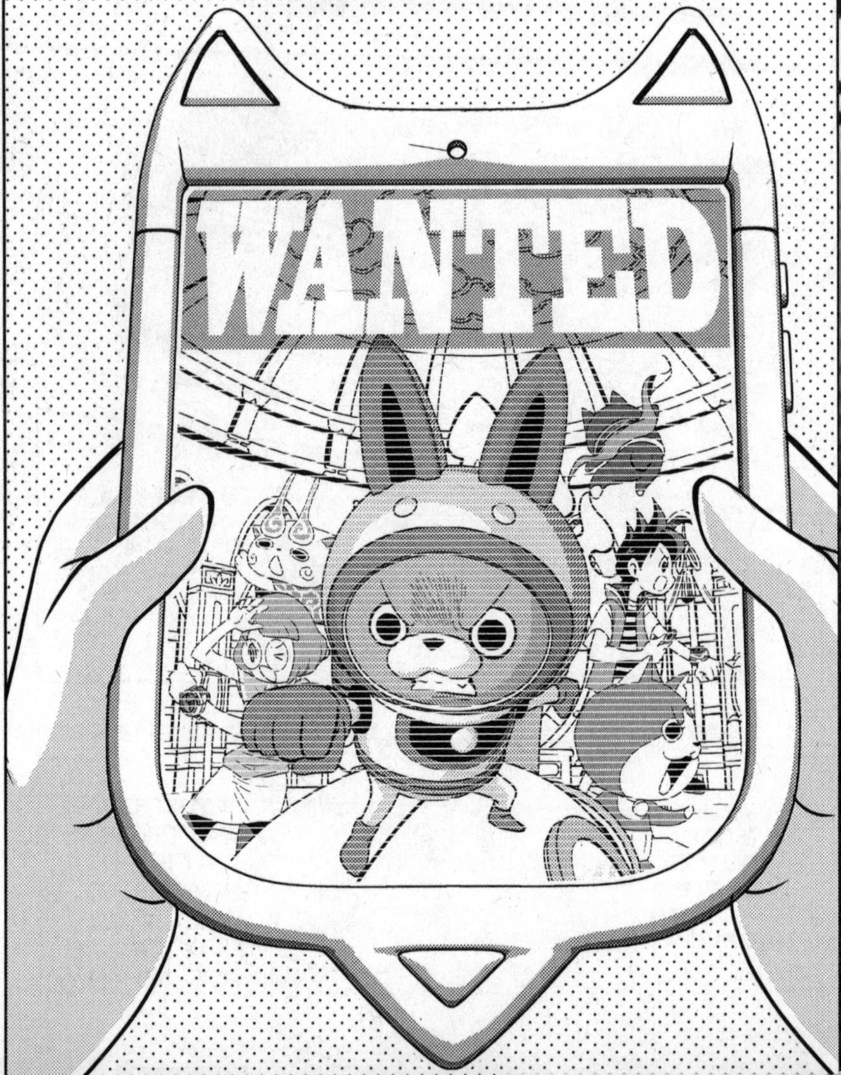
WANTED

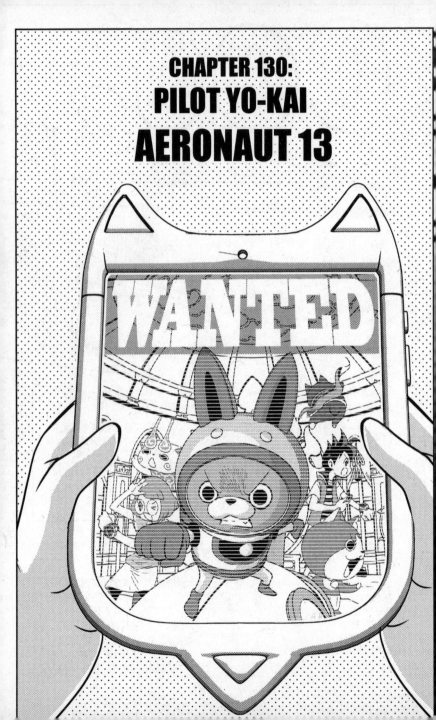

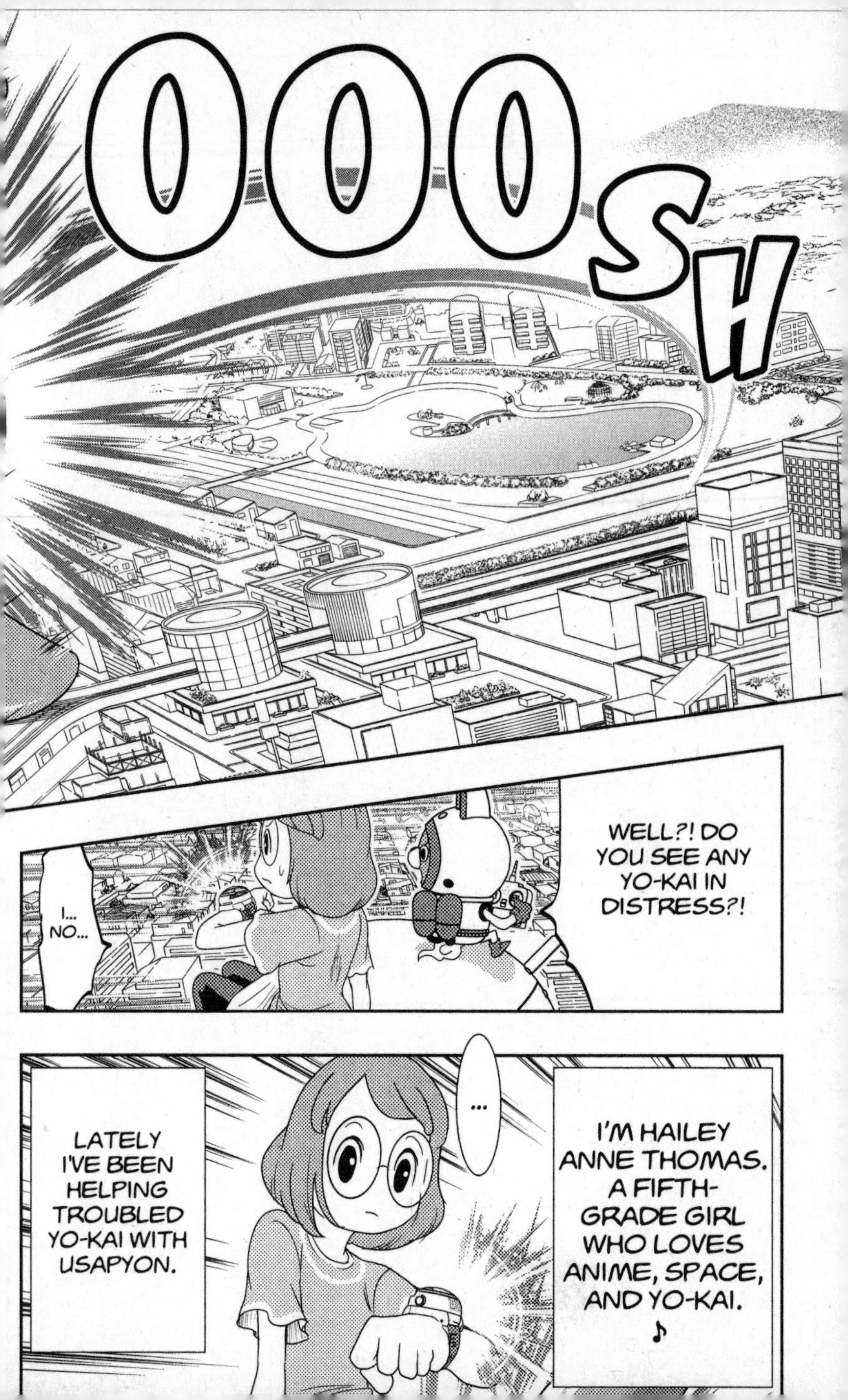
OOOOSH
WELL?! DO YOU SEE ANY YO-KAI IN DISTRESS?!
I... NO...
I'M HAILEY ANNE THOMAS. A FIFTH-GRADE GIRL WHO LOVES ANIME, SPACE, AND YO-KAI. ♪
...
LATELY I'VE BEEN HELPING TROUBLED YO-KAI WITH USAPYON.

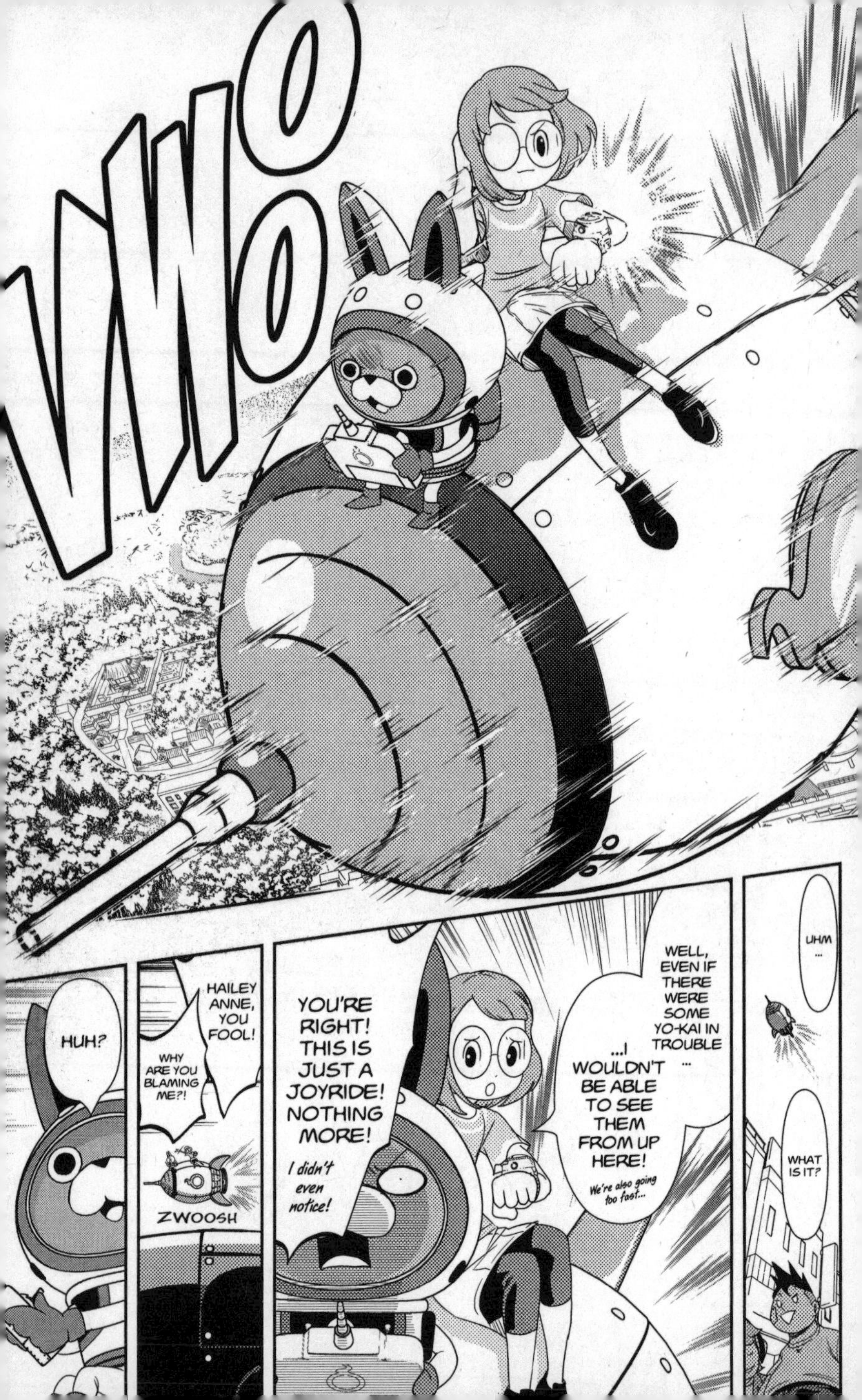
VWOO
UHM ...
WHAT IS IT?
WELL, EVEN IF THERE WERE SOME YO-KAI IN TROUBLE ...
...I WOULDN'T BE ABLE TO SEE THEM FROM UP HERE!
We're also going too fast...
YOU'RE RIGHT! THIS IS JUST A JOYRIDE! NOTHING MORE!
I didn't even notice!
HAILEY ANNE, YOU FOOL!
WHY ARE YOU BLAMING ME?!
ZWOOSH
HUH?

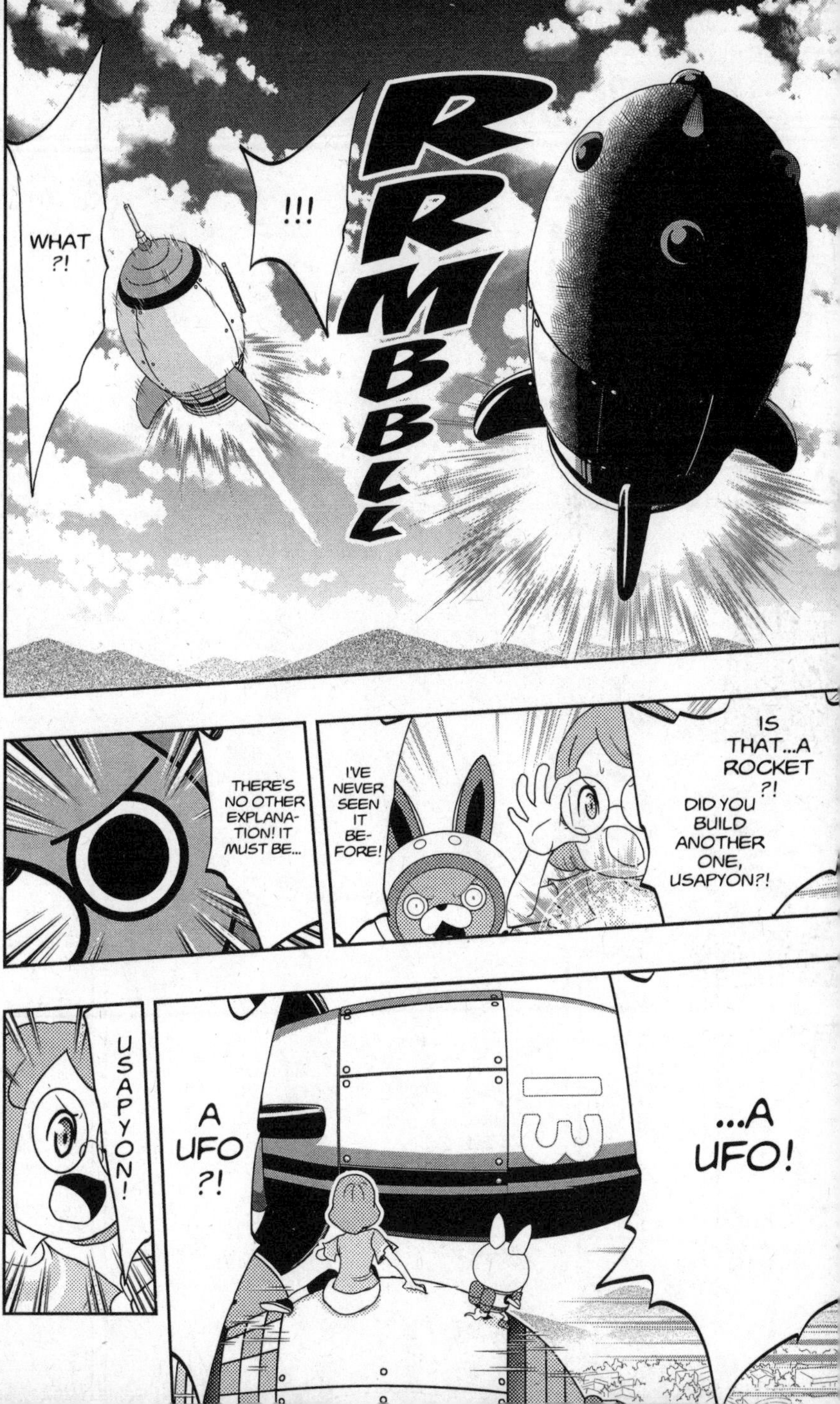
RRMBBLL
!!!
WHAT ?!
IS THAT...A ROCKET ?!
DID YOU BUILD ANOTHER ONE, USAPYON?!
I'VE NEVER SEEN IT BE-FORE!
THERE'S NO OTHER EXPLANA-TION! IT MUST BE...
...A UFO!
A UFO ?!
USAPYON!

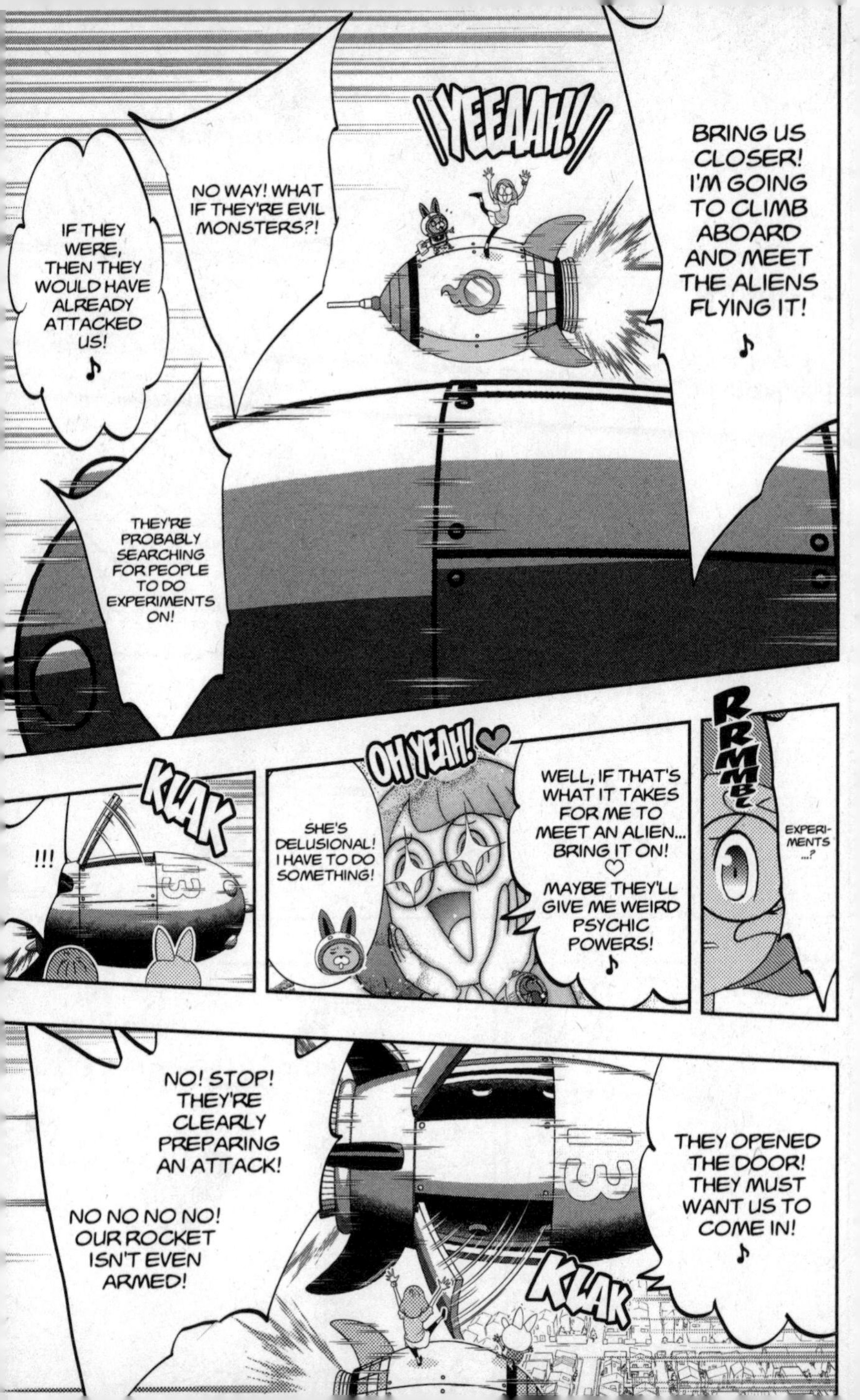
BRING US CLOSER! I'M GOING TO CLIMB ABOARD AND MEET THE ALIENS FLYING IT! ♪
YEEAAH!
NO WAY! WHAT IF THEY'RE EVIL MONSTERS?!
IF THEY WERE, THEN THEY WOULD HAVE ALREADY ATTACKED US! ♪
THEY'RE PROBABLY SEARCHING FOR PEOPLE TO DO EXPERIMENTS ON!
RRMMBL
EXPERI-MENTS ...?
OH YEAH! ♡
WELL, IF THAT'S WHAT IT TAKES FOR ME TO MEET AN ALIEN... BRING IT ON! ♡
MAYBE THEY'LL GIVE ME WEIRD PSYCHIC POWERS! ♪
SHE'S DELUSIONAL! I HAVE TO DO SOMETHING!
KLAK
!!!
THEY OPENED THE DOOR! THEY MUST WANT US TO COME IN! ♪
KLAK
NO! STOP! THEY'RE CLEARLY PREPARING AN ATTACK!
NO NO NO NO! OUR ROCKET ISN'T EVEN ARMED!

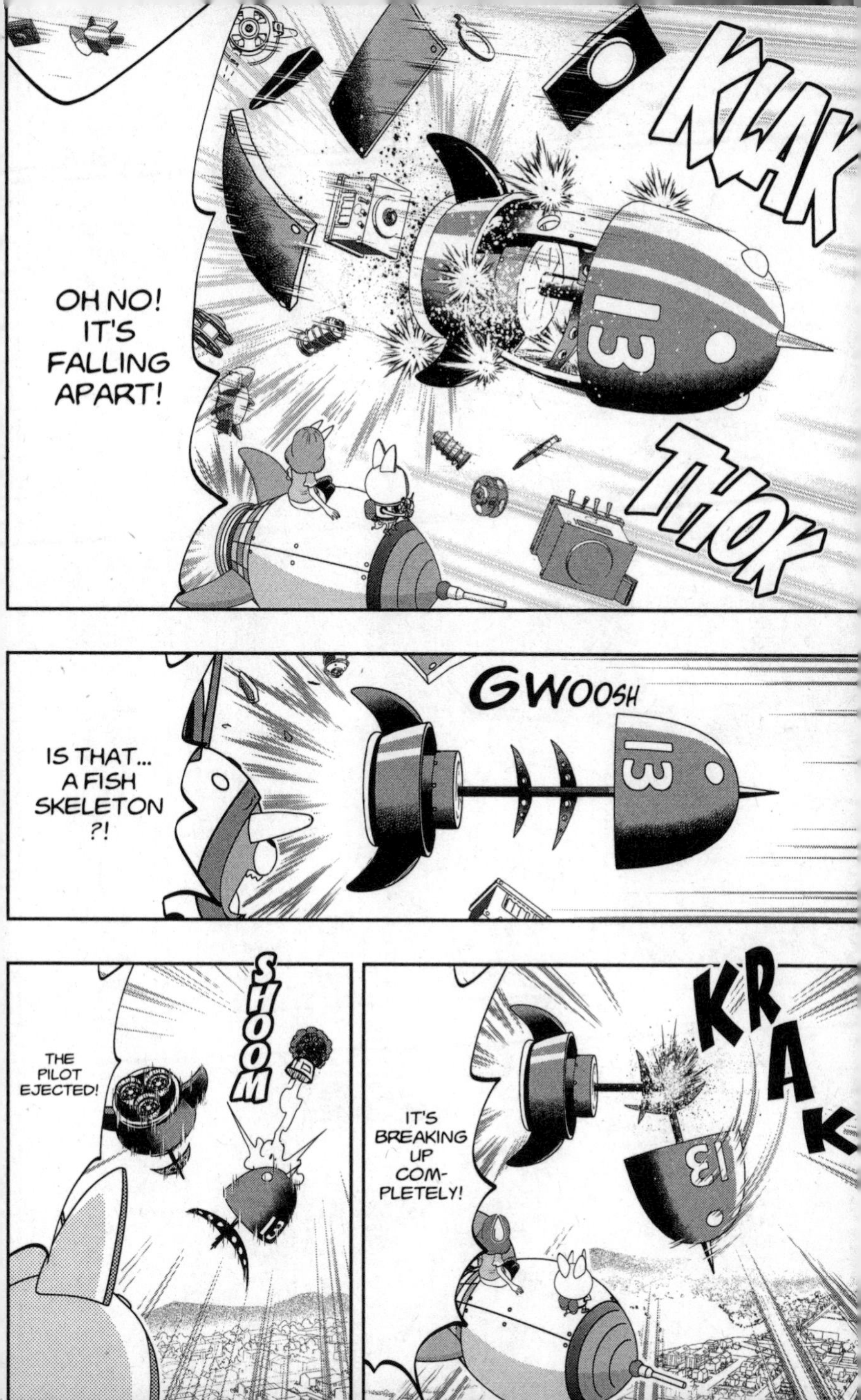
KWAK
OH NO! IT'S FALLING APART!
THOK
GWOOSH
IS THAT... A FISH SKELETON ?!
KRAK
IT'S BREAKING UP COM-PLETELY!
SHOOM
THE PILOT EJECTED!

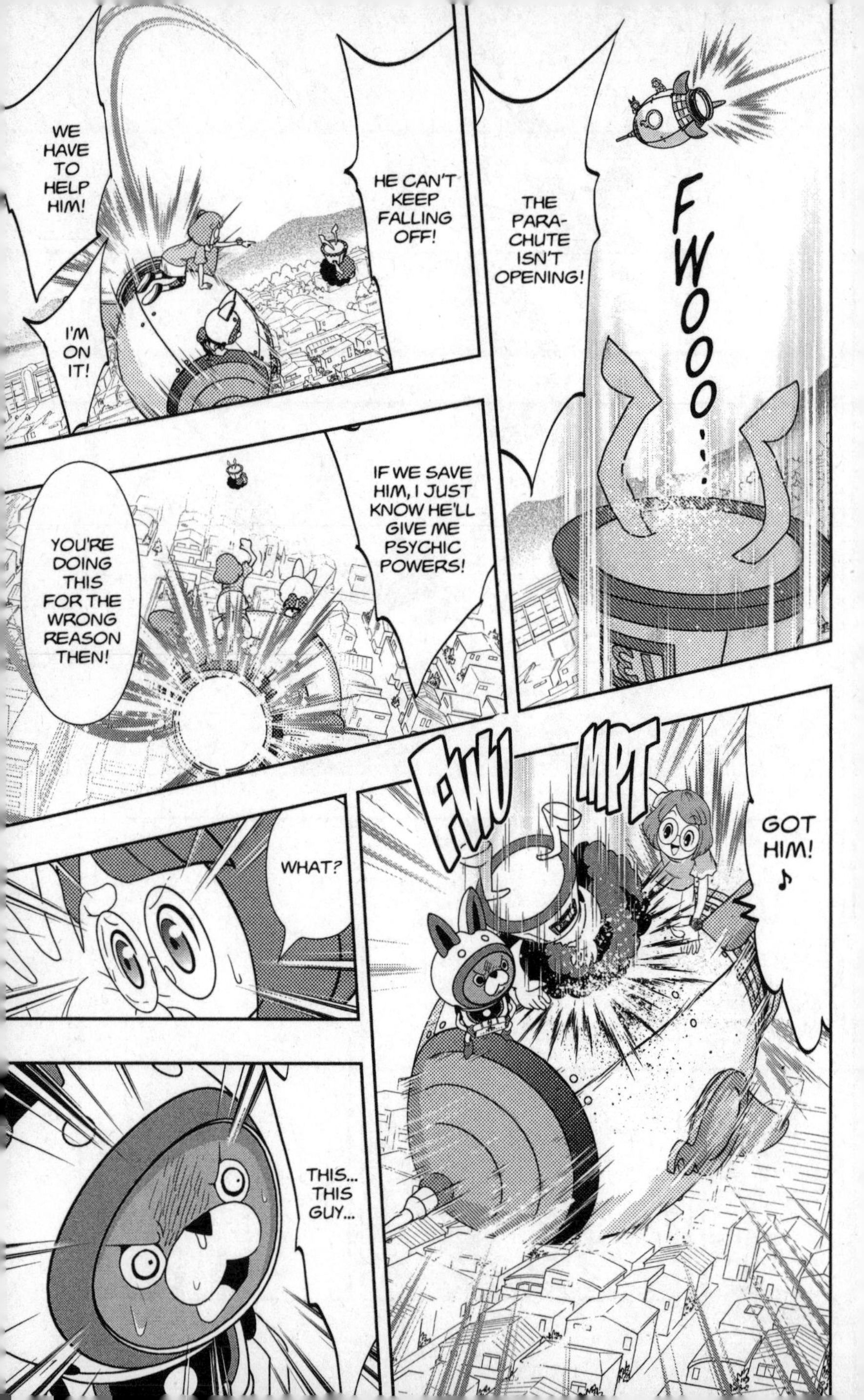

THE PARACHUTE ISN'T OPENING!
FWOOO...
HE CAN'T KEEP FALLING OFF!
WE HAVE TO HELP HIM!
I'M ON IT!
IF WE SAVE HIM, I JUST KNOW HE'LL GIVE ME PSYCHIC POWERS!
YOU'RE DOING THIS FOR THE WRONG REASON THEN!
FWUMPT
GOT HIM! ♪
WHAT?
THIS... THIS GUY...

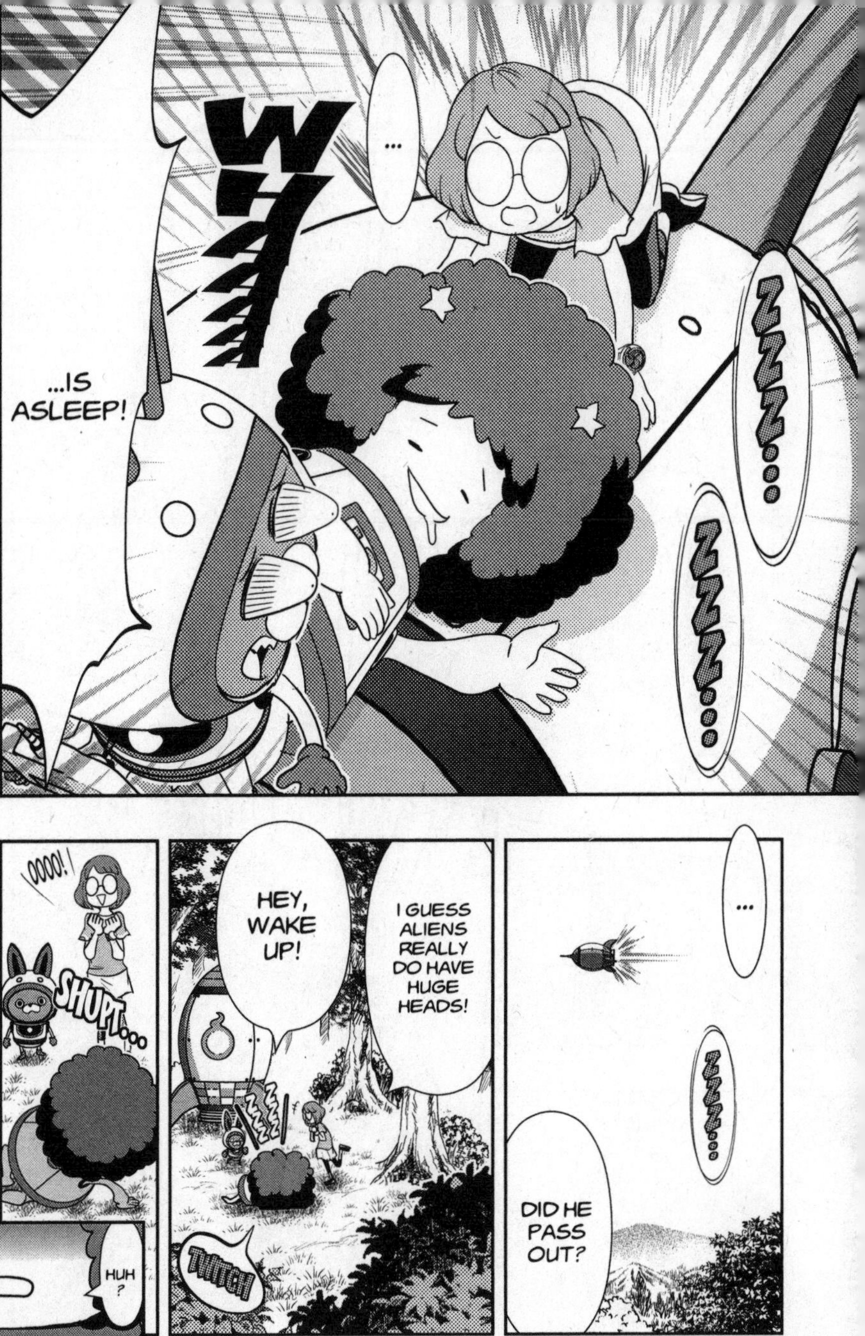
...
...IS ASLEEP!
ZZZZ...
ZZZZ...
...
ZZZZ...
DID HE PASS OUT?
I GUESS ALIENS REALLY DO HAVE HUGE HEADS!
HEY, WAKE UP!
TWITCH
OOOO!
SHUPT...
HUH?

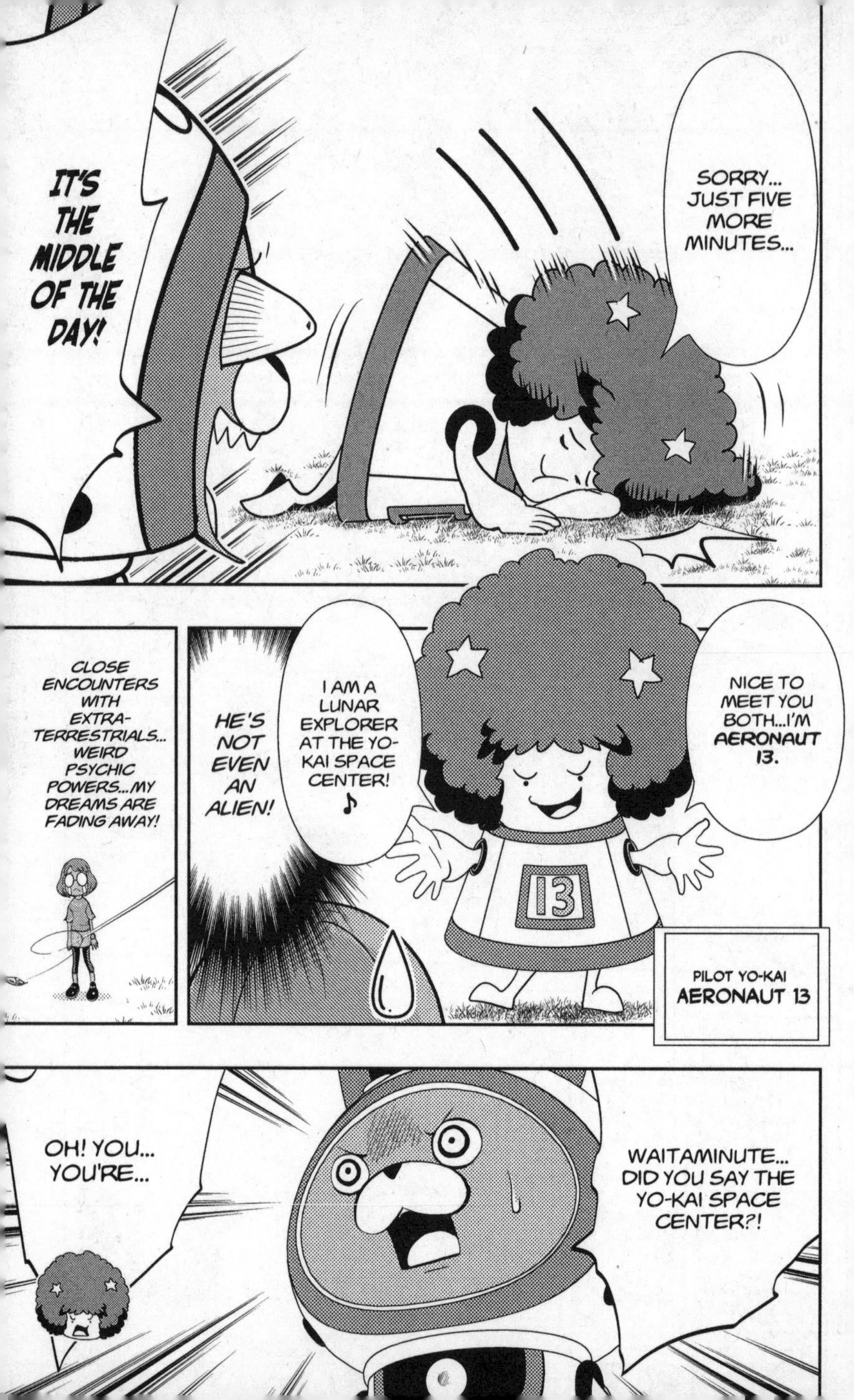
SORRY... JUST FIVE MORE MINUTES...
IT'S THE MIDDLE OF THE DAY!
NICE TO MEET YOU BOTH...I'M AERONAUT 13.
I AM A LUNAR EXPLORER AT THE YO-KAI SPACE CENTER! ♪
HE'S NOT EVEN AN ALIEN!
PILOT YO-KAI AERONAUT 13
CLOSE ENCOUNTERS WITH EXTRA-TERRESTRIALS... WEIRD PSYCHIC POWERS...MY DREAMS ARE FADING AWAY!
WAITAMINUTE... DID YOU SAY THE YO-KAI SPACE CENTER?!
OH! YOU... YOU'RE...
13

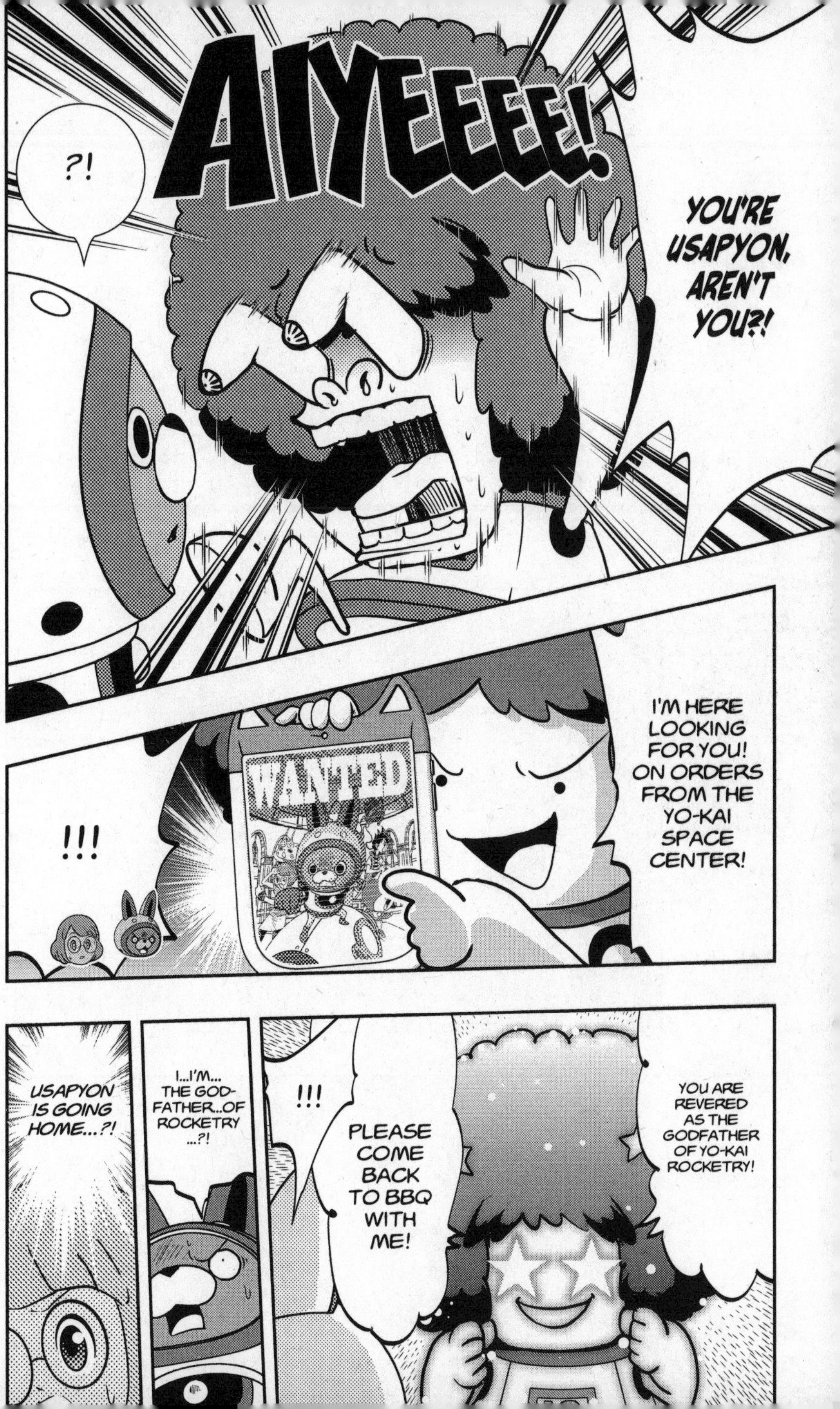
AIYEEEEE!
YOU'RE USAPYON, AREN'T YOU?!
?!
I'M HERE LOOKING FOR YOU! ON ORDERS FROM THE YO-KAI SPACE CENTER!
WANTED
!!!
YOU ARE REVERED AS THE GODFATHER OF YO-KAI ROCKETRY!
PLEASE COME BACK TO BBQ WITH ME!
!!!
I...I'M... THE GOD-FATHER...OF ROCKETRY ...?!
USAPYON IS GOING HOME...?!

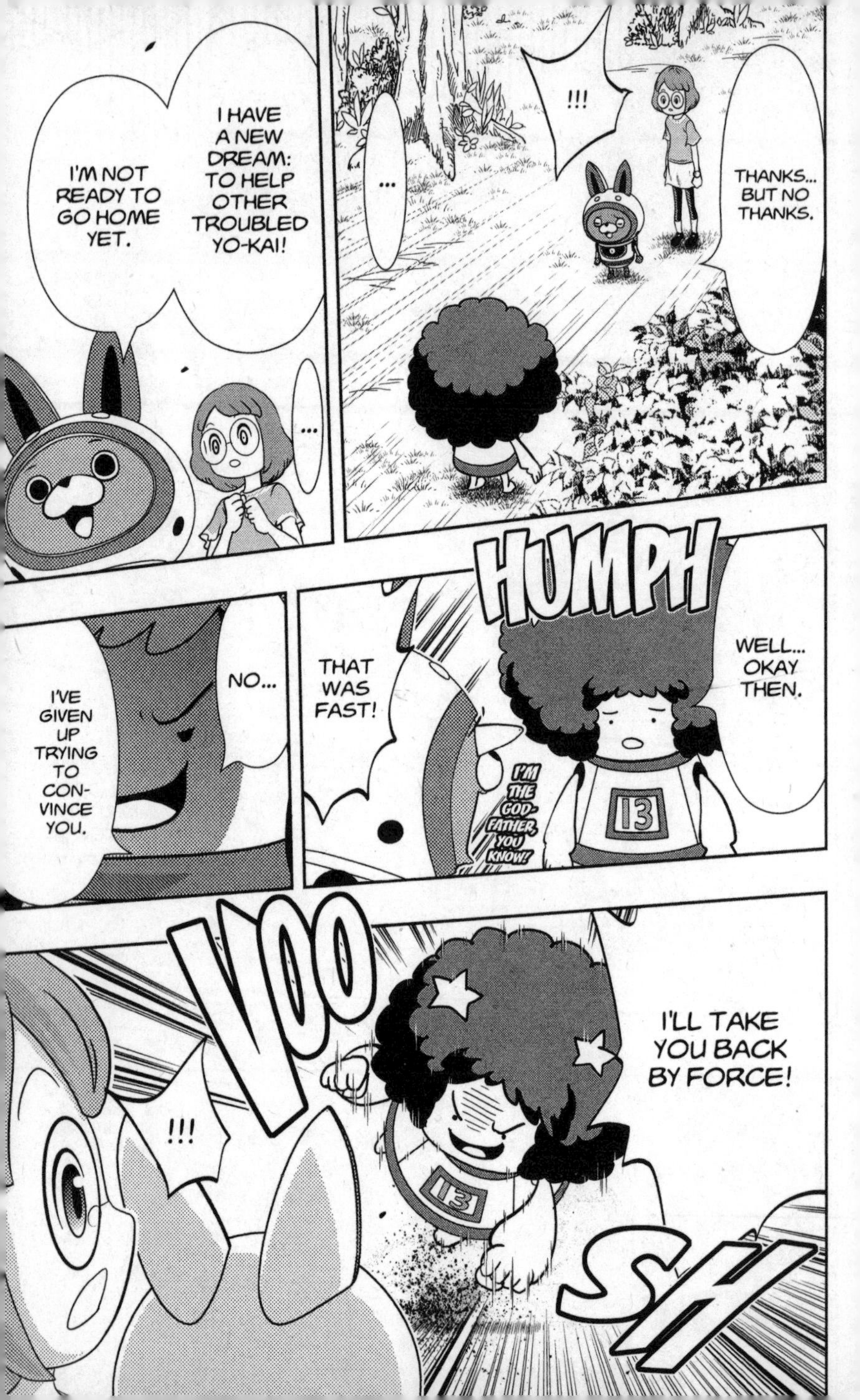
THANKS... BUT NO THANKS.
!!!
...
I HAVE A NEW DREAM: TO HELP OTHER TROUBLED YO-KAI!
I'M NOT READY TO GO HOME YET.
...
HUMPH
WELL... OKAY THEN.
THAT WAS FAST!
I'M THE GOD-FATHER, YOU KNOW!
NO...
I'VE GIVEN UP TRYING TO CON-VINCE YOU.
I'LL TAKE YOU BACK BY FORCE!
VOO
!!!
SH

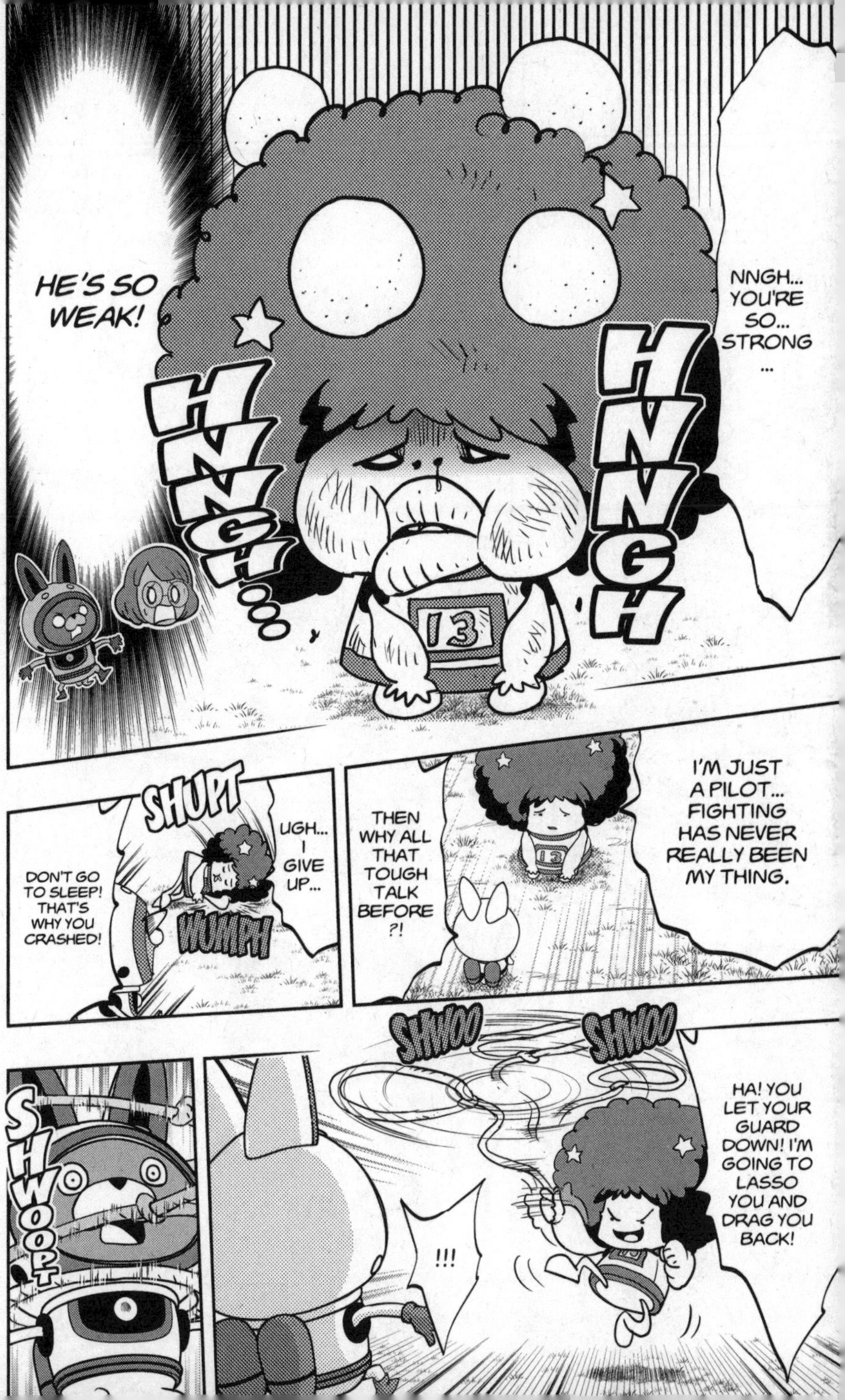
NNGH... YOU'RE SO... STRONG ...
HNNGH
HNNGHOOO
HE'S SO WEAK!
I'M JUST A PILOT... FIGHTING HAS NEVER REALLY BEEN MY THING.
THEN WHY ALL THAT TOUGH TALK BEFORE ?!
SHUPT
UGH... I GIVE UP...
WUMPH
DON'T GO TO SLEEP! THAT'S WHY YOU CRASHED!
SHWOO
SHWOO
HA! YOU LET YOUR GUARD DOWN! I'M GOING TO LASSO YOU AND DRAG YOU BACK!
!!!
SHWOOPT

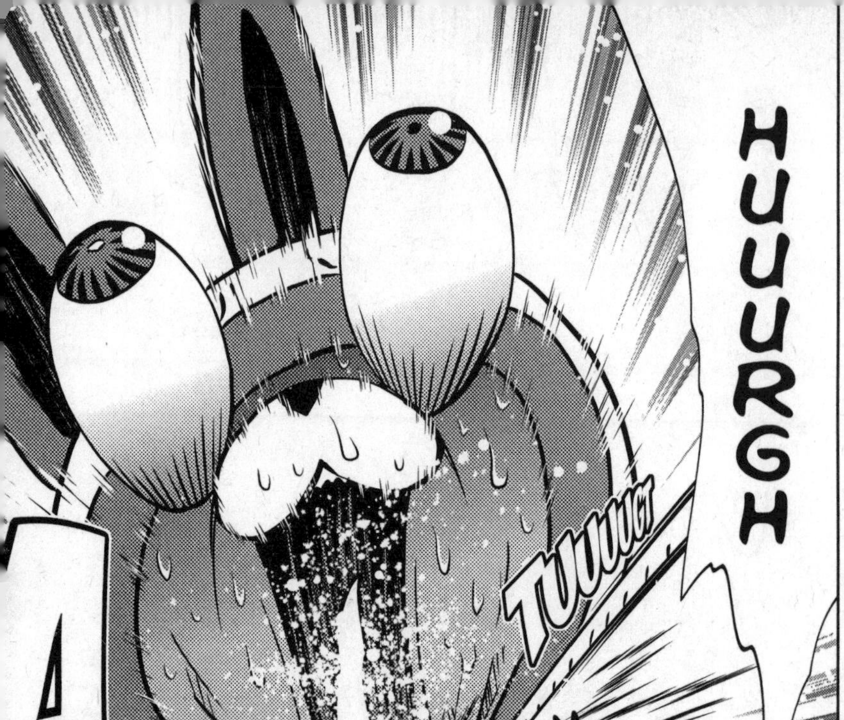
HUUURGH
TUUUUGT
AGGGHH

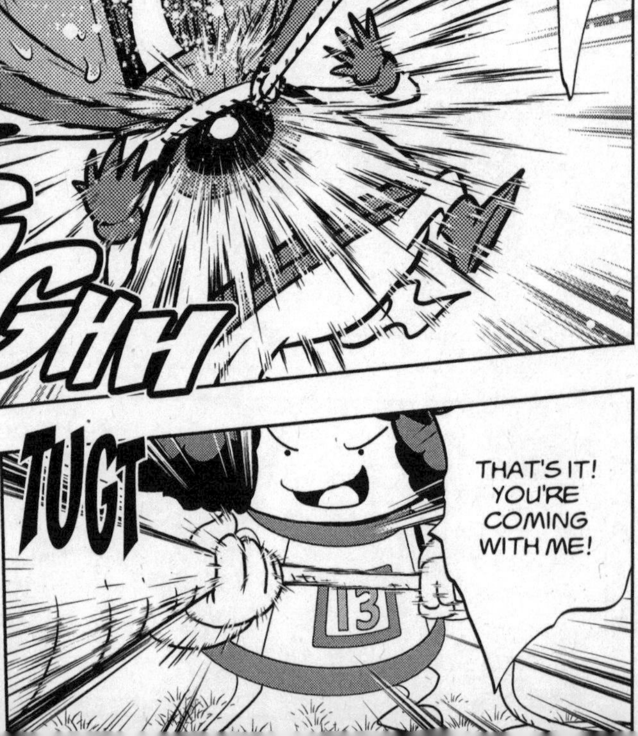
TUGT
THAT'S IT! YOU'RE COMING WITH ME!

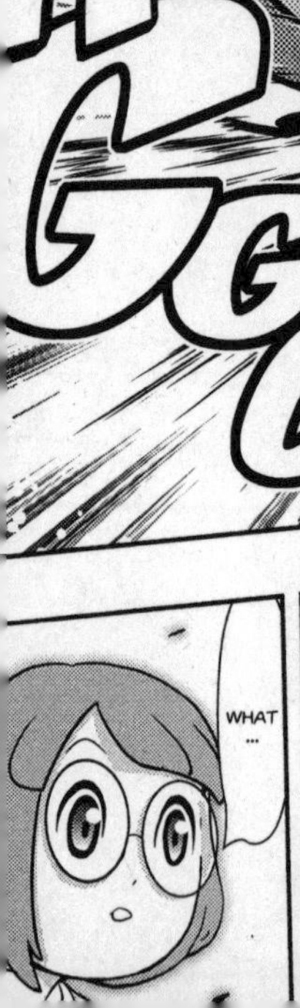
WHAT ...

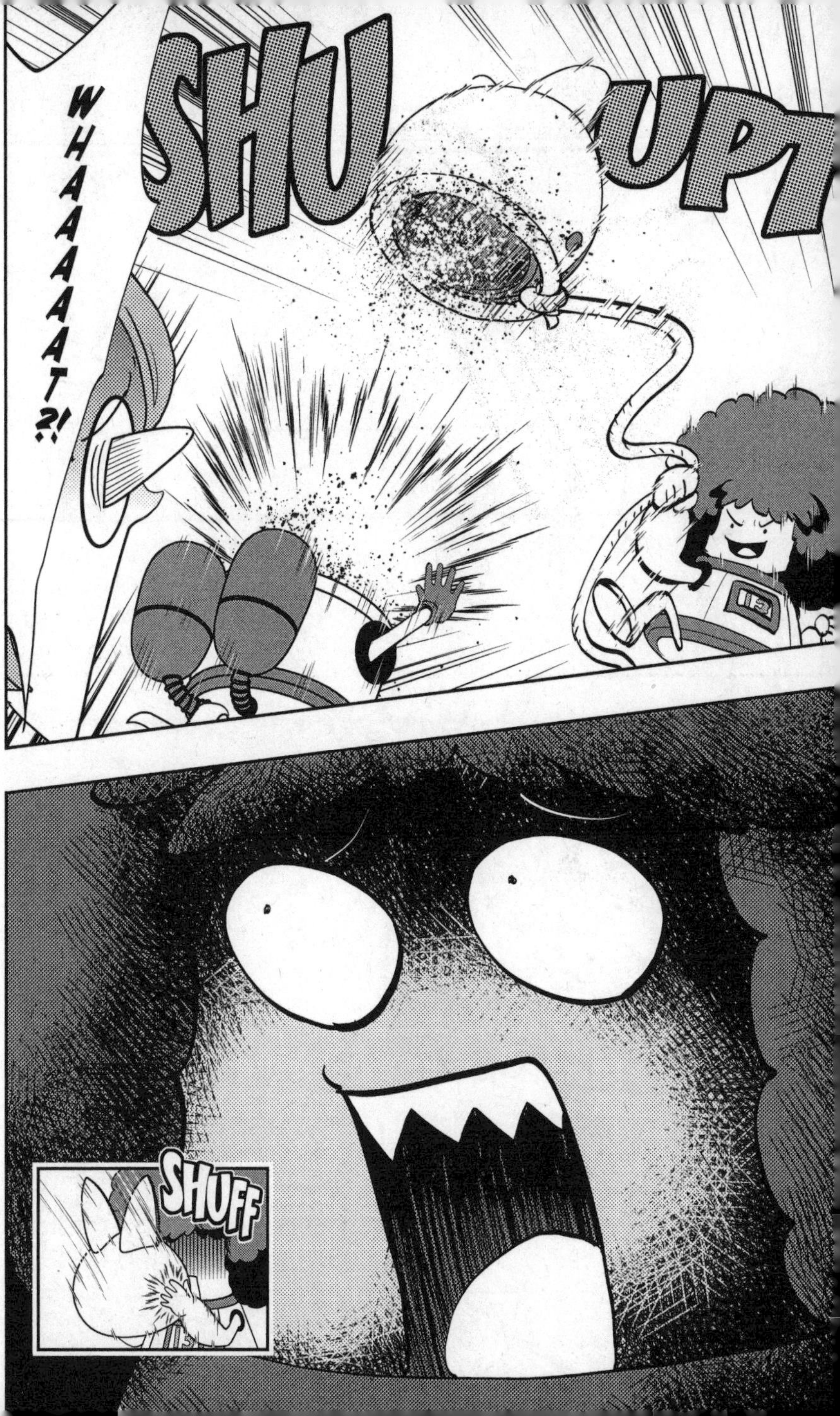
SHU UPT
WHAAAAAAAT?!
SHUFF

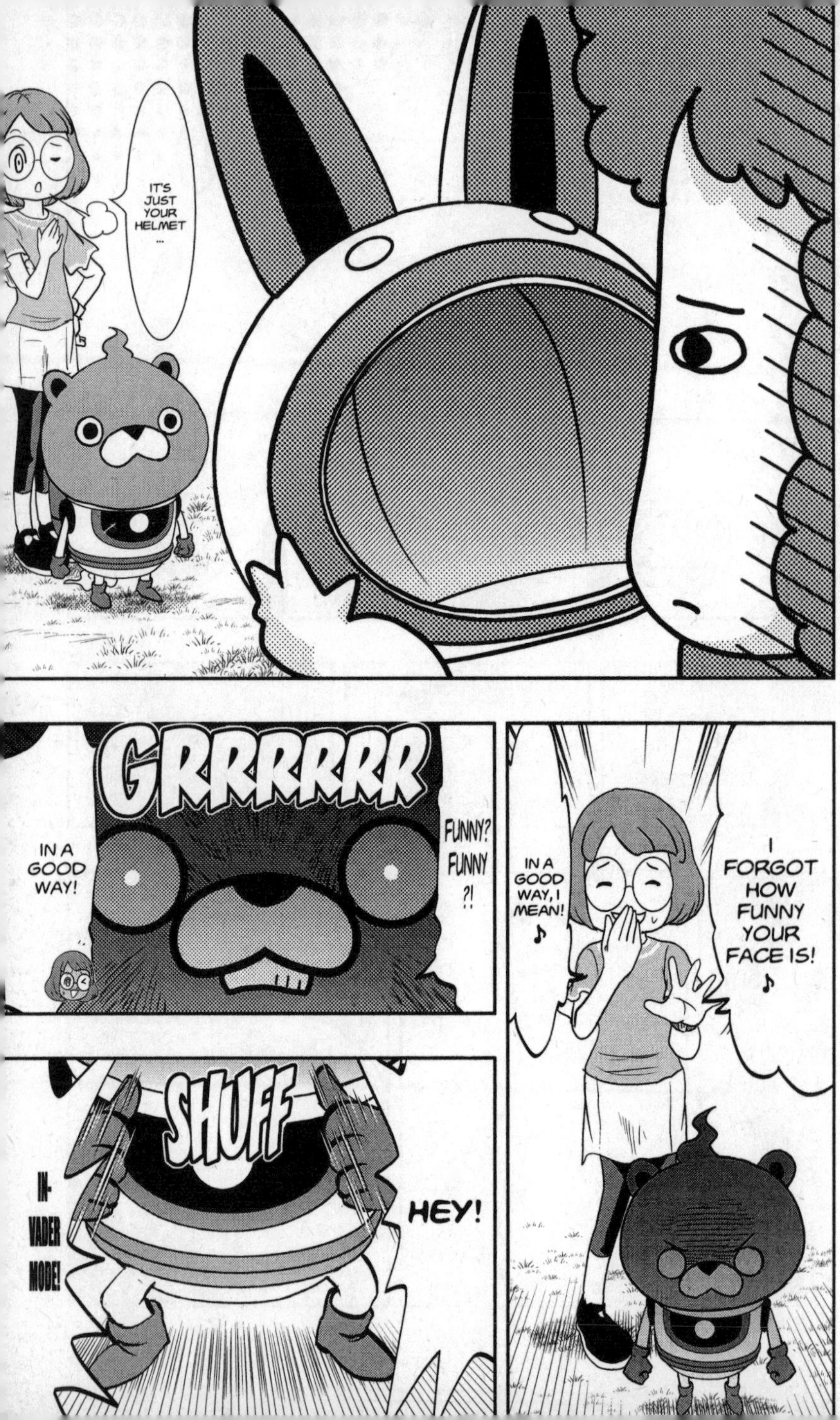
IT'S JUST YOUR HELMET ...
I FORGOT HOW FUNNY YOUR FACE IS! ♪
IN A GOOD WAY, I MEAN! ♪
GRRRRRRR
FUNNY? FUNNY ?!
IN A GOOD WAY!
SHUFF
HEY!
IN-VADER MODE!

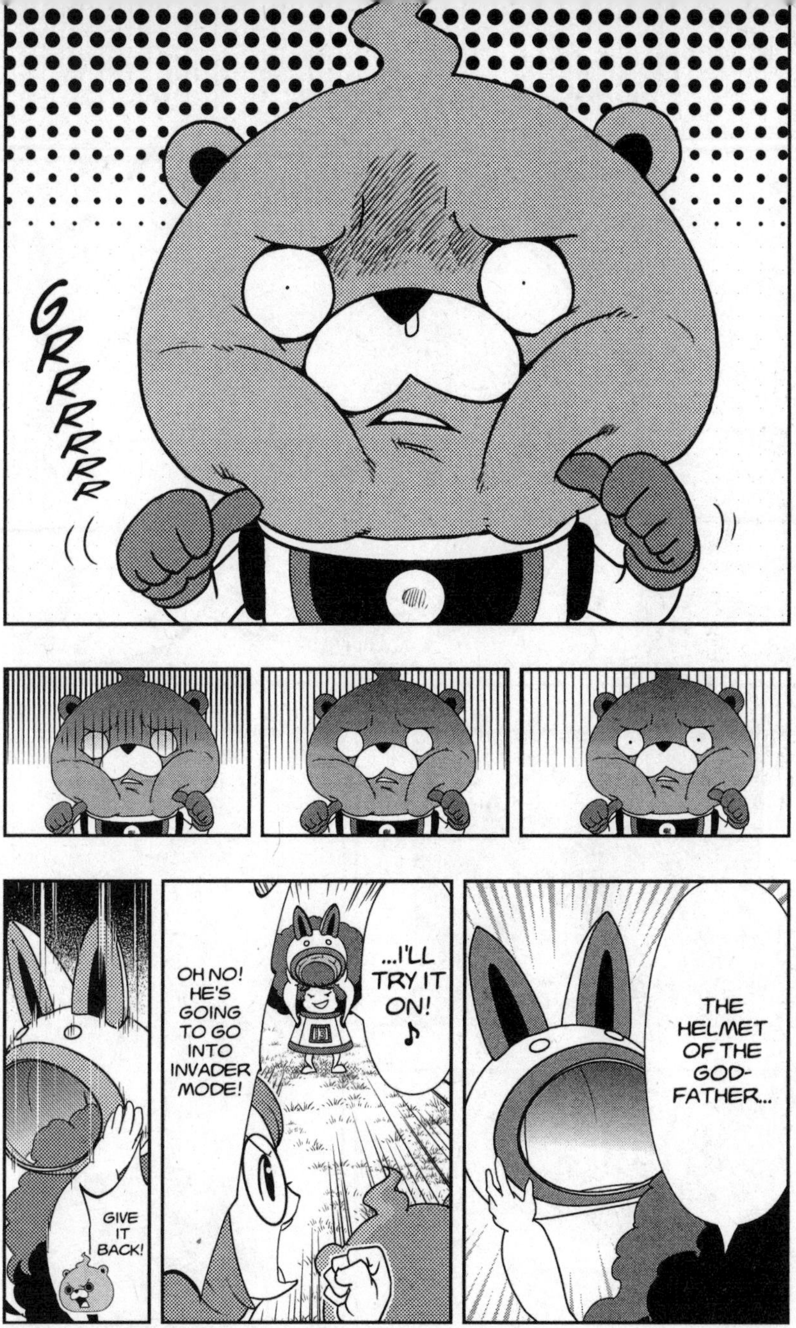
GRRRRRR
THE HELMET OF THE GOD-FATHER...
...I'LL TRY IT ON! ♪
OH NO! HE'S GOING TO GO INTO INVADER MODE!
GIVE IT BACK!

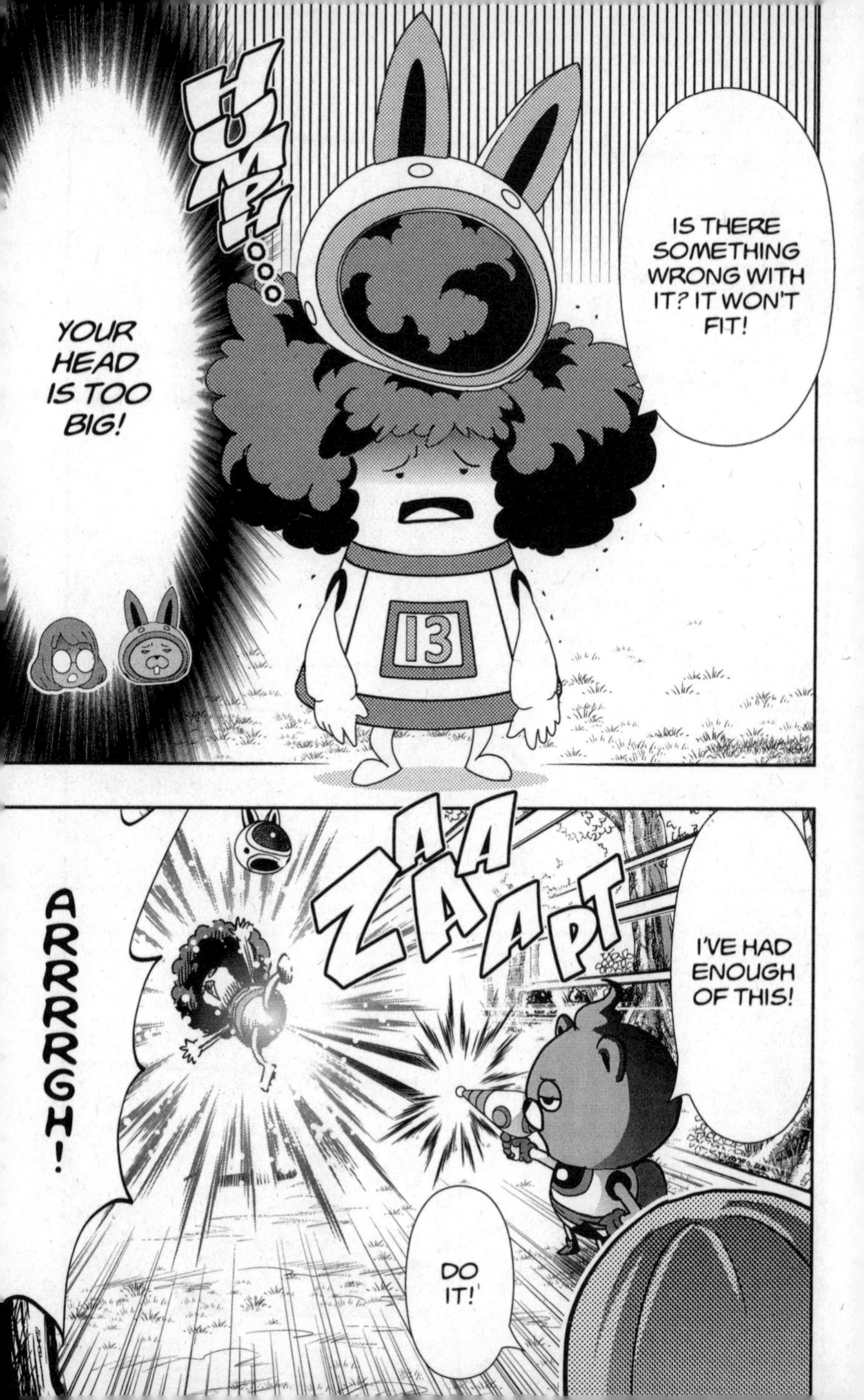
IS THERE SOMETHING WRONG WITH IT? IT WON'T FIT!
HUMPH...
YOUR HEAD IS TOO BIG!
I'VE HAD ENOUGH OF THIS!
DO IT!
ZAAAAPT
ARRRRRGH!

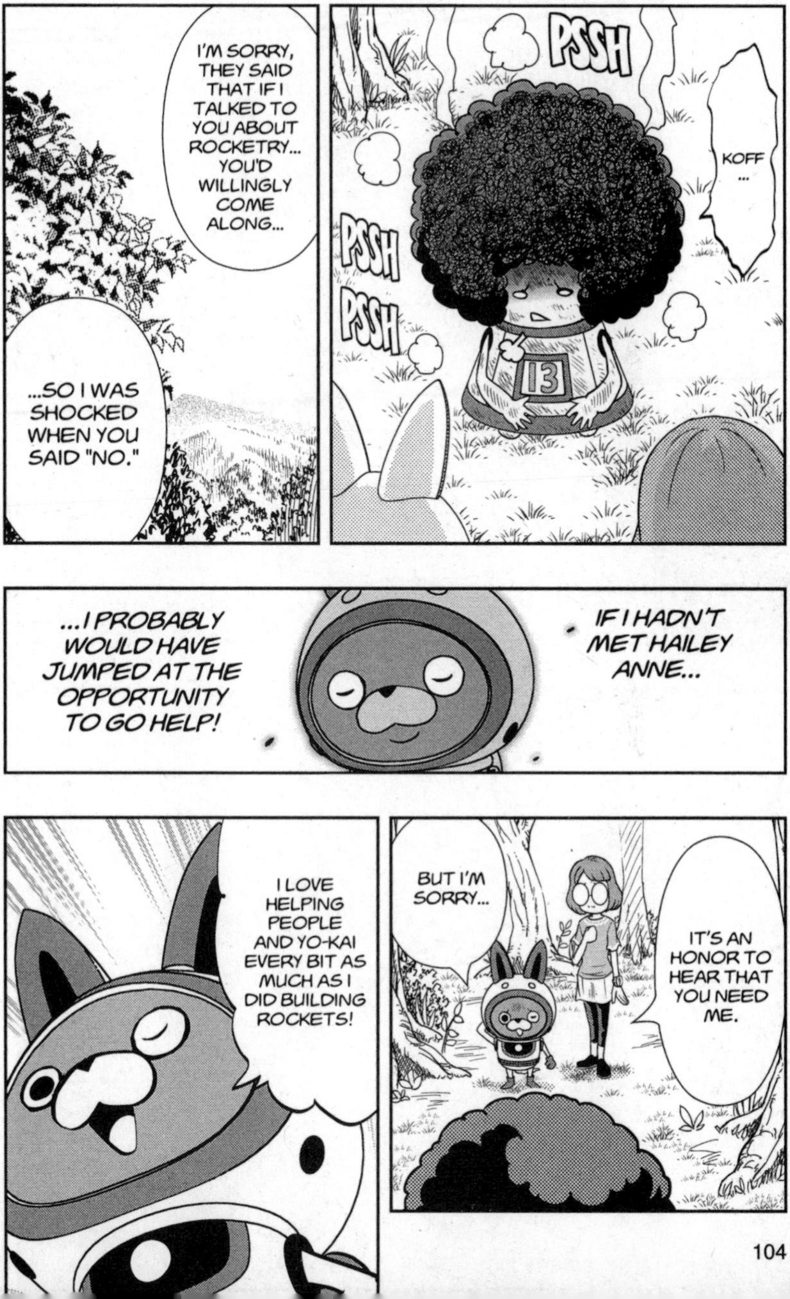
PSSH
KOFF ...
PSSH
PSSH
I'M SORRY, THEY SAID THAT IF I TALKED TO YOU ABOUT ROCKETRY... YOU'D WILLINGLY COME ALONG...
...SO I WAS SHOCKED WHEN YOU SAID "NO."
IF I HADN'T MET HAILEY ANNE...
...I PROBABLY WOULD HAVE JUMPED AT THE OPPORTUNITY TO GO HELP!
IT'S AN HONOR TO HEAR THAT YOU NEED ME.
BUT I'M SORRY...
I LOVE HELPING PEOPLE AND YO-KAI EVERY BIT AS MUCH AS I DID BUILDING ROCKETS!

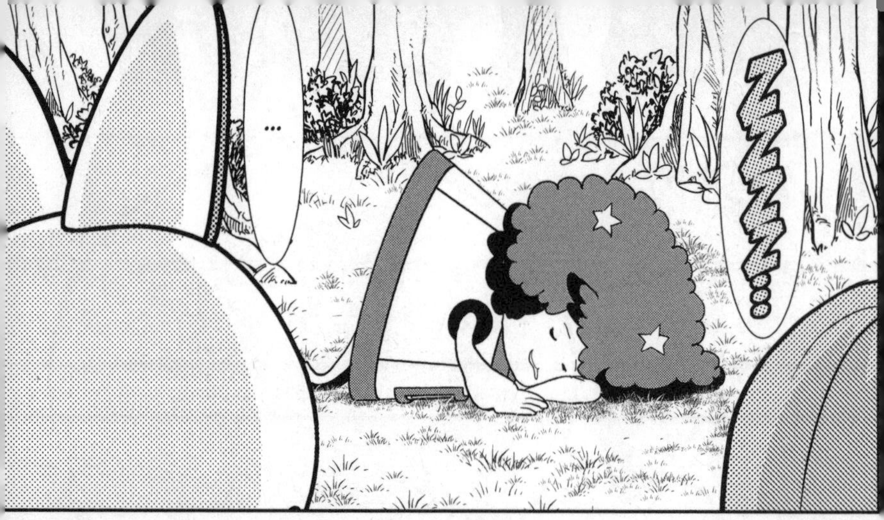
ZZZZZ...
...

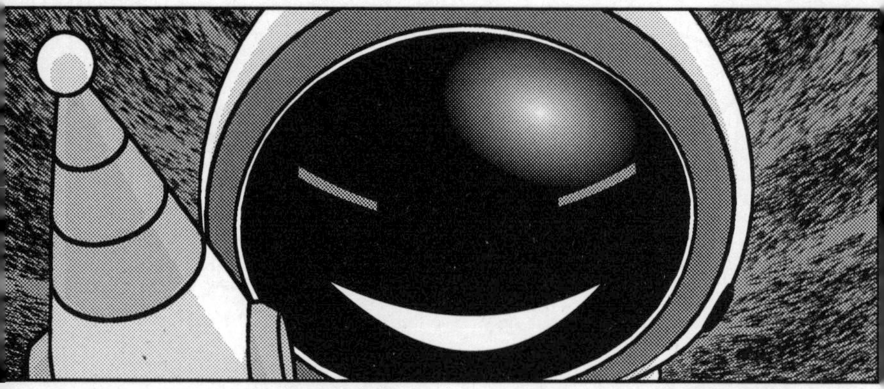

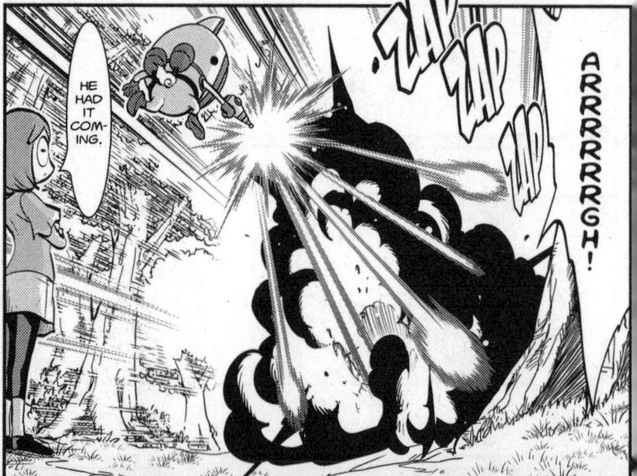
ARRRRRGH!
ZAP ZAP ZAP
HE HAD IT COMING.

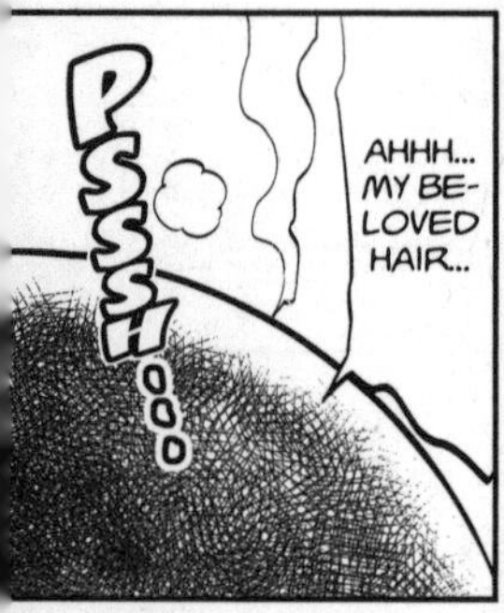
AHHH... MY BE-LOVED HAIR...
PSSSHOOO

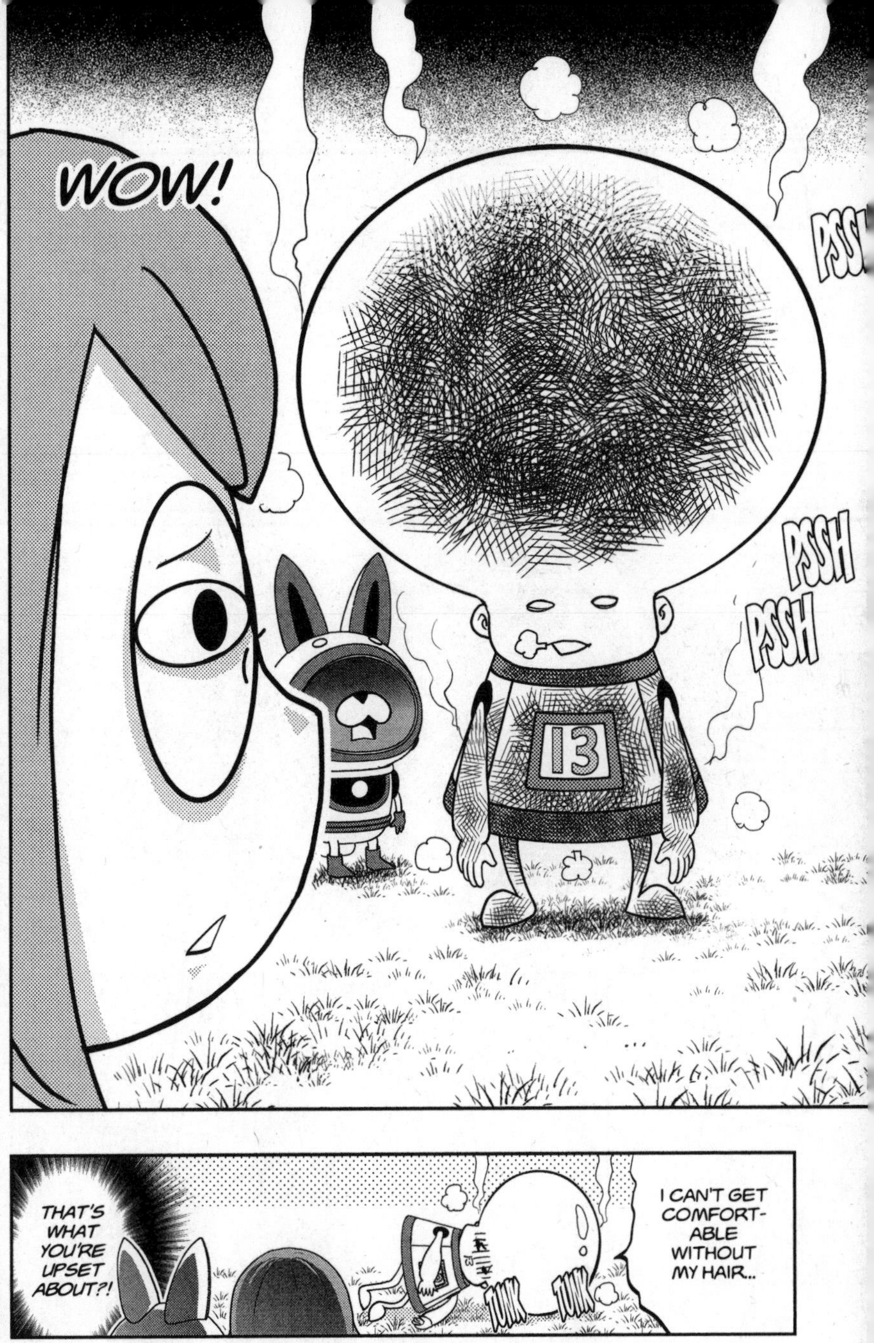
PSSH
PSSH
PSSH
WOW!
I CAN'T GET COMFORT-ABLE WITHOUT MY HAIR..
TUNK
TUNK
THAT'S WHAT YOU'RE UPSET ABOUT?!

CHAPTER 131:
SHOCK YO-KAI
HAIRUM SCARUM

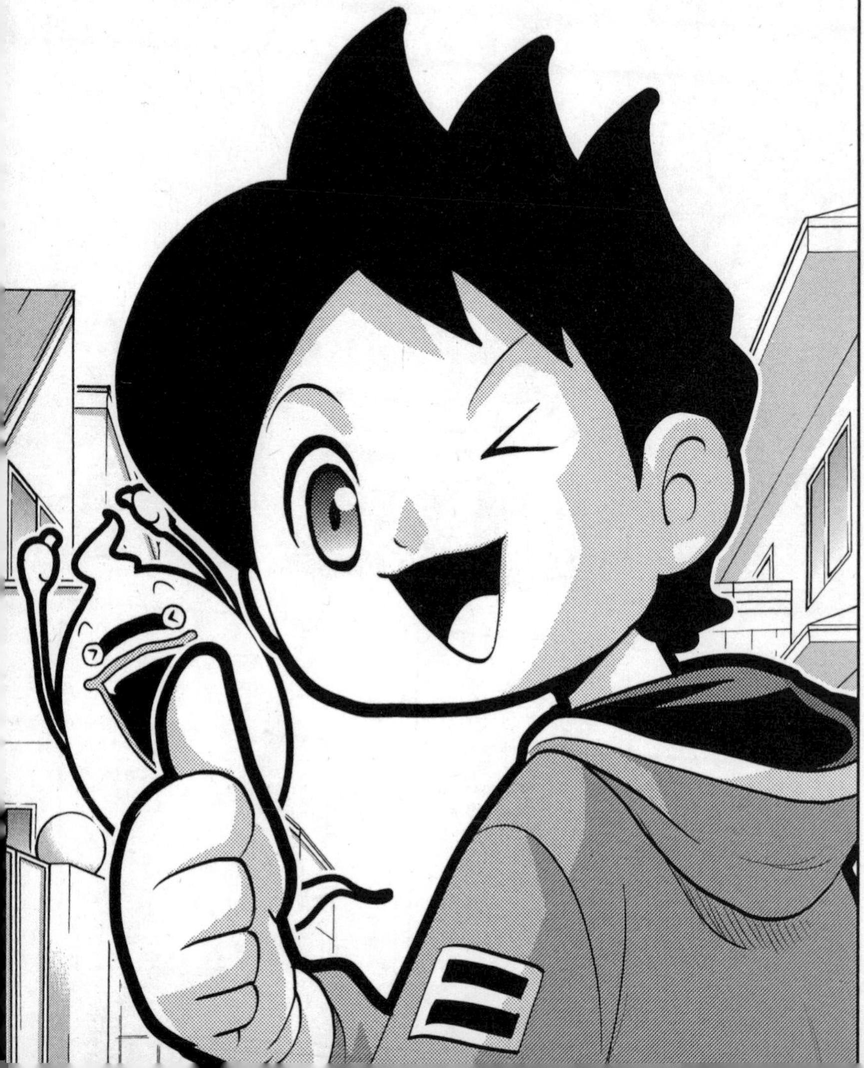

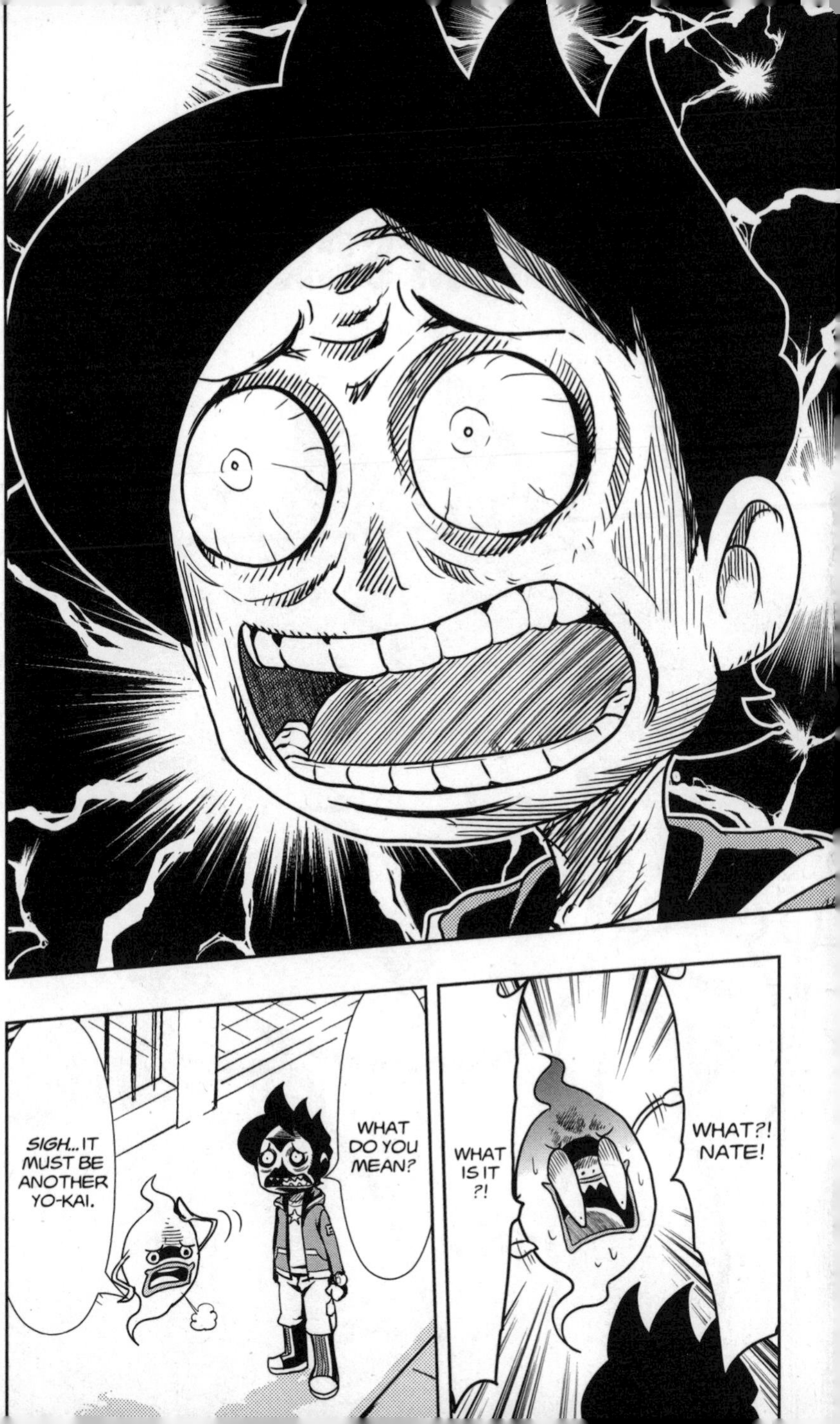
WHAT?! NATE!
WHAT IS IT ?!
WHAT DO YOU MEAN?
SIGH... IT MUST BE ANOTHER YO-KAI.

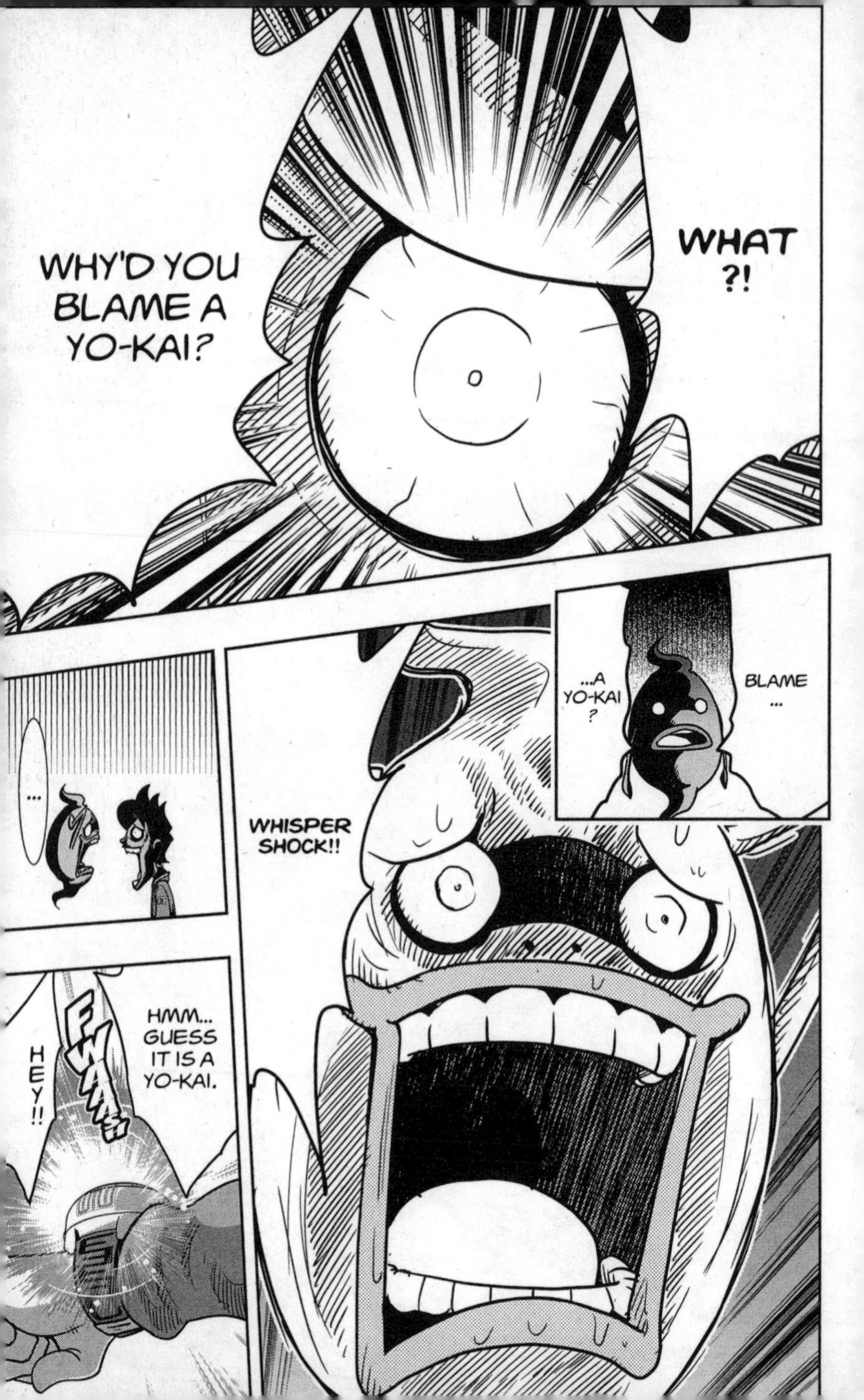
WHAT ?!
WHY'D YOU BLAME A YO-KAI?
BLAME ...
...A YO-KAI ?
WHISPER SHOCK!!
...
HMM... GUESS IT IS A YO-KAI.
FWAAS!
HEY!!

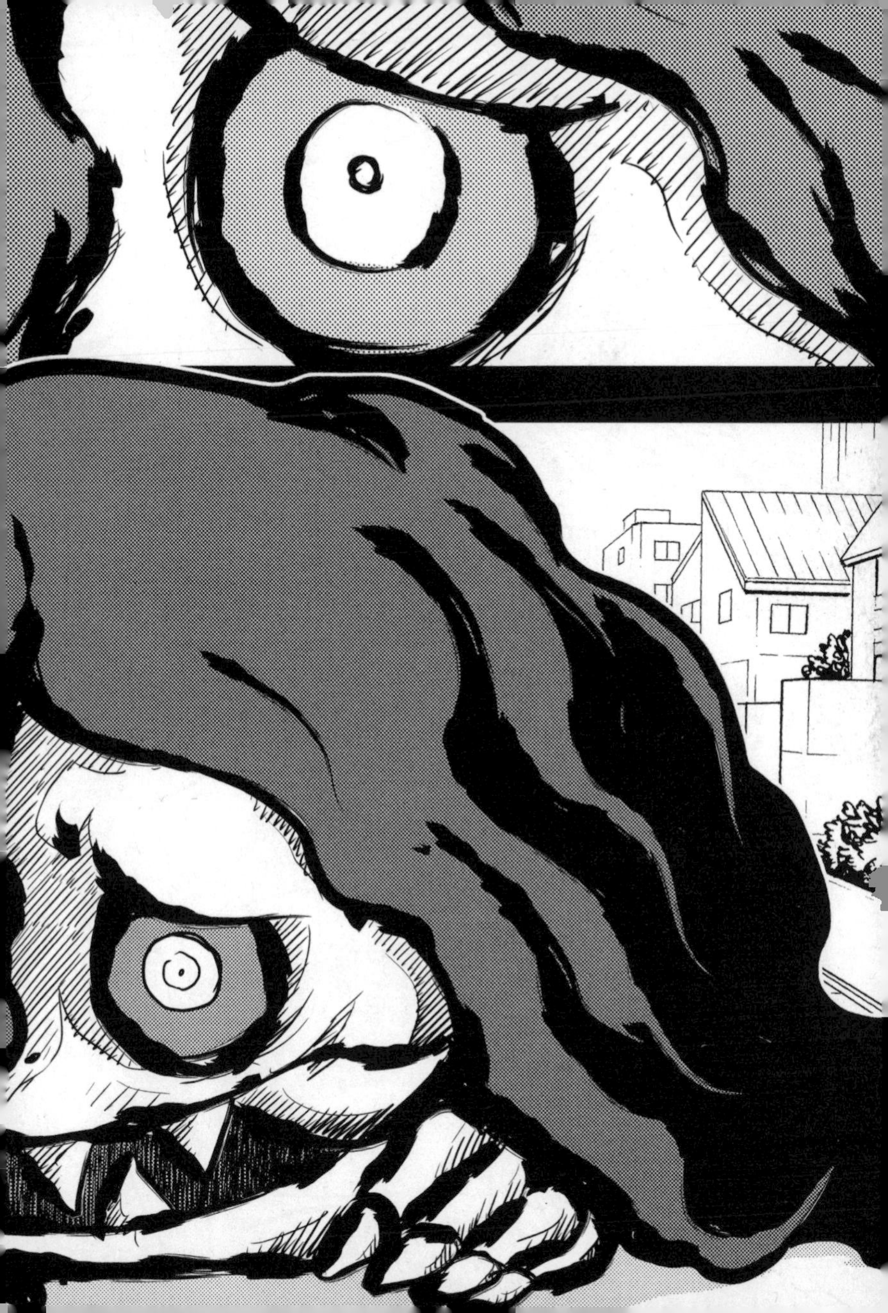

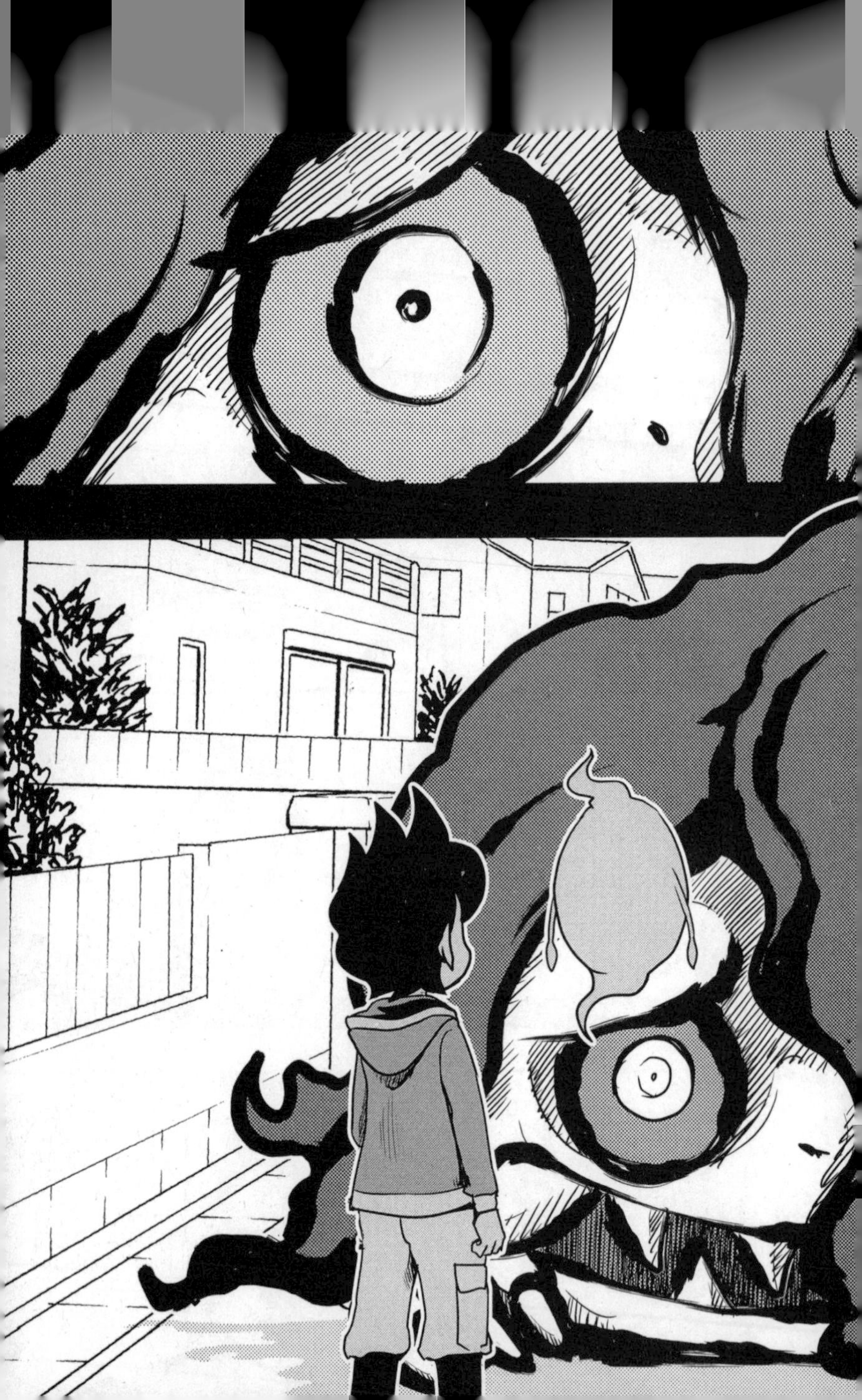

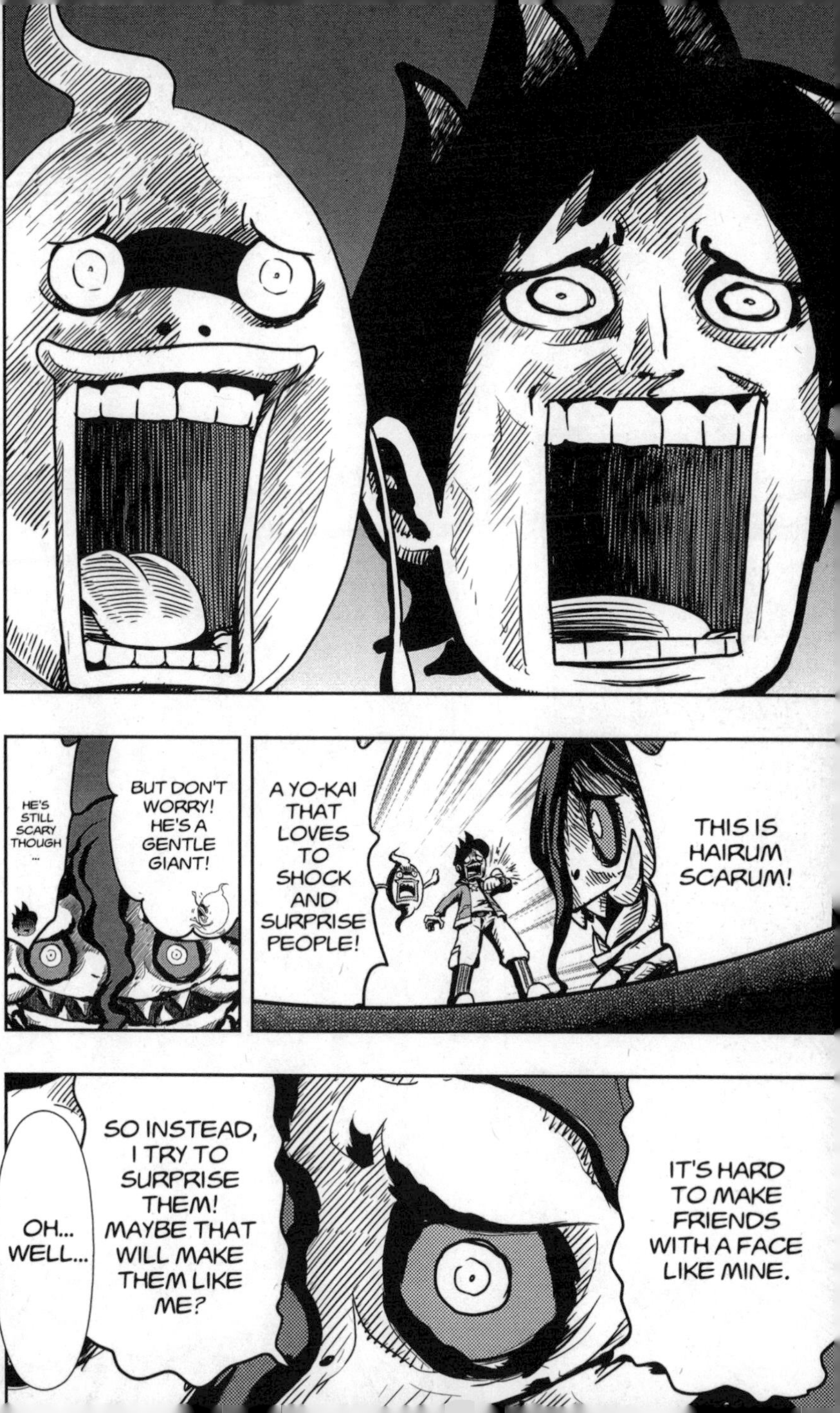
THIS IS HAIRUM SCARUM!
A YO-KAI THAT LOVES TO SHOCK AND SURPRISE PEOPLE!
BUT DON'T WORRY! HE'S A GENTLE GIANT!
HE'S STILL SCARY THOUGH ...
IT'S HARD TO MAKE FRIENDS WITH A FACE LIKE MINE.
SO INSTEAD, I TRY TO SURPRISE THEM! MAYBE THAT WILL MAKE THEM LIKE ME?
OH... WELL...

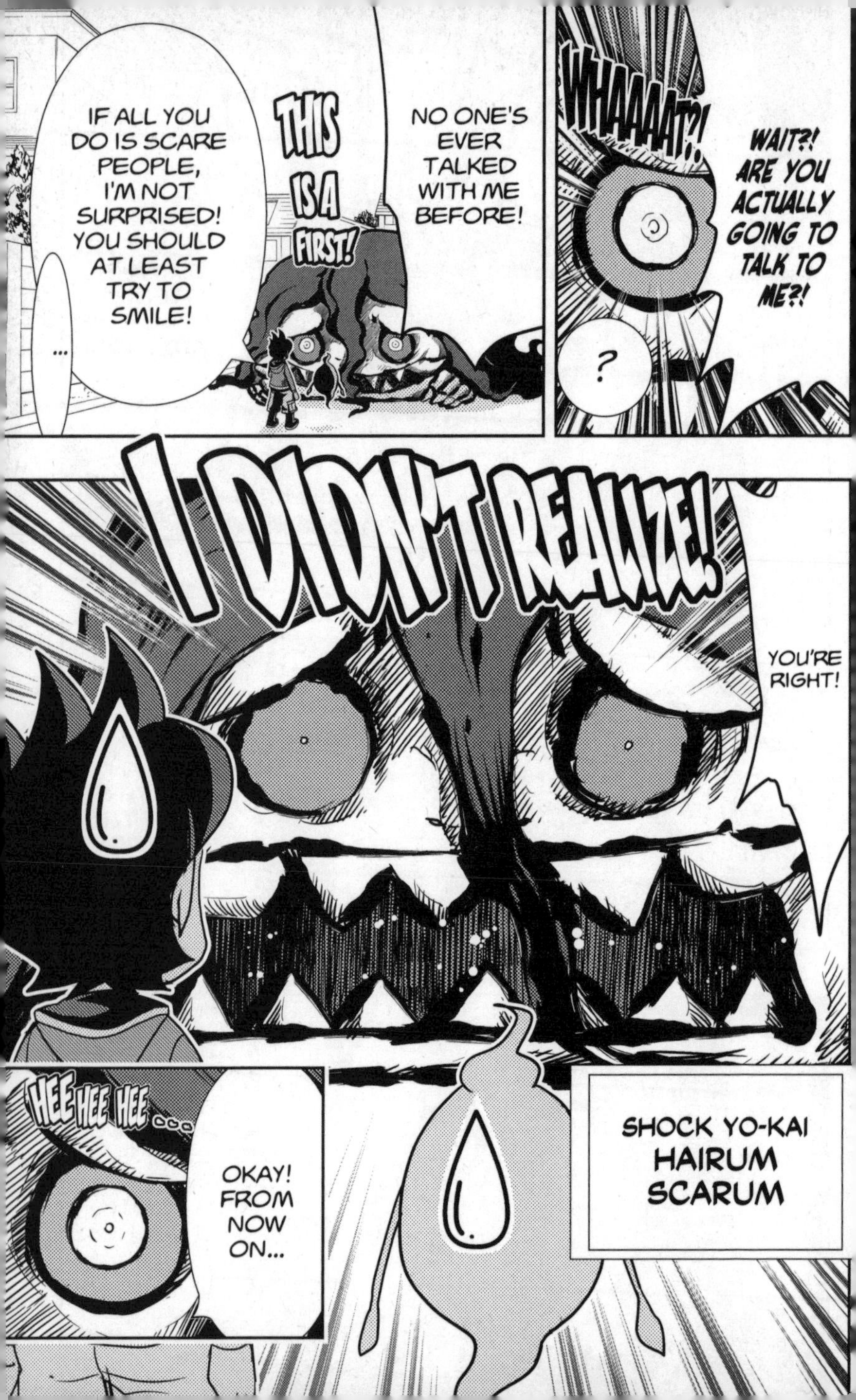
WHAAAAT?!
WAIT?! ARE YOU ACTUALLY GOING TO TALK TO ME?!
?
NO ONE'S EVER TALKED WITH ME BEFORE!
THIS IS A FIRST!
IF ALL YOU DO IS SCARE PEOPLE, I'M NOT SURPRISED! YOU SHOULD AT LEAST TRY TO SMILE!
...
YOU'RE RIGHT!
I DIDN'T REALIZE!
SHOCK YO-KAI HAIRUM SCARUM
OKAY! FROM NOW ON...
HEE HEE HEE...

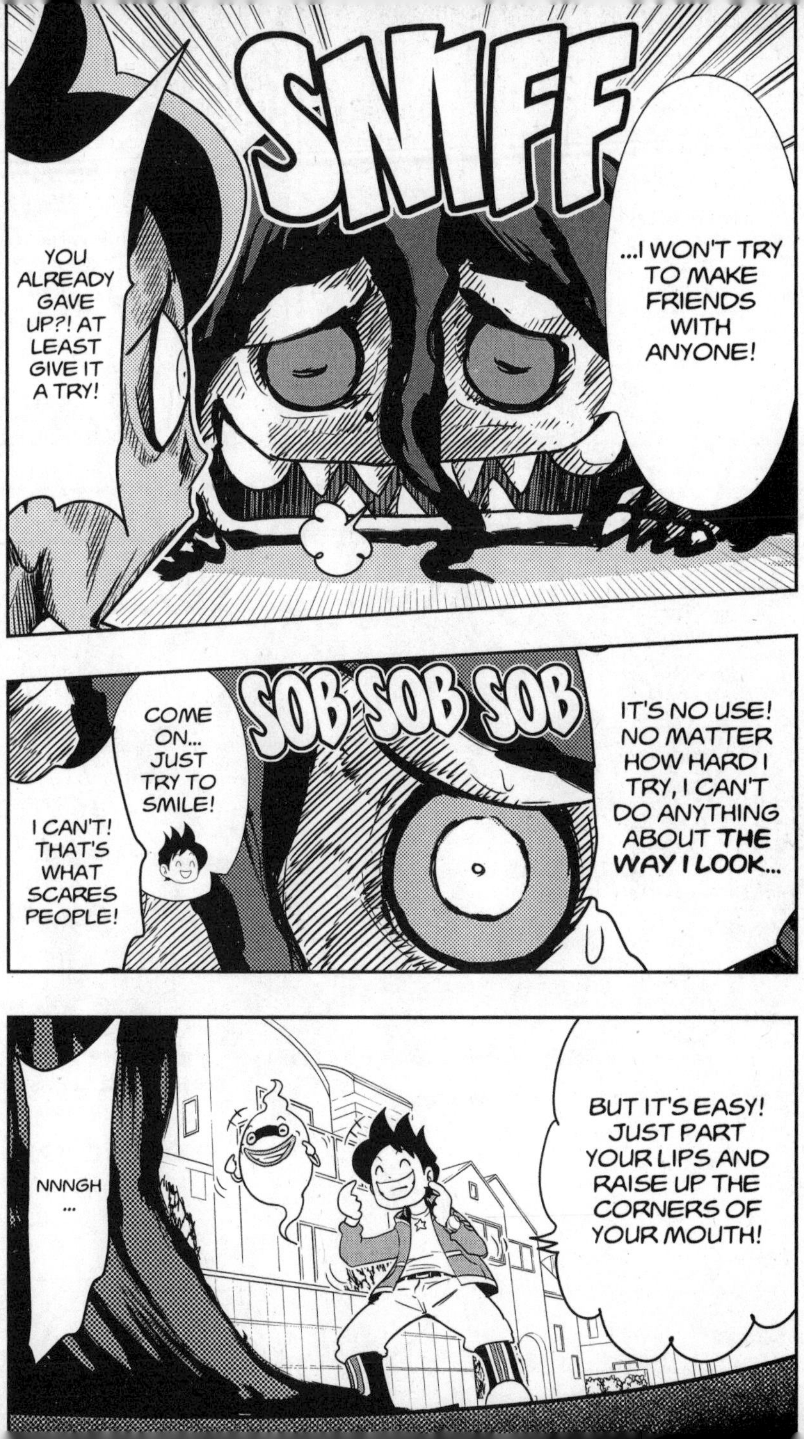
SNIFF
...I WON'T TRY TO MAKE FRIENDS WITH ANYONE!
YOU ALREADY GAVE UP?! AT LEAST GIVE IT A TRY!
IT'S NO USE! NO MATTER HOW HARD I TRY, I CAN'T DO ANYTHING ABOUT THE WAY I LOOK...
SOB SOB SOB
COME ON... JUST TRY TO SMILE!
I CAN'T! THAT'S WHAT SCARES PEOPLE!
BUT IT'S EASY! JUST PART YOUR LIPS AND RAISE UP THE CORNERS OF YOUR MOUTH!
NNNGH ...

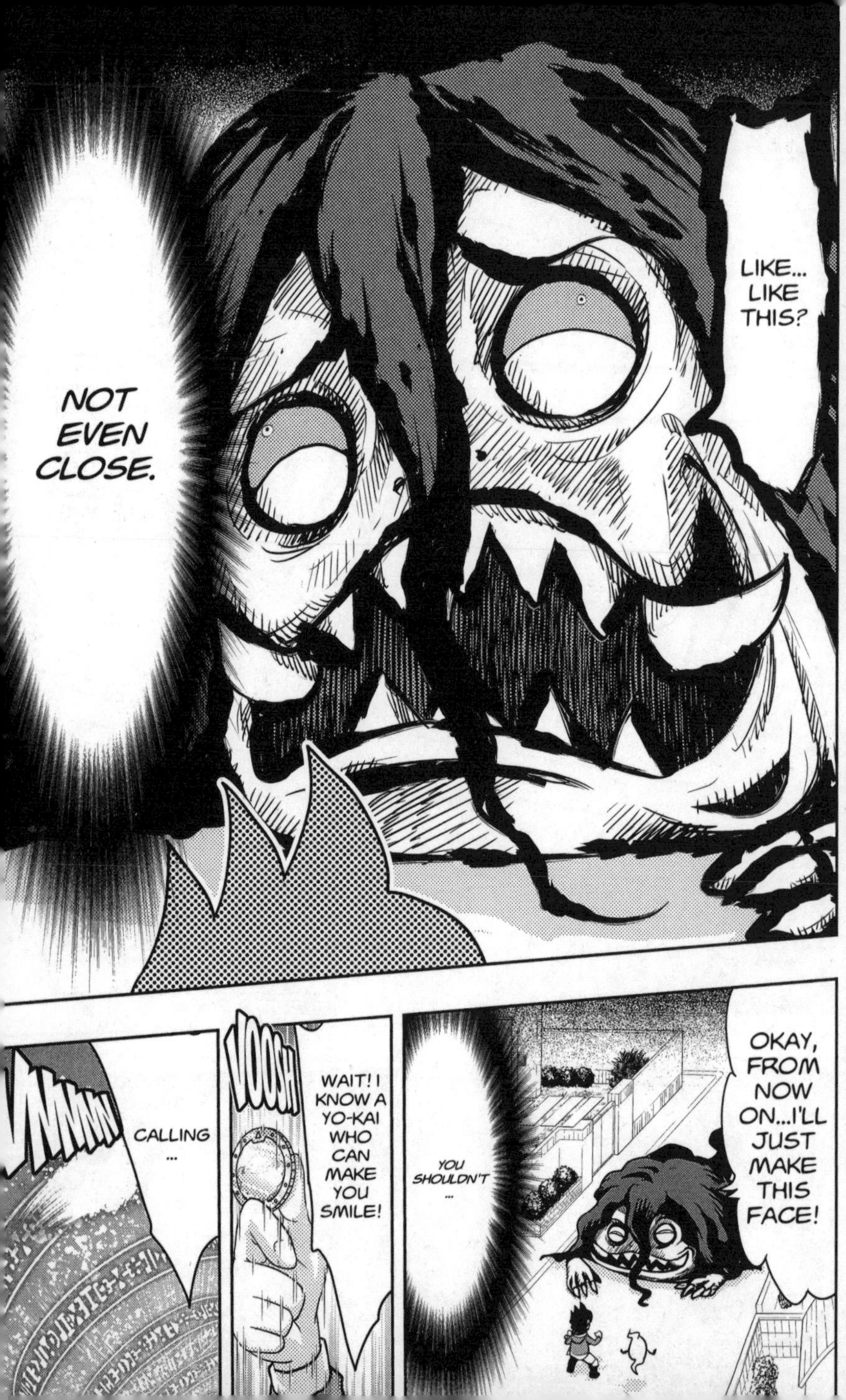
LIKE... LIKE THIS?
NOT EVEN CLOSE.
OKAY, FROM NOW ON...I'LL JUST MAKE THIS FACE!
YOU SHOULDN'T ...
VOOSH
WAIT! I KNOW A YO-KAI WHO CAN MAKE YOU SMILE!
CALLING ...

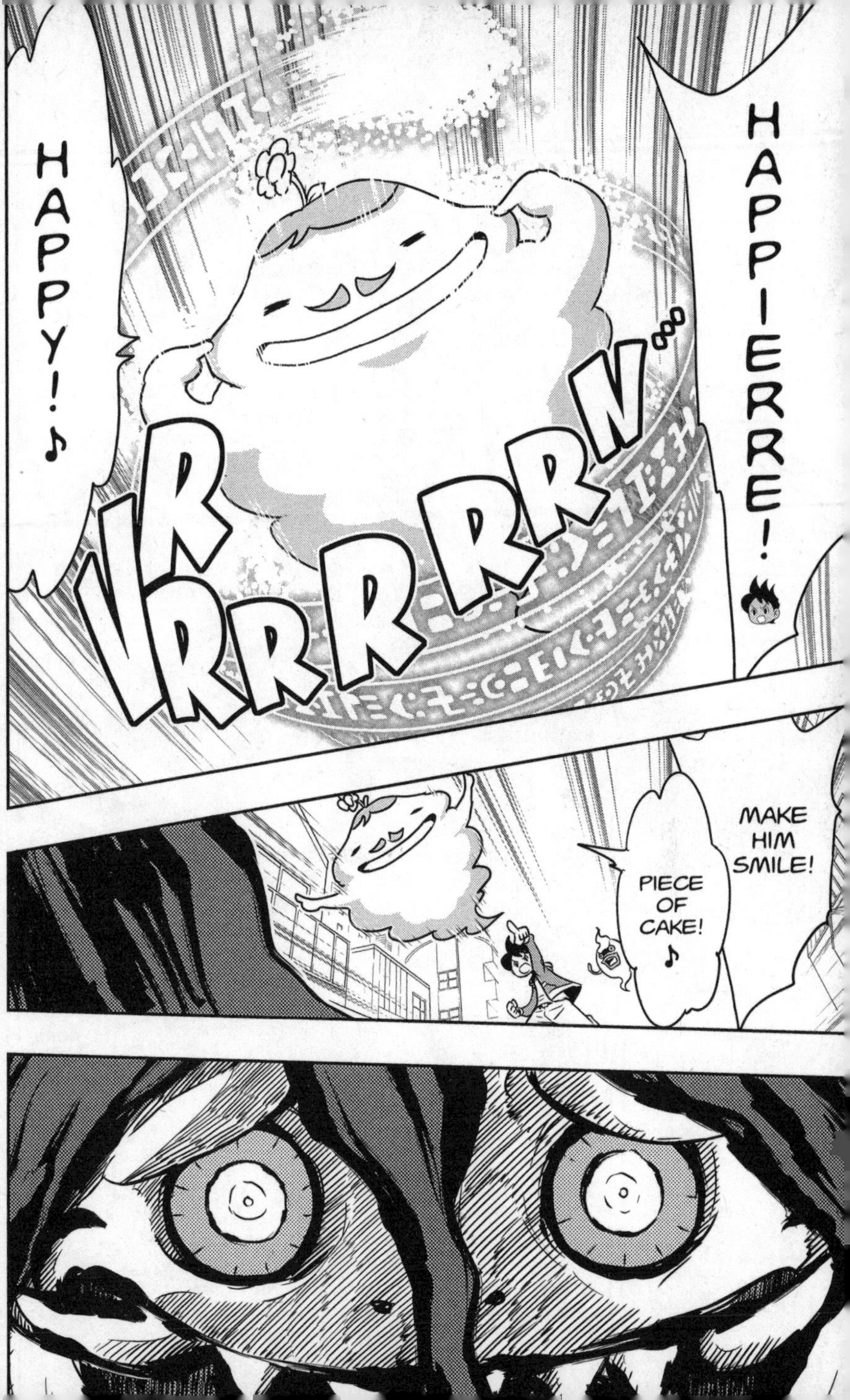
HAPPIERRE!
HAPPY! ♪
VRRRRRN...
MAKE HIM SMILE!
PIECE OF CAKE! ♪

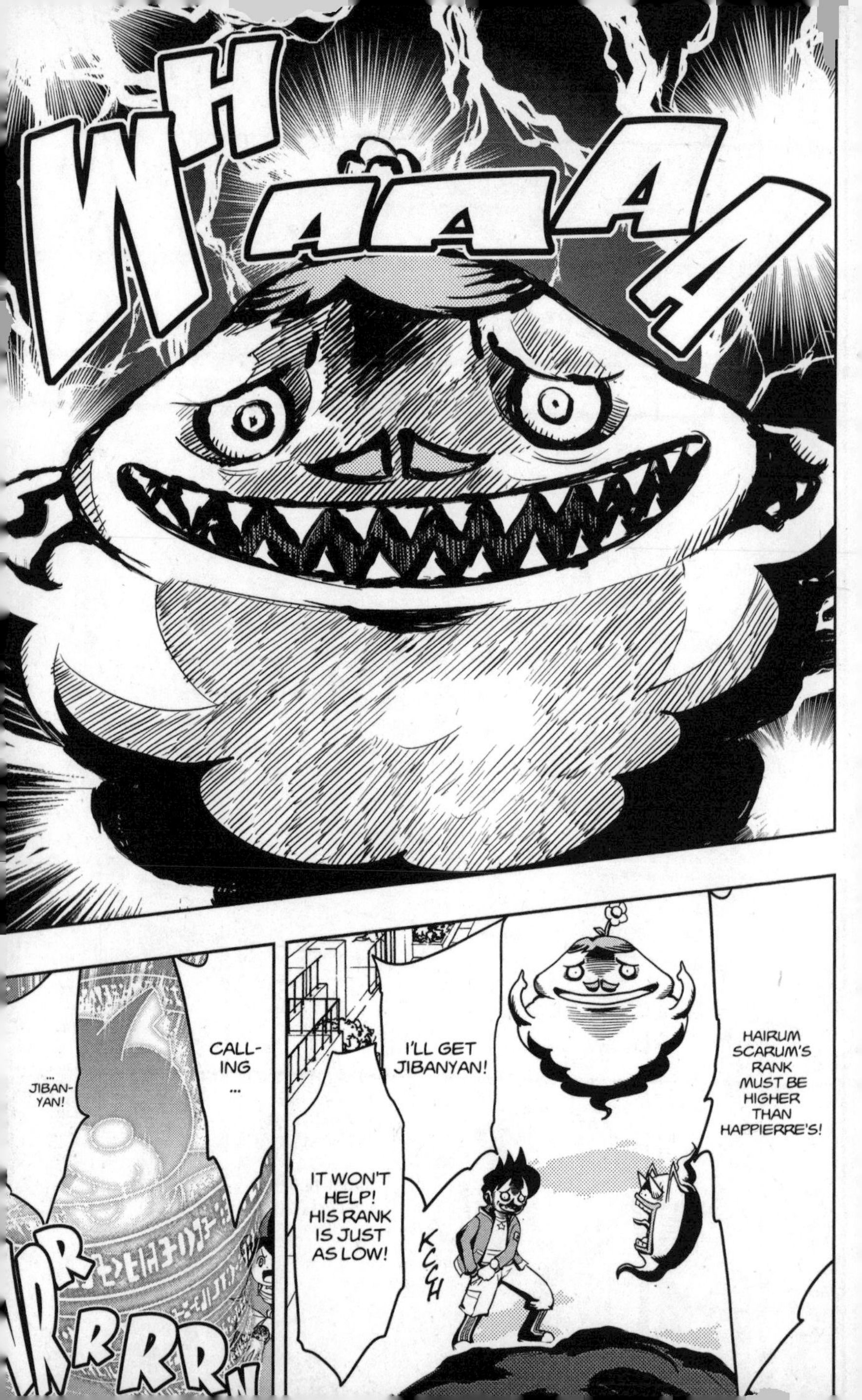
WHAAAA
HAIRUM SCARUM'S RANK MUST BE HIGHER THAN HAPPIERRE'S!
I'LL GET JIBANYAN!
IT WON'T HELP! HIS RANK IS JUST AS LOW!
KCCH
CALLING...
...JIBANYAN!
RRRRRN

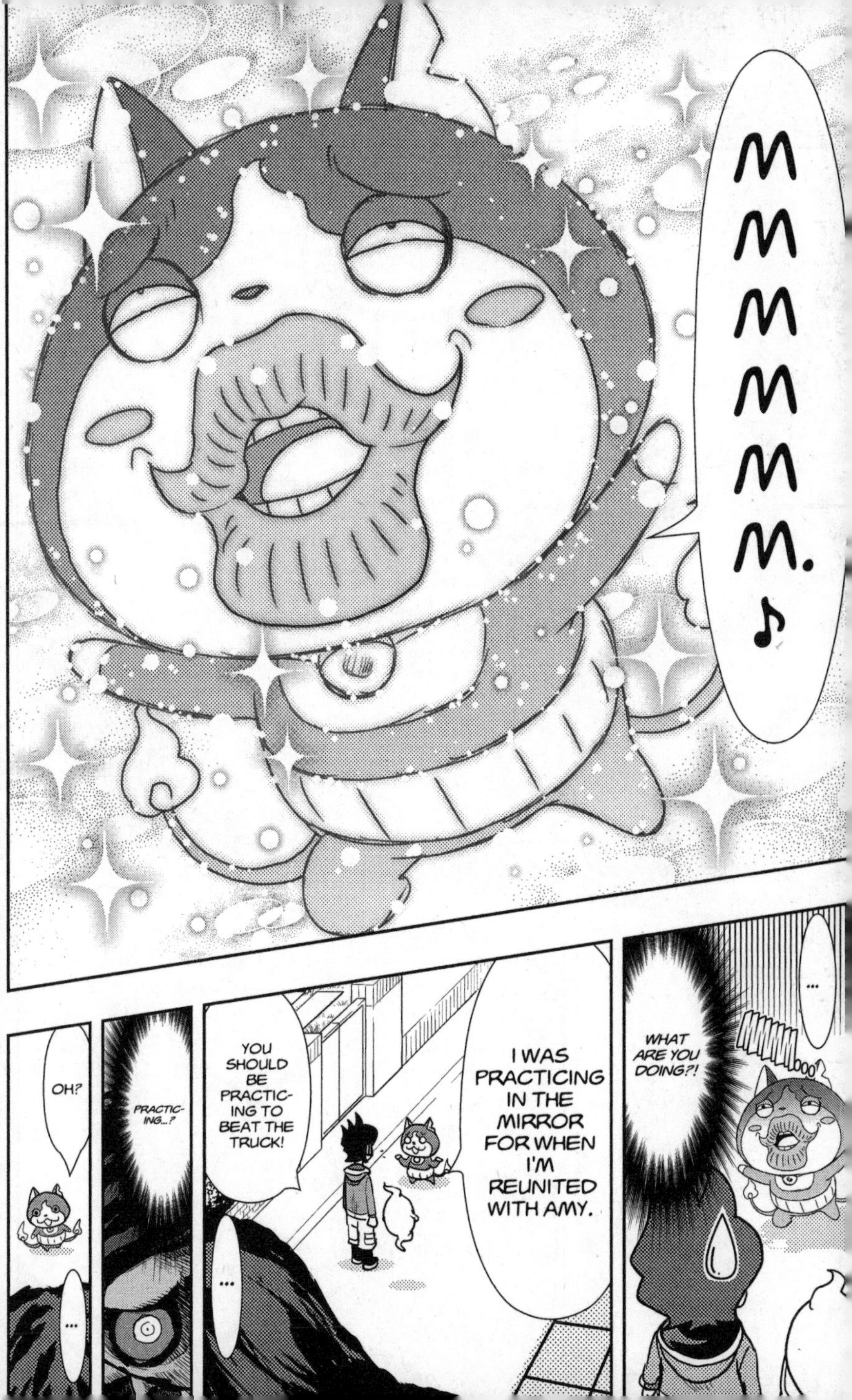
MMMMMM.♪
...
WHAT ARE YOU DOING?!
I WAS PRACTICING IN THE MIRROR FOR WHEN I'M REUNITED WITH AMY.
YOU SHOULD BE PRACTIC-ING TO BEAT THE TRUCK!
...
PRACTIC-ING...?
OH?
...

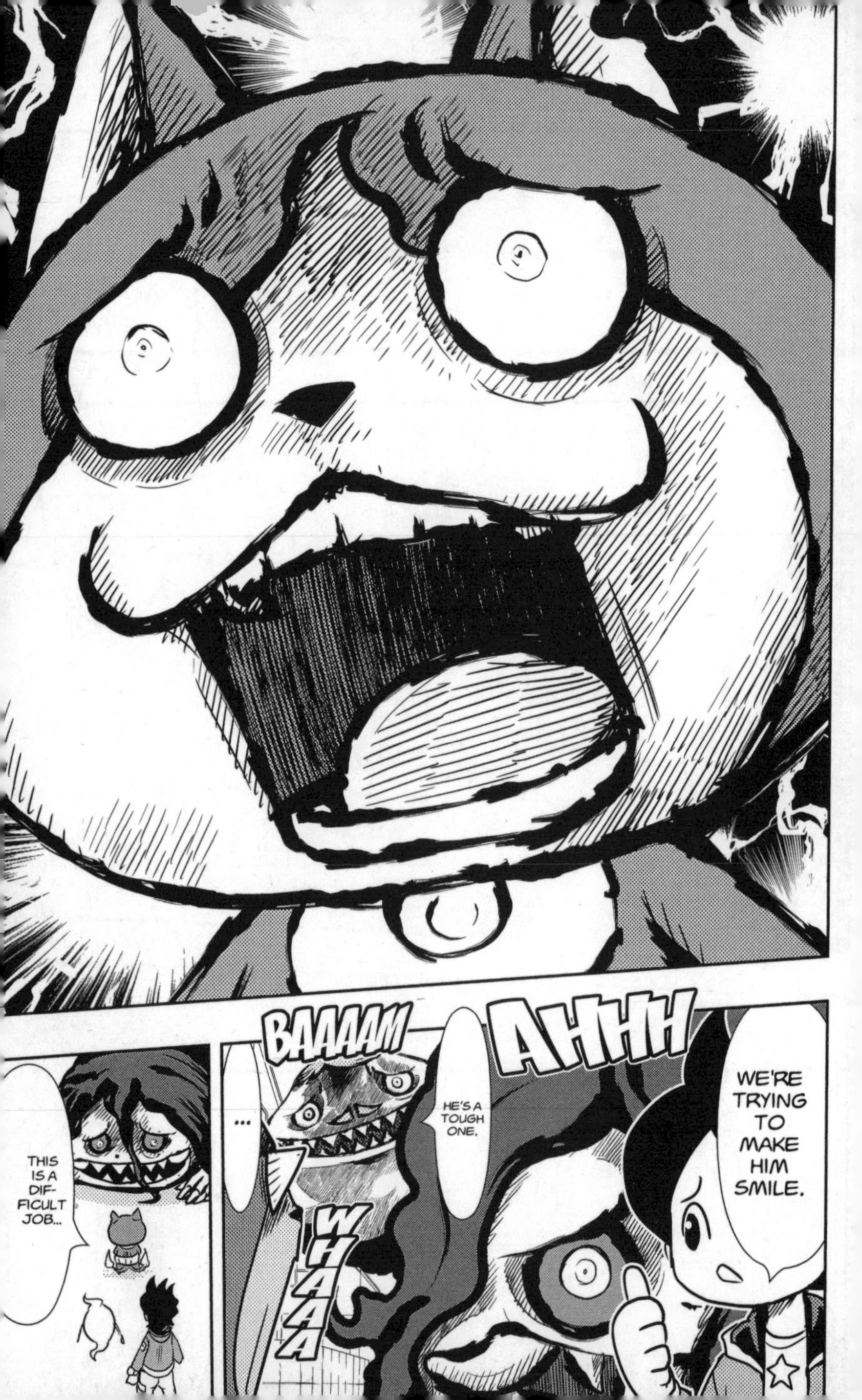
AHHH
WE'RE TRYING TO MAKE HIM SMILE.
HE'S A TOUGH ONE.
WHAAAA
BAAAAM
...
THIS IS A DIF-FICULT JOB...

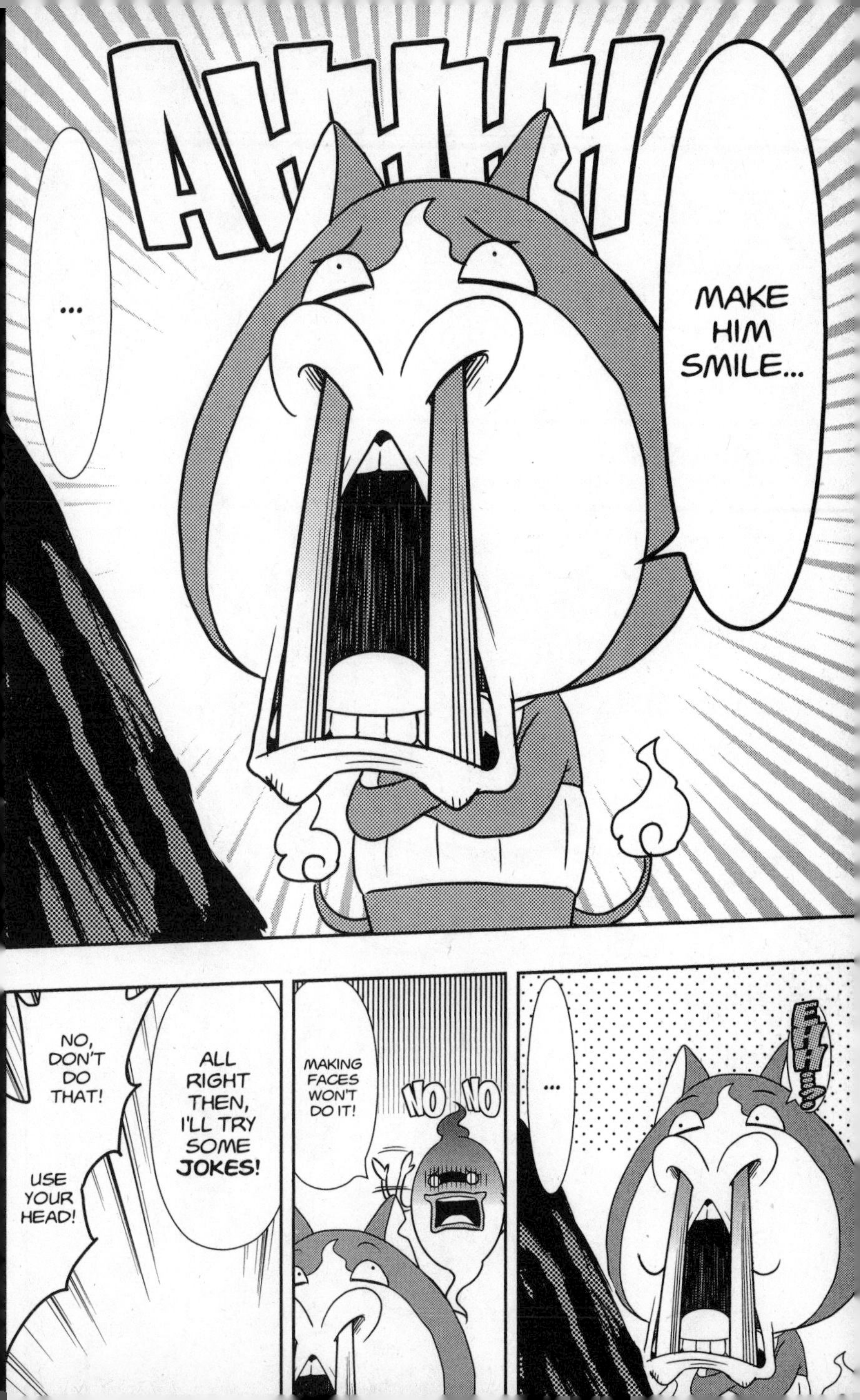
MAKE HIM SMILE...
AHHHH
...
...
MAKING FACES WON'T DO IT!
NO NO
ALL RIGHT THEN, I'LL TRY SOME JOKES!
NO, DON'T DO THAT!
USE YOUR HEAD!

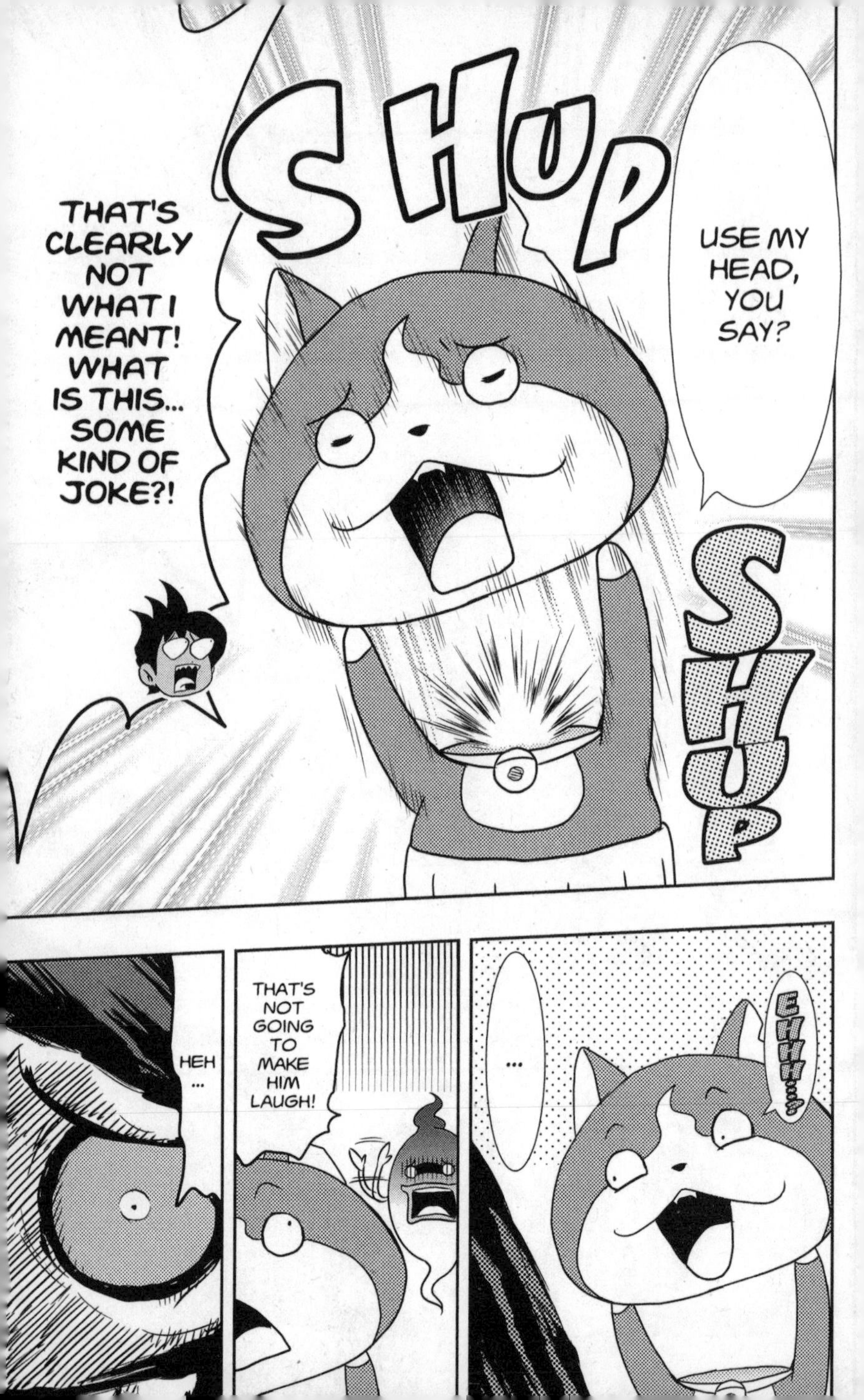
USE MY HEAD, YOU SAY?
SHUP
THAT'S CLEARLY NOT WHAT I MEANT! WHAT IS THIS... SOME KIND OF JOKE?!
SHUP
EHHH
...
THAT'S NOT GOING TO MAKE HIM LAUGH!
HEH...

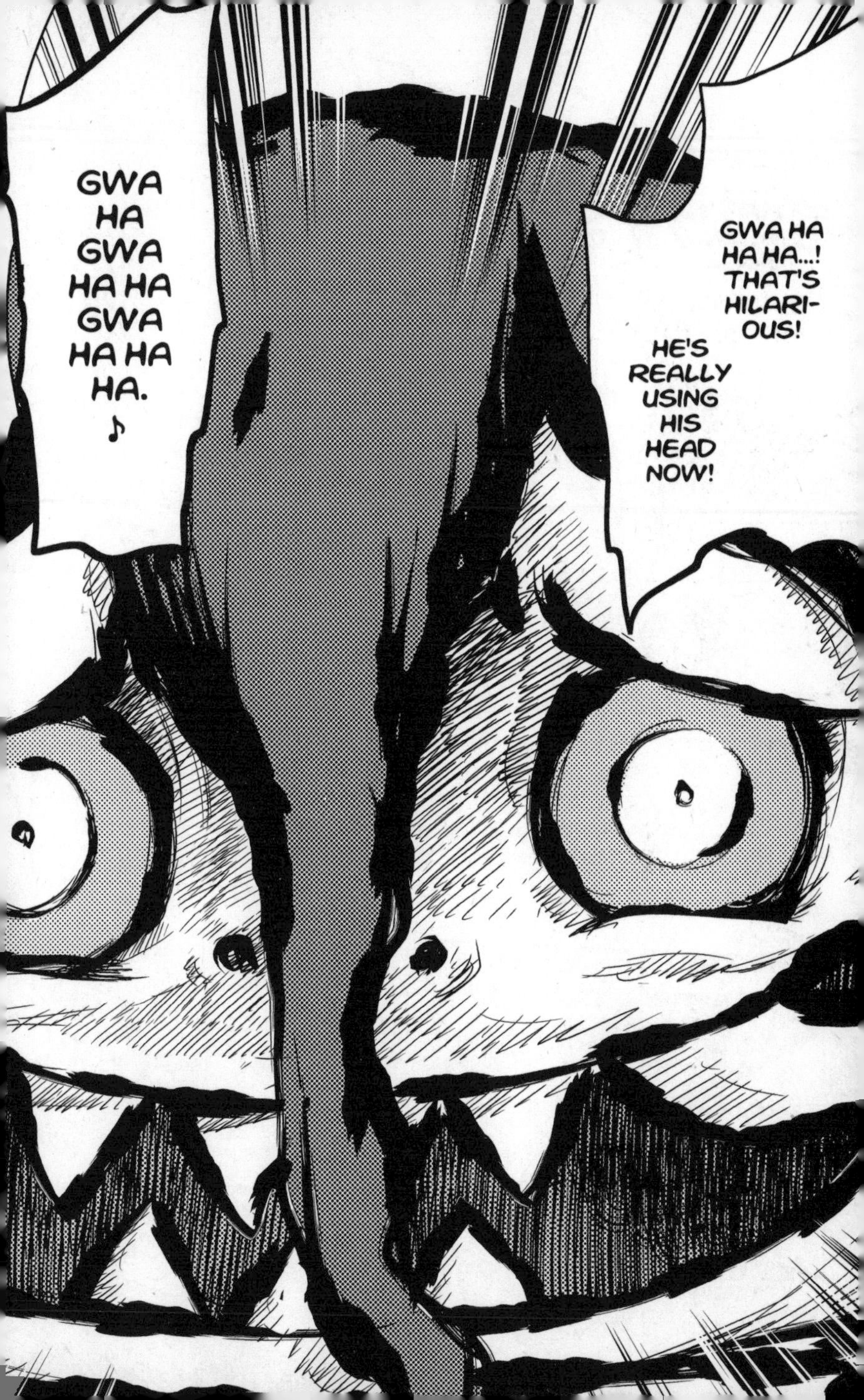
GWA HA HA HA...! THAT'S HILARI-OUS!
HE'S REALLY USING HIS HEAD NOW!
GWA HA GWA HA HA GWA HA HA HA. ♪

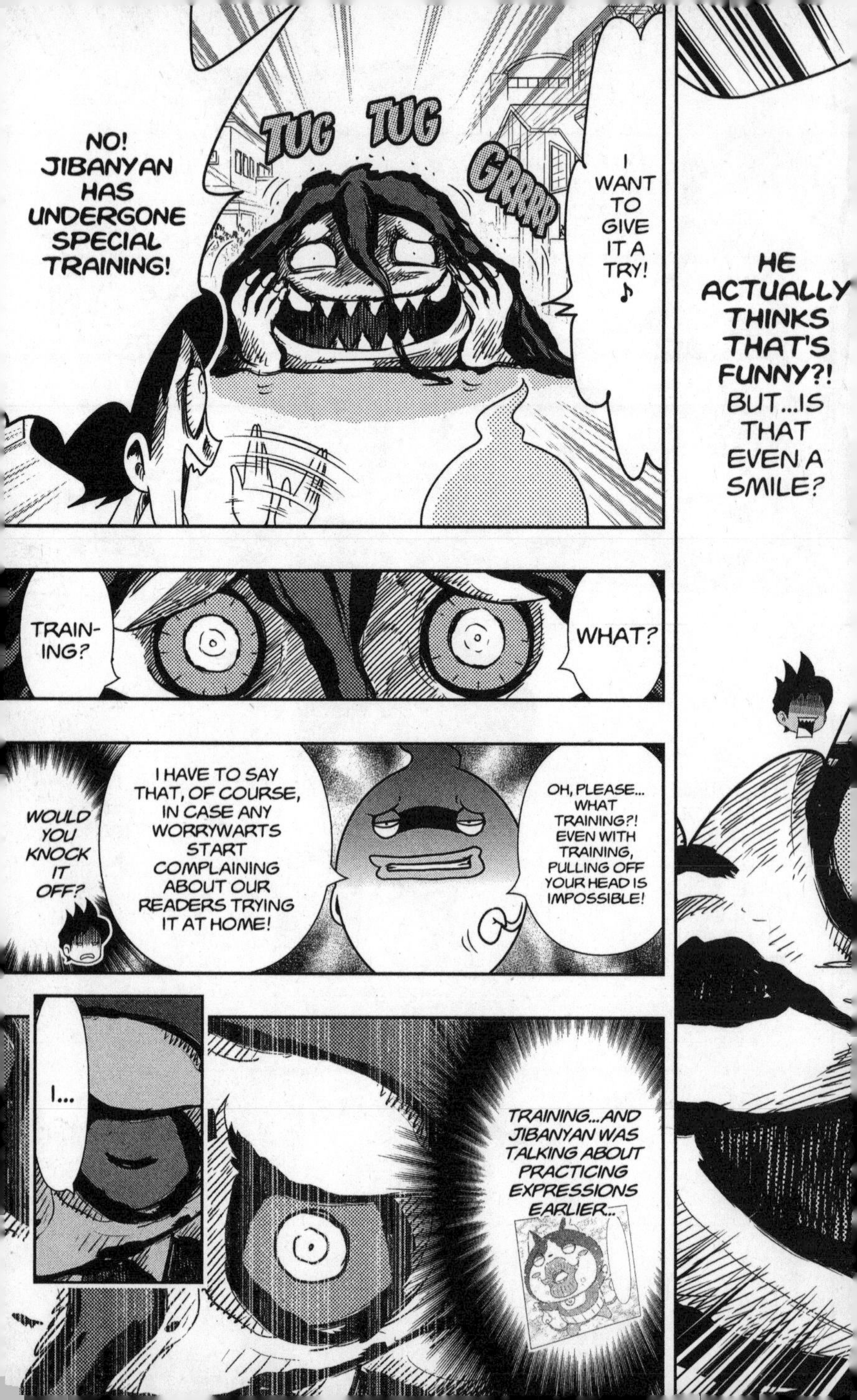
HE ACTUALLY THINKS THAT'S FUNNY?! BUT...IS THAT EVEN A SMILE?
I WANT TO GIVE IT A TRY! ♪
GRRRR
TUG TUG
NO! JIBANYAN HAS UNDERGONE SPECIAL TRAINING!
WHAT?
TRAIN-ING?
OH, PLEASE... WHAT TRAINING?! EVEN WITH TRAINING, PULLING OFF YOUR HEAD IS IMPOSSIBLE!
I HAVE TO SAY THAT, OF COURSE, IN CASE ANY WORRYWARTS START COMPLAINING ABOUT OUR READERS TRYING IT AT HOME!
WOULD YOU KNOCK IT OFF?
TRAINING...AND JIBANYAN WAS TALKING ABOUT PRACTICING EXPRESSIONS EARLIER...
I...

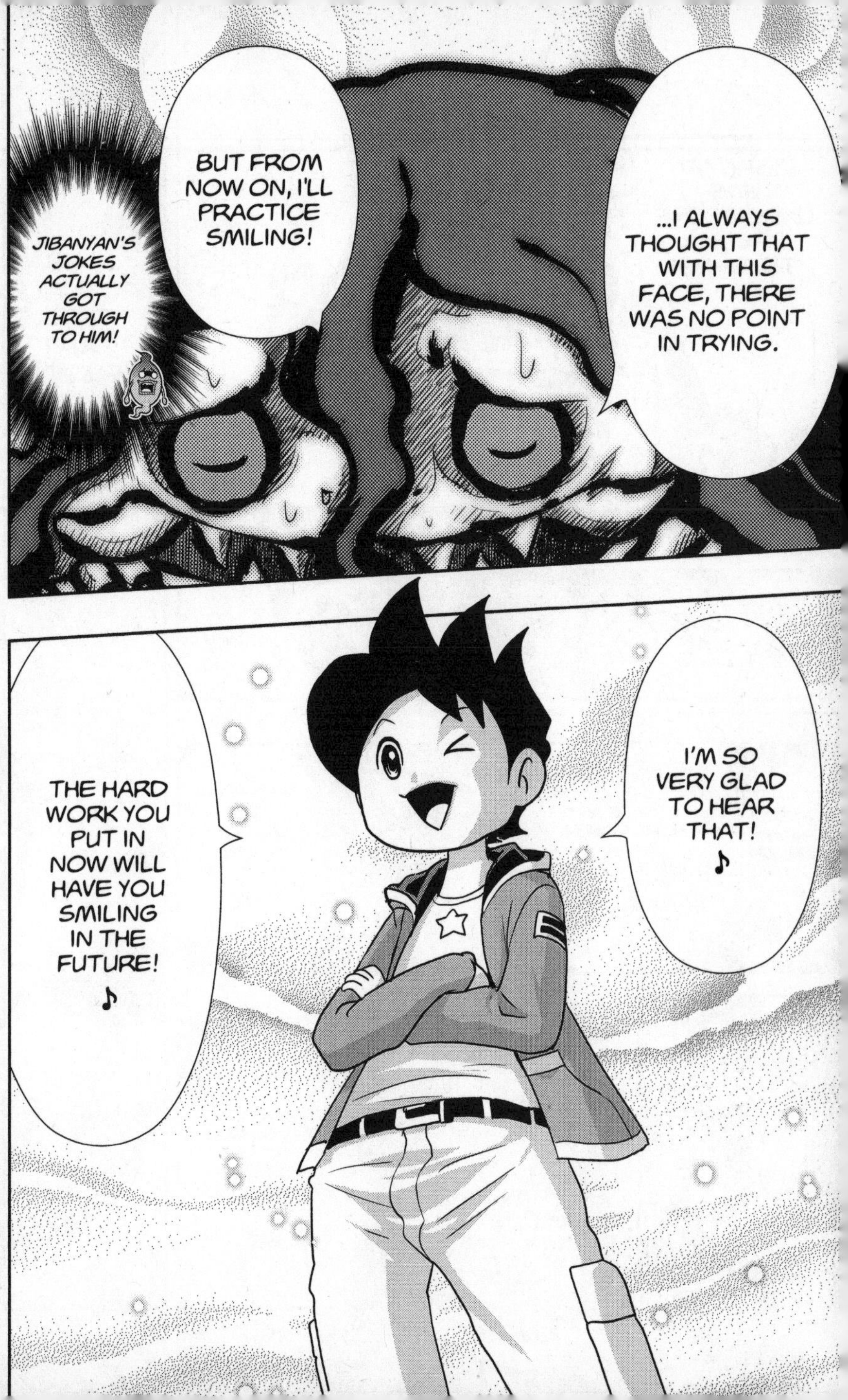
...I ALWAYS THOUGHT THAT WITH THIS FACE, THERE WAS NO POINT IN TRYING.
BUT FROM NOW ON, I'LL PRACTICE SMILING!
JIBANYAN'S JOKES ACTUALLY GOT THROUGH TO HIM!
I'M SO VERY GLAD TO HEAR THAT! ♪
THE HARD WORK YOU PUT IN NOW WILL HAVE YOU SMILING IN THE FUTURE! ♪

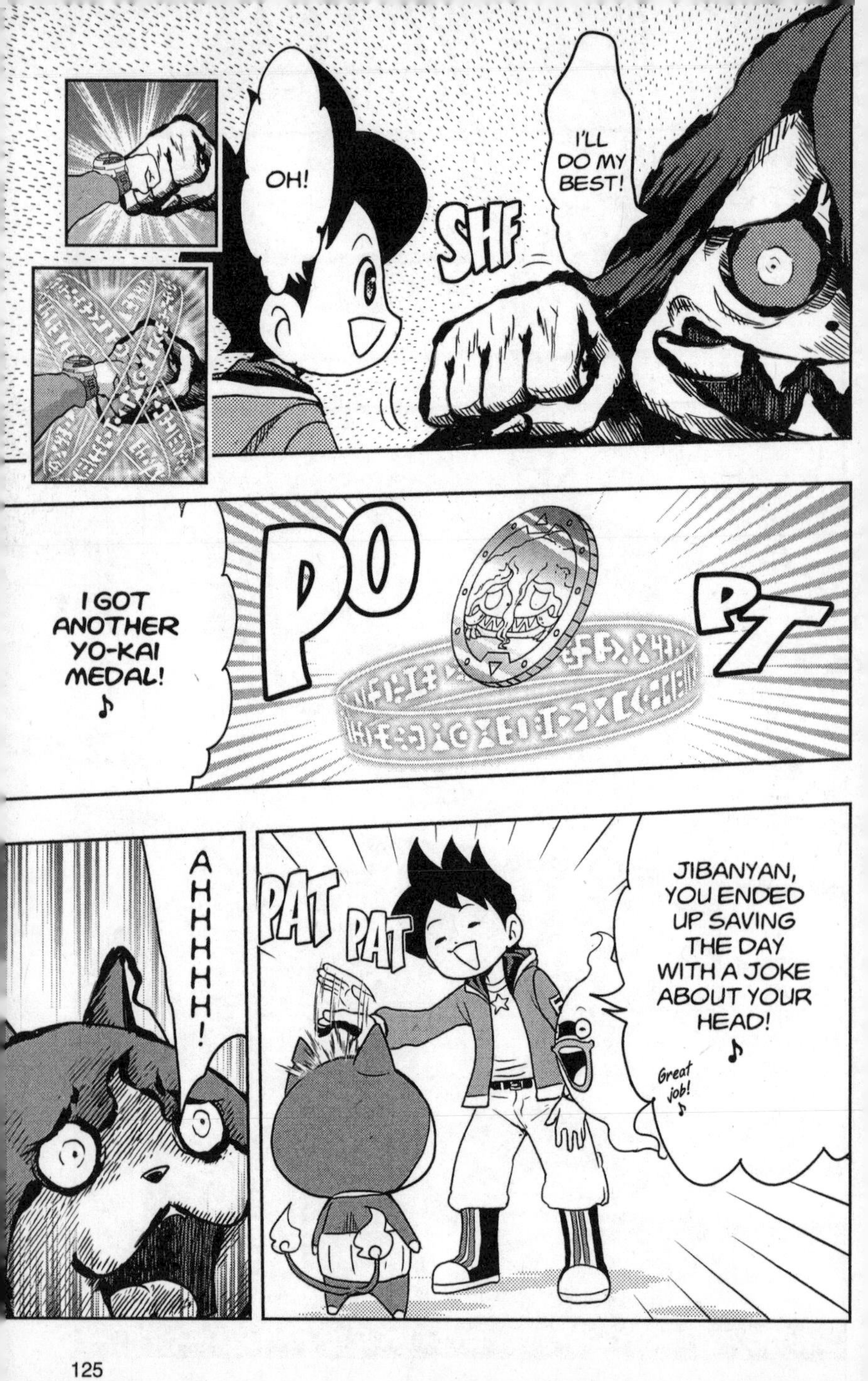
I'LL DO MY BEST!
SHF
OH!
PO
PT
I GOT ANOTHER YO-KAI MEDAL! ♪
JIBANYAN, YOU ENDED UP SAVING THE DAY WITH A JOKE ABOUT YOUR HEAD! ♪
Great job! ♪
PAT
PAT
AHHHHH!

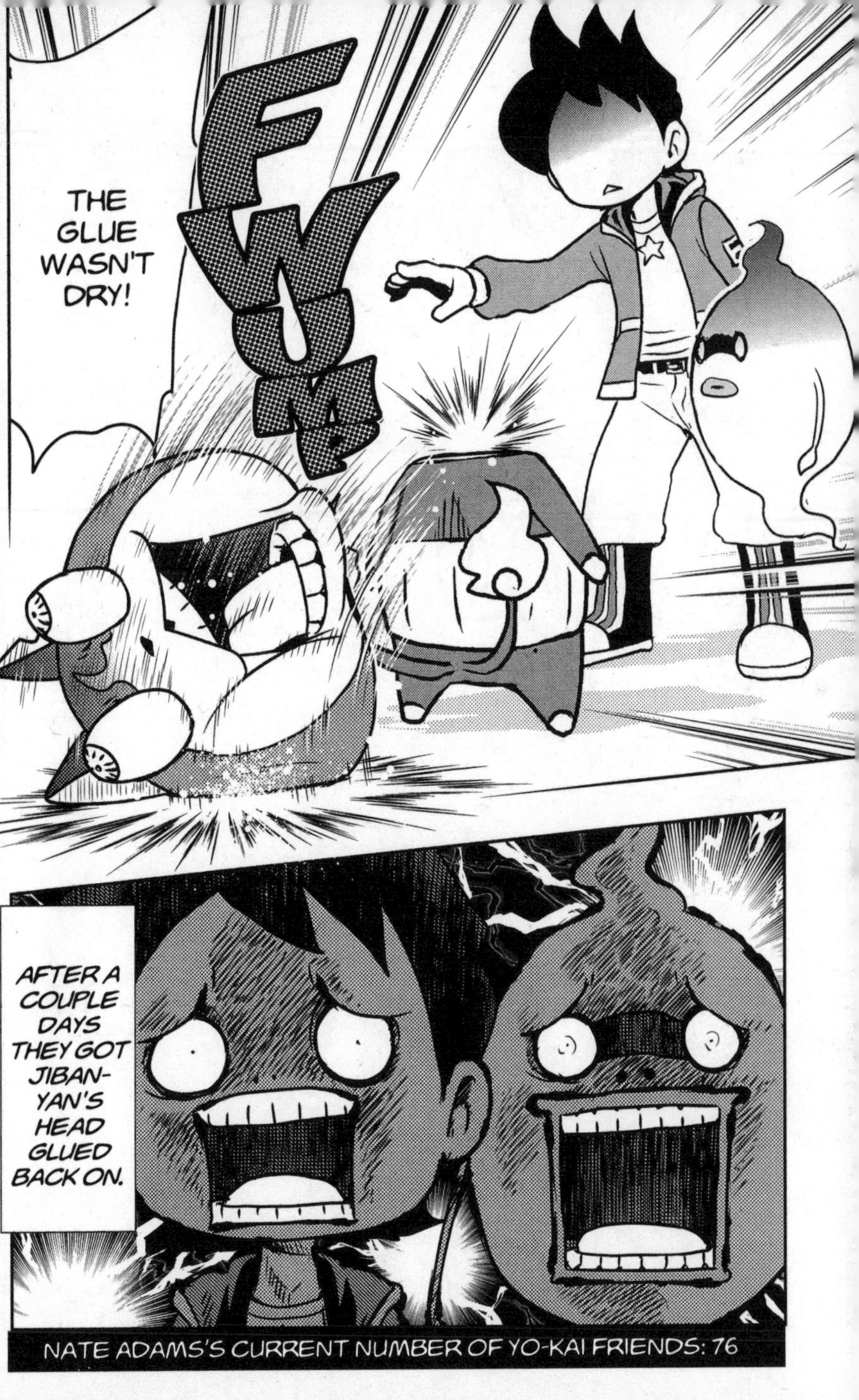
FWUMP
THE GLUE WASN'T DRY!
AFTER A COUPLE DAYS THEY GOT JIBAN-YAN'S HEAD GLUED BACK ON.
NATE ADAMS'S CURRENT NUMBER OF YO-KAI FRIENDS: 76

CHAPTER 132:
LORD YO-KAI OF THE SEWERS
FROGETMENOT

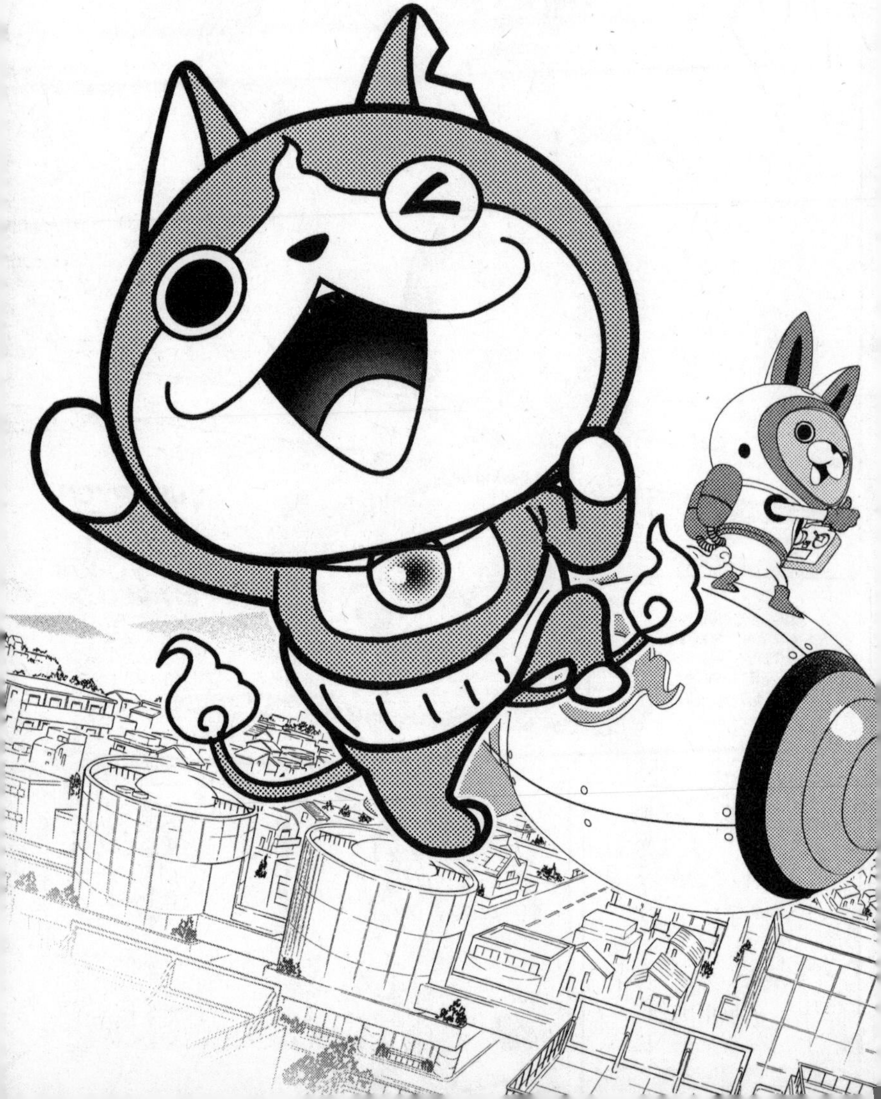

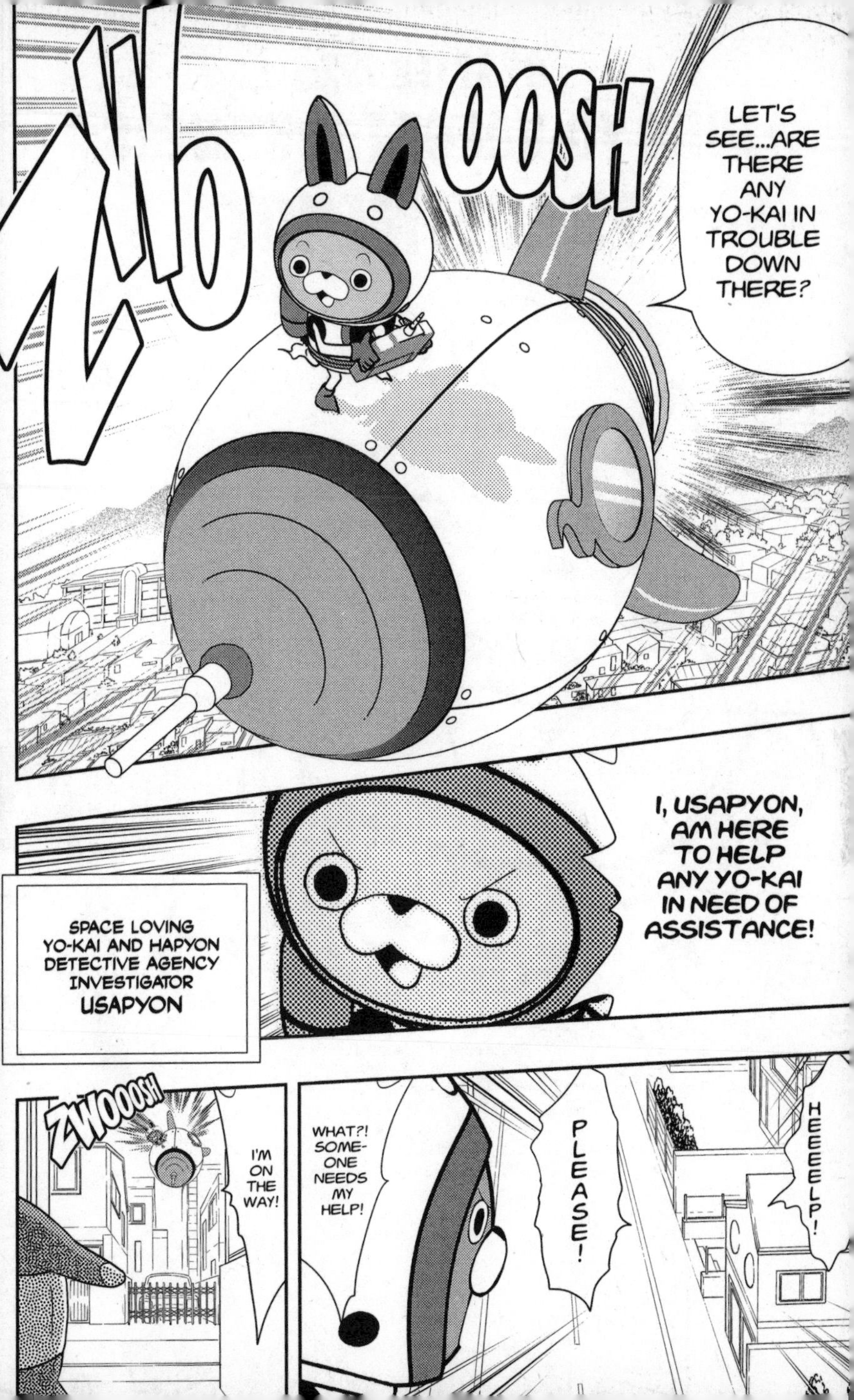
ZWOOOSH
LET'S SEE...ARE THERE ANY YO-KAI IN TROUBLE DOWN THERE?
I, USAPYON, AM HERE TO HELP ANY YO-KAI IN NEED OF ASSISTANCE!
SPACE LOVING YO-KAI AND HAPYON DETECTIVE AGENCY INVESTIGATOR USAPYON
HEEEELP!
PLEASE!
WHAT?! SOME-ONE NEEDS MY HELP!
ZWOOOSH
I'M ON THE WAY!

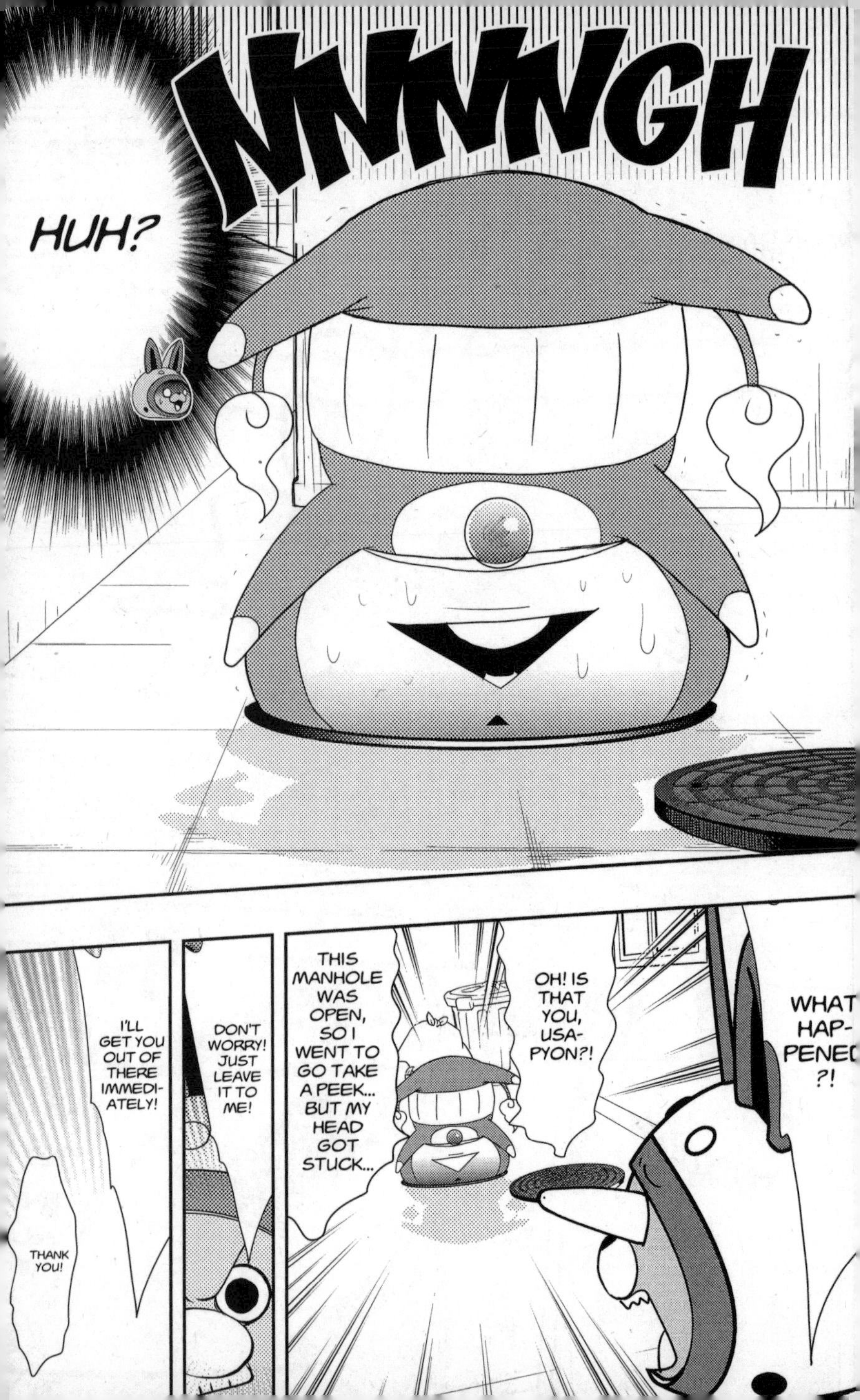
MNNNGH
HUH?
WHAT HAP-PENED?!
OH! IS THAT YOU, USA-PYON?!
THIS MANHOLE WAS OPEN, SO I WENT TO GO TAKE A PEEK... BUT MY HEAD GOT STUCK...
DON'T WORRY! JUST LEAVE IT TO ME!
I'LL GET YOU OUT OF THERE IMMEDI-ATELY!
THANK YOU!

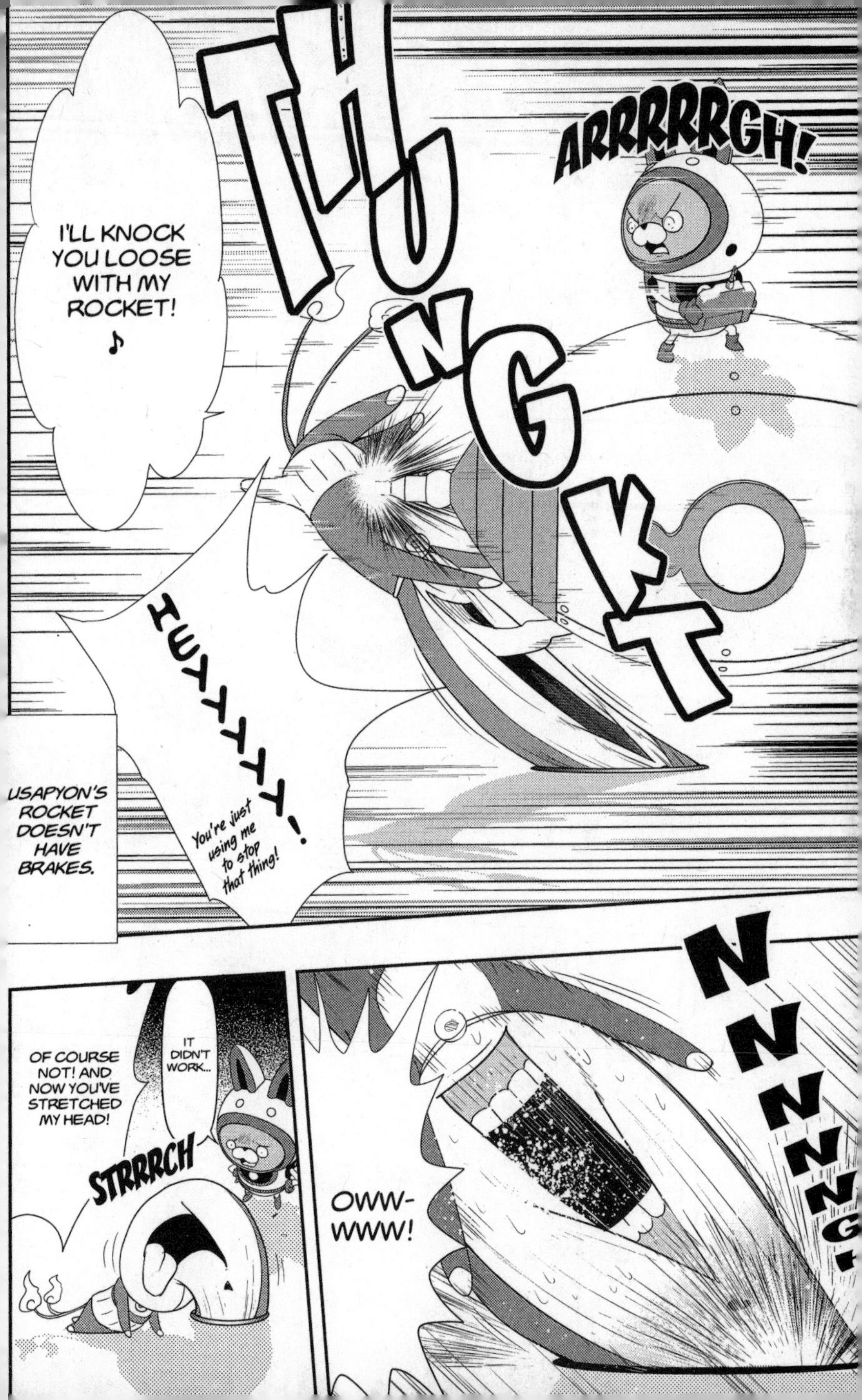
ARRRRRGH!
THUNGK
I'LL KNOCK YOU LOOSE WITH MY ROCKET! ♪
HEYYYYYY!
You're just using me to stop that thing!
USAPYON'S ROCKET DOESN'T HAVE BRAKES.
NNNNNG!
OWW-WWW!
IT DIDN'T WORK...
OF COURSE NOT! AND NOW YOU'VE STRETCHED MY HEAD!
STRRRCH

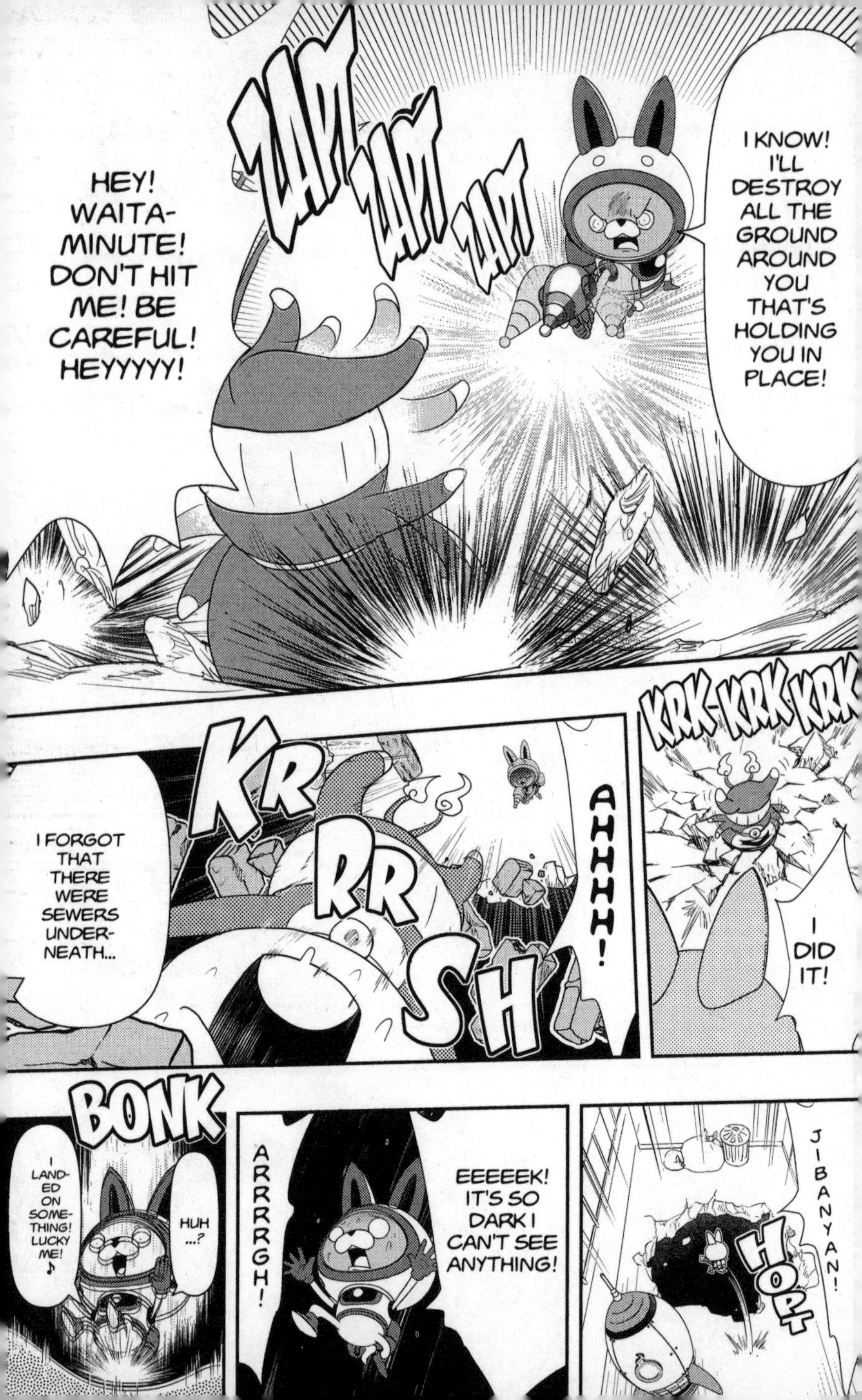
I KNOW! I'LL DESTROY ALL THE GROUND AROUND YOU THAT'S HOLDING YOU IN PLACE!
ZAP! ZAP! ZAP!
HEY! WAITA-MINUTE! DON'T HIT ME! BE CAREFUL! HEYYYYY!
KRK-KRK-KRK
I DID IT!
AHHHH!
KRRRSH
I FORGOT THAT THERE WERE SEWERS UNDER-NEATH...
JIBANYAN!
HOP
EEEEEK! IT'S SO DARK I CAN'T SEE ANYTHING!
ARRRRGH!
BONK
HUH ...?
I LANDED ON SOME-THING! LUCKY ME! ♪

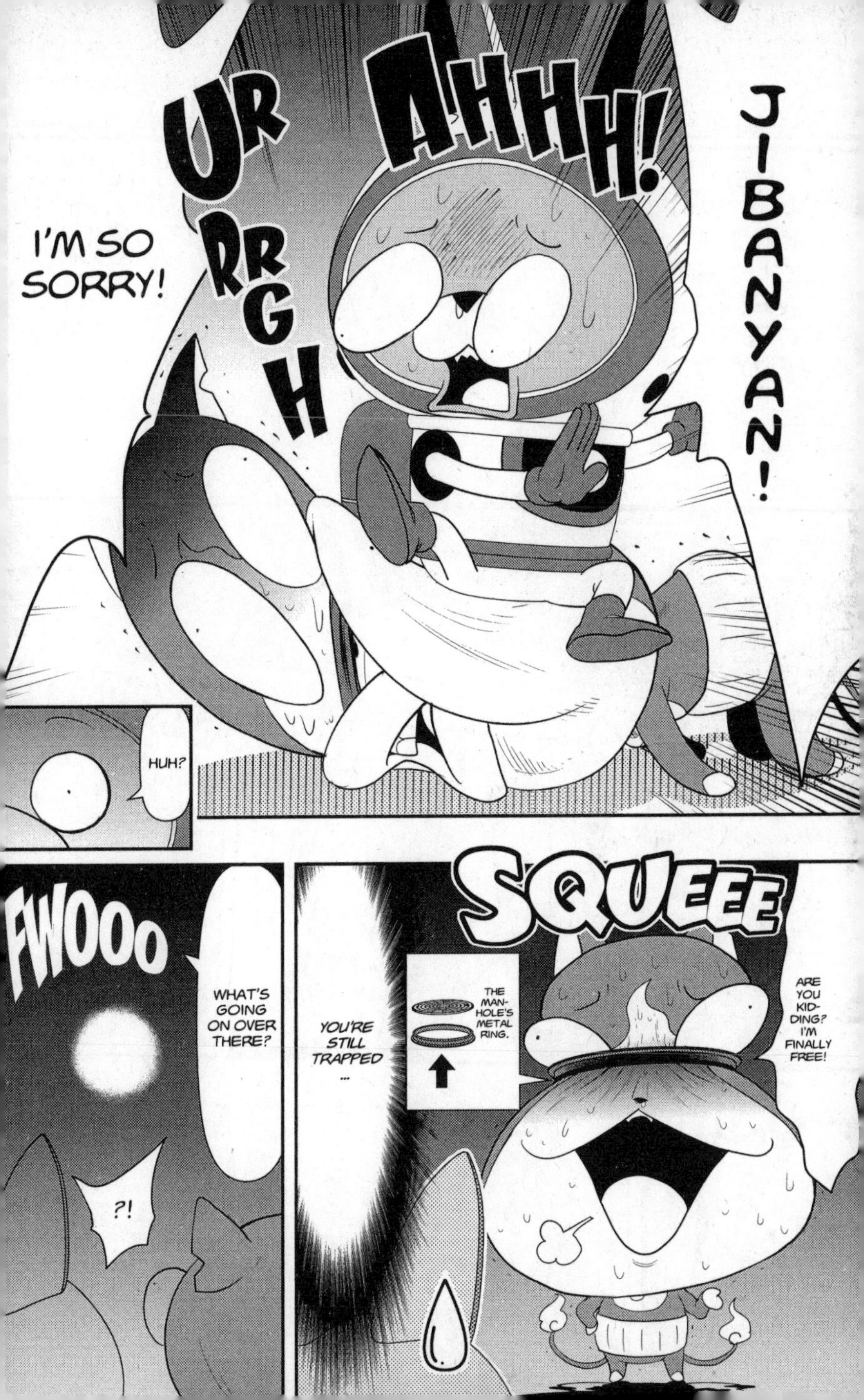
JIBANYAN!
AHHHH!
URRRGH
I'M SO SORRY!
HUH?
SQUEEE
ARE YOU KID-DING? I'M FINALLY FREE!
THE MAN-HOLE'S METAL RING.
YOU'RE STILL TRAPPED ...
FWOOO
WHAT'S GOING ON OVER THERE?
?!

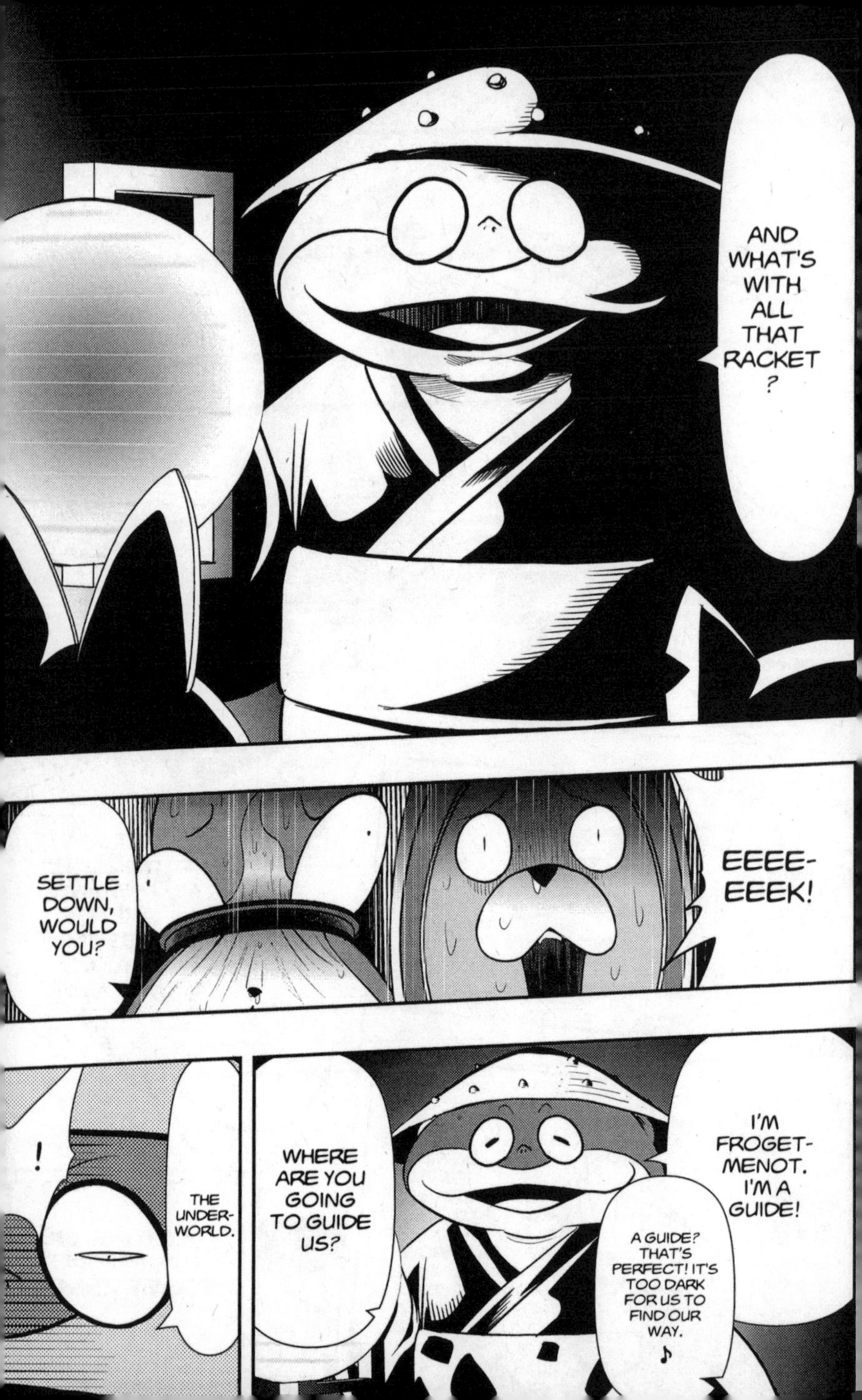
AND WHAT'S WITH ALL THAT RACKET?
EEEE-EEEK!
SETTLE DOWN, WOULD YOU?
I'M FROGET-MENOT. I'M A GUIDE!
A GUIDE? THAT'S PERFECT! IT'S TOO DARK FOR US TO FIND OUR WAY. ♪
WHERE ARE YOU GOING TO GUIDE US?
THE UNDER-WORLD.
!

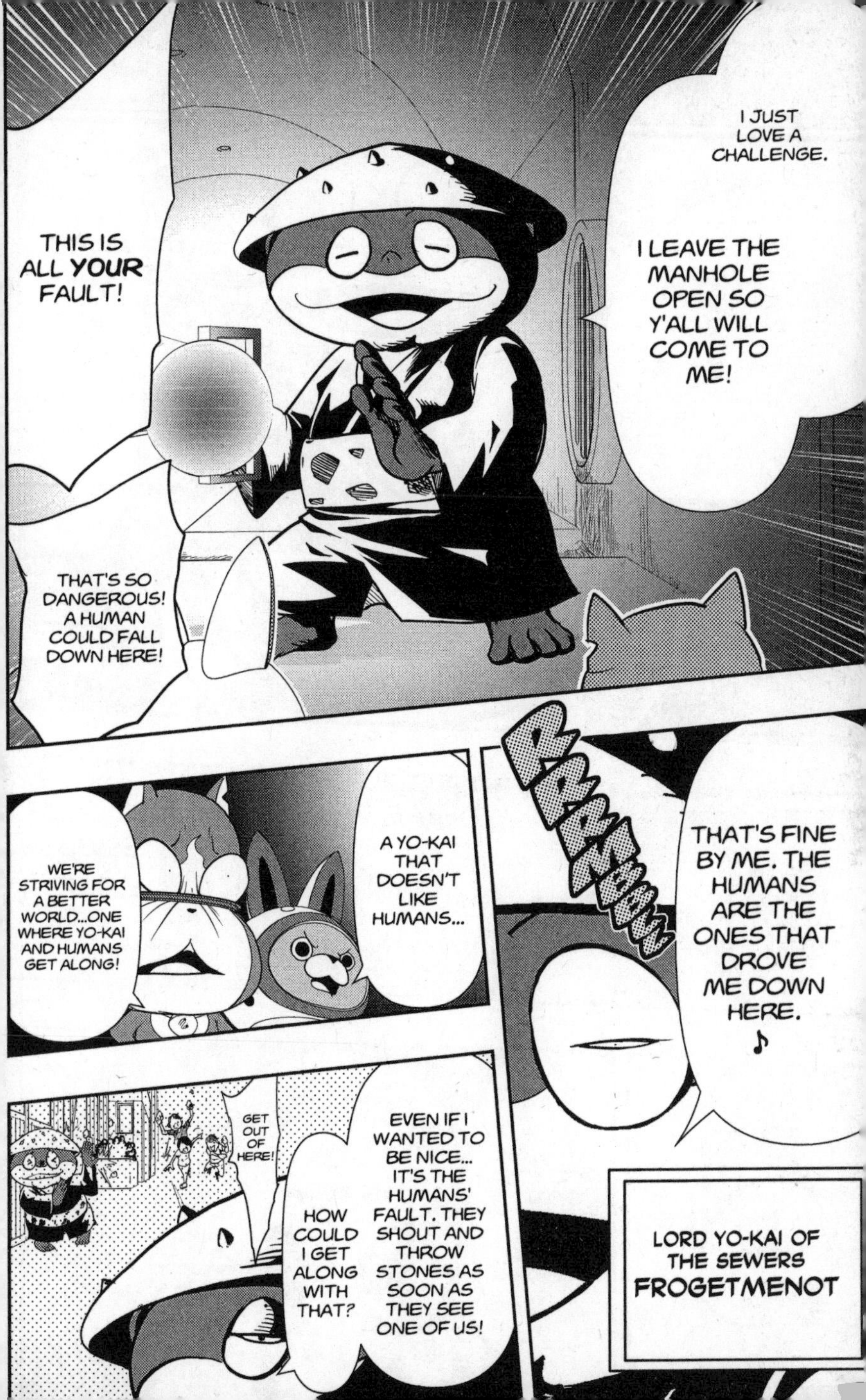
I JUST LOVE A CHALLENGE.
I LEAVE THE MANHOLE OPEN SO Y'ALL WILL COME TO ME!
THIS IS ALL **YOUR** FAULT!
THAT'S SO DANGEROUS! A HUMAN COULD FALL DOWN HERE!
THAT'S FINE BY ME. THE HUMANS ARE THE ONES THAT DROVE ME DOWN HERE. ♪
LORD YO-KAI OF THE SEWERS **FROGETMENOT**
A YO-KAI THAT DOESN'T LIKE HUMANS...
WE'RE STRIVING FOR A BETTER WORLD...ONE WHERE YO-KAI AND HUMANS GET ALONG!
EVEN IF I WANTED TO BE NICE... IT'S THE HUMANS' FAULT. THEY SHOUT AND THROW STONES AS SOON AS THEY SEE ONE OF US!
HOW COULD I GET ALONG WITH THAT?
GET OUT OF HERE!

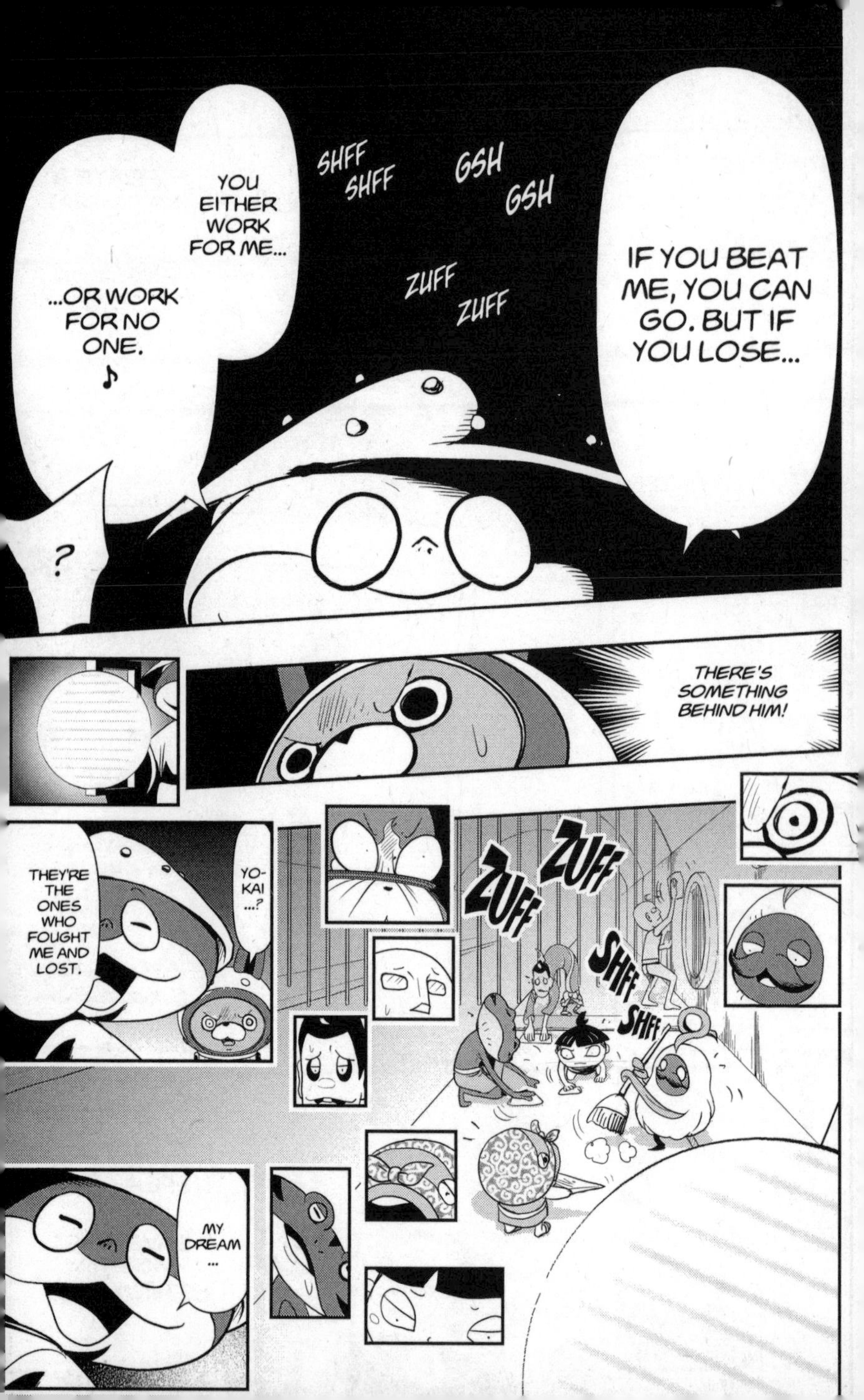
IF YOU BEAT ME, YOU CAN GO. BUT IF YOU LOSE...
GSH GSH
SHFF SHFF
ZUFF ZUFF
YOU EITHER WORK FOR ME...
...OR WORK FOR NO ONE. ♪
?
THERE'S SOMETHING BEHIND HIM!
ZUFF ZUFF
SHFF SHFF
YO-KAI...?
THEY'RE THE ONES WHO FOUGHT ME AND LOST.
MY DREAM...

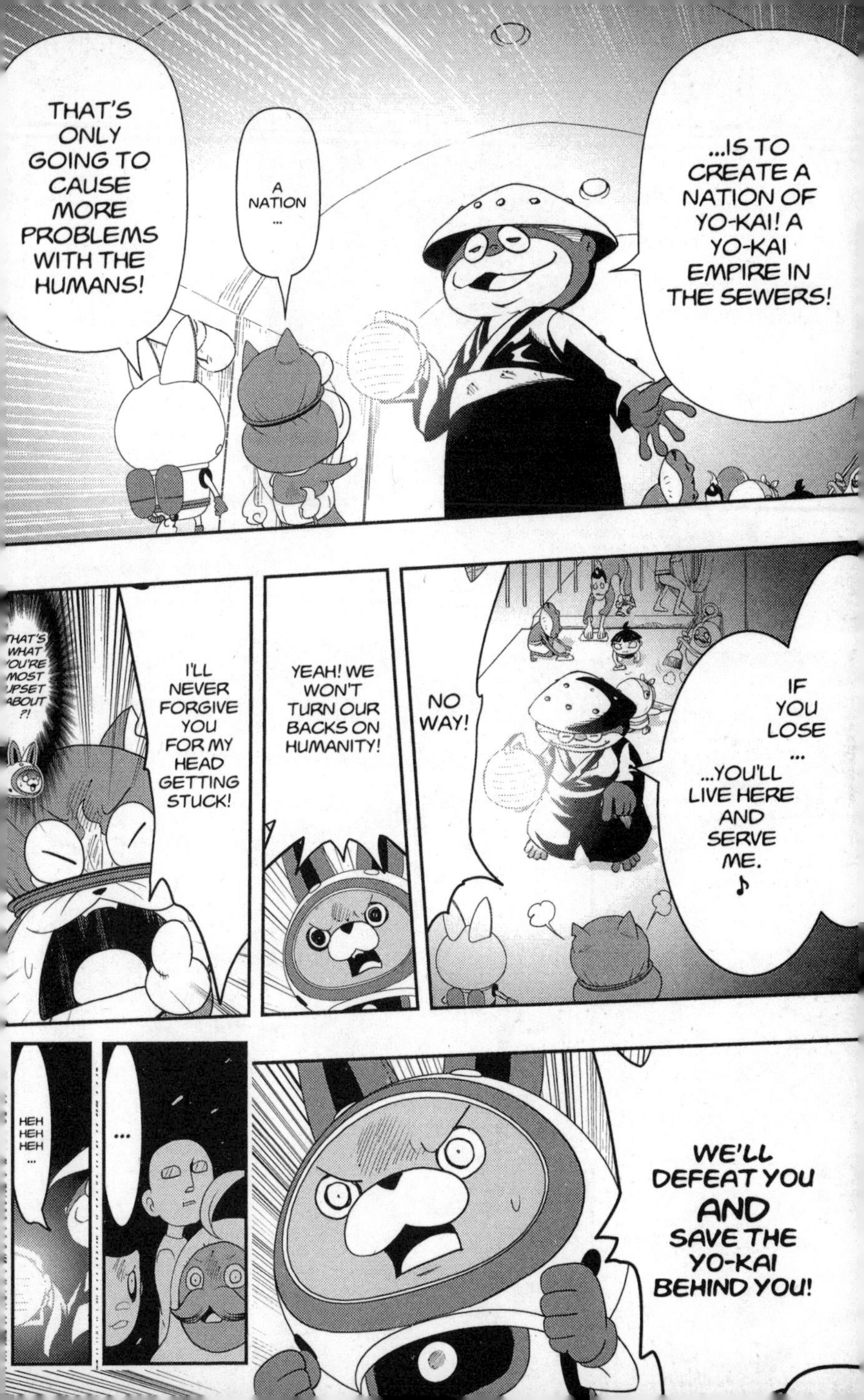
...IS TO CREATE A NATION OF YO-KAI! A YO-KAI EMPIRE IN THE SEWERS!
A NATION ...
THAT'S ONLY GOING TO CAUSE MORE PROBLEMS WITH THE HUMANS!
IF YOU LOSE ...
...YOU'LL LIVE HERE AND SERVE ME. ♪
NO WAY!
YEAH! WE WON'T TURN OUR BACKS ON HUMANITY!
I'LL NEVER FORGIVE YOU FOR MY HEAD GETTING STUCK!
THAT'S WHAT 'OU'RE MOST JPSET ABOUT ?!
WE'LL DEFEAT YOU AND SAVE THE YO-KAI BEHIND YOU!
...
HEH HEH HEH ...

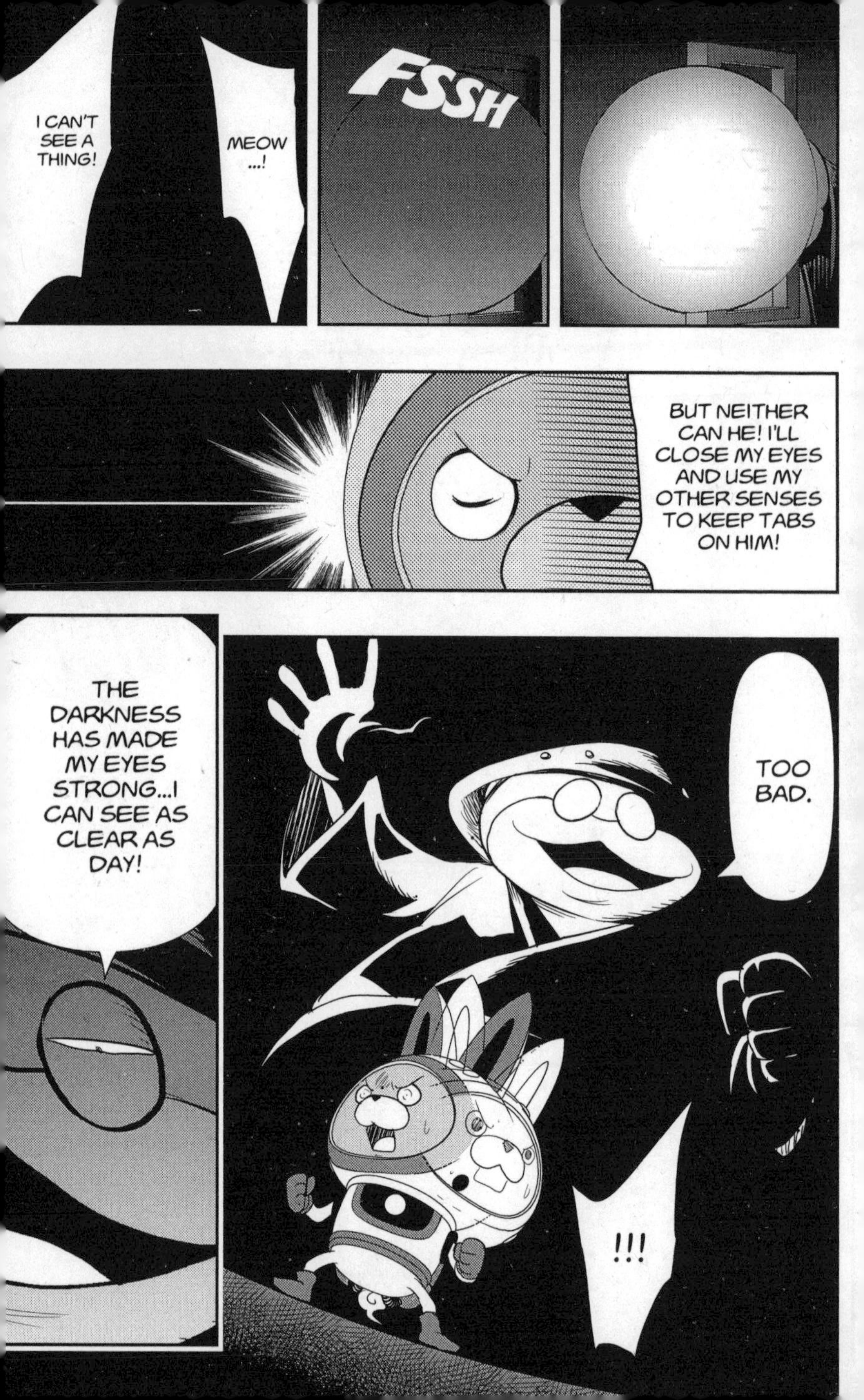
FSSH
MEOW ...!
I CAN'T SEE A THING!
BUT NEITHER CAN HE! I'LL CLOSE MY EYES AND USE MY OTHER SENSES TO KEEP TABS ON HIM!
TOO BAD.
!!!
THE DARKNESS HAS MADE MY EYES STRONG...I CAN SEE AS CLEAR AS DAY!

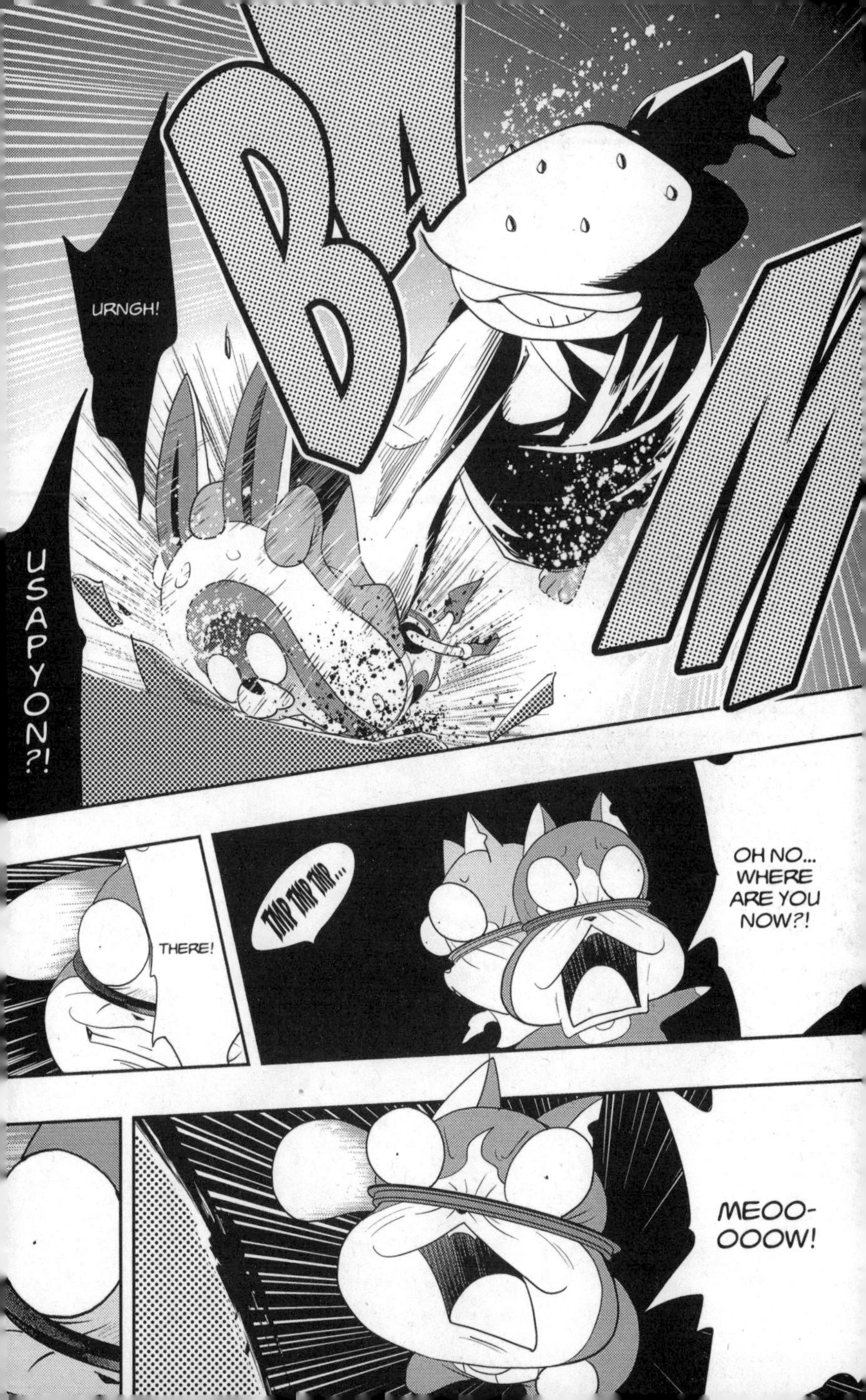
BAM
URNGH!
USAPYON?!
OH NO... WHERE ARE YOU NOW?!
TMP TMP TMP...
THERE!
MEOO-OOOW!

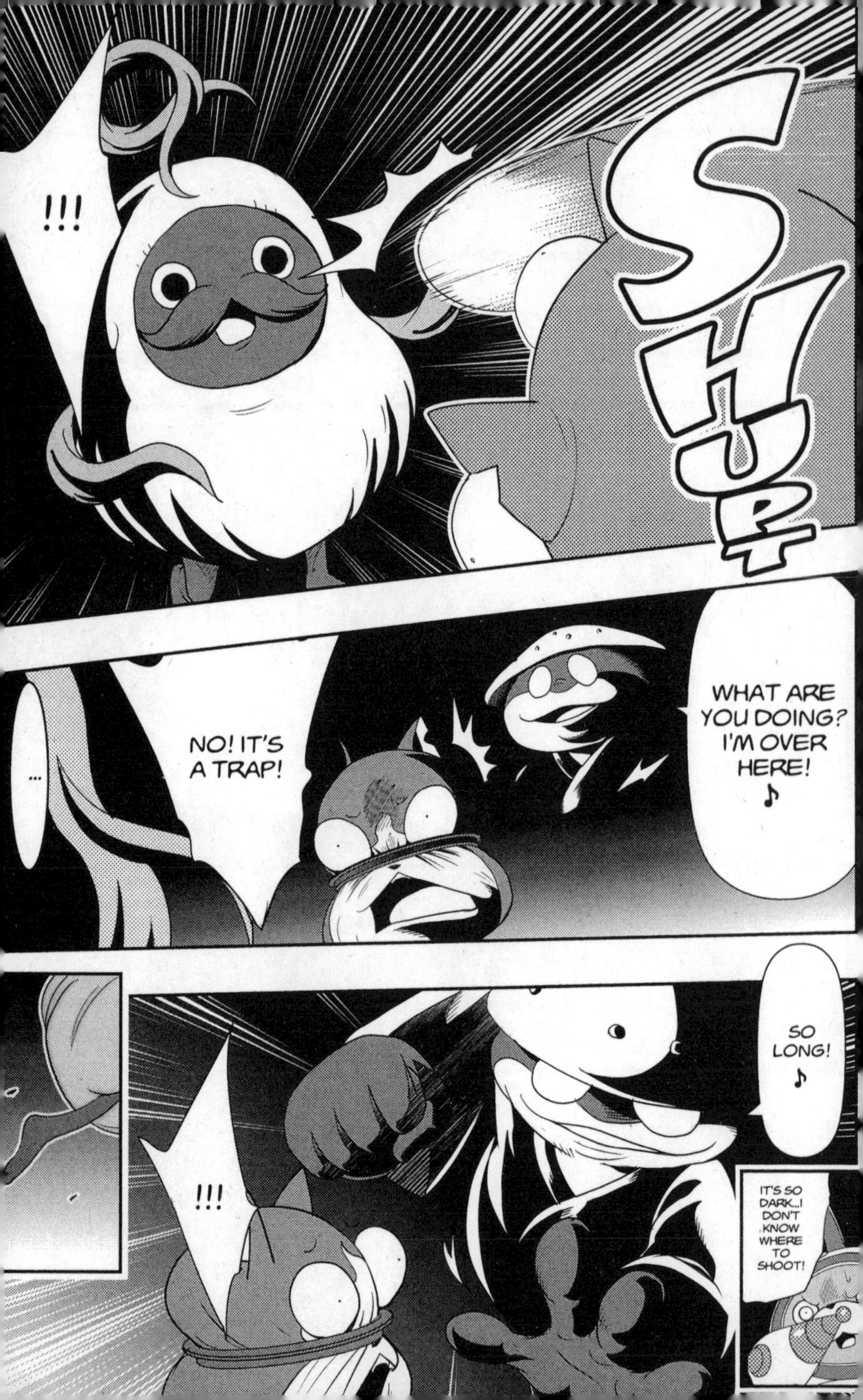
SHUPT
!!!
WHAT ARE YOU DOING? I'M OVER HERE! ♪
NO! IT'S A TRAP!
...
SO LONG! ♪
IT'S SO DARK...I DON'T KNOW WHERE TO SHOOT!
!!!

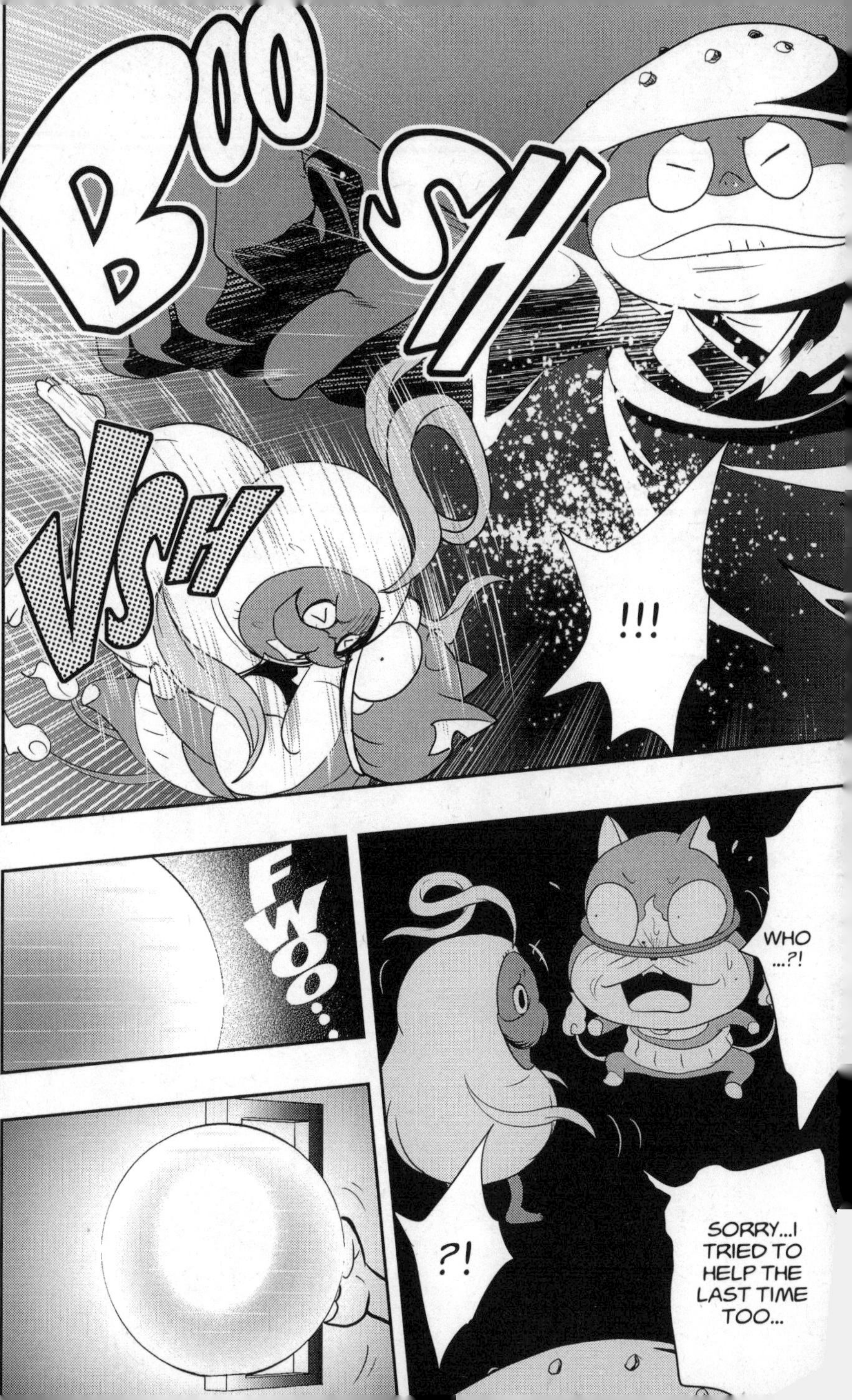
BOOSH
VISH
!!!
WHO ...?!
SORRY...I TRIED TO HELP THE LAST TIME TOO...
?!
FWOO...

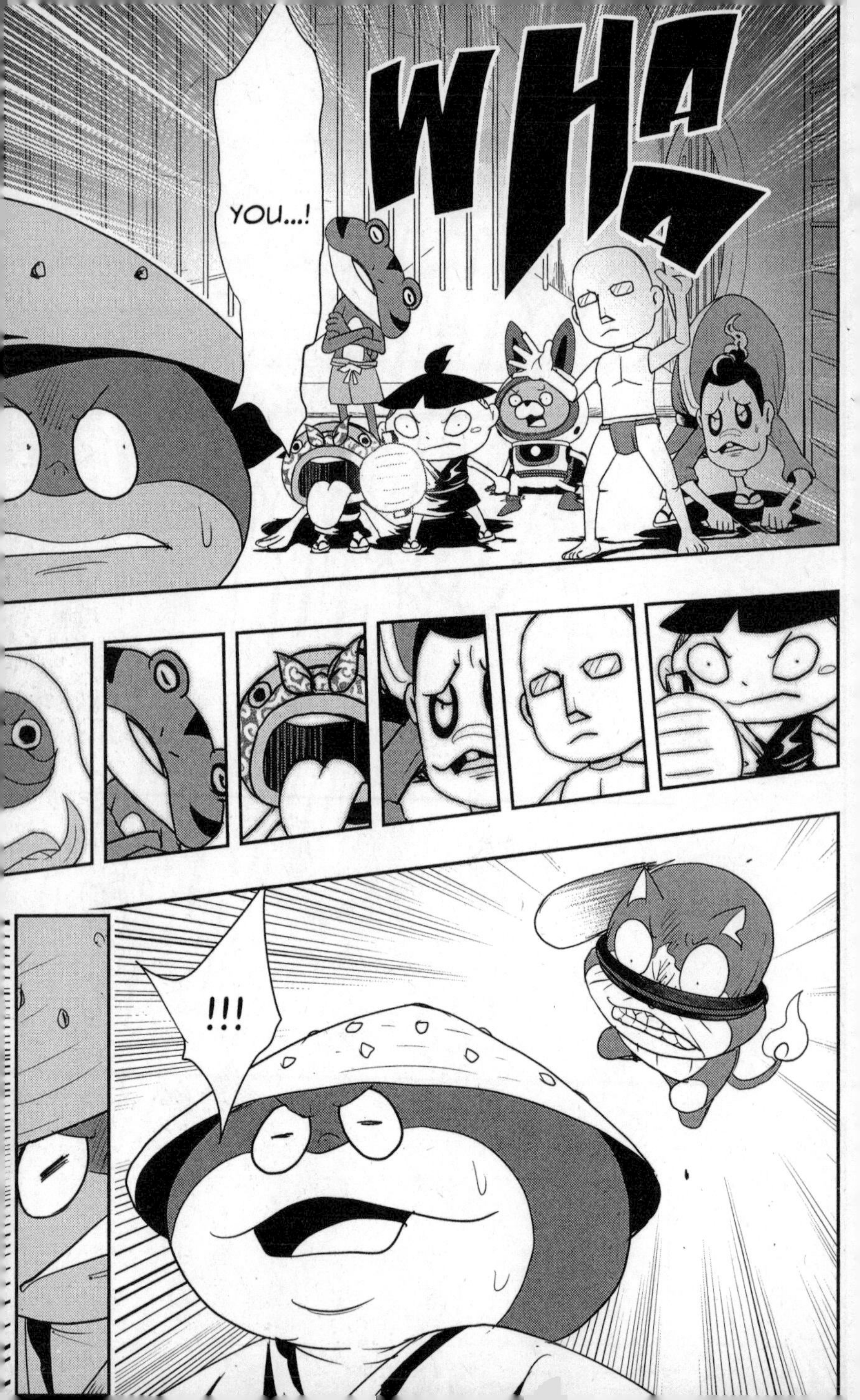
WHA
YOU...!
!!!

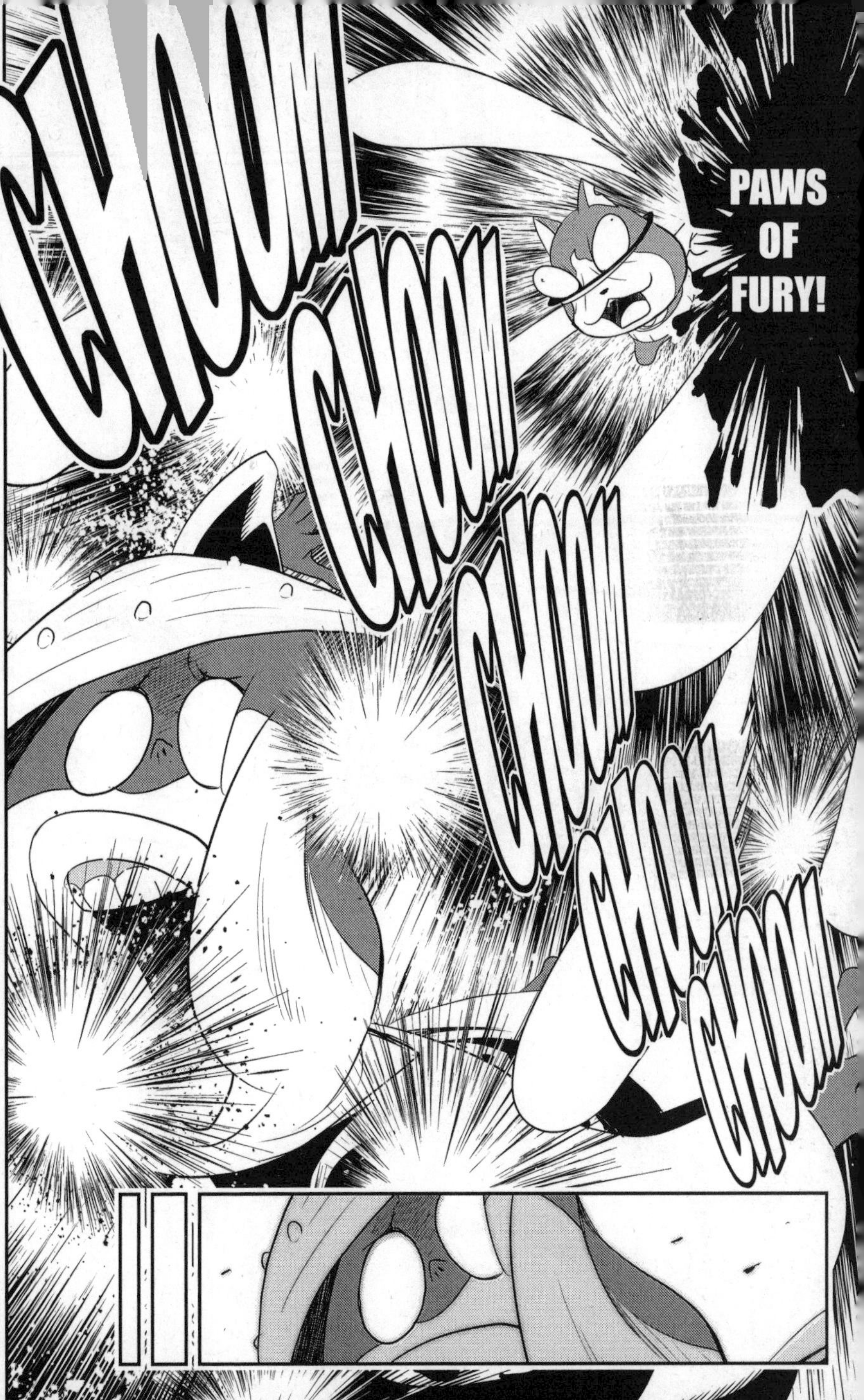
PAWS OF FURY!
CHOOM
CHOOM
CHOOM
CHOOM
CHOOM

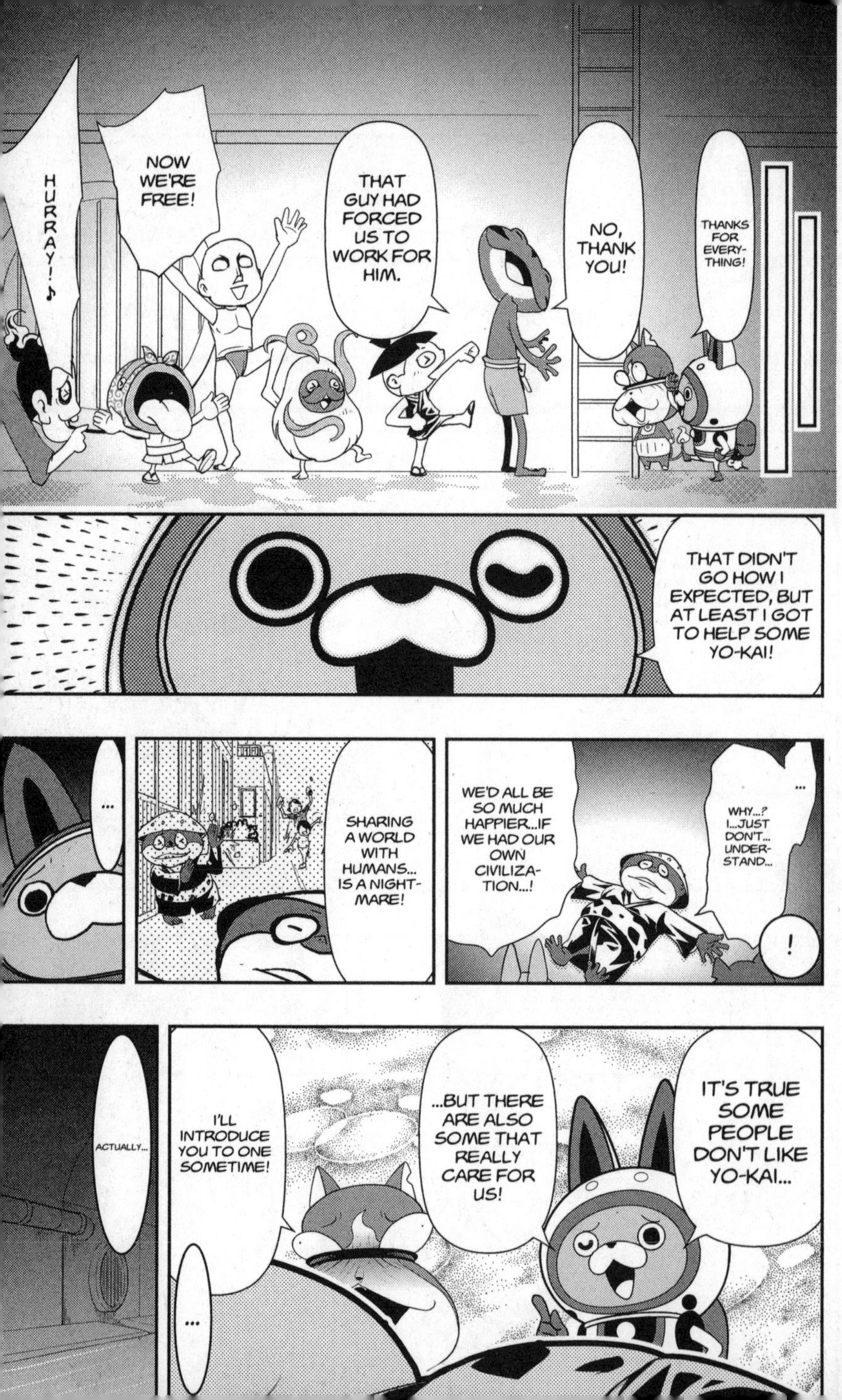
THANKS FOR EVERY-THING!
NO, THANK YOU!
THAT GUY HAD FORCED US TO WORK FOR HIM.
NOW WE'RE FREE!
HURRAY!♪
THAT DIDN'T GO HOW I EXPECTED, BUT AT LEAST I GOT TO HELP SOME YO-KAI!
...
WHY...? I...JUST DON'T... UNDER-STAND...
!
WE'D ALL BE SO MUCH HAPPIER...IF WE HAD OUR OWN CIVILIZA-TION...!
SHARING A WORLD WITH HUMANS... IS A NIGHT-MARE!
...
IT'S TRUE SOME PEOPLE DON'T LIKE YO-KAI...
...BUT THERE ARE ALSO SOME THAT REALLY CARE FOR US!
I'LL INTRODUCE YOU TO ONE SOMETIME!
...
ACTUALLY...

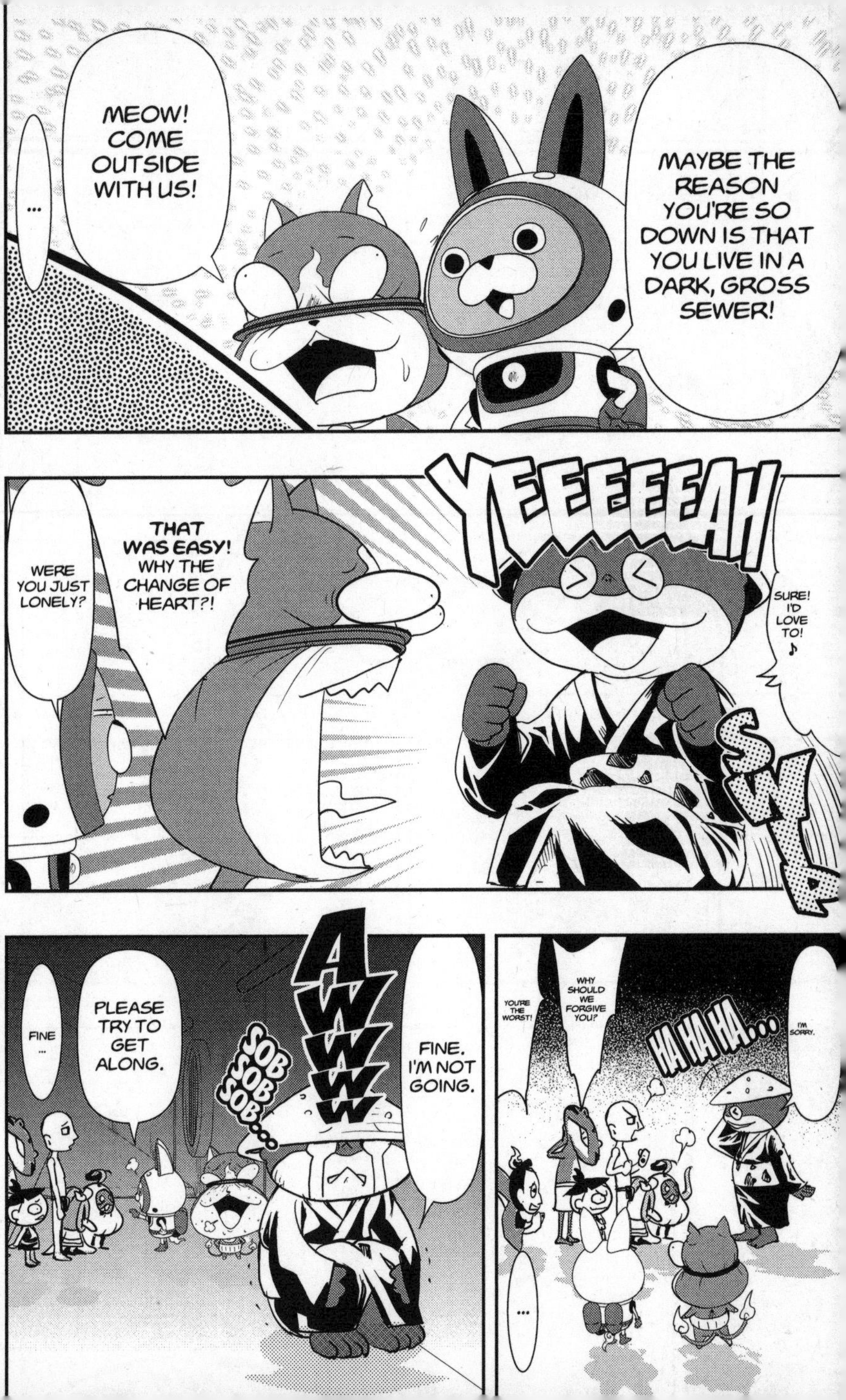
MAYBE THE REASON YOU'RE SO DOWN IS THAT YOU LIVE IN A DARK, GROSS SEWER!
MEOW! COME OUTSIDE WITH US!
...
YEEEEEAH
SURE! I'D LOVE TO! ♪
THAT WAS EASY! WHY THE CHANGE OF HEART?!
WERE YOU JUST LONELY?
...
I'M SORRY.
HA HA HA...
WHY SHOULD WE FORGIVE YOU?
YOU'RE THE WORST!
...
FINE. I'M NOT GOING.
AWWWW
SOB SOB SOB...
PLEASE TRY TO GET ALONG.
FINE ...

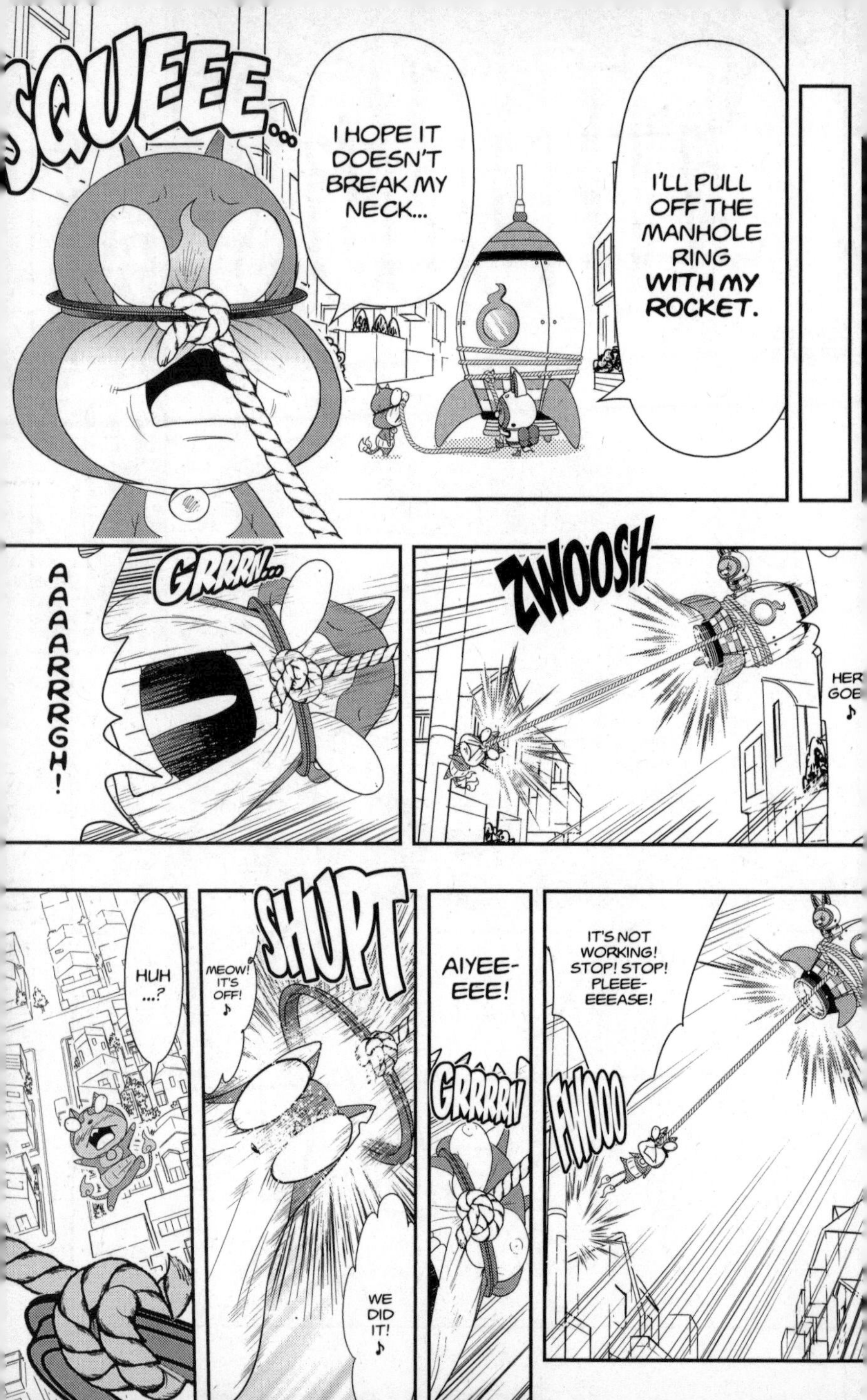
I'LL PULL OFF THE MANHOLE RING WITH MY ROCKET.
I HOPE IT DOESN'T BREAK MY NECK...
SQUEEE...
ZWOOSH
HER GOE ♪
GRRRN...
AAAAARRRGH!
IT'S NOT WORKING! STOP! STOP! PLEEE-EEEASE!
FWOOO
AIYEE-EEE!
GRRRRN
SHUPT
MEOW! IT'S OFF! ♪
WE DID IT! ♪
HUH ...?

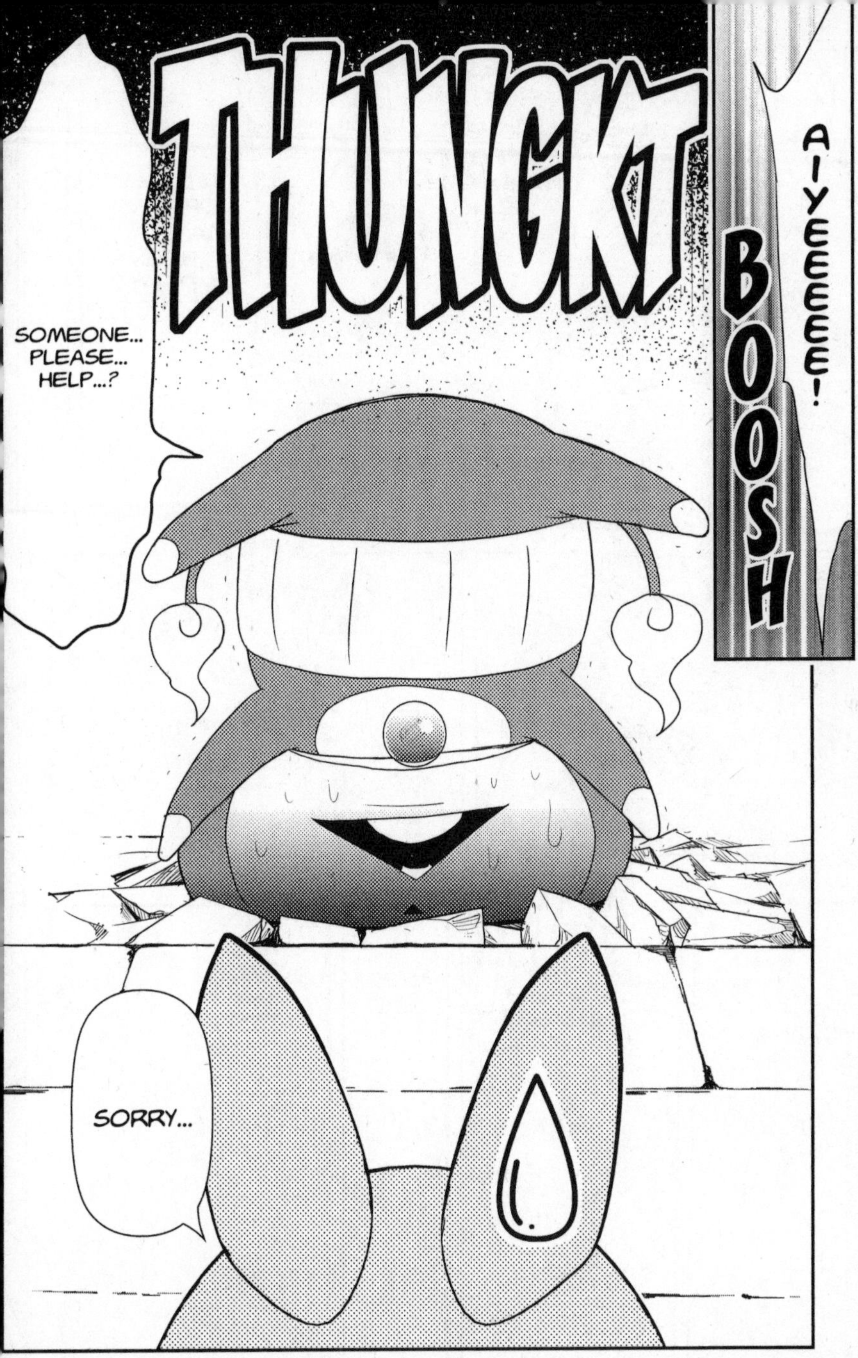
AIYEEEE!
BOOSH
THUNCK!
SOMEONE... PLEASE... HELP...?
SORRY...

CHAPTER 133:
HERO YO-KAI SILVER LINING

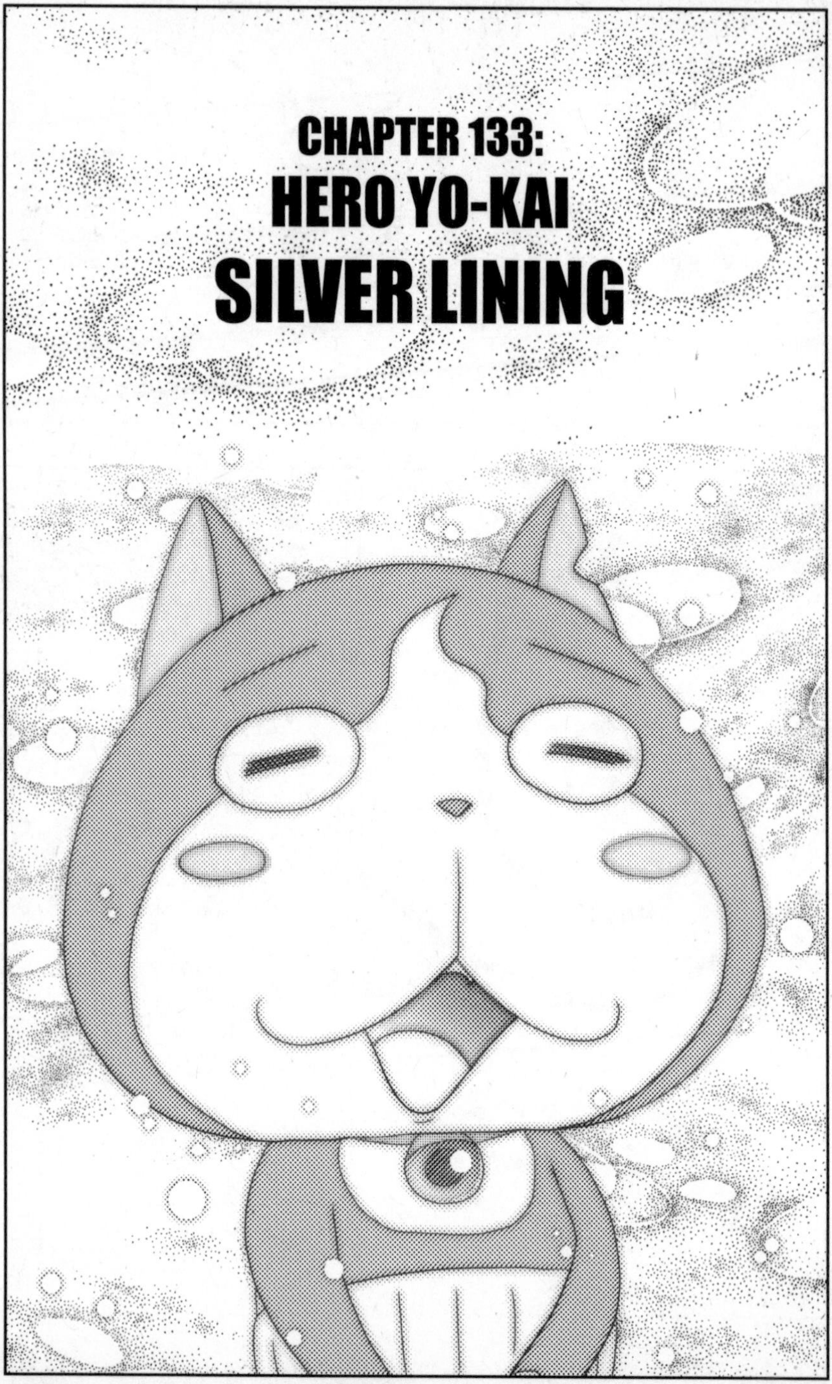

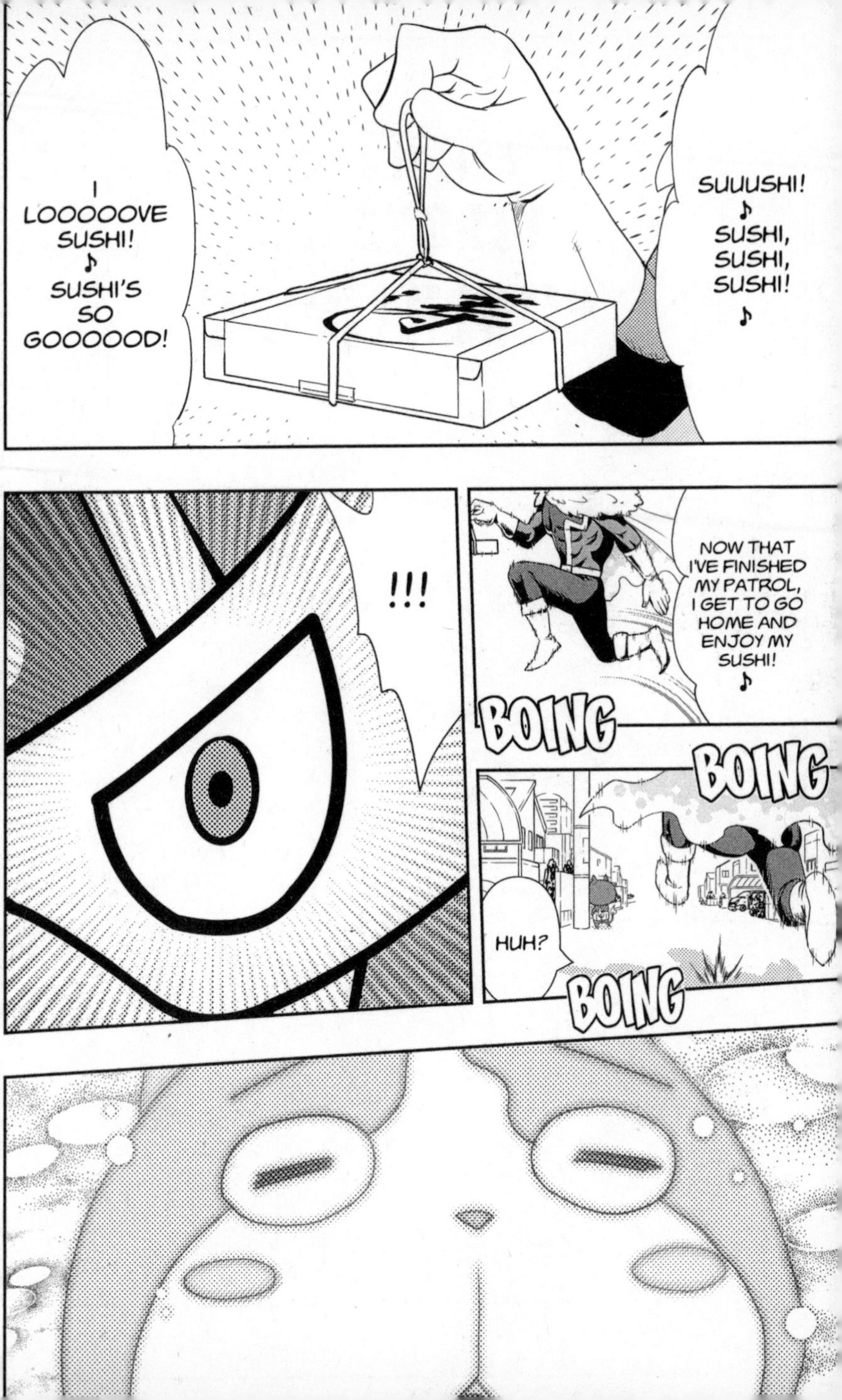
SUUUSHI! ♪ SUSHI, SUSHI, SUSHI! ♪
I LOOOOOVE SUSHI! ♪ SUSHI'S SO GOOOOOD!
NOW THAT I'VE FINISHED MY PATROL, I GET TO GO HOME AND ENJOY MY SUSHI! ♪
BOING
BOING
HUH?
BOING
!!!

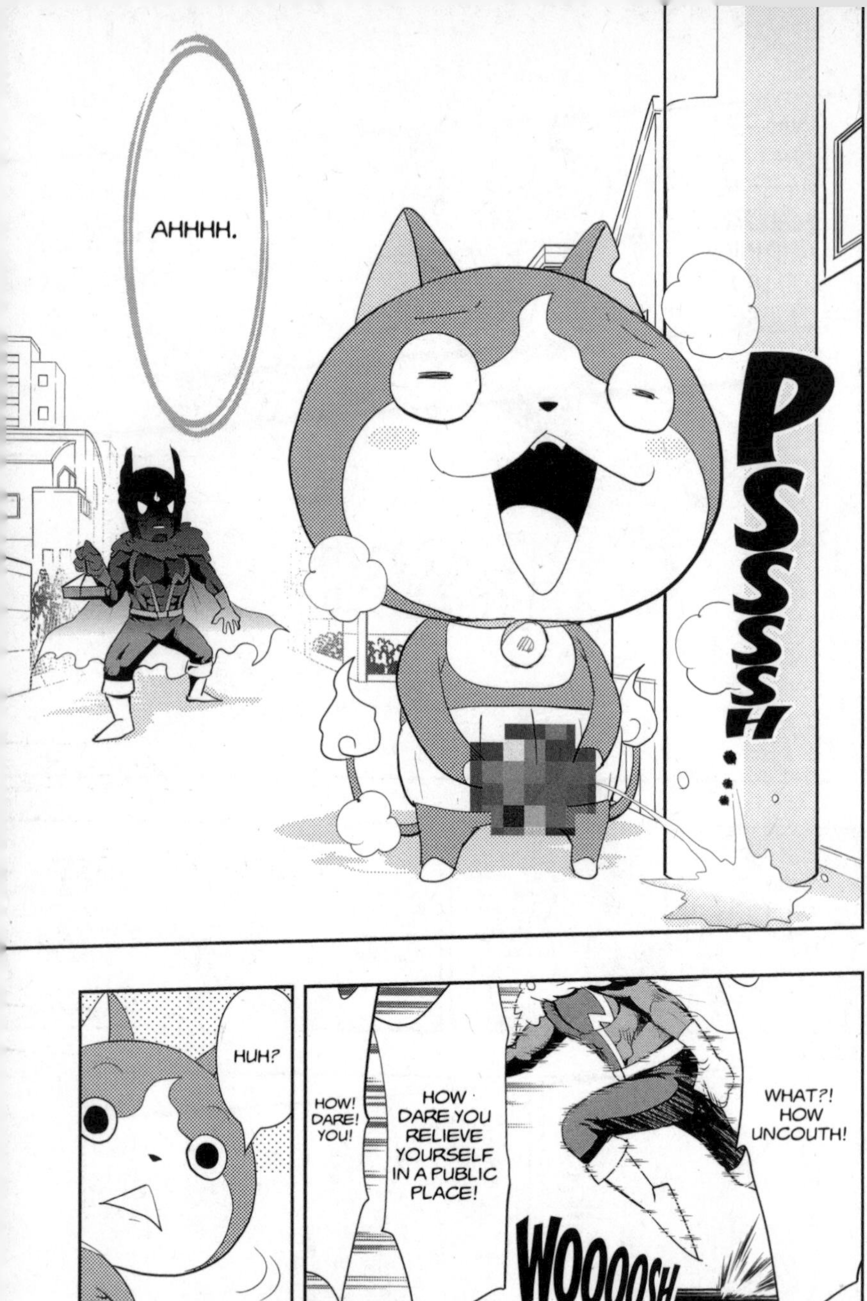
AHHHH.
PSSSSH...
WHAT?! HOW UNCOUTH!
HOW DARE YOU RELIEVE YOURSELF IN A PUBLIC PLACE!
HOW! DARE! YOU!
WOOOOSH
HUH?

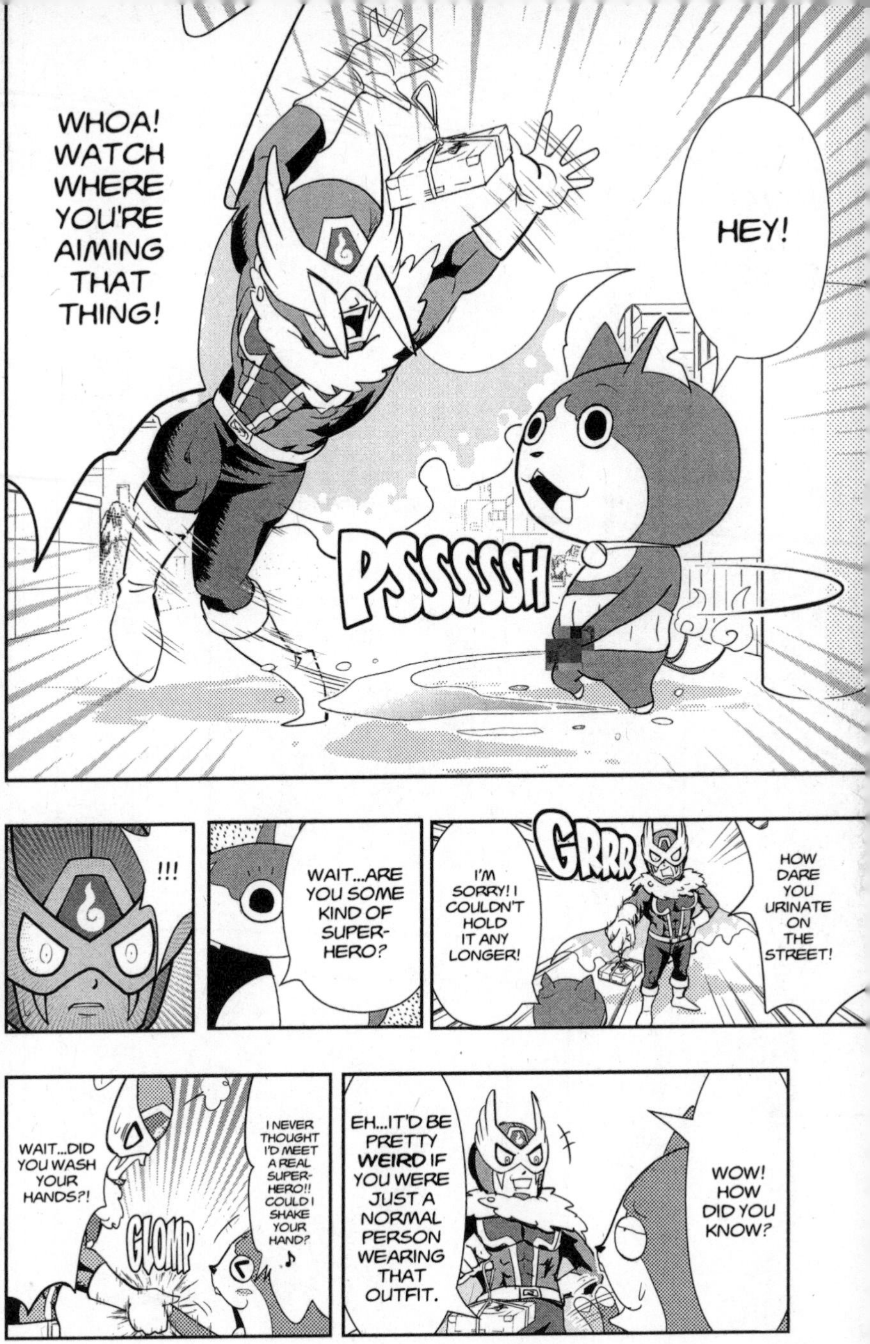
HEY!
WHOA! WATCH WHERE YOU'RE AIMING THAT THING!
PSSSSSH
HOW DARE YOU URINATE ON THE STREET!
GRRR
I'M SORRY! I COULDN'T HOLD IT ANY LONGER!
WAIT...ARE YOU SOME KIND OF SUPER-HERO?
!!!
WOW! HOW DID YOU KNOW?
EH...IT'D BE PRETTY **WEIRD** IF YOU WERE JUST A NORMAL PERSON WEARING THAT OUTFIT.
I NEVER THOUGHT I'D MEET A REAL SUPER-HERO!! COULD I SHAKE YOUR HAND? ♪
GLOMP
WAIT...DID YOU WASH YOUR HANDS?!

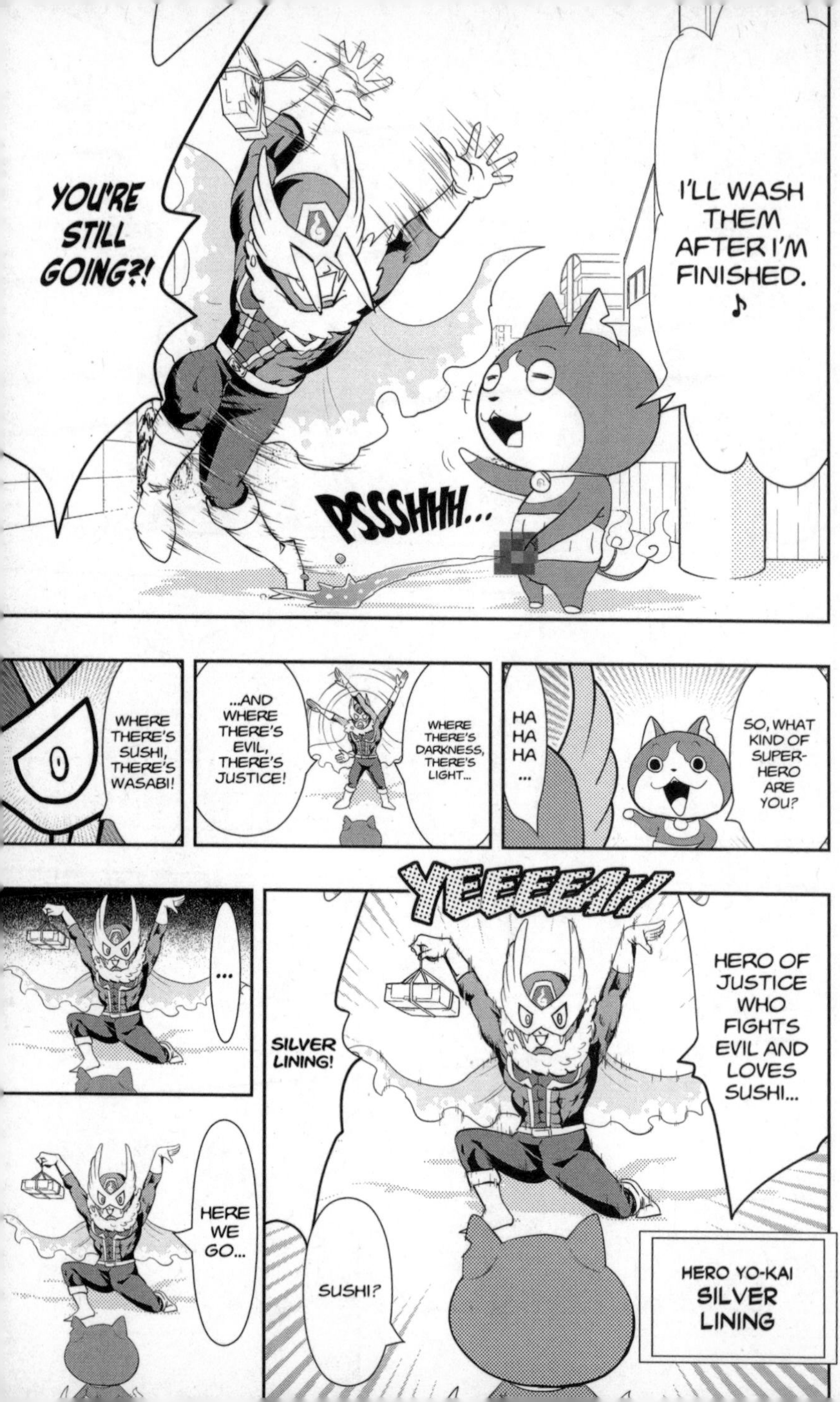
I'LL WASH THEM AFTER I'M FINISHED. ♪
YOU'RE STILL GOING?!
PSSSHHH...
SO, WHAT KIND OF SUPER-HERO ARE YOU?
HA HA HA ...
WHERE THERE'S DARKNESS, THERE'S LIGHT...
...AND WHERE THERE'S EVIL, THERE'S JUSTICE!
WHERE THERE'S SUSHI, THERE'S WASABI!
YEEEEAH!
HERO OF JUSTICE WHO FIGHTS EVIL AND LOVES SUSHI...
SILVER LINING!
HERO YO-KAI SILVER LINING
SUSHI?
...
HERE WE GO...

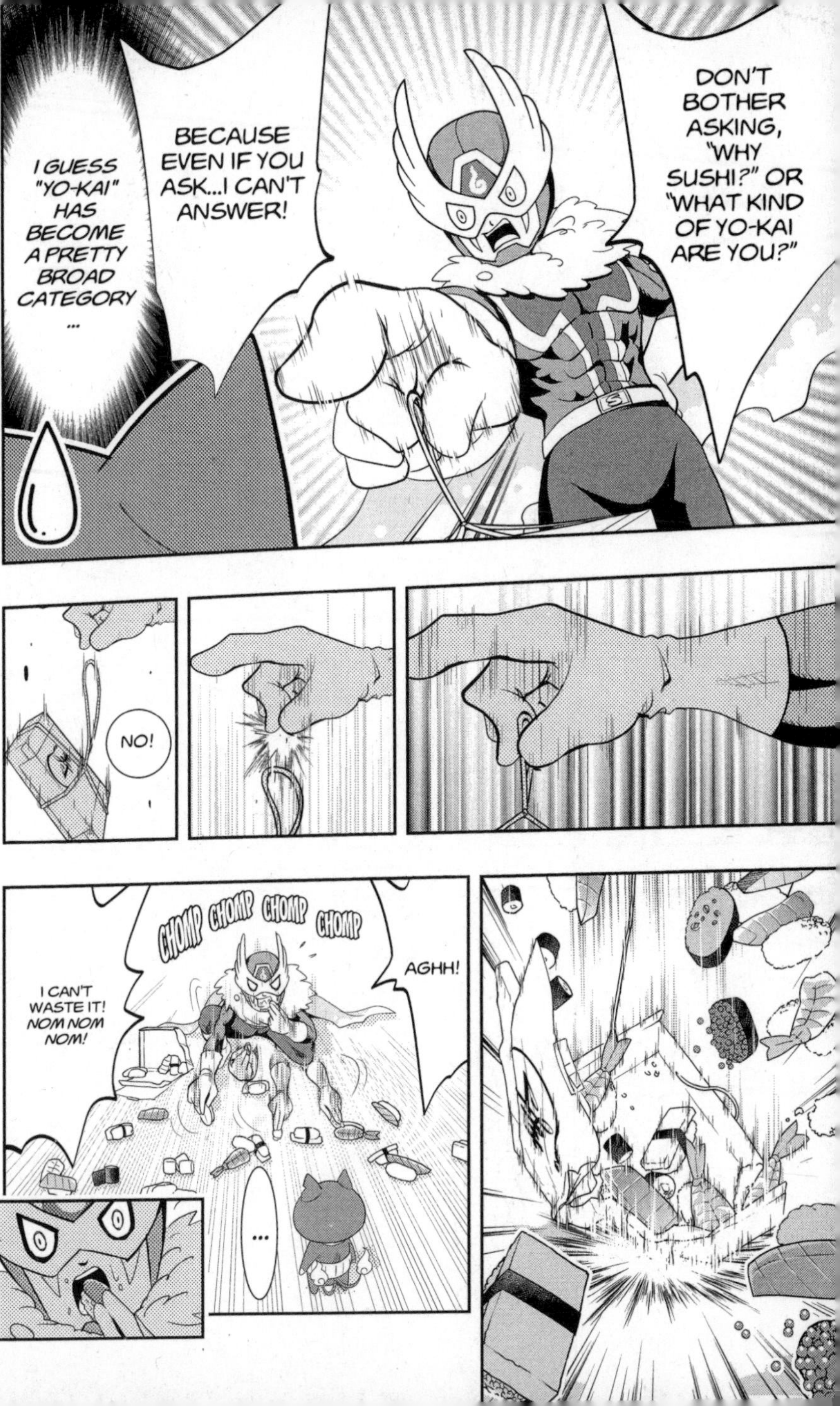
DON'T BOTHER ASKING, "WHY SUSHI?" OR "WHAT KIND OF YO-KAI ARE YOU?"
BECAUSE EVEN IF YOU ASK...I CAN'T ANSWER!
I GUESS "YO-KAI" HAS BECOME A PRETTY BROAD CATEGORY ...
NO!
AGHH!
CHOMP CHOMP CHOMP CHOMP
I CAN'T WASTE IT! NOM NOM NOM!
...

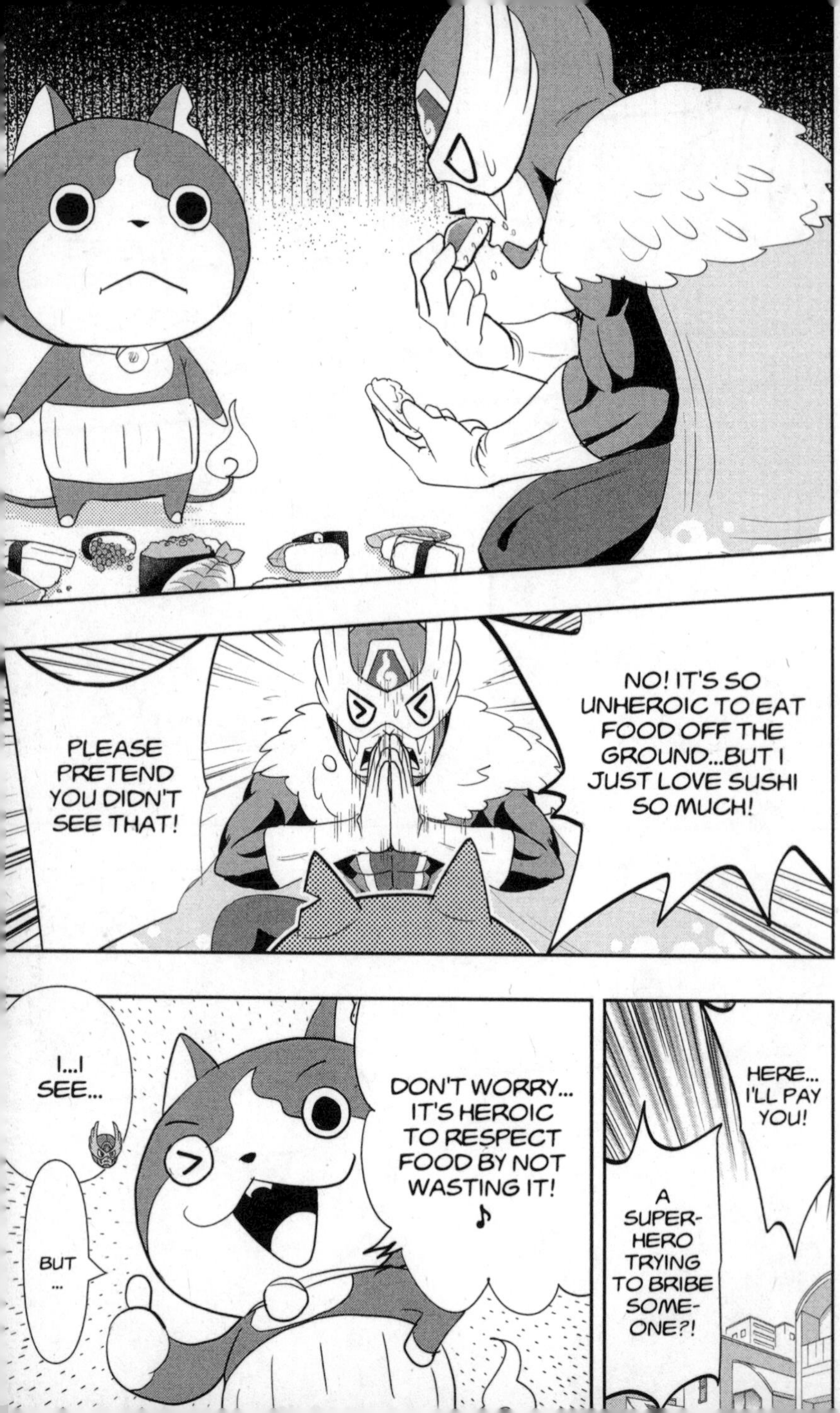
NO! IT'S SO UNHEROIC TO EAT FOOD OFF THE GROUND...BUT I JUST LOVE SUSHI SO MUCH!
PLEASE PRETEND YOU DIDN'T SEE THAT!
HERE... I'LL PAY YOU!
A SUPER-HERO TRYING TO BRIBE SOME-ONE?!
DON'T WORRY... IT'S HEROIC TO RESPECT FOOD BY NOT WASTING IT! ♪
I...I SEE...
BUT ...

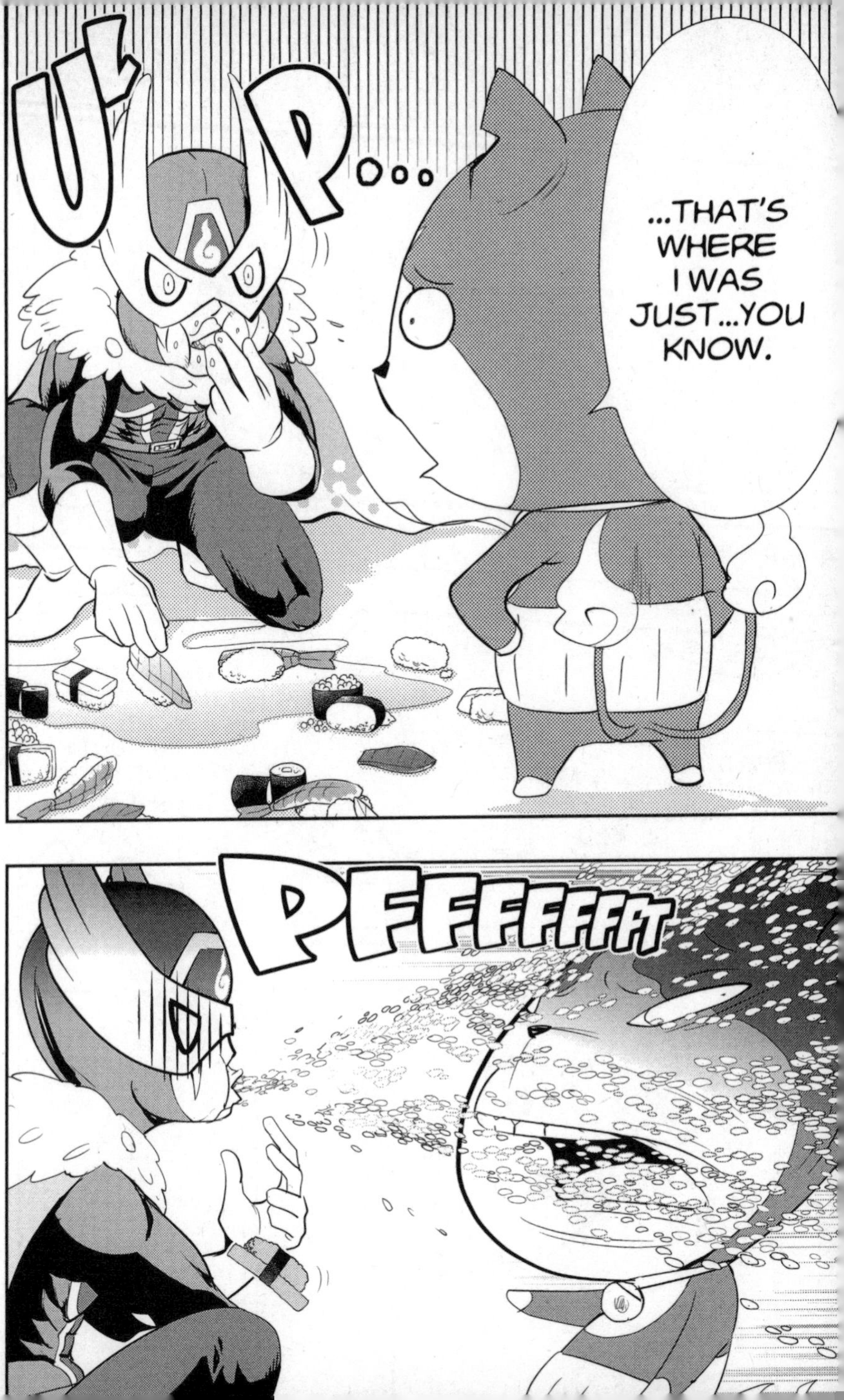
...THAT'S WHERE I WAS JUST...YOU KNOW.
ULP...
PFFFFFFFT

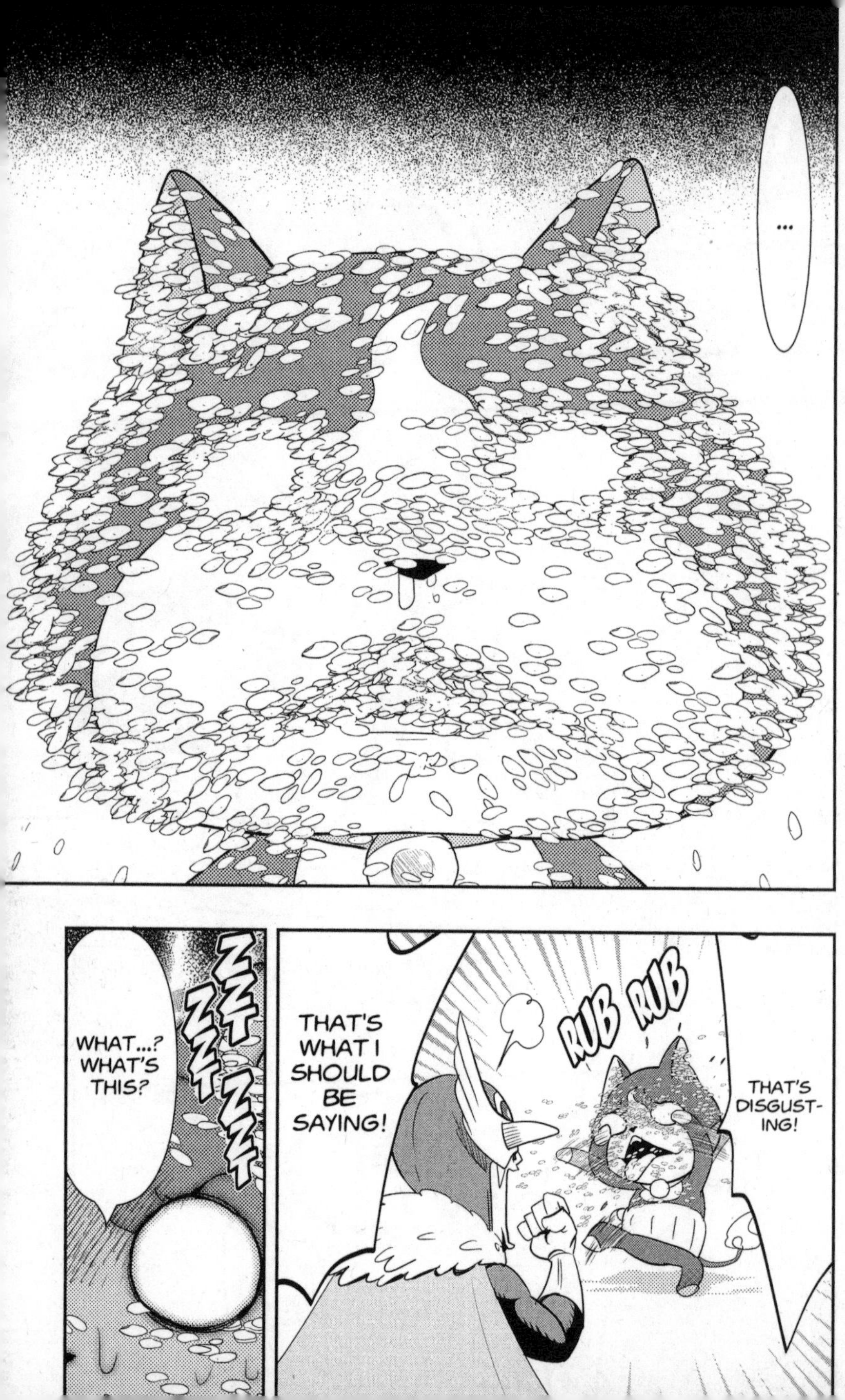
...
RUB RUB
THAT'S DISGUSTING!
THAT'S WHAT I SHOULD BE SAYING!
ZZZT ZZZT ZZZT
WHAT...? WHAT'S THIS?

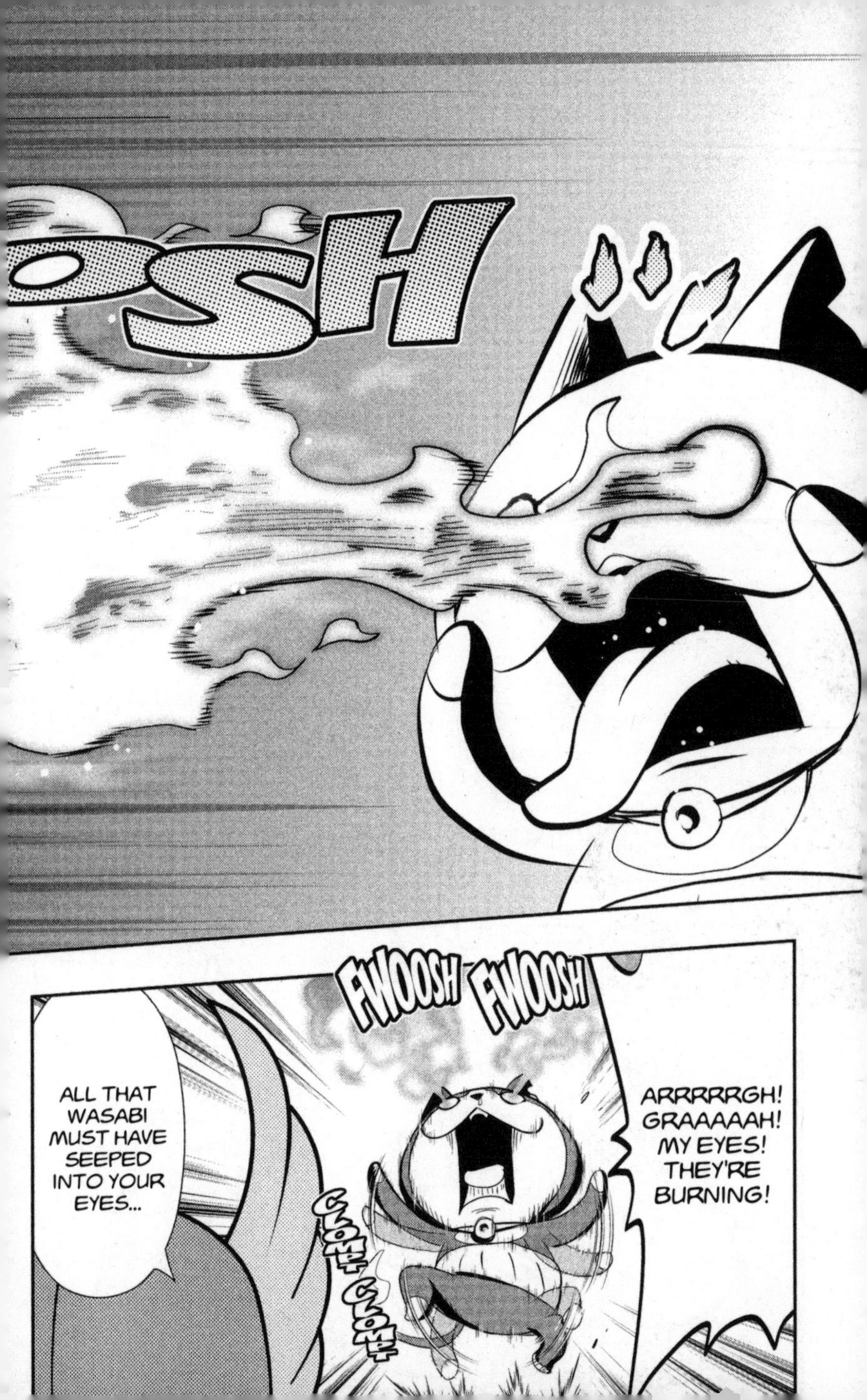
OSH
FWOOSH FWOOSH
ARRRRRGH! GRAAAAAH! MY EYES! THEY'RE BURNING!
CLOMP CLOMP
ALL THAT WASABI MUST HAVE SEEPED INTO YOUR EYES...

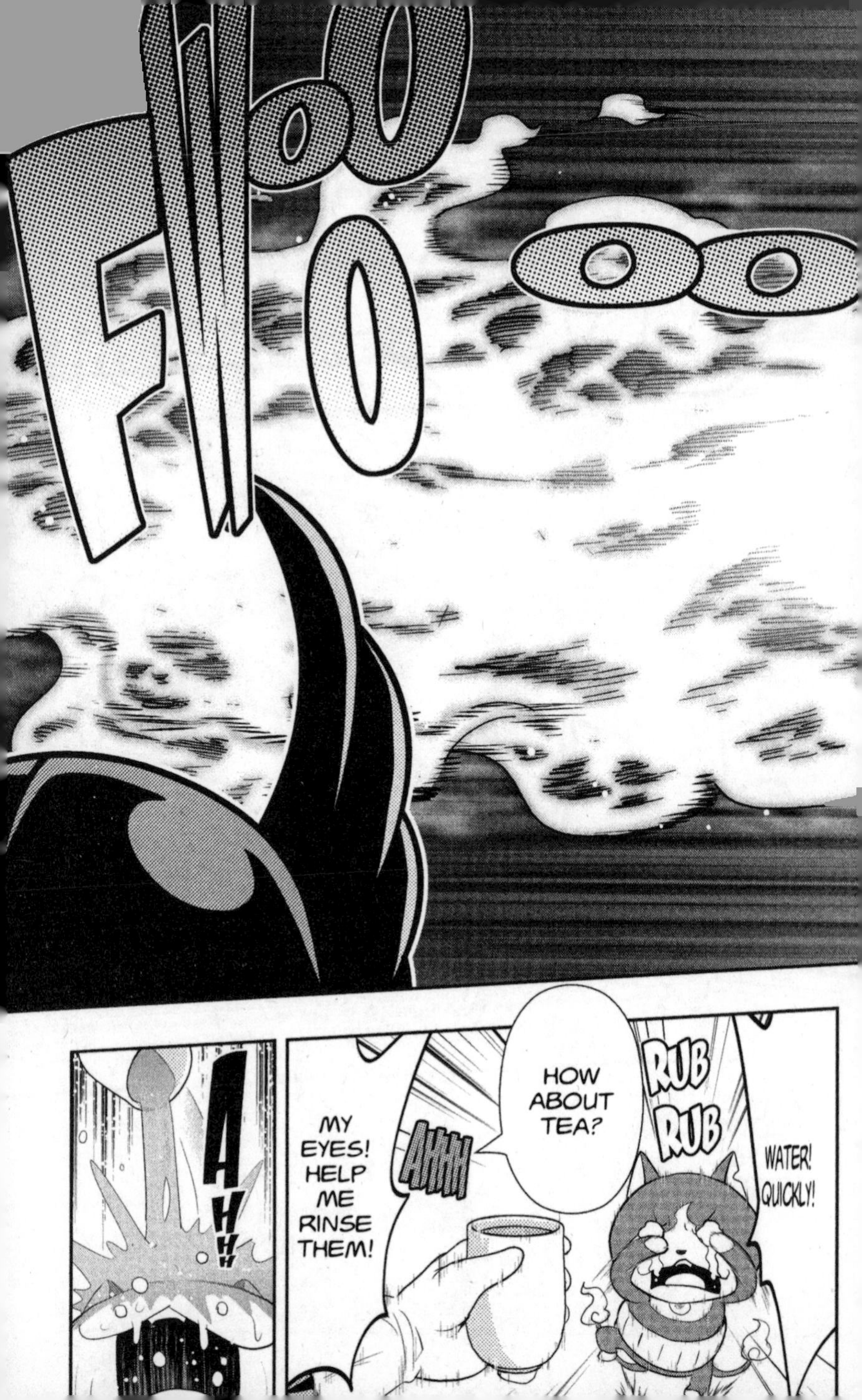
FWOO
OOO
RUB RUB
WATER! QUICKLY!
HOW ABOUT TEA?
AHHH
MY EYES! HELP ME RINSE THEM!
AHHH!!

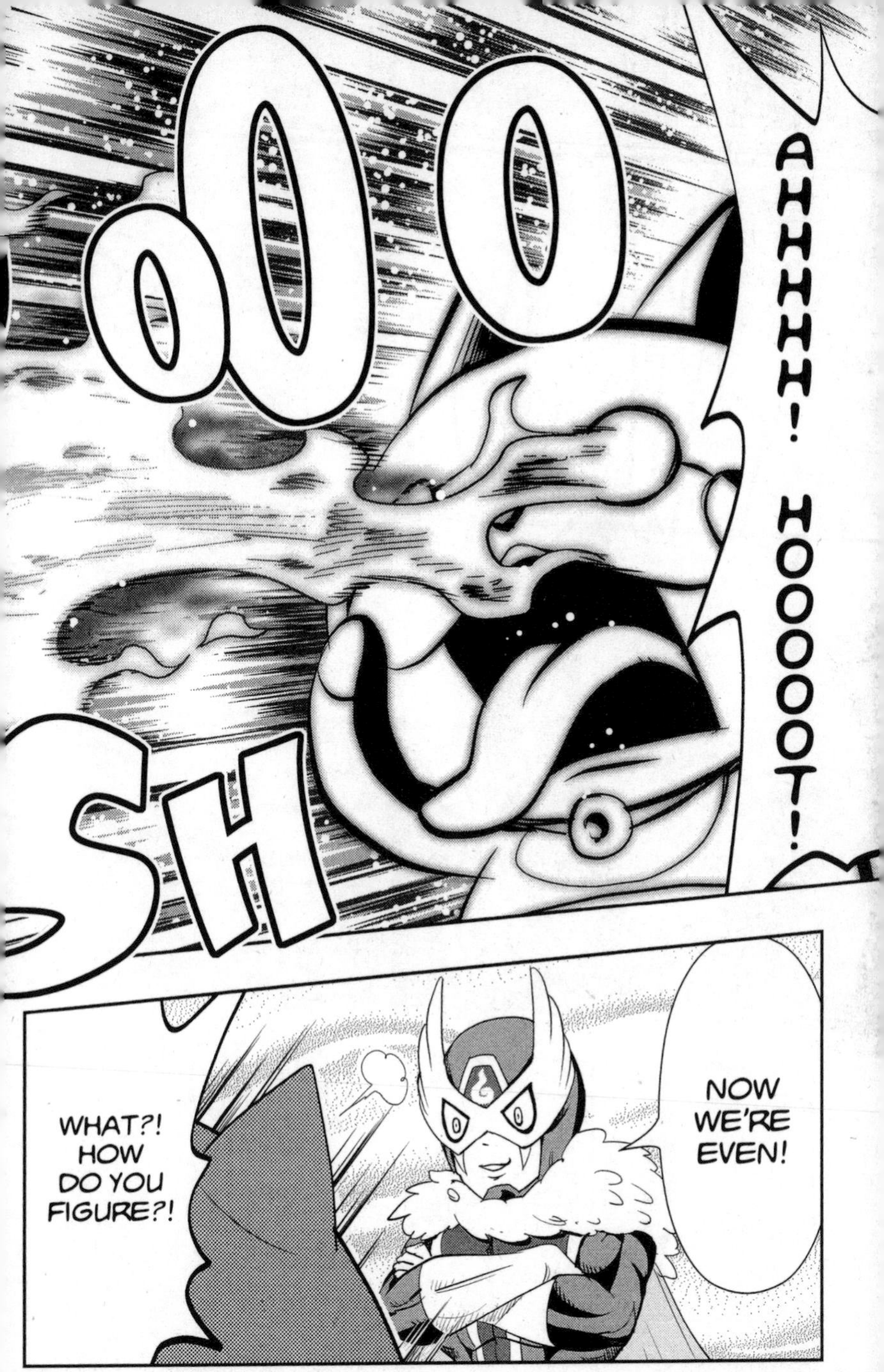
AHHHHH! HOOOOOT!
SHOOO
NOW WE'RE EVEN!
WHAT?! HOW DO YOU FIGURE?!

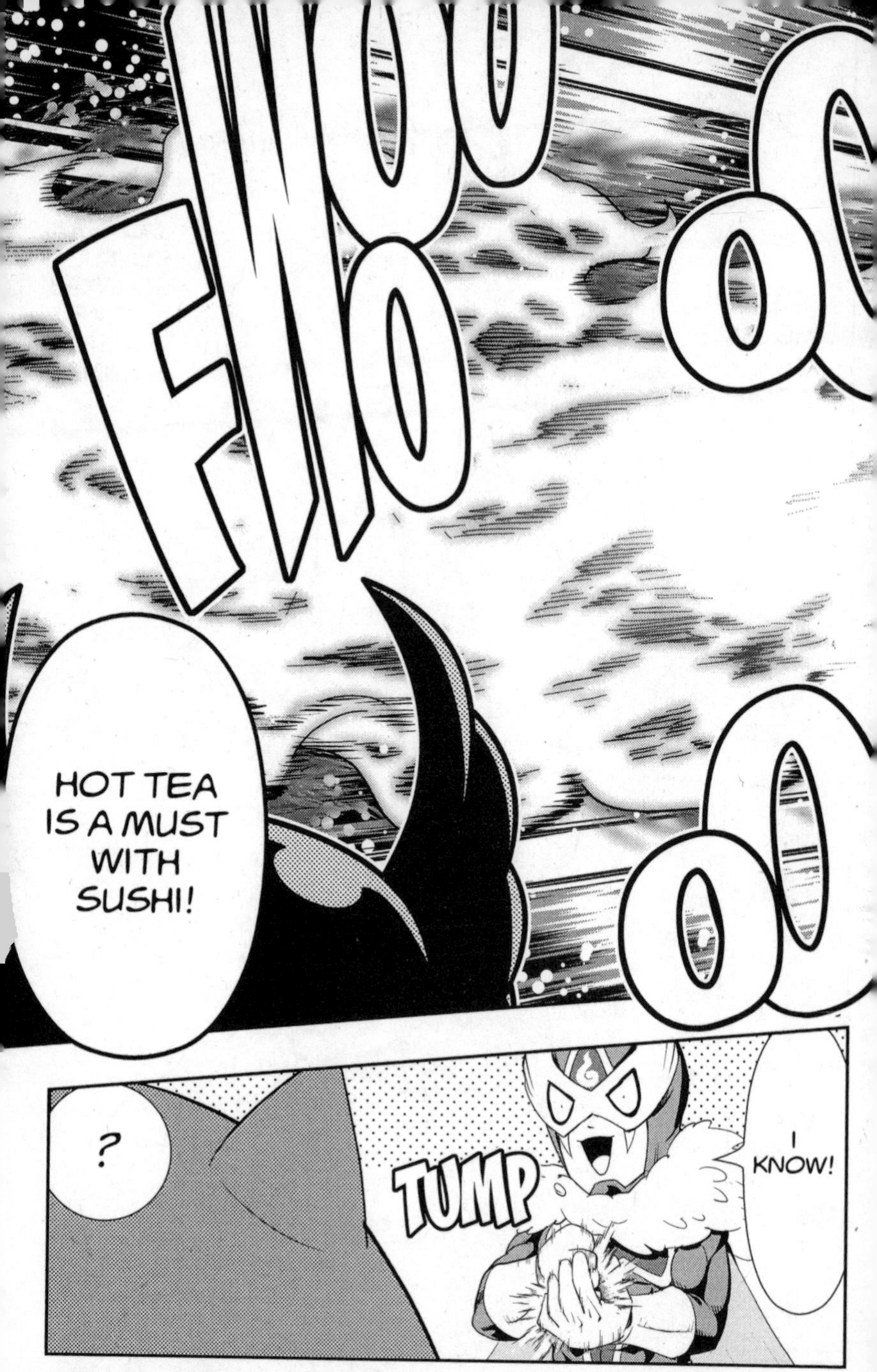
FWOOOOOO
HOT TEA IS A MUST WITH SUSHI!
I KNOW!
TUMP
?

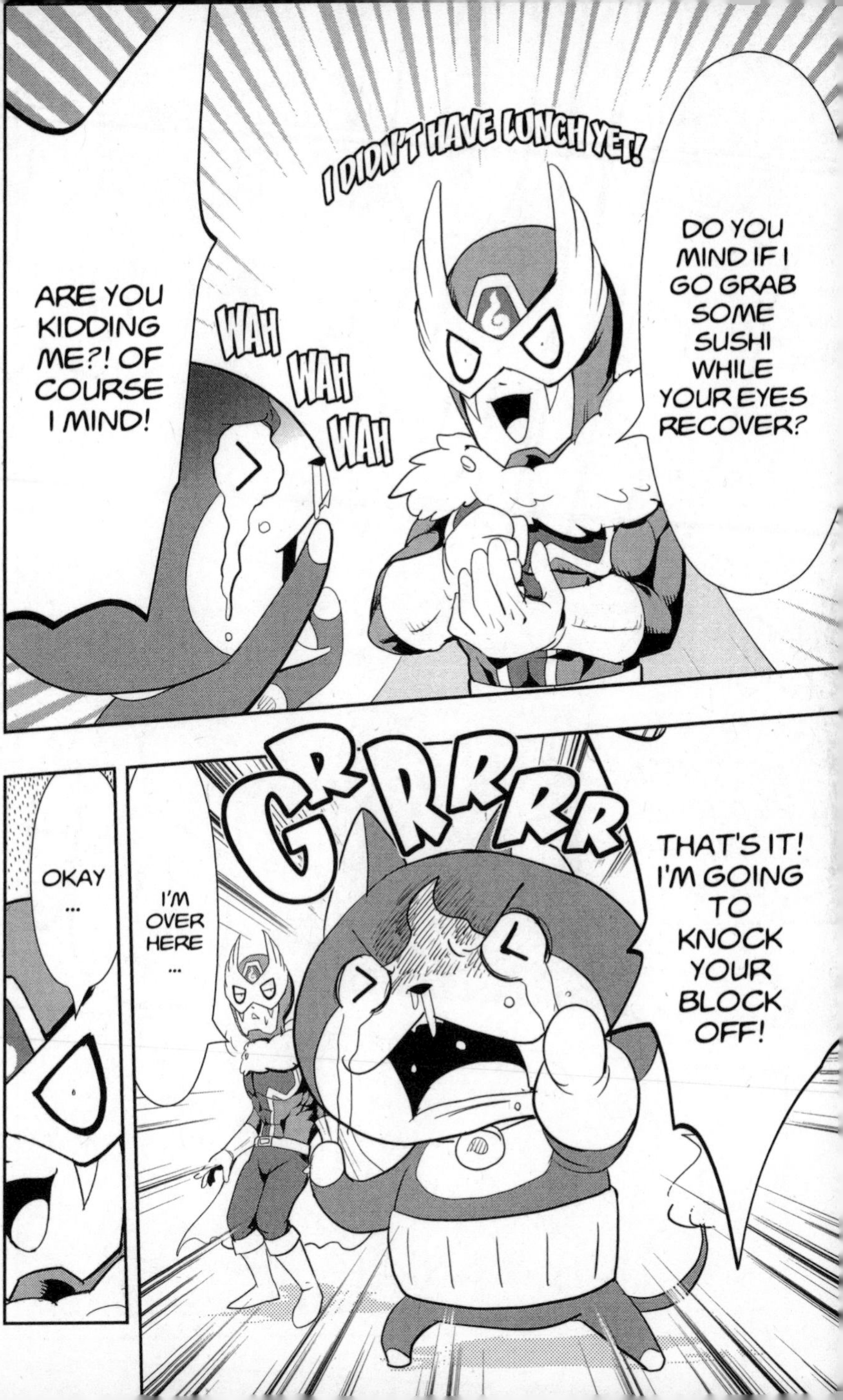
DO YOU MIND IF I GO GRAB SOME SUSHI WHILE YOUR EYES RECOVER?
I DIDN'T HAVE LUNCH YET!
WAH WAH WAH
ARE YOU KIDDING ME?! OF COURSE I MIND!
GRRRRR
THAT'S IT! I'M GOING TO KNOCK YOUR BLOCK OFF!
I'M OVER HERE ...
OKAY ...

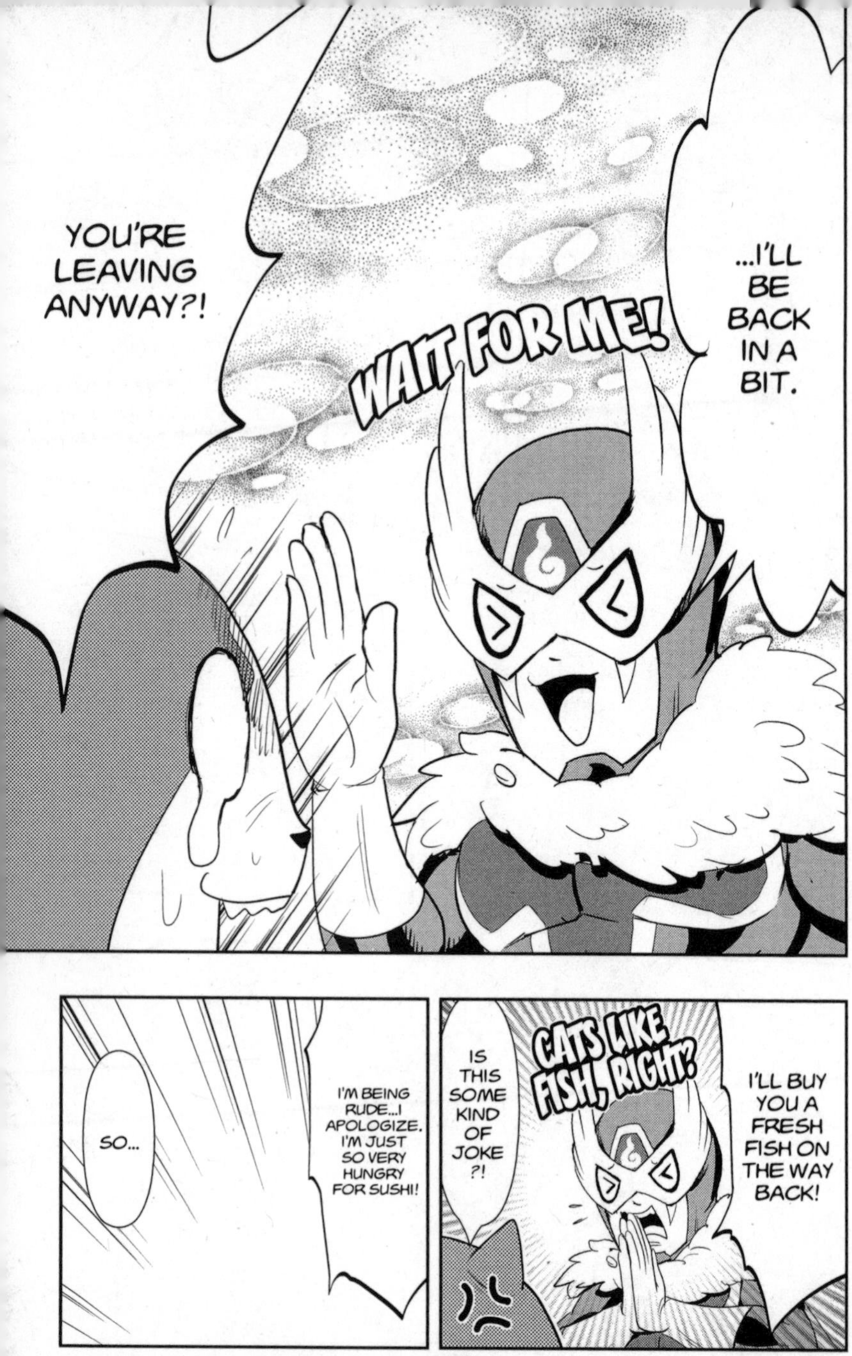
...I'LL BE BACK IN A BIT.
WAIT FOR ME!
YOU'RE LEAVING ANYWAY?!
I'LL BUY YOU A FRESH FISH ON THE WAY BACK!
CATS LIKE FISH, RIGHT?
IS THIS SOME KIND OF JOKE?!
I'M BEING RUDE...I APOLOGIZE. I'M JUST SO VERY HUNGRY FOR SUSHI!
SO...

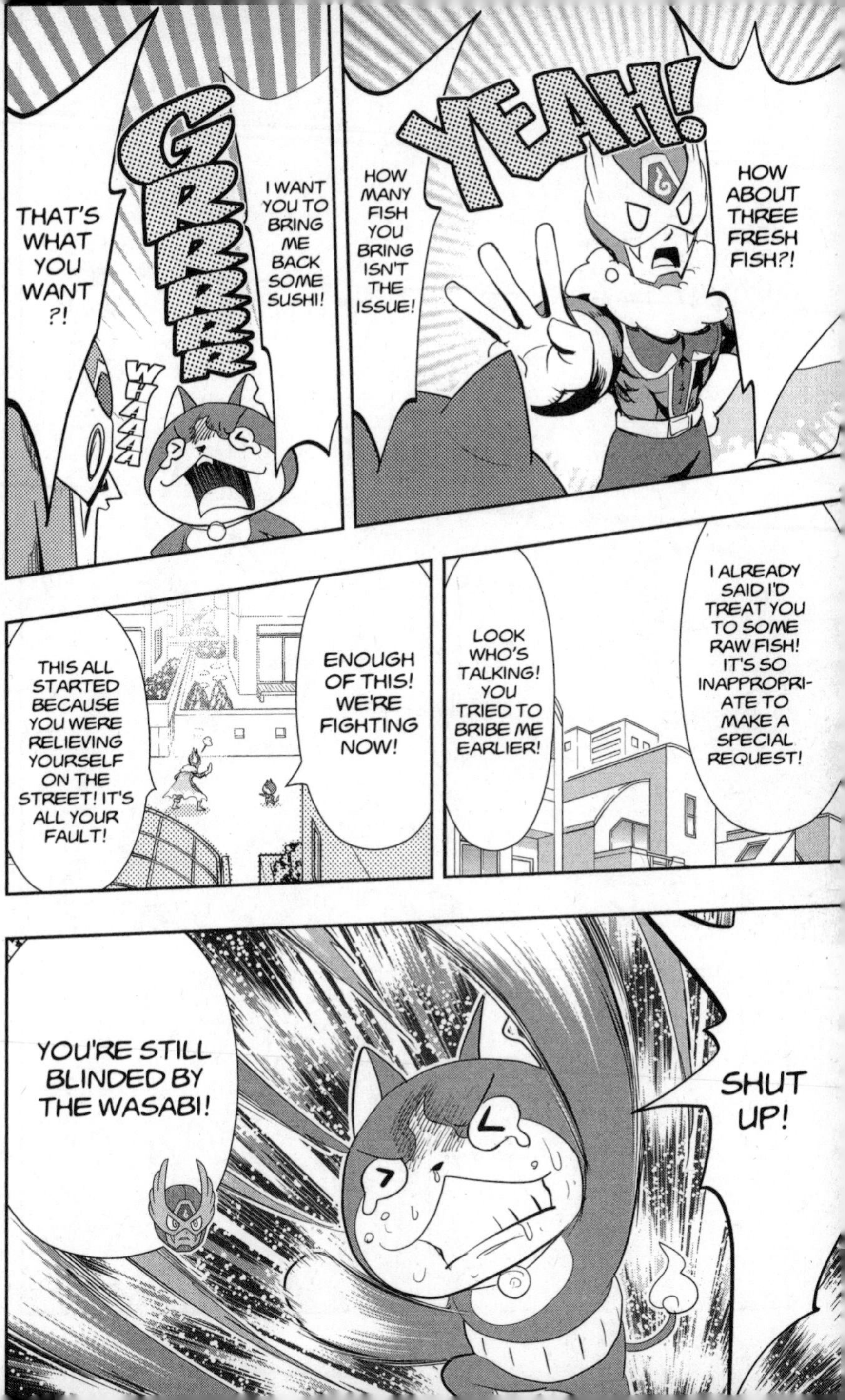
YEAH!
HOW ABOUT THREE FRESH FISH?!
HOW MANY FISH YOU BRING ISN'T THE ISSUE!
I WANT YOU TO BRING ME BACK SOME SUSHI!
GRRRRR
THAT'S WHAT YOU WANT?!
WHAAAA
I ALREADY SAID I'D TREAT YOU TO SOME RAW FISH! IT'S SO INAPPROPRI-ATE TO MAKE A SPECIAL REQUEST!
LOOK WHO'S TALKING! YOU TRIED TO BRIBE ME EARLIER!
ENOUGH OF THIS! WE'RE FIGHTING NOW!
THIS ALL STARTED BECAUSE YOU WERE RELIEVING YOURSELF ON THE STREET! IT'S ALL YOUR FAULT!
SHUT UP!
YOU'RE STILL BLINDED BY THE WASABI!

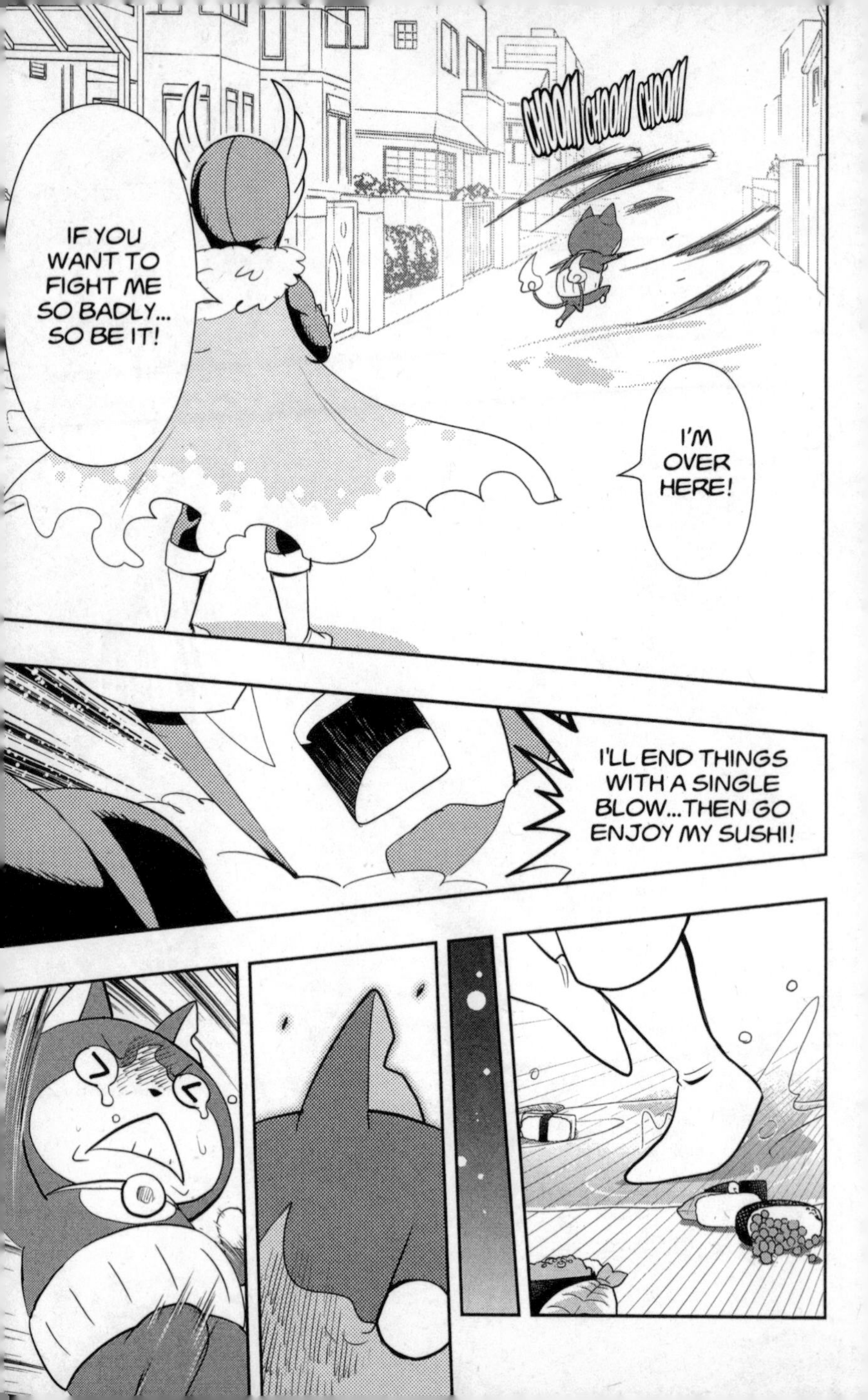
CHOOM CHOOM CHOOM
IF YOU WANT TO FIGHT ME SO BADLY... SO BE IT!
I'M OVER HERE!
I'LL END THINGS WITH A SINGLE BLOW...THEN GO ENJOY MY SUSHI!

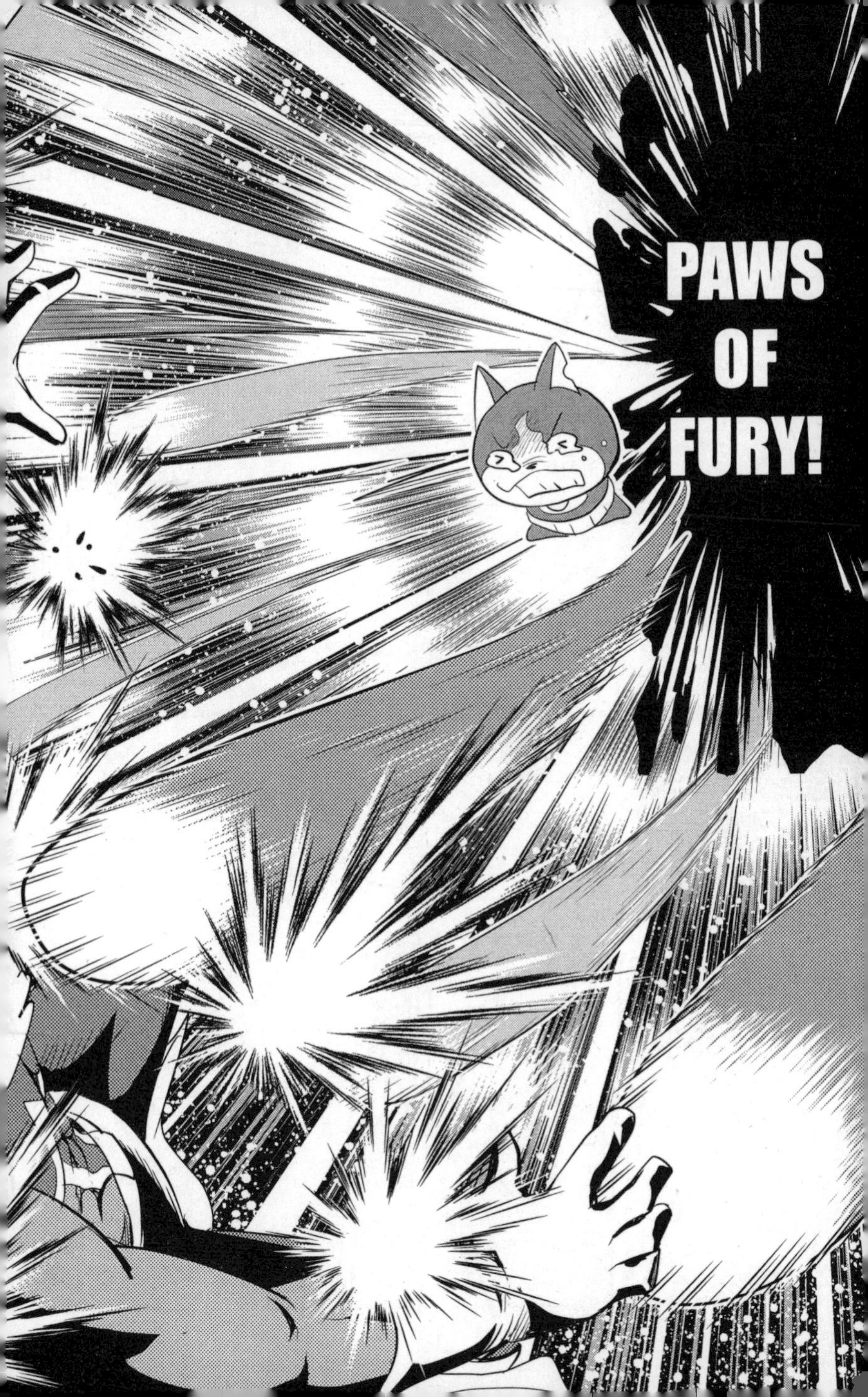
PAWS OF FURY!

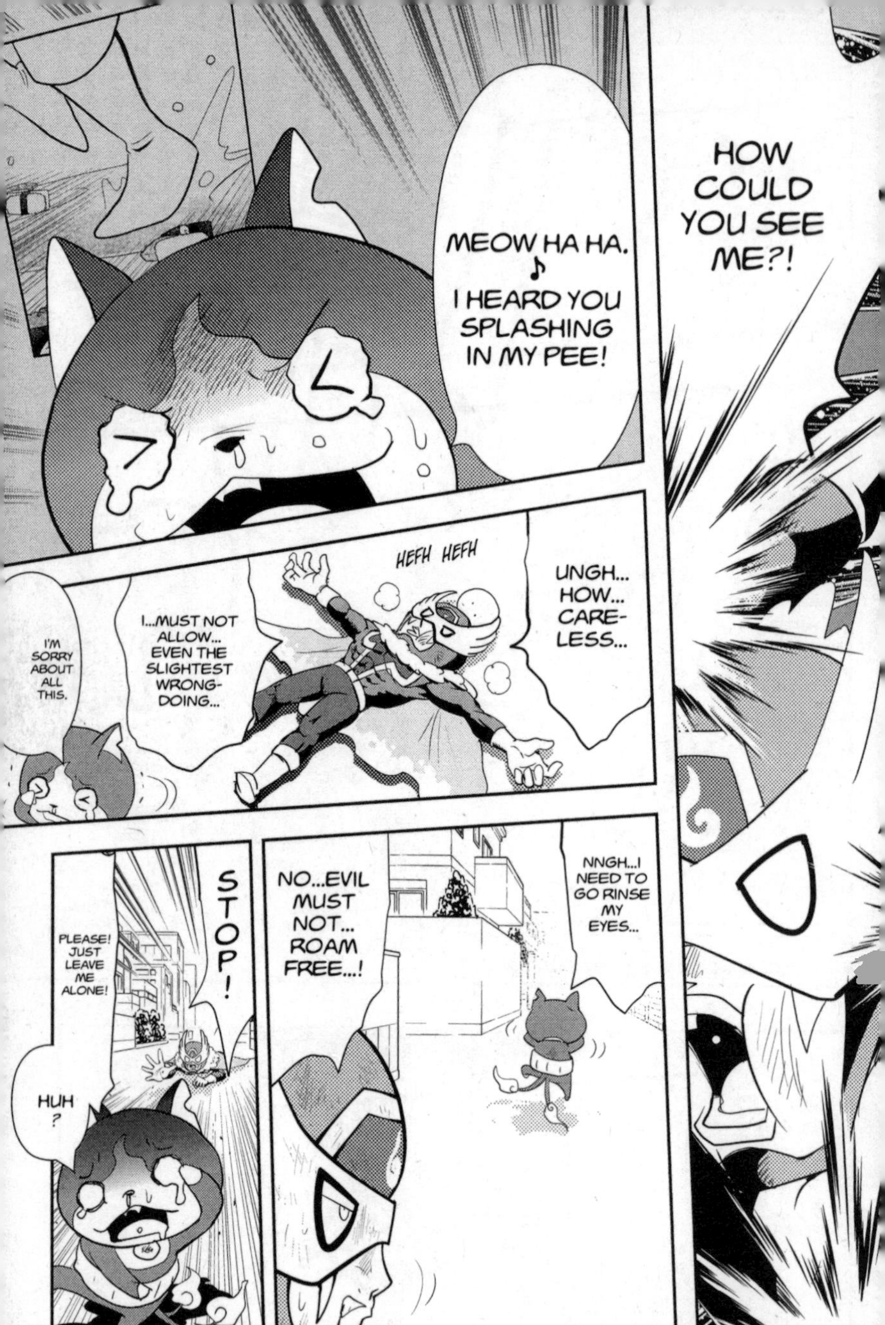
HOW COULD YOU SEE ME?!
MEOW HA HA. ♪ I HEARD YOU SPLASHING IN MY PEE!
UNGH... HOW... CARE-LESS...
HEFH HEFH
I...MUST NOT ALLOW... EVEN THE SLIGHTEST WRONG-DOING...
I'M SORRY ABOUT ALL THIS.
NNGH...I NEED TO GO RINSE MY EYES...
NO...EVIL MUST NOT... ROAM FREE...!
STOP!
PLEASE! JUST LEAVE ME ALONE!
HUH?

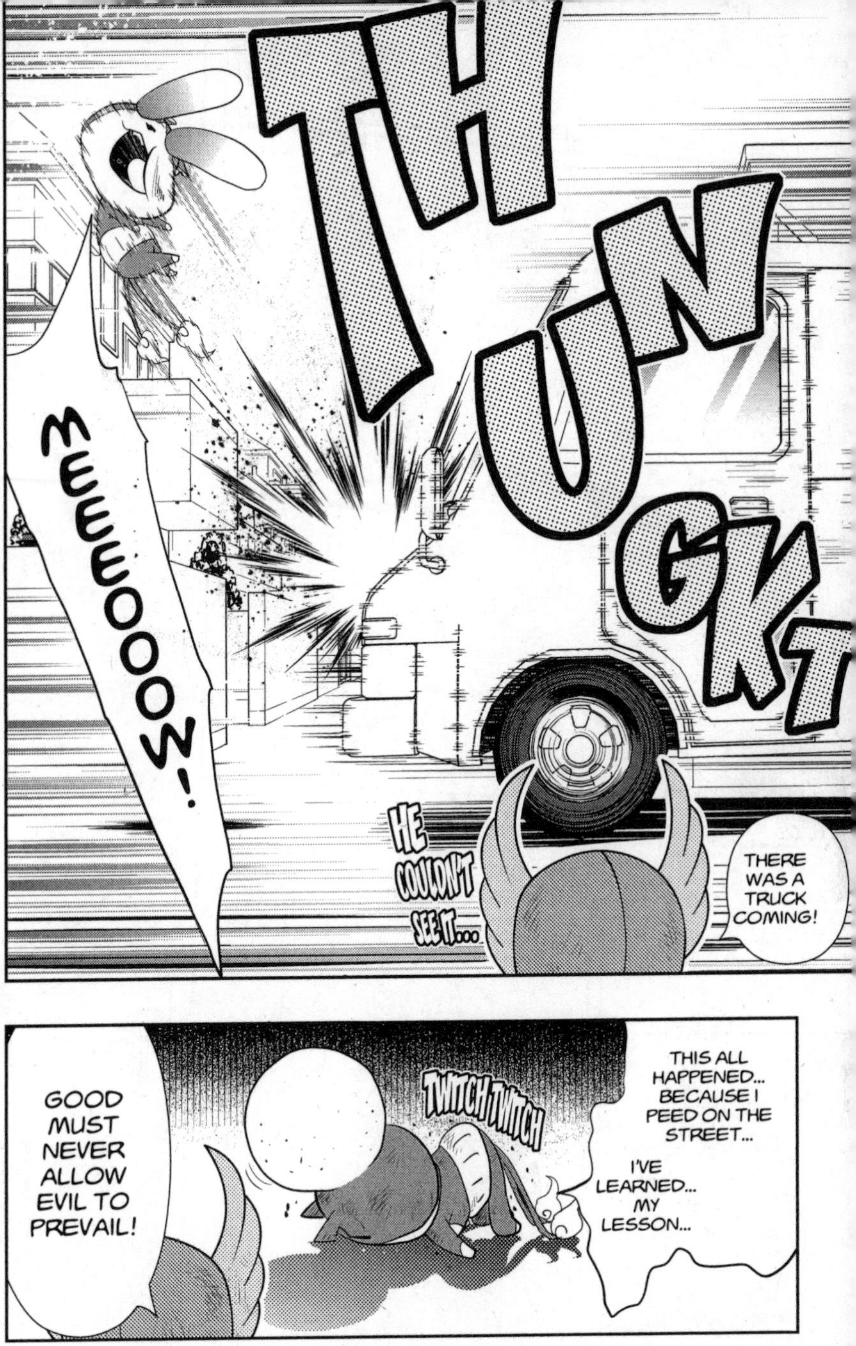
THUNGKT
MEEEOOOW!
THERE WAS A TRUCK COMING!
HE COULDN'T SEE IT...
THIS ALL HAPPENED... BECAUSE I PEED ON THE STREET...
I'VE LEARNED... MY LESSON...
TWITCH TWITCH
GOOD MUST NEVER ALLOW EVIL TO PREVAIL!

CHAPTER 134: IDLE YO-KAI IMAGENIUS

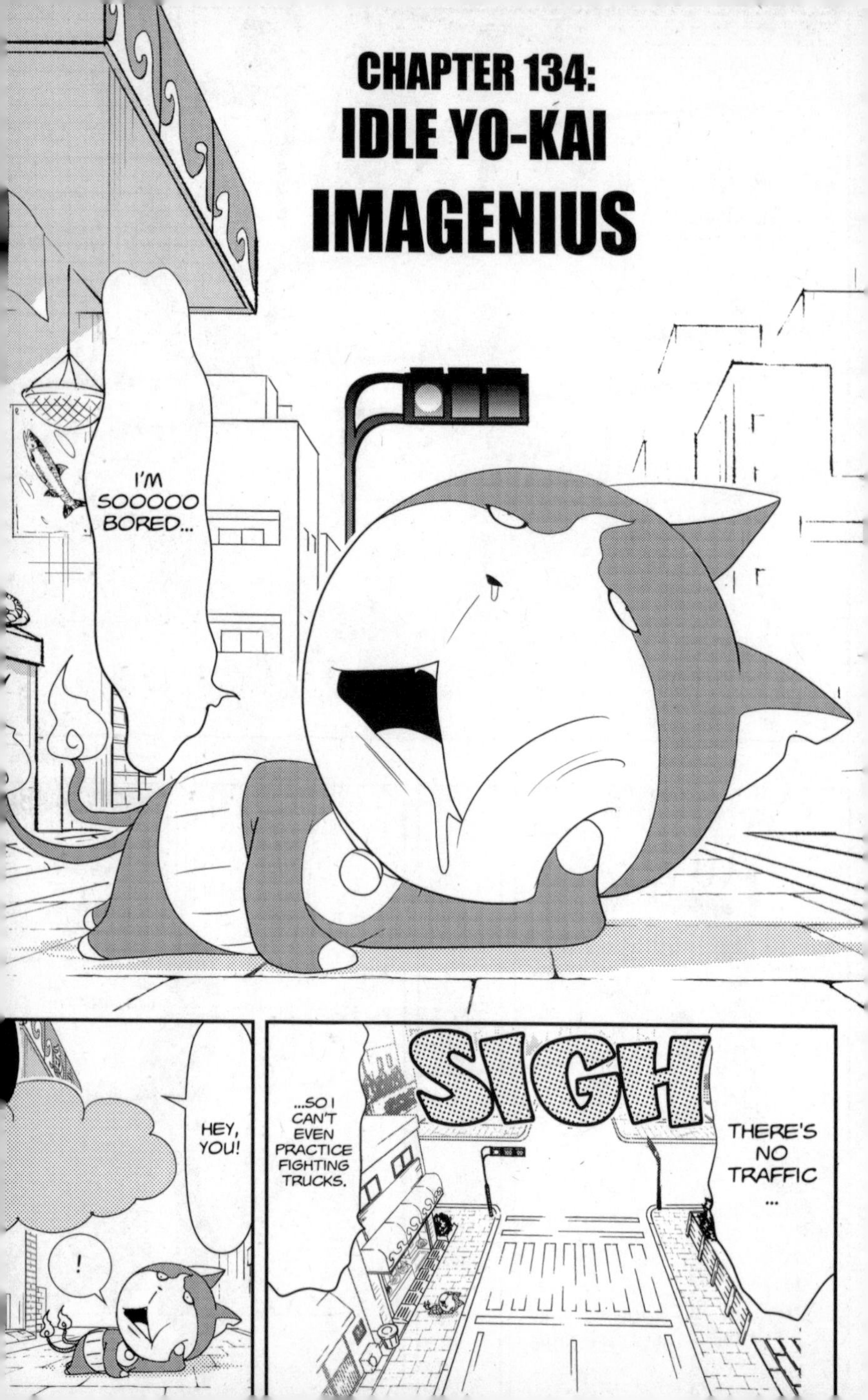
I'M SOOOOO BORED...
THERE'S NO TRAFFIC ...
SIGH
...SO I CAN'T EVEN PRACTICE FIGHTING TRUCKS.
HEY, YOU!
!

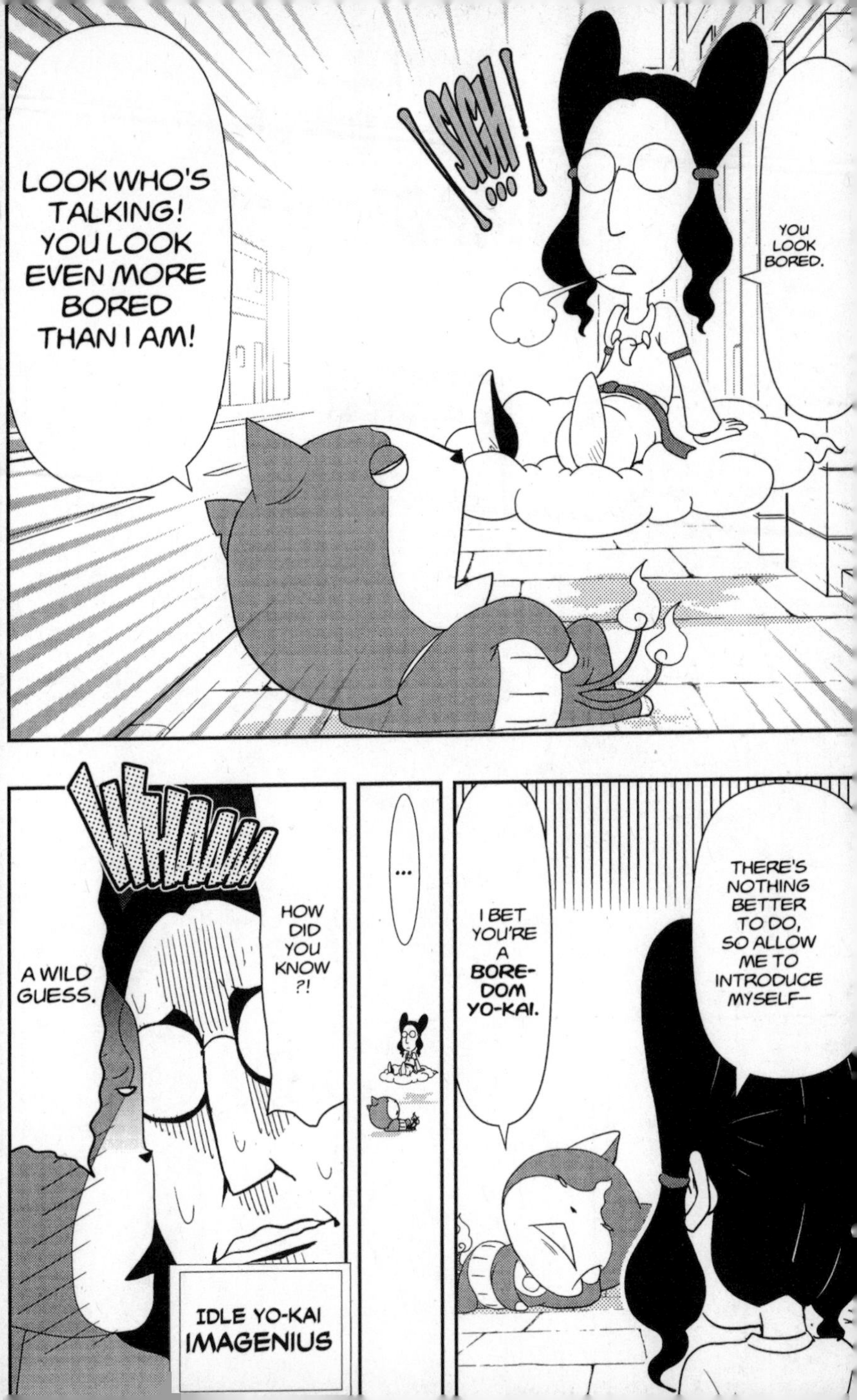
YOU LOOK BORED.
SIGH...
LOOK WHO'S TALKING! YOU LOOK EVEN MORE BORED THAN I AM!
THERE'S NOTHING BETTER TO DO, SO ALLOW ME TO INTRODUCE MYSELF—
I BET YOU'RE A BORE-DOM YO-KAI.
...
WHAAA
HOW DID YOU KNOW?!
A WILD GUESS.
IDLE YO-KAI IMAGENIUS

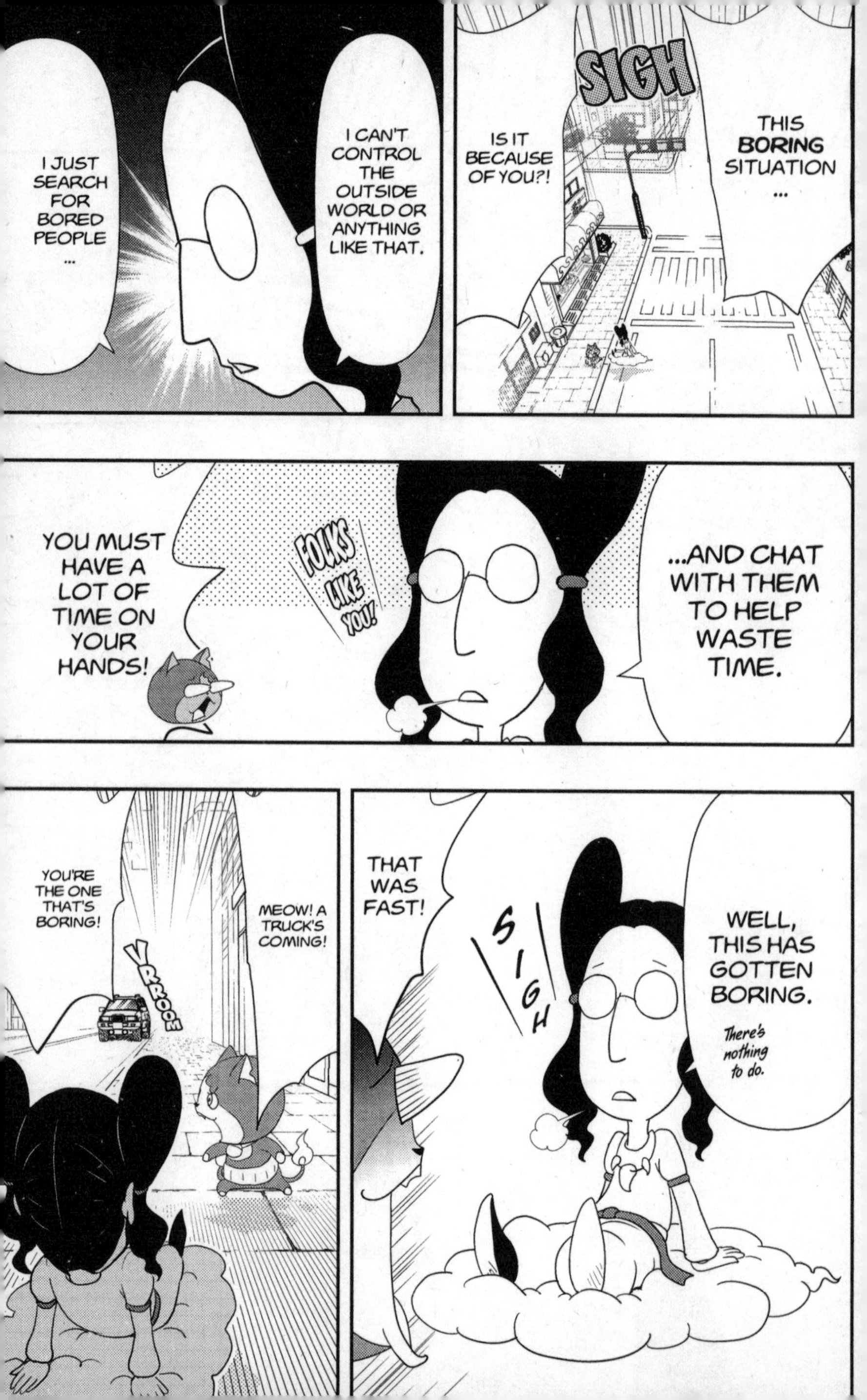
SIGH
THIS BORING SITUATION ...
IS IT BECAUSE OF YOU?!
I CAN'T CONTROL THE OUTSIDE WORLD OR ANYTHING LIKE THAT.
I JUST SEARCH FOR BORED PEOPLE ...
...AND CHAT WITH THEM TO HELP WASTE TIME.
FOLKS LIKE YOU!
YOU MUST HAVE A LOT OF TIME ON YOUR HANDS!
WELL, THIS HAS GOTTEN BORING.
There's nothing to do.
SIGH
THAT WAS FAST!
MEOW! A TRUCK'S COMING!
VRROOM
YOU'RE THE ONE THAT'S BORING!

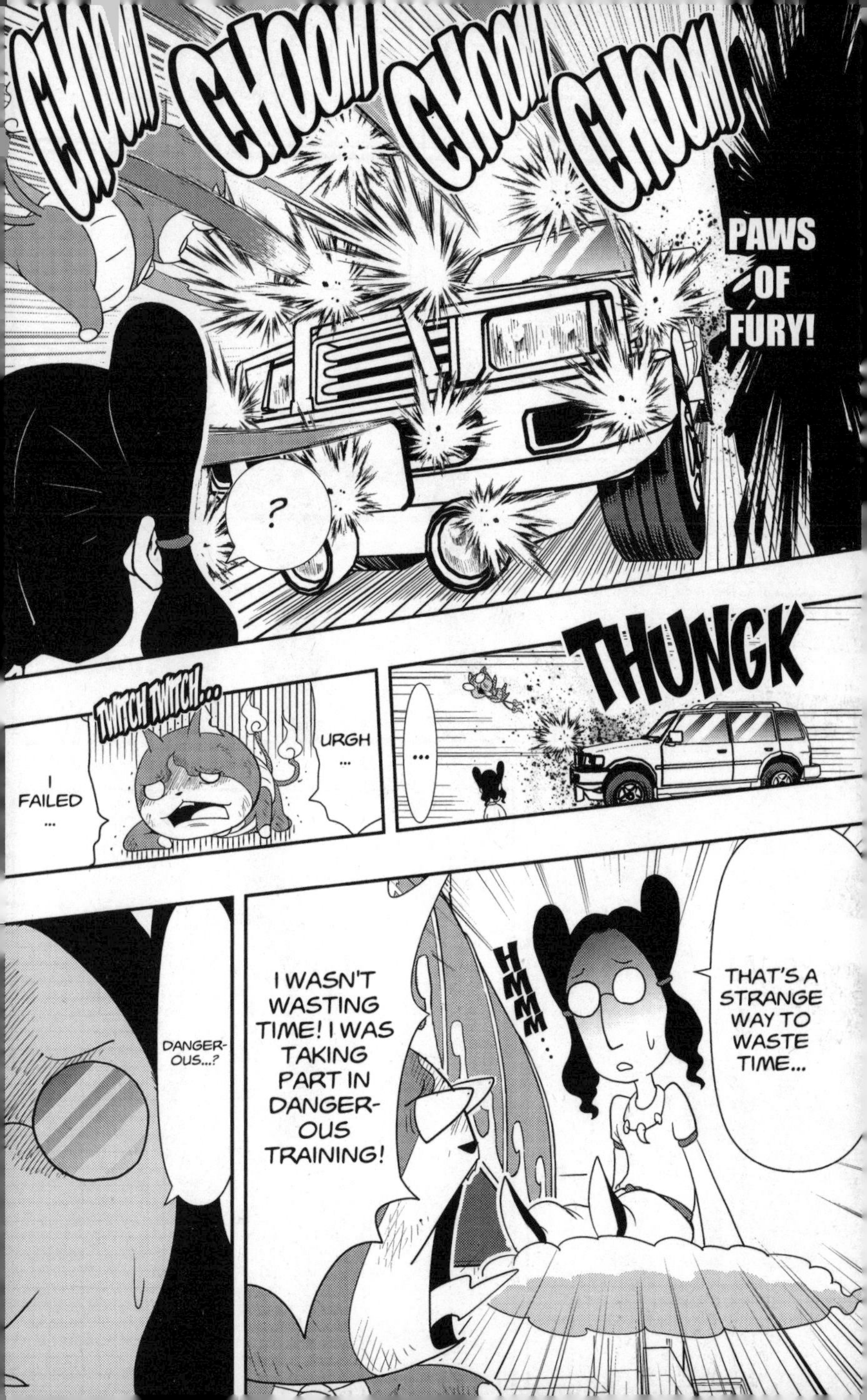
CHOOM CHOOM CHOOM CHOOM
PAWS OF FURY!
?
THUNGK
...
TWITCH TWITCH...
URGH ...
I FAILED ...
THAT'S A STRANGE WAY TO WASTE TIME...
HMMM...
I WASN'T WASTING TIME! I WAS TAKING PART IN DANGEROUS TRAINING!
DANGEROUS...?

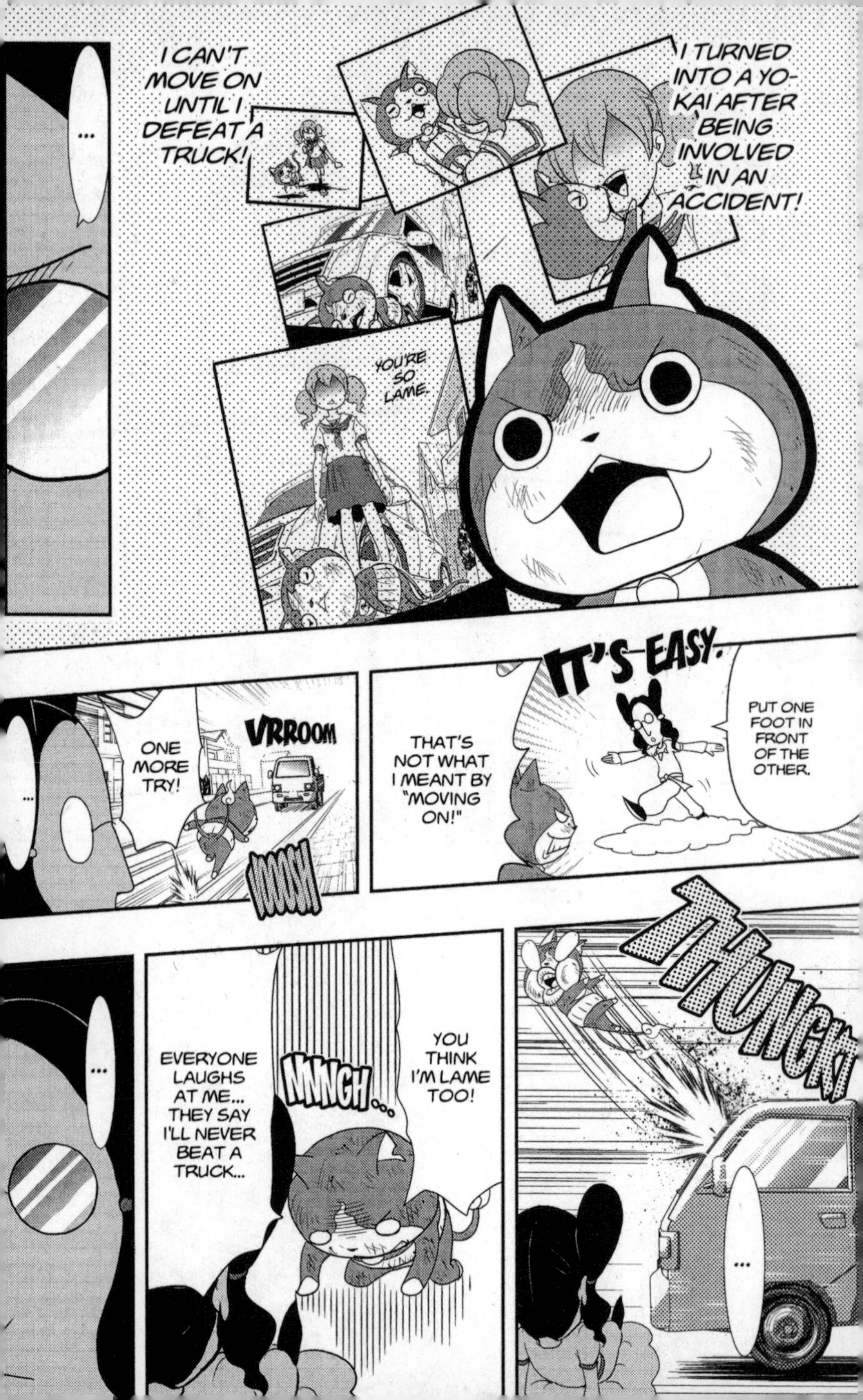
I TURNED INTO A YO-KAI AFTER BEING INVOLVED IN AN ACCIDENT!
I CAN'T MOVE ON UNTIL I DEFEAT A TRUCK!
YOU'RE SO LAME.
...
IT'S EASY.
PUT ONE FOOT IN FRONT OF THE OTHER.
THAT'S NOT WHAT I MEANT BY "MOVING ON!"
VRROOM
ONE MORE TRY!
VOOOSH
...
THUNGK!
...
YOU THINK I'M LAME TOO!
NNNGH...
EVERYONE LAUGHS AT ME... THEY SAY I'LL NEVER BEAT A TRUCK...
...

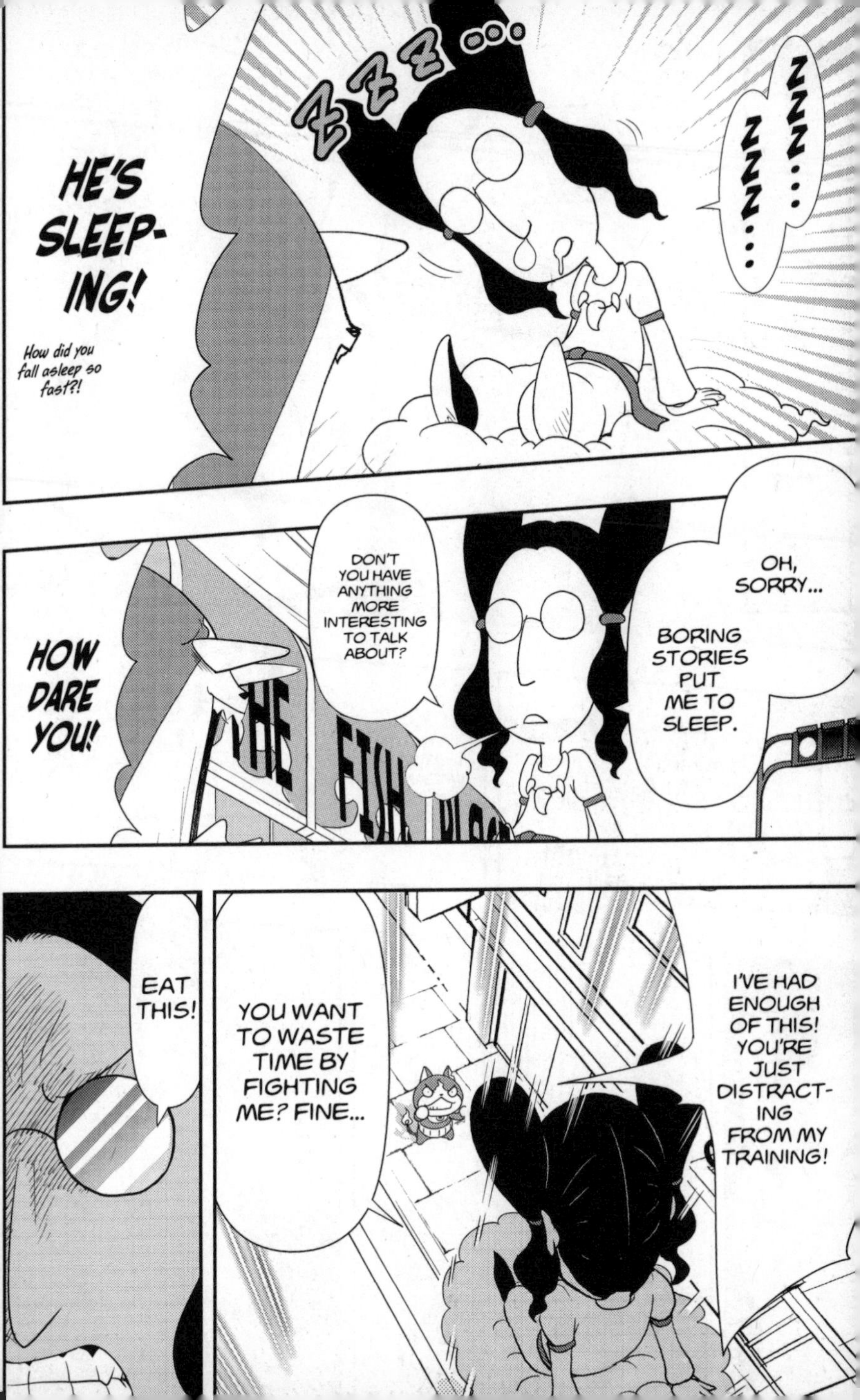
ZZZ... ZZZ...
ZZZ...
HE'S SLEEP-ING!
How did you fall asleep so fast?!
OH, SORRY...
BORING STORIES PUT ME TO SLEEP.
DON'T YOU HAVE ANYTHING MORE INTERESTING TO TALK ABOUT?
HOW DARE YOU!
I'VE HAD ENOUGH OF THIS! YOU'RE JUST DISTRACT-ING FROM MY TRAINING!
YOU WANT TO WASTE TIME BY FIGHTING ME? FINE...
EAT THIS!

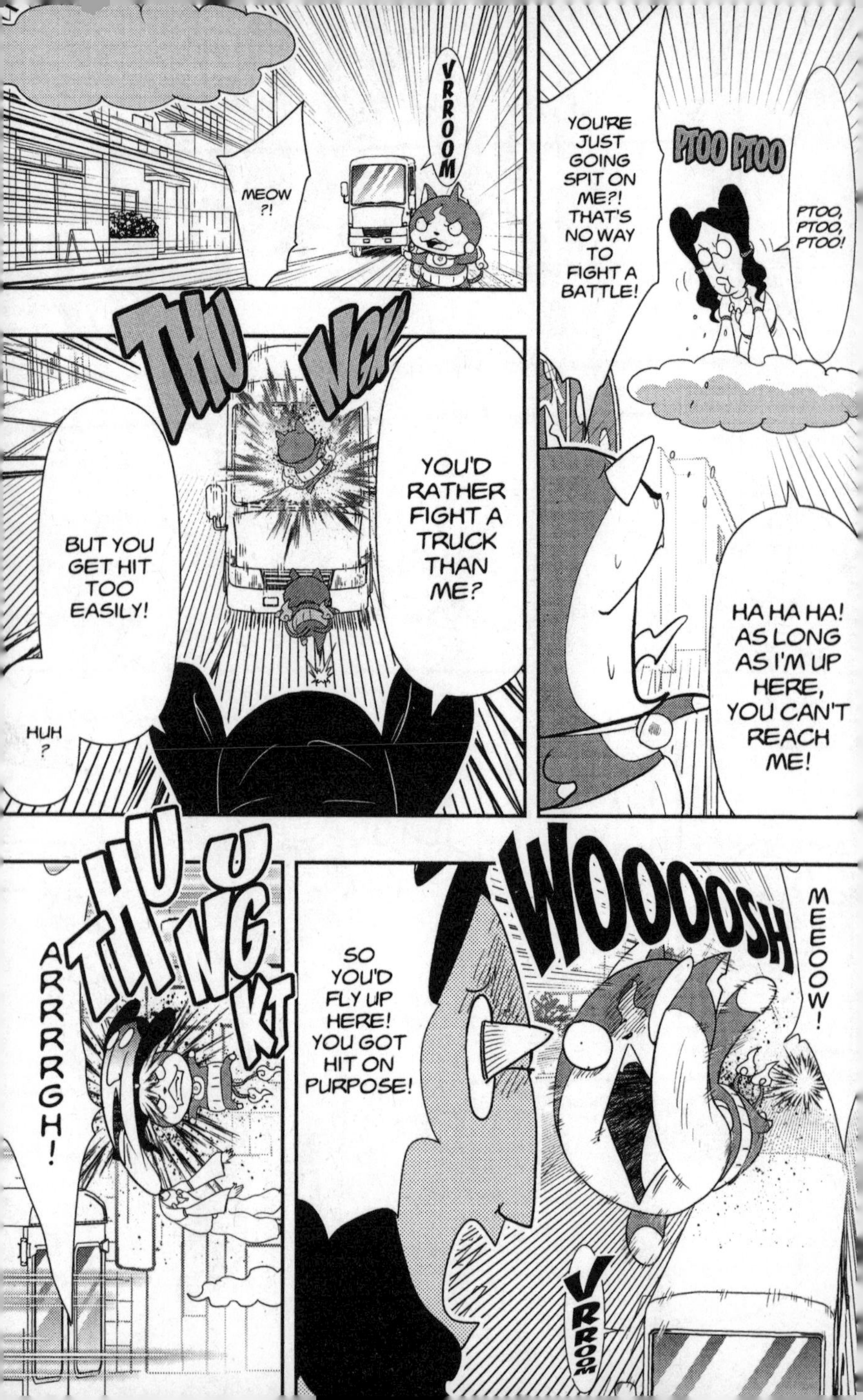
PTOO PTOO
PTOO, PTOO, PTOO!
YOU'RE JUST GOING SPIT ON ME?! THAT'S NO WAY TO FIGHT A BATTLE!
HA HA HA! AS LONG AS I'M UP HERE, YOU CAN'T REACH ME!
VRROOM
MEOW?!
THUNCK!
YOU'D RATHER FIGHT A TRUCK THAN ME?
BUT YOU GET HIT TOO EASILY!
HUH?
MEEOOOW!
WOOOOSH
SO YOU'D FLY UP HERE! YOU GOT HIT ON PURPOSE!
VRROOM
THUUNGKT
ARRRRGH!

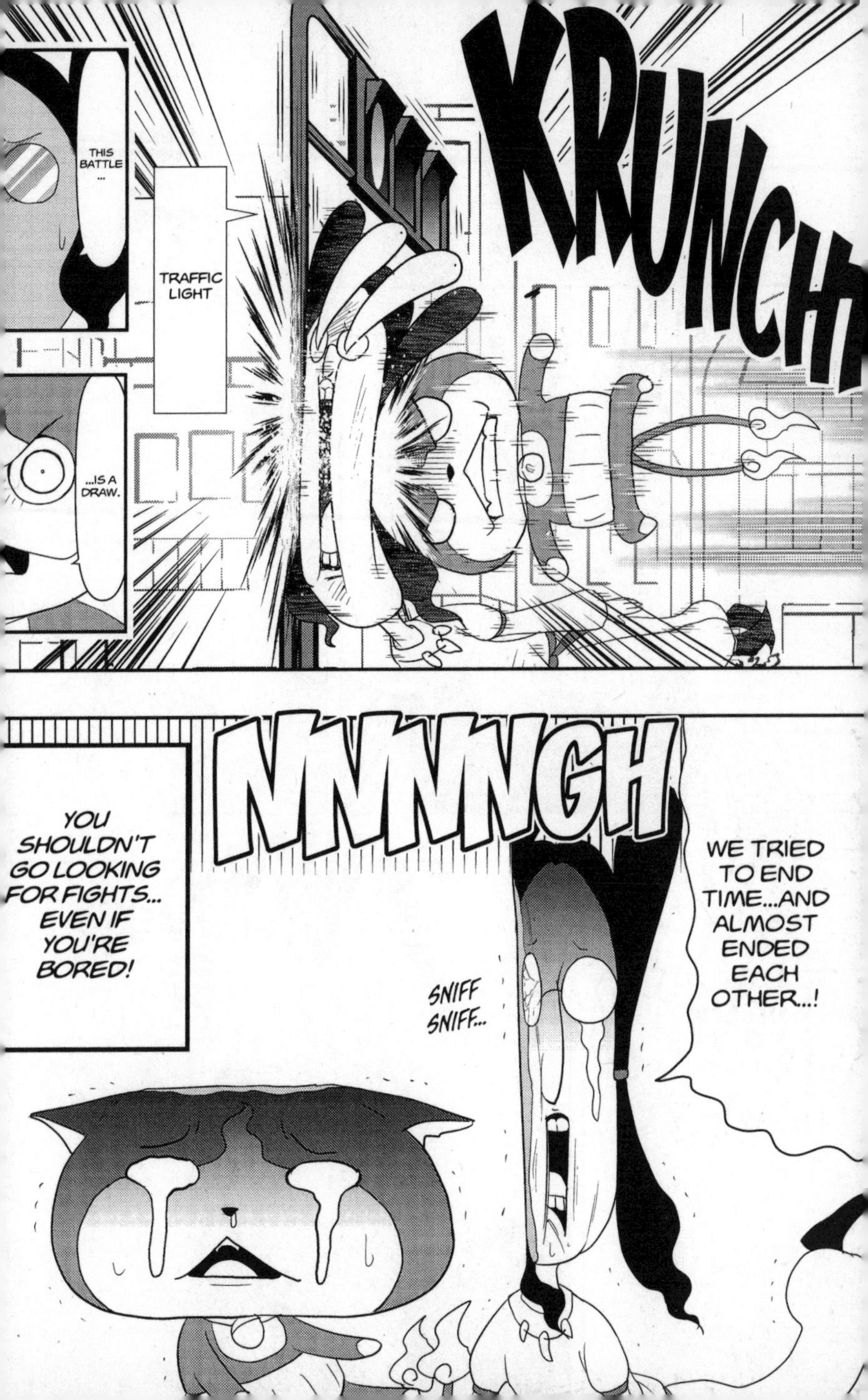
KRUNCH!
TRAFFIC LIGHT
THIS BATTLE...
...IS A DRAW.
NNNNNGH
WE TRIED TO END TIME...AND ALMOST ENDED EACH OTHER...!
SNIFF SNIFF...
YOU SHOULDN'T GO LOOKING FOR FIGHTS... EVEN IF YOU'RE BORED!

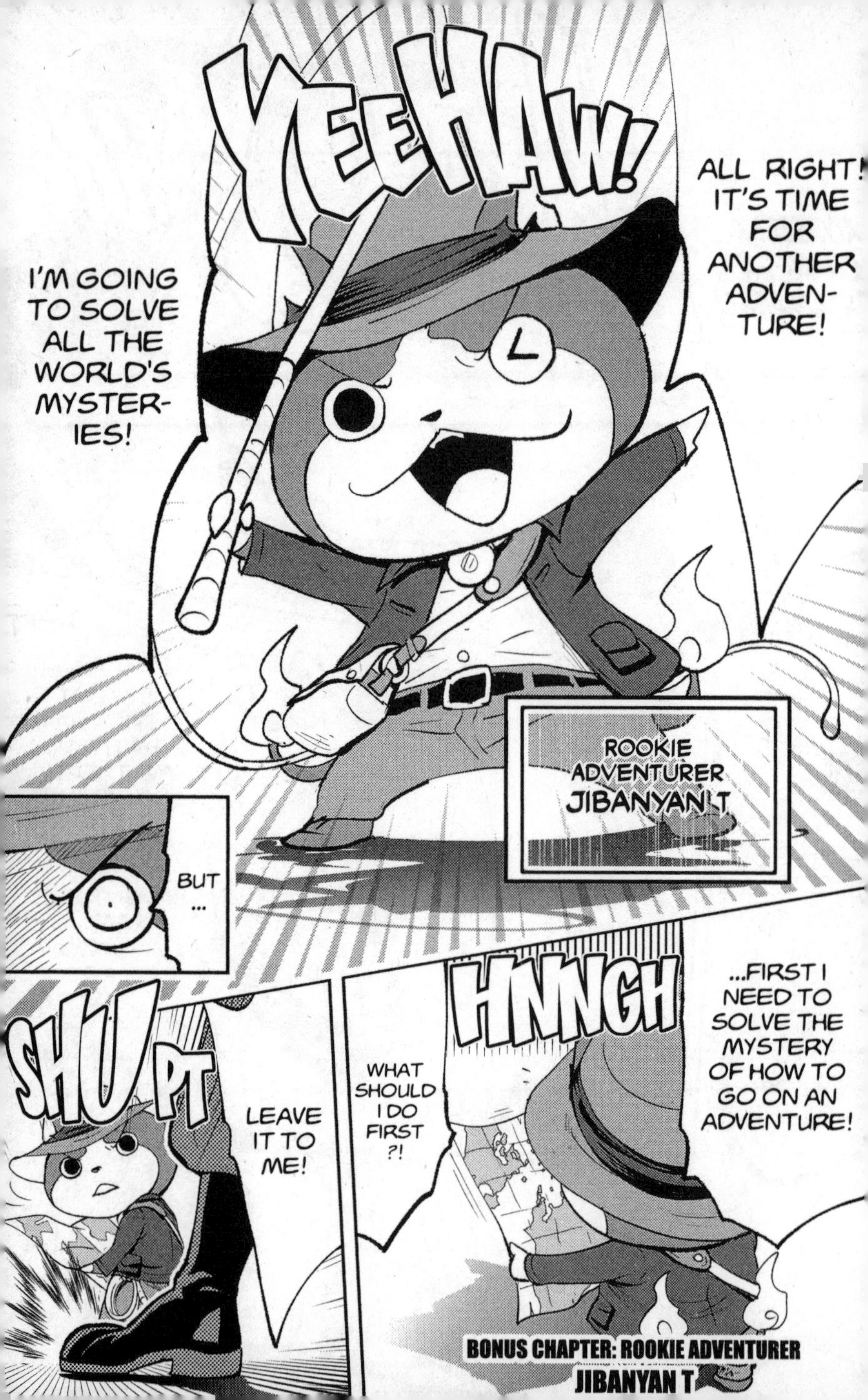
YEEHAW!
ALL RIGHT! IT'S TIME FOR ANOTHER ADVEN-TURE!
I'M GOING TO SOLVE ALL THE WORLD'S MYSTER-IES!
ROOKIE ADVENTURER JIBANYAN T
BUT ...
HNNGH
...FIRST I NEED TO SOLVE THE MYSTERY OF HOW TO GO ON AN ADVENTURE!
WHAT SHOULD I DO FIRST ?!
SHUPT
LEAVE IT TO ME!
BONUS CHAPTER: ROOKIE ADVENTURER JIBANYAN T

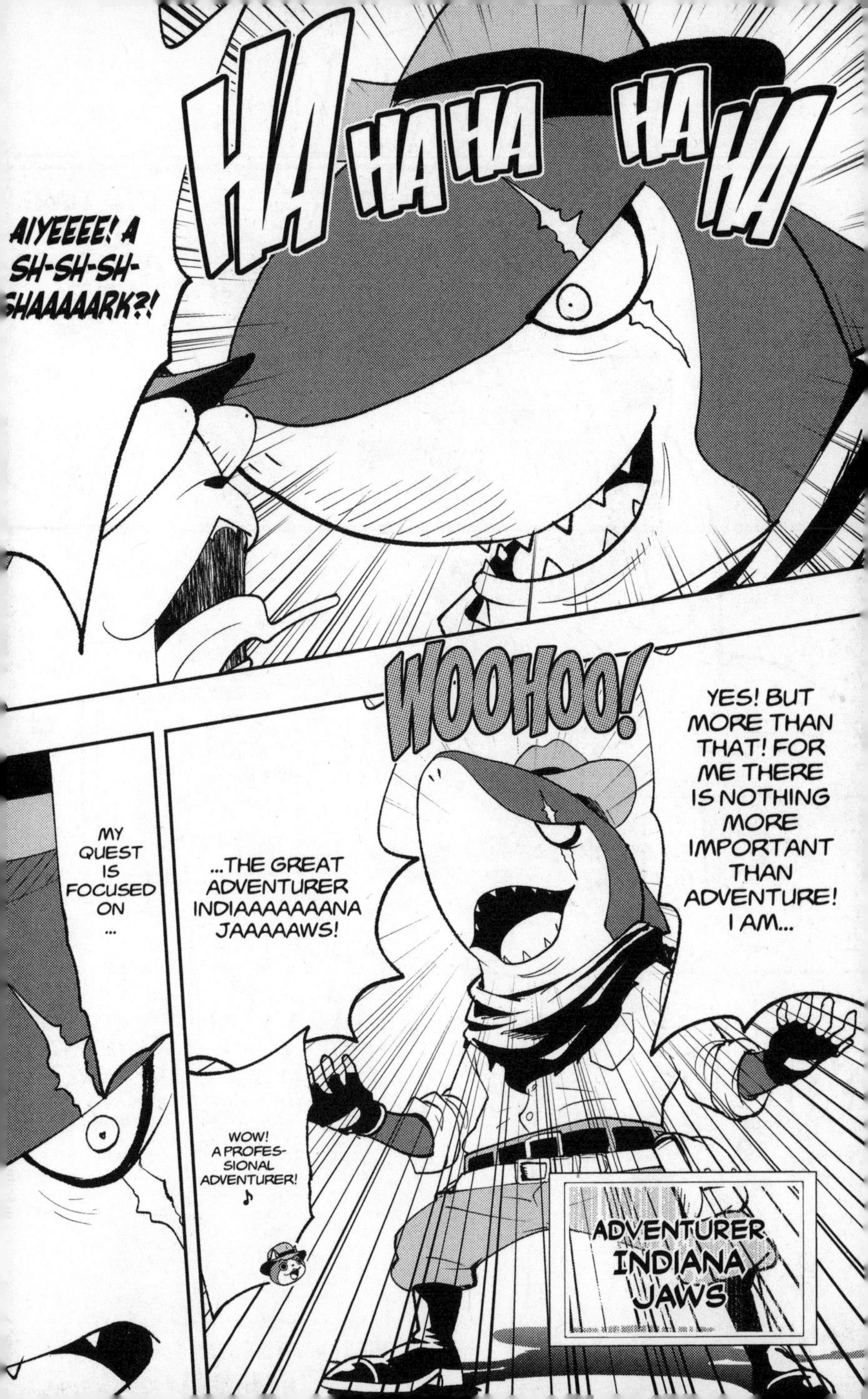
HA HAHA HA HAHA
AIYEEEE! A SH-SH-SH-SHAAAAARK?!
WOOHOO!
YES! BUT MORE THAN THAT! FOR ME THERE IS NOTHING MORE IMPORTANT THAN ADVENTURE! I AM...
...THE GREAT ADVENTURER INDIAAAAAAAANA JAAAAAWS!
ADVENTURER INDIANA JAWS
WOW! A PROFES-SIONAL ADVENTURER! ♪
MY QUEST IS FOCUSED ON ...

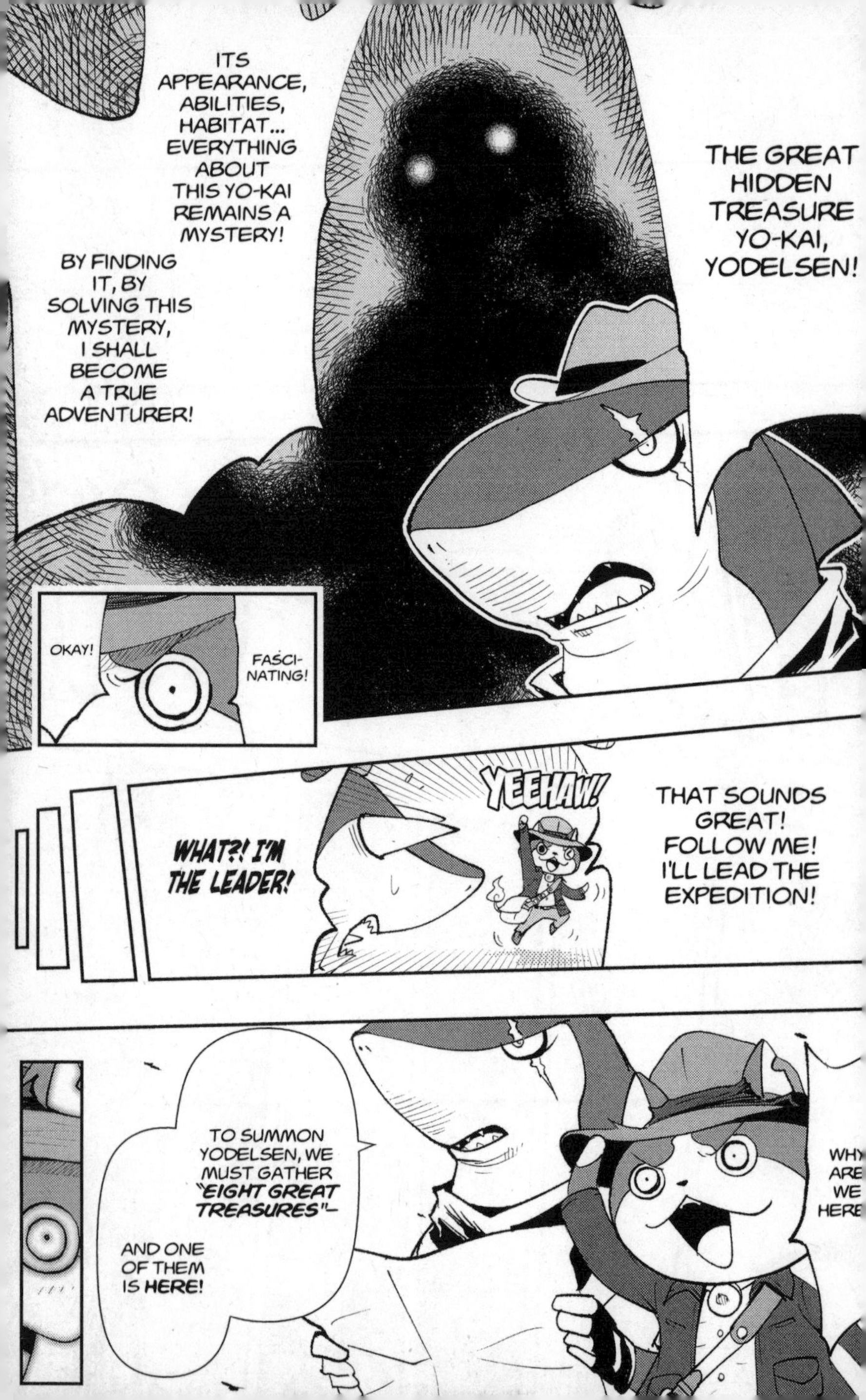
THE GREAT HIDDEN TREASURE YO-KAI, YODELSEN!
ITS APPEARANCE, ABILITIES, HABITAT... EVERYTHING ABOUT THIS YO-KAI REMAINS A MYSTERY!
BY FINDING IT, BY SOLVING THIS MYSTERY, I SHALL BECOME A TRUE ADVENTURER!
FASCI-NATING!
OKAY!
THAT SOUNDS GREAT! FOLLOW ME! I'LL LEAD THE EXPEDITION!
YEEHAW!
WHAT?! I'M THE LEADER!
WHY ARE WE HERE
TO SUMMON YODELSEN, WE MUST GATHER "EIGHT GREAT TREASURES"—
AND ONE OF THEM IS HERE!

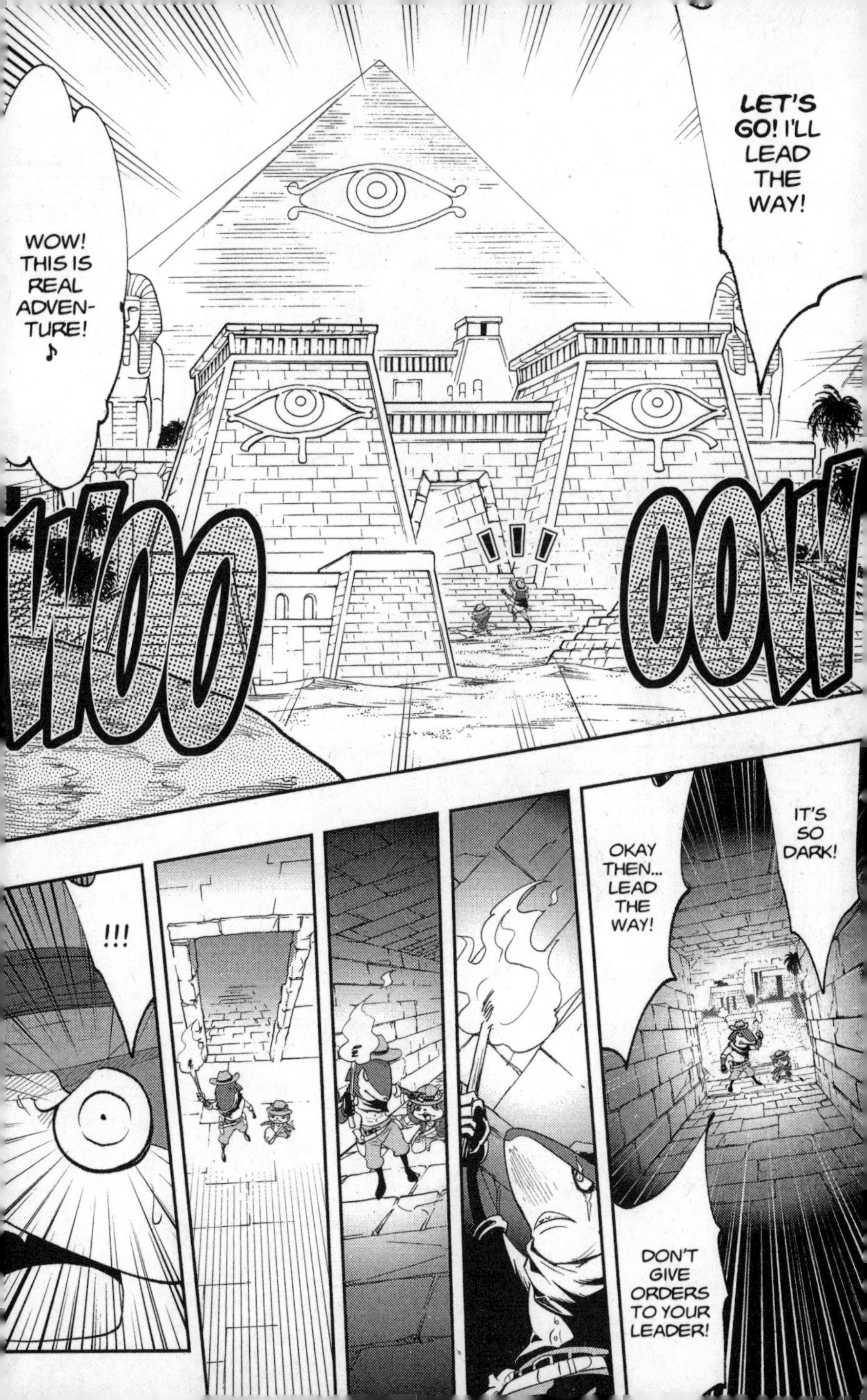
LET'S GO! I'LL LEAD THE WAY!
WOW! THIS IS REAL ADVEN-TURE! ♪
!!!
WOO
OOW
IT'S SO DARK!
OKAY THEN... LEAD THE WAY!
DON'T GIVE ORDERS TO YOUR LEADER!
!!!

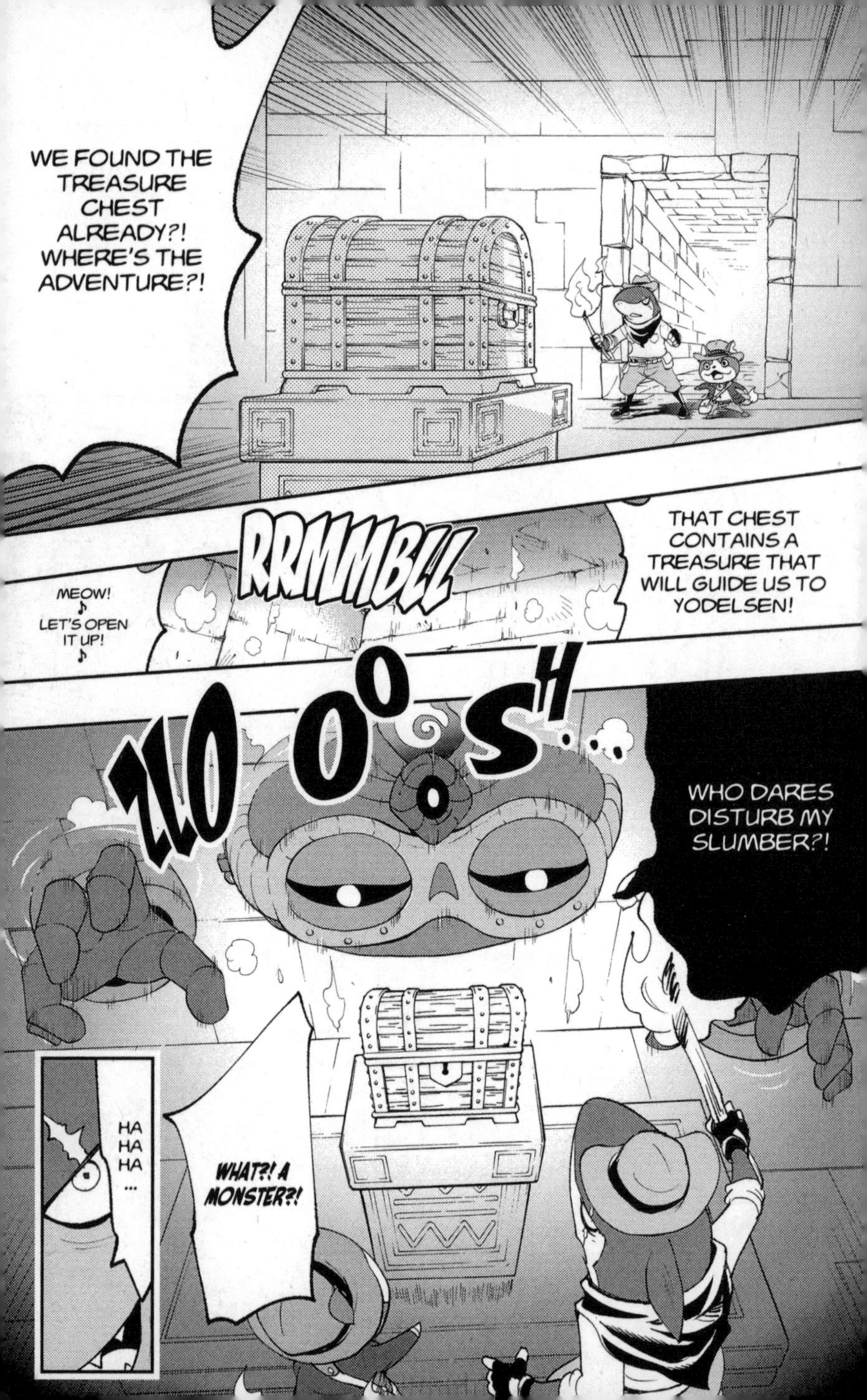
WE FOUND THE TREASURE CHEST ALREADY?! WHERE'S THE ADVENTURE?!
THAT CHEST CONTAINS A TREASURE THAT WILL GUIDE US TO YODELSEN!
RRMMBLL
MEOW! ♪ LET'S OPEN IT UP! ♪
ZLOOOSH!
WHO DARES DISTURB MY SLUMBER?!
WHAT?! A MONSTER?!
HA HA HA ...

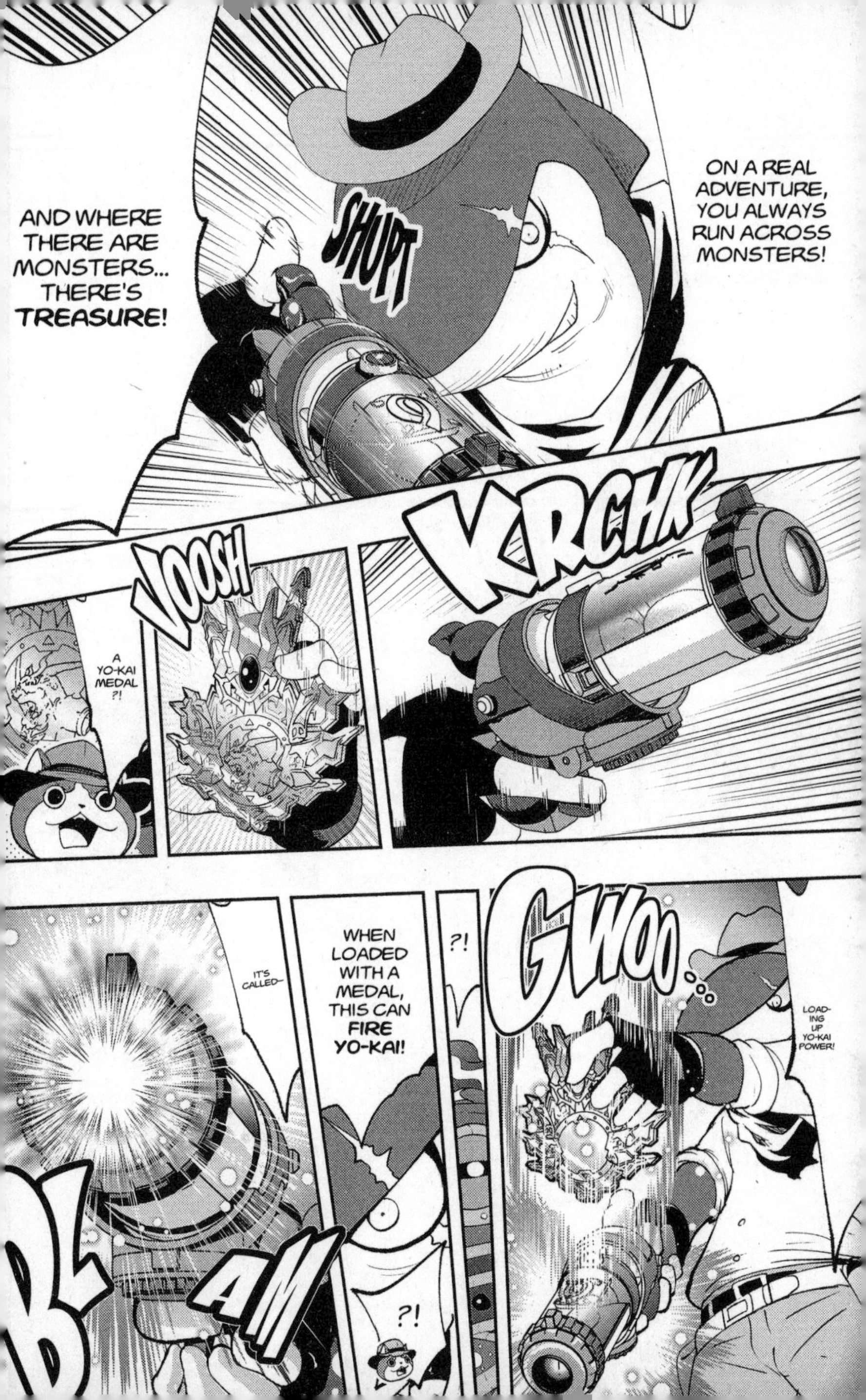
ON A REAL ADVENTURE, YOU ALWAYS RUN ACROSS MONSTERS!
SHUPT
AND WHERE THERE ARE MONSTERS... THERE'S **TREASURE!**
KRCHK
VOOSH
A YO-KAI MEDAL ?!
LOADING UP YO-KAI POWER!
GWOO...
?!
WHEN LOADED WITH A MEDAL, THIS CAN **FIRE YO-KAI!**
?!
IT'S CALLED—
BLAM

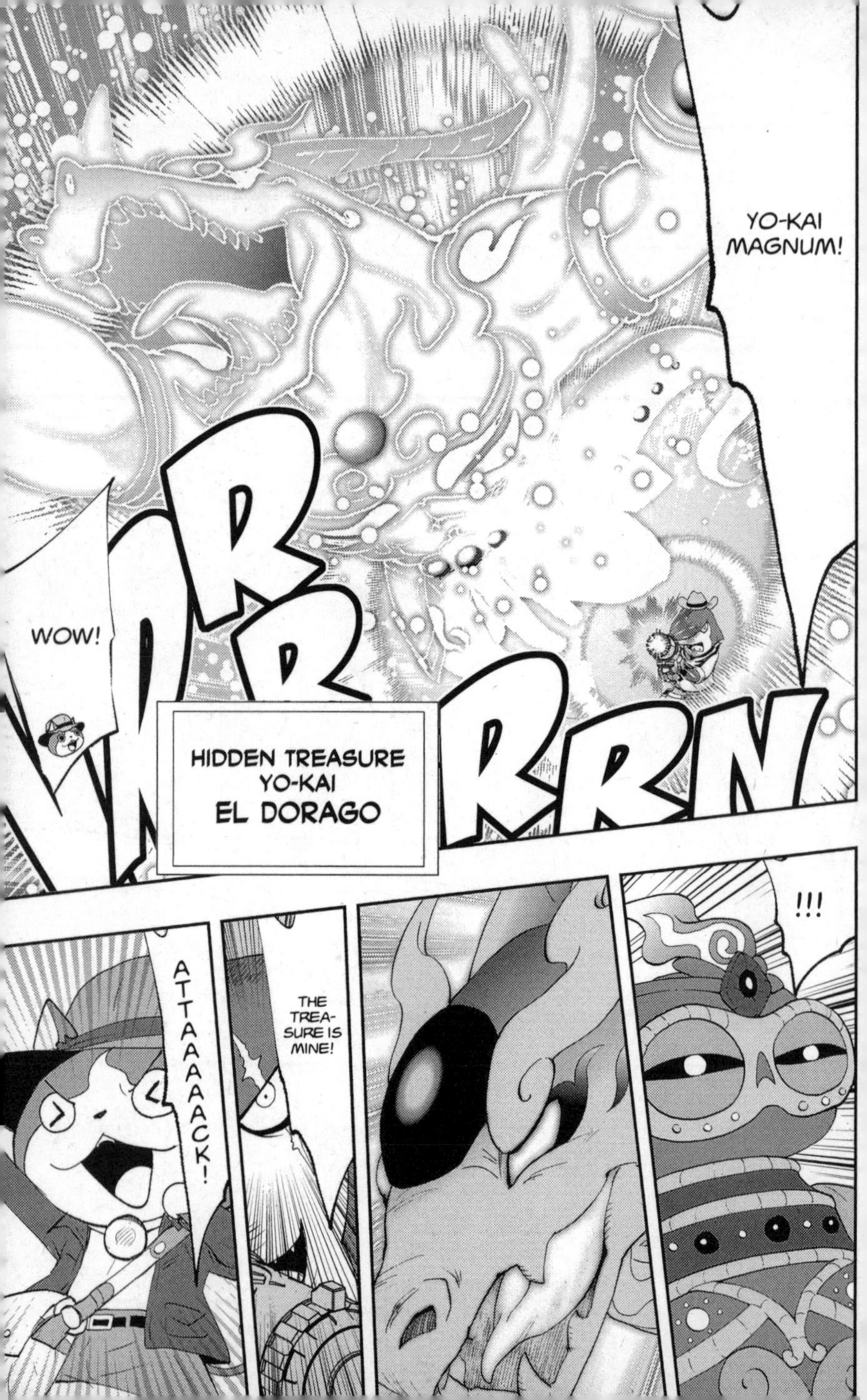
YO-KAI MAGNUM!
HIDDEN TREASURE YO-KAI EL DORAGO
WOW!
!!!
THE TREA-SURE IS MINE!
ATTAAAAACK!

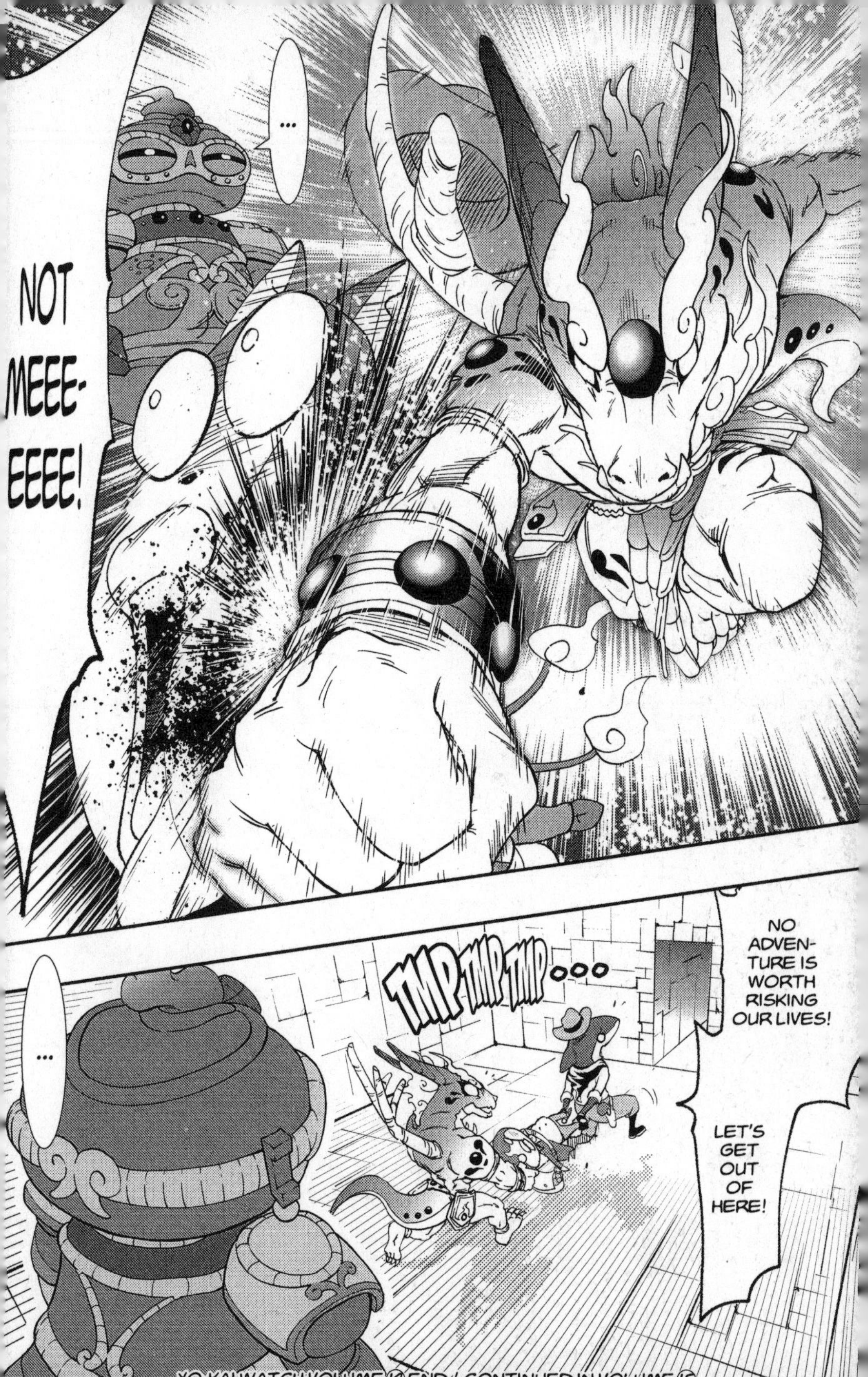
...
NOT MEEEE-EEEEE!
NO ADVENTURE IS WORTH RISKING OUR LIVES!
LET'S GET OUT OF HERE!
TMP TMP TMP
...

YO-KAI WATCH VOLUME 14 END / CONTINUED IN VOLUME 15

AUTHOR BIO

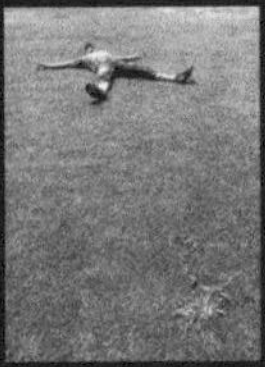

I don't have many pictures of myself. That's why volume 13's photo looked like it did.

Unlike the last book, with volume 14 we're back to being a gag manga! I hope you enjoy them both!

— Noriyuki Konishi

Noriyuki Konishi hails from Shimabara City in Nagasaki Prefecture, Japan. He debuted with the one-shot *E-CUFF* in *Monthly Shonen Jump Original* in 1997. He is known in Japan for writing manga adaptations of *AM Driver* and *Mushiking: King of the Beetles*, along with *Saiyuki Hiro Go-Kū Den!*, *Chōhenshin Gag Gaiden!! Card Warrior Kamen Riders*, *Go-Go-Go Saiyuki: Shin Gokūden* and more. Konishi was the recipient of the 38th Kodansha manga award in 2014 and the 60th Shogakukan manga award in 2015.

THIS IS THE END OF THIS GRAPHIC NOVEL!

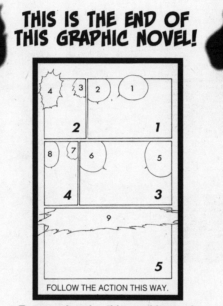

FOLLOW THE ACTION THIS WAY.

To properly enjoy this graphic novel, please turn it around and begin reading from right to left.